GHOSTS AND SHADOWS

A "Cadillac" Holland Mystery

H. Max Hiller

INDIES UNITED PUBLISHING HOUSE, LLC

Published June 2020
By Indies United Publishing House, LLC

ISBN: 978-1-64456-141-6
Library of Congress Control Number: 2020938199

INDIES UNITED PUBLISHING HOUSE, LLC
P.O. BOX 3071
QUINCY, IL 62305-3071
www.indiesunited.net

For
Brian Fitzgerald
Boss, mentor, and friend.

Chapter 1

I worked with a guy in Iraq whose pet phrase was, "Your tax dollars at work." He used it the way other people punctuated their sentences with the F-word. He would watch Apache helicopters rip apart a tree line full of Al-Qaeda gunmen then turn to me and say it. He especially liked dropping it in the middle of Intelligence and Special Forces debriefings about missions that went belly-up. He said it when he advised me to get out of the intelligence business after the agency responsible for an operation he asked me to organize disavowed knowledge of my mission.

None of that was on my mind when my phone rang as I enjoyed breakfast on the Tuesday morning after Christmas in 2009. I spent most of the previous night helping NOPD detectives clear the French Quarter of pickpockets honing their craft in preparation for Mardi Gras. The call was from Ken Hammond, my Captain at the State Police. Any call from him was surprising because he transferred me to the command of NOPD's Chief of Detectives the same week I graduated from the Louisiana State Police academy.

"Good morning." I tried to sound as if his call were a normal occurrence.

"Are you busy?" He did not wait for a response. "I need you meet one of our arson investigators right now."

"Sure." Arson investigation is not normally so time sensitive.

Captain Hammond gave me an address in New Orleans East, but no further details. It was not even clear that I was to investigate anything. I had just washed down a half dozen beignets at Café du Monde with a hot cup of café au lait, so it only took me about five minutes to get to my car.

I own a pair of Cadillacs that I alternate as my patrol car. The Chief of Detectives provided me with a Cadillac sedan when I joined NOPD's ranks nearly a year after Hurricane Katrina. NOPD appropriated it from the Sewell Cadillac dealership in the CBD just days after the storm. The department destroyed its own squad cars using them to patrol the brackish floodwaters covering eighty percent of the sprawling city. I have supplied my own Cadillac ever since, which has earned me the nickname "Cadillac." This name is meant to be far more derisive than I choose to take it, but then again, I drive a nicer car than the police officers trying to insult me get to.

I drove to the Plum Orchard Neighborhood on the lakeside of Chef Menteur Highway. Chef is the old road leading to Mississippi. Vietnamese refugees made up the dominant population along there before Katrina devastated the tight-knit community. What housing was available after the storm was divided nearly equally between returning residents and the influx of Hispanics filling the city's need for cheap labor. I heard Mexican gangs were moving into the area, and was not looking forward to a gang war between the Mexican cartels and the sons of men who fought the Viet Cong and NVA.

State Fire Marshal Clyde Wheeler was standing in front of the address Hammond gave me. Wheeler was talking on his cell phone with considerable animation beside his department-issued GMC Acadia. I parked my red Cadillac XLR coupe with its COP CAR vanity plates behind his marked vehicle. Clyde was a thin-framed guy in his late fifties standing barely taller than my kid sister. I could not immediately see what managed to stir him up this early in the morning. I also could not understand why there was no evidence of a fire anywhere on the block.

"Captain Hammond sent me. I'm Detective Holland." I tried to get him to smile and shook his hand. "How can I be of service?"

"I don't know that you can, Detective. Not unless you can explain where my crime scene went to overnight." He pointed to the address in question. A bulldozer was leveling a fresh load of dirt on the newly vacant lot. I lacked useful responses to either the question or the situation. "This is the third suspicious fire scene that's been demolished this way."

"There was a fire here last night and an empty lot this morning?" The Fire Marshal had my full attention.

"I even secured the building as evidence. Uniformed NOPD officers were protecting the scene. They claim they were told to stand down and then watched a pair of dump trucks from Mississippi haul the building away."

"Who claimed jurisdiction over your crime scene?"

"Nobody seems to be able to answer that." Wheeler tossed up his hands in frustration. He then explained that the NOPD officers told him someone in a nice suit flashed a badge and told them to leave. The demolition contractor already had city permits for the demolition work.

"Did they remember the agent's name?" I knew better, but asked the question so he would know I was interested.

"Of course not. He said his name, flashed his badge, and sent them on their way. What do you make of it?" Wheeler was calmer now that there was someone with whom to share his problem.

"I take it you called the ATF's duty officer and they claimed they didn't know what you were talking about." Wheeler just nodded. The ATF would be the only Federal agency with any reason to be involved in a suspicious fire that would outrank the State Fire Marshal. "Have you called the city about the demolition?"

"I got off the phone with them just as you pulled up. The planning office said they put the building on the demolition list last week. Today just happened to be their day to tear it down. They did seem surprised that the crew was here so early. They ask for the work to be done between ten and four so that there are fewer people around to complain."

"What was so special about the fire?" I decided to start at the beginning and look for anything else out of whack besides someone not wanting the crime scene investigated.

"It was one of the hottest house fires I have ever seen. That's what has me bothered. Two other houses that were demolished before I could get a good look were also hot fires. They all involved an accelerant I haven't seen used in the thirty years I've been at this. It was literally white hot in places," Wheeler tried to explain what piqued his interest.

"Apparently, someone wants you to believe the Federal government is blocking your investigation. This is the sort of thing that ordinarily gets the Feds all excited."

"That's what's bugging me the most. I'm used to the ATF taking over my fire scenes, but I've never seen them just throw one away."

"We're also standing here assuming it was the ATF that took

your house. Maybe it's an arsonist with a connection in the city planning office."

"That's a reach at best, Detective." Wheeler argued.

"True, but it's also the only conspiracy theory that explains what happened here. Most likely this is just a bad case of our tax dollars at work." Wheeler grinned at this sentiment, but neither of us was prepared to believe my arsonist theory was the actual solution to the mystery.

"What should we do next?" Wheeler wondered aloud.

"Go get some sleep. Call me if you get another fire like this." I patted him on the shoulder and sent him on his way. It was all I could do. Solving crimes requires having a crime scene. I handed him my card with my cell phone number and thought about that old spook named Jack "Casper" Rickman and his favorite mantra for the first time in five years.

Chapter 2

Wheeler's problem bothered me more than most situations tossed my way because of the way it stirred up the memory of Jack Rickman like burnt beans from the bottom of a cast iron pot. "Casper" Jack was the intelligence handler that disavowed me when my work for him nearly caused a diplomatic incident.

I called the Fire Marshal and jotted down the addresses of the two other fires he connected to the latest one. The first scene was located in the heart of the Sixth District, lately known as Little Baghdad for the neighborhood's combination of violence and painfully slow rebuilding after Katrina's flooding. The other was in Hollygrove, a notorious neighborhood in the Seventeenth District. Drug dealing likely connected those two, but that failed to link them to the third fire. Arson is too impersonal to be a means of gang retaliation in New Orleans. I was looking for a vigilante arsonist if I wanted to make any drug war or gang-related theory work. It was going to be easier to come up with a new theory than to find a suspect matching such a narrow profile.

I decided to speak in person with the officers shooed off the site earlier in the morning. NOPD's Fifth District Headquarters flooded during Katrina and the "temporary" station was still a hastily converted furniture store on St. Bernard Avenue five years after the storm. FEMA and the City Council agreed on nothing more than tearing down the damaged station house to stop people from asking when it would reopen.

The duty Sergeant told me I might catch the two police officers

I came to see before they clocked out. I found them finishing their daily reports. This was a good thing for me because it meant the details I was interested in should still be fresh in their minds.

"What can you tell me about the Fed that ran you off?" I asked, trying not to sound critical of their quick acceptance of the mystery agent's authority.

"He drove up in an unmarked Charger with government plates. He was about your height, with short salt and pepper hair. There was a creepy look about him and he had this really weird smile."

This was a strange detail for the officers to remember. It must have been a very odd look, indeed.

"Yeah. He looked like the sort of creep you would stop and question if you saw him anywhere near a playground without a kid of his own. There was just something wrong about him, but he shoved his badge in our faces and wasn't taking no for an answer." The partner's description was less precise yet far more telling. It actually reminded me of someone I once knew.

"How good of a look did you get at the badge?"

"Not very. It was one I had never seen one like it before, but that just means it was not DEA or ATF. Like I said, he flashed it and ordered us to leave."

"Was he alone?"

"I didn't see anyone else in the car, did you?"

The partner answered with a shake of his head, "The heavy equipment showed up as we left."

"About that. Did you get the name of the company doing the demolition?" They should have been able to get that much since it was probably painted on the side of the equipment or the truck door.

"That's what really made me think something was going on," the second officer said and grabbed his report. "Olmstead Incinerator. They're out of Biloxi. I can't figure out why anyone would take what's left of a burnt up house all the way to Mississippi to burn it again."

"Unless you knew there was something really toxic in the house. I could see them incinerating a house with a meth lab in it, but I don't think this place did. They smell like cat pee," the first officer offered.

"What did this place smell like?"

"I don't know. Like something metallic burnt up?"

The police officers looked at one another in hopes they might come up the name of the metal, but neither could. I was getting near the end of their reliable information. They would keep talking if I kept asking questions, but I sensed we were getting closer and closer to them just giving me nothing but useless speculation.

Chapter 3

I am fairly new to police work despite my detective's rank. I came to my present job directly from a career in military intelligence and working with those three-letter agencies that keep to the shadows. That work involved hours of picking through piles of raw data followed by a few brief moments of intense action when I led a raid based on what I found. Understanding why something happened, or why anyone would have done it, was only my starting point. My task was to take that knowledge and formulate a plan of action to stop the perpetrator from carrying out their next attack. It took surprisingly little tweaking of my skill set to go from eliminating jihadist cells in the Middle East to arresting criminals in New Orleans.

One thing that helped my transition to civilian life was that, in Katrina's aftermath, my hometown struck me as an English-speaking version of Baghdad. My own government destroyed both, using bombs on one and a woefully ineffective recovery bureaucracy against the other.

Washington also liked to blame the local government officials for every delay and obstacle in both of these flawed recovery efforts. Government bureaucrats and their no-bid private contractors spent more time making big plans than actually laying bricks. The widespread dissatisfaction with the haphazard rebuilding of Iraq, and especially the people handling it, made Al Qaeda's recruiting easier in devastated cities such as Mosul. I recognized this dynamic at work in New Orleans, where I was fighting the toxic combination of thugs rebuilding their gangs and the white-collar criminals siphoning off FEMA recovery dollars. I took no satisfaction in having my comparisons of the two validated when politically motivated knee-jerk reactions and solutions only worsened the situation in either location.

The National Guard, private security contractors, and most of the borrowed police left town as the FEMA money to pay them ran out. I was the last remaining State Police Detective assigned to the personal discretion of Bill Avery, NOPD's Chief of Detectives. Had I consulted Bill first, he still would have sent me to talk to Wheeler about an arson case that seemed to make absolutely no sense. It is the sort of make-work case he likes giving me to conserve NOPD's limited resources and manpower.

Chief of Detectives Bill Avery was not happy with the solutions I gave him to my last two petty cases. The first involved the dog mauling of a rap music mogul. That case uncovered evidence that a rogue FBI agent was behind my father's disappearance after Katrina. The second investigation was into a corporate interest in buying houses in the Lower Ninth Ward. I wound up linking an influential City Councilwoman to the Dixie Mafia and derailed a redevelopment project the City Council was counting on to rebuild the city's poorest neighborhood. Avery barred me from City Hall after the Councilwoman's arrest.

Among the many pieces of advice my father gave me in my youth were to never ask a question I did not already have an answer to, never pull on any string unless I knew where both ends were attached, and to never push against anything I didn't know where the far end was headed.

It was difficult to think of a now weed-covered lot as one end of a loose thread, but it was. Wheeler was worried about the wrong thing. The thread we needed to follow didn't lead to the method. It led to the motive. One end or the other of this thread would explain why someone erased Wheeler's crime scenes in a fashion that gave new meaning to the phrase "scorched earth."

I called Captain Hammond to let him know I was willing to work with the Fire Marshal. My second call was to Chief Avery. I offered to buy him lunch because he is calmer when he is eating; my pursuing a case with no obvious suspects was not going to relax him in the least.

Chapter 4

I have a mostly silent interest in a popular Creole-Italian bistro named Strada Ammazarre on Decatur Street, close to the French Market. My partner in this venture, Tony Vento, is also the chef. We put the day-to-day management of the place in the hands of Joaquin, our Cuban-born maître d'. Chef Tony managed to steal him from a fancier restaurant because Joaquin gets to be more openly gay under our roof. He also knows he will get a receptive response when he tells us what he believes needs done to improve the business rather than the two of us sending him in opposite directions with our own ideas.

"Ah, I see you have invited Chief Cochon to lunch," Joaquin said just loud enough for me alone to hear before he gave the massive hulk of NOPD's Chief of Detectives a welcoming embrace.

Joaquin is well aware of how uncomfortable it makes the Chief when he hugs him. I could not decide whether the term "Chief Pig" was a slang term for a cop or referred to the man's voracious appetite. It could be both.

I led the way to the kitchen and we took our usual positions at the Chef's Table directly across from the cook's line. Dinner guests can pay extra for the dubious pleasure of witnessing the kitchen in operation while having Chef Tony personally cook and serve their meal. The table offers the Chief and me the bistro's highest level of discretion and privacy.

I ordered a crab salad, consisting of three kinds of chopped greens and crisp vegetables topped by fresh lump crabmeat drizzled with a citrus-tinged vinaigrette dressing. Chief Avery ate his normal mid-day meal of a portion and a half of the day's pasta special. Today's was grilled Italian sausage with bell peppers and onions sautéed in olive oil with garlic and a spicy blend of herbs and spices tossed with linguini. I watched Chef Tony cringe as our overweight friend reached for the bottle of Louisiana Hot Sauce before he even tasted a bite of his meal. One of the servers left us with a pitcher of freshly made sweet tea and warm baguettes from Leidenheimer's bakery.

"Captain Hammond called me this morning," I began. Chief Avery's head snapped towards me. "There have been three suspicious fires in the past couple of weeks where the house was demolished and hauled away before the Fire Marshal could even get inside for a good look."

"It is strange that the houses were hauled away so fast." Chief Avery agreed, even as he shrugged indifferently.

"Do you have any problem with me nosing around in this?" I waited until his mouth was full to ask the question.

"I've never objected to any of your nosing around. At least not until the damage is already done."

I laughed at this, but he was serious.

"What's the worst you'll find?" Avery wondered aloud.

"Well, the cops guarding the last scene were kicked out by a supposed Federal Agent right before the building was hauled to an incinerator in Mississippi. I may kick over another Federal case neither of us knows anything about. It was a mess the last time I did that."

"True dat." The Chief of Detectives was finally able to make a joke about my exposing the FBI's undercover operation that went off the rails.

"The only thing I have been informed about is some sort of special intelligence operation the DEA has running in preparation for a huge drug sweep next year. This doesn't sound connected to that," Avery advised.

"The patrolmen said the guy's badge wasn't DEA, anyway." I added this tidbit to support Avery's instinct that the cases were unrelated.

"What do you have so far?"

"Three fires. One was in the Sixth District, one in the Fifth District and one in the Seventeenth District. All three involved intensely hot fires and all three were very close to I-10. Even so, only the accelerant seems to link them. The Fire Marshal said there were spots that glowed white hot in last night's fire. That has to be a chemical fire of some sort. Whether the DEA can shed any light on this or not, I still have to believe there is a drug angle."

"What's the DEA willing to tell you?"

"I haven't checked with them. I wanted to talk to you first. I can call them, or you can check with them about it, but I need any useful information they can provide."

"I'll call," Chief Avery immediately decided. What he was really saying was that he was prepared to be diplomatic and to play nice while in the DEA's sandbox.

"I'll swing by City Hall this afternoon to find out who owned the houses. Maybe something else links the houses and provides a motive for the fires."

"You're probably right. I'll let you know what the DEA says," Avery agreed before changing the subject so he could enjoy the rest of his meal.

Chapter 5

My hour at the City Assessor's office was less helpful than I hoped. The clerk said a known slumlord owned the first property on my list. A group of African-American attorneys owned the second property, as well as a dozen other rental properties in Central City. A real estate development company from Arizona owned the last house on my list, which was the one Hammond sent me to that morning. I saw no way to link the three sets of investors. This left open the possibility that the fires tied back to the occupants.

Calls to the property owners proved to be only marginally fruitful. The foul-mouthed slumlord swore his property was unoccupied at the time of the fire. He suggested squatters might have used it or that neighborhood drug dealers made it into a stash house. He claimed to have repeatedly boarded up the doors and windows to no avail. The Black attorney I spoke with said their rental property was leased to a young couple, and there were never been any problems with them. He also had not spoken to the tenants since the fire, which he felt was out of character for them. He suspected they might have started the fire accidently and fled rather than be questioned by the police. The last house was in the best neighborhood of the three. It was not where I would choose to live, but Plum Orchard was certainly a nicer neighborhood than Hollygrove. The owner's agent in Arizona gave me a local number to call, and the cheerful woman I spoke with told me the couple who rented the house were on vacation when the place caught fire and she apologized for not having their new address.

I hoped to piece more of the story together from what any neighbors might have to say about the properties and their occupants. I started in Hollygrove. The area has fallen on hard times since the opening of Interstate-10 put an end to Airline Highway's glory days as the western pathway into New Orleans. Hollygrove is now just another part of town where dope and gunfire compete for taking the most lives each day. The landmarks of the Town and Country Motel, where Carlos Marcello ruled his Mafia franchise, and the seedy Travel Inn, where Jimmy Swaggart's televangelist days ended in the arms of a hooker, were leveled years earlier to make room for an upscale neighborhood.

Traffic on Airline Highway was light so early in the afternoon. NOPD officers were patting down the adolescent occupants of a late-model Mustang near my crime scene. I gave up harassing petty crooks soon after I came to New Orleans. Most street dealers just need to feed their families. These corner-boys also know everything going on in their community. They usually have reliable information to share, but would not speak a word if I were constantly arresting them. I pulled into a gas-and-go store and pumped five dollars of gas into my car for all to see. I wanted to question the clerk without being too obvious.

"I need to ask you a couple of questions." I showed the clerk my badge and leaned towards him as I paid for the fuel. The clerk was Lebanese or Syrian and accustomed to speaking nearly nose to nose. It is a massively discomforting tradition for most Americans when they first deal with men from the Middle East.

"What can you tell me about the fire last week?"

"In the pink house?" Apparently, more than one fire occurred in the past week. "Those kids, the ones selling drugs, they used it to hide their money and guns. One of the gangs, they met there every day."

"Which gang?"

"I try not to know those things. I would just see a car pull up every morning and then they would go inside for a while and come out to start selling their filth once again." I understood he wanted to know as little as possible, but he was still unable to ignore an obvious daily routine.

"Can you at least describe the car?"

"It was a white Hummer, one of those H2s, maybe a couple of years old. A thin young Black boy drove it and an older man went inside."

"So, someone in an SUV delivered drugs to the dealers there?"

The clerk looked at me as if he thought I doubted him.

"It is what I saw with my own eyes." He knew what he witnessed and could not care less if it was what I wanted to hear.

"Do you know where they moved their deliveries after the fire?"

"No."

Answering that question would have required him to be far more involved than he was prepared to be. It was one thing to look out his window and witness something suspicious, or even an obvious crime. It was something else entirely for him to ask about such things. He worked among criminals and junkies who did not like being dimed out, so I bought a soda and candy to make it look like that was why I took so long to pay for my gas.

The second address was half a block off Louisiana Avenue near the rebuilt CJ Peete Apartments. I parked a block from the tooth gap the burned-out house left in the block of ramshackle shotgun houses. These houses were always home to some of the city's very poorest citizens, many of whom held legitimate, though low-paying, jobs. I looked at the overhead power lines for the athletic shoes that would mark a gang's territory, but saw none. That only meant I was already deep inside some gang's turf. It crossed off any theory about a gang trying to burn a rival's stash house. No rival gang member would risk being caught this far behind enemy lines.

I noticed a woman standing on the balcony of a newer apartment building in the next block. I could not tell if she was watching me or not, but I decided she probably witnessed the comings and goings from the burned-out house. The wine cooler in her hand diminished the chances she was just getting out of bed for her night job. It suggested her having a steady day job was unlikely as well. I was not going to get any answers from her by shouting back and forth for her neighbors to hear. I drove to her building and figured out her unit number, found her name on the mailbox, and called 411 for her telephone number.

"Hello?" My phone number does not appear as a blocked number on caller ID, but her not recognizing the number accomplished about the same thing.

"Good afternoon. I'm the cop parked down the street and I was hoping you might be willing to answer a question or two over the phone so I don't have to knock on your door." The best threats are implied ones.

"What sort of questions?"

"What can you tell me about the house across the street, the one that burned?"

"Nothing."

"Knock. Knock."

"Okay," she said in a tone that made me glad we were talking over the phone. "A guy named Richie lived there. He's with the Pistol Peetes."

"And what is Richie's job?"

"He runs the route for the gang. He keeps the corner boys supplied and picks up their cash."

"Any idea where he's staying now?" She was in the gang if she did.

I was starting to suspect she was anyway. Her balcony provided an impressive over-watch of the gang's turf. She could have seen cops coming from blocks away and sounded an alarm to the occupants of the house.

"No."

"One last question." I nearly shouted this because I could tell she was about to disconnect the call. "What's Richie drive?"

"A white Hummer." The questions this response brought to mind were ones she was not going to answer. Our short chat left me optimistic about linking the third fire to the first two.

I took a moment to call an NOPD narcotics detective I hoped felt he owed me a favor. I asked him four questions about the Pistol Peetes, all but one of which he said he would need to ask somebody else about or look something up before he could answer. The one question he did answer was where the gang got its name. The members grew up playing basketball on the open-air basketball courts across Washington Avenue from the CJ Peete projects. The name was a perfect fit for a trigger-happy gang from the projects.

The Detective gave me my other answers within an hour. Richie was Richard "Richie Rich" Franklin. He was twenty-three years old with a sealed juvenile record and a half dozen drug and firearms arrests as an adult. All but one of the charges were eventually dismissed or plea-bargained to misdemeanors. The narcotics detective told me Ritchie drove a white Hummer H2 with spinner wheels so I put out a BOLO for the vehicle. I wanted to know where it was, but I did not want whoever spotted it to pull it over.

The most recent fire caused roof damage to one of the houses next door. I found the Vietnamese homeowner standing in his side yard watching the repair work on his home like a hawk. His

English was far better than that of the men standing on his roof, but he would never shake the lingering traces of his native dialect in his pronunciation. The man looked to be in his sixties, but I figured there must be a better way to start our conversation than asking if he served in the ARVN during the final months of the Vietnam War.

"Heck of a way to get a new roof," I said with an extra wide smile.

The homeowner glanced back at me, spotted my badge on its lanyard, and let his face show his anger about the roof damage.

"You gonna catch the men that started the fire? We have enough bad people here. We don't need people that start fires, too."

"I'm working on it." I stopped in my tracks and let the distance between us cool his attitude off a bit. "I was hoping you might help me do so. I have a few questions about your neighbor and the fire."

"There was six Mexicans living here. They said they ran a lawn care business but I never see no work trucks. I never even knew their names."

He did not know their names but he knew all about their nationality and the number of people living next door, as well as their daily routine. This living arrangement was also quite a bit different from what the rental agent told me. I wondered how the lease went from a nice couple to a half dozen Mexican laborers. I was prepared to accept that she never visited the residence after leasing it rather than believe she was intentionally lying to me.

"I don't suppose one of their visitors drove a Hummer H2?" This was a long shot at best.

"Big white thing? Yes. There was a Black man came in one every couple of days. He always came early in the morning and he never stayed very long. They were selling drugs. That's what I think." I was not going to discuss it with him. I just nodded my head as if I agreed.

"Who called in the fire alarm?" I assumed it was him because of the way he seemed to keep an eye on the place.

"I don't know. They woke me up with their fighting a couple of hours before the fire and I went back to bed when they stopped."

"What was the argument about?"

"It sounded like one of them was chasing someone with a nail gun."

"Were nail gun fights something they did a lot?" The very idea put a nasty image in my mind. Nails fired from one will pierce a

Kevlar vest.

"They were usually very quiet neighbors. This was the first time."

"Why do you think it was a nail gun?

"It sounded like what those guys use." He pointed to his roofers. "I know what a real gun sounds like."

"But, you're sure someone really was shooting at them? He nodded, obviously displeased that I questioned what he told me. I thanked him for his help and let him get back to supervising the roofers.

I could understand why he might think he heard a nail gun. The pneumatic popping was a familiar sound to anyone who rebuilt a home in the wake of Hurricane Katrina. Between framers and roofers, the sound filled the air for nearly two solid years. It was unlikely the snooping neighbor was familiar with the sound of suppressed automatic weapons. They make a sound that the untrained ear could easily mistake for a pneumatic nail gun.

Any rival gang raiding the house, including the Pistol Peetes, were unlikely to have made use of suppressors. Making a lot of noise encourages potential witnesses to keep their heads down. Besides that, possessing an unregistered or improvised suppressor would bring a Federal firearms charge.

Chapter 6

My maternal grandparents started our family's tradition of celebrating new Year's Eve in an upper-floor suite of the Marriott Hotel on Canal Street the year it opened. We have enjoyed the midnight fireworks display from that balcony every year since. It allows us to avoid the huddled masses and act like the third world despots my mother's side of our family brings to mind. My grandparents and uncles were always quick to denigrate my father's position because their idea of working in civil service was doing political dirty work for Louisiana's shadiest politicians. My maternal grandfather and uncles all served in the shadows of Louisiana's governors and as political advisors to state-level politicians of both parties. Uncle Felix is the go-to person to get out of a scandal or to put someone else into one. He likes to describe my being a detective as a working vacation from the sorts of thing I should be doing for him. It was a scary thought that my black-ops skills were in high demand in state-level politics.

My grandparents were long dead and most of my aunts and uncles would not spend the night in New Orleans now that they need not fear angering their king and queen with their absence. My mother insisted on holding the reservation though, and now fills the room each year with people who still want to believe old-money royalty matters. My sister and I accept that our presence is required, as are being properly attired and on our best behavior. My sister, Tulip, and my date were wearing gowns from Saks in Canal Place, with their hair and make-up done by an Uptown salon. I stood around in my tuxedo trying not to look like a waiter at Antoine's.

Tulip spent most of the evening looking for an opportunity to escape so she could meet Chef Tony once he closed down the bistro. My long-standing edict against my business partner dating my sister softened as I slowly came to the realization that this was never my decision to make. My mother was uncharacteristically silent on the prospect of a working-class foreigner climbing her family tree.

Most of my evening involved bouncing between acting the part of the good son and being a worthy boyfriend. I had yet to cook breakfast in bed for the beauty I'd been dating for barely four months, but my mother was already planning my high-society wedding to State's Attorney Katie Reilly. Cooking that first breakfast was my only New Year's resolution. I was hoping my mother's wedding talk did not spook Katie. There would be absolutely no discussion about my mother's increasingly apparent romantic relationship with Roger Kline, the dog trainer I used to solve a recent homicide case. Roger stayed around to console my mother in the weeks after I uncovered the details of my father's death. I was unsure of my mother's purpose in always referring to Roger as her 'escort' when they were seen in public rather than using any terms suggesting a romance, and I have politely avoided any references to his ability to handle all sorts of vicious mammals.

Chief Avery and his wife were on the guest list, along with their two oldest children and their spouses. Tulip and Katie's legal opinion were that my mother inviting my boss to the suite for an evening of free food and liquor was not technically influence peddling. Besides, Chief Avery was the one who would benefit the most from being in a room of my mother's politically connected guests.

"Any progress on the case?" Avery asked while we stood on the balcony overlooking the packed French Quarter. The Algiers Point bonfire was roaring skyward across the Mississippi River. This year the wood was from a pair of demolished crack houses condemned by the City Council. There seemed to be a large crowd standing downwind of the smoke.

"I've made enough forward progress to hurt my nose hitting a brick wall." Avery was looking for a simple yes or no answer, not a full report. He was not going to like hearing all three fires bore a connection to the Pistol Peetes. They were a new gang, and it was not a good thing for them to be gaining traction. Avery lived in constant fear of a gang war breaking out during Mardi Gras.

"So the Chief has you on something new?" Katie asked once Avery went inside for a beer. I tried distracting her by kissing along her bare shoulder to her neck while hugging her from behind. She shrugged me off and stepped away to turn and face me. Her expression let me know I was failing to keep my promise of giving her full transparency. Failure to do so risk an abrupt end to our relationship.

"As of about one o'clock this afternoon. I wanted to tell you about it as foreplay later." Making an excuse doomed any kind of foreplay later. I tried to save the evening by telling Katie everything I knew for sure. "Someone is burning drug dealers out of their homes. I think whoever set the fires may be trying to work their way up the supply chain."

"Arson isn't really part of the usual way gangs work. Has anyone been killed?" Katie stepped back into my arms, saving what she wanted to say for later.

"I have no idea. The first fire was just a couple of weeks ago, but I wasn't called in until this morning. Captain Hammond put me on the case, not Bill. He sent me to talk to a State Fire Marshal, who was complaining to him about somebody destroying his crime scenes."

"Hammond decided you were the guy to call?" Katie laughed at the potentially regrettable judgment my boss displayed in making such an assignment. "You're their expert at complicating simple things."

"Hey, now."

"You're the only cop I know who could start out looking into a legal offer to buy a house and end up disrupting an entire election. I love you, but you sure can make a mess."

"So you love me, hmm?" I gave her my best soulful look.

"That's what you took out of all that, Detective?" Katie laughed again. "It's amazing you haven't been fired."

"I can always fall back on the bistro." I certainly wasn't buying any Cadillacs on my detective's paycheck. I went back to nibbling on Katie's neck. She wore her long brown hair braided down her back, which left her neck exposed.

"Yes, my love. You and your friend have a very nice clubhouse to play in." Katie smooched my cheek and turned her attention to the glass of French champagne she plucked from a passing server's tray.

"You make such a cute couple." My mother seemed intent on making a photo album of the evening with her cell phone's camera. She and Roger were watching the bonfire's embers glowing in the distance. It is as close as my mother will ever approach Algiers or the West Bank.

"So do the two of you," I said to cool her enthusiasm a bit. Roger smirked nearly as much as my mother frowned.

"Enough about me." My mother abruptly closed that topic. She turned to other items on her agenda. "I just wish your sister had someone to share the evening with."

"She's fine. She's meeting someone in time for the fireworks." Katie would have been wise to stop at the end of her first sentence.

"Oh, so she does have a date? Are you sure he isn't married? I mean, if he can't join us now, whatever is he doing?" My mother's passive-aggressiveness about Chef Tony and Tulip is comical, but not very funny.

"He has to work late." Katie looked to me for help.

"What does your psychic have to say about next year?" I asked to change the subject entirely. This question never fails to distract my mother. She began consulting an online psychic when her life unraveled in the wake of Hurricane Katrina. The combination of the premature report of my death, my father vanishing in the midst of their divorce, and the complete obliteration of our home in town and the extensive damage to the weekend house in the Rigolets nearly destroyed her. She never ceases to amaze me with her quite rational and pertinent interpretations of what I perceive to be the cryptic babblings of a stranger who knows her credit card number.

"That I should let myself be the person I have always wanted to be, that my son should look for answers and not questions, and that I should accept my daughter as she truly is and not as I expect her to be."

"Three strikes and you're out," I grumbled to myself while showing my best poker face. Katie squeezed my hand and cracked a grin. I chose my audible response more carefully. "And how much did that cost you?"

"Much less than therapy would after the year you and your sister have put me through."

She did endure an admittedly bad year at the hands of her children. I discovered my father was murdered and Tulip volunteered to kick-start the campaign of a former Black Panther's nephew for the City Council seat vacated by my investigation into crooked real estate schemes.

My mother's festive mood returned by the time fireworks began exploding above the river across from Jackson Square. My sister slipped out moments before they began to catch a cab to Strada Ammazarre. Tulip and Tony planned to watch the pyrotechnics from the balcony of his apartment above the bistro. Katie and I would have been on my balcony had we not stayed to cover Tulip's escape. We enjoyed the fireworks show and weathered my mother for another hour before we made an excuse about the next day being a workday in the justice system.

It was nearly dawn before I started cooking my long-anticipated romantic breakfast for Katie. She sat on the small rolling island in my kitchen, dangling her long legs between us, as if her long brown hair lying tangled across her shoulders and wearing nothing but my unbuttoned tuxedo shirt, were not distraction enough. Katie was the first woman I dated since returning to New Orleans to see my apartment. I was wary of sharing my space during my first few years back in town and spent my nights with the sort of women accustomed to meeting in hotels.

Katie commented on the aptness of my owning one of Manny Chevrolet's banners from the city's 2006 mayoral race. His slogan was "A troubled man for troubled times." I adopted the banner at a time when my own motto could have been "A troubled cop for troubling crimes." Manny's campaign was my sister's first foray into local politics, but mother was less embarrassed by that than by Tulip's backing Lionel Batiste in the current City Council race.

I raided the bistro's pantry to present Katie with a breakfast of eggs Benedict, freshly sliced cantaloupe tightly wrapped in salty prosciutto, and fried Yukon Gold potatoes. We washed it down with the chilled bottle of Moet et Chandon champagne I snatched from the caterer on our way out of the suite.

"Do you need to go to the office today?" I assumed justice was taking a holiday whether or not crime did.

"I'm trying to avoid the place right now. Bob is still throwing a tantrum about the Justice Department abruptly shutting down our grand jury investigation into a heroin ring out in New Orleans East. They claim they're preparing indictments of their own." I could commiserate with the DA's sentiments because I stood down more times than I could count while in the Special Forces.

"Then his loss is my gain." I smiled and topped off her

champagne. We curled up on my sofa to watch LSU, my alma mater, play Penn State in the Capital One Bowl. LSU lost by a field goal in the final minute. Katie did her best to console me once I stopped yelling at the television set. She was kind enough to keep to herself how little she cares about college football.

I heard Tony start the elevator as the game began. The elevator is the only means of accessing our apartments on the third floor. We were only open for dinner on New Year's Day. This still meant a long day of work for the chef. It also put an end to any intimacy he shared with Tulip. I put images of that out of my mind as best I could.

Chapter 7

lyde Wheeler's next phone call came well after midnight the next Monday night. I took his call while trailing a trio of teenagers I suspected of a string of armed robberies on Dauphine Street. I kept a block between us and walked on the opposite side of the street. This provided a line of cars to duck behind if they decided to open fire on me. I needed to be close by if they accosted anyone stumbling away from Bourbon Street. They were only six blocks away from the safety of the Treme Neighborhood if they made a run for home. I was not about to follow them across Rampart and into that dimly lit jungle at that hour of the night.

"Where are you?" I asked when I saw his number on the screen. There was only one reason for him to call me after the sun went down.

"Seventy-six hundred block of Gannon Road. Hurry, it's going fast."

I ran back to Bourbon Street and asked a First District officer to drive me to the scene in his squad car. It saved me ten minutes in response time, which proved to be valuable.

The entire block was as bright as mid-day. Flames engulfed a small brick ranch-style house except for its metal roof. I felt heat from the fire half a block away. Units from a second fire station approached the scene as I arrived. There was an ambulance on the scene, but the EMTs had no survivors to treat.

"When did this get called in?" I asked Wheeler once I located him.

"An hour ago. The neighbor on the left said they smelled fireworks and looked outside. The fire started while they were looking at the house. They barely got out of theirs before smoke filled it."

"Do you really think this started because of fireworks?"

"Not a fire this hot."

Firefighters were spraying down the homes to either side of the house, which was well beyond saving. The Fire Marshal led me to the right-hand side of the burning structure and pointed to a spot in the middle of an exterior wall of the totally engulfed house. It was where the bathroom was located. He pointed out a hole in the brick siding. It looked to me as though lava was pouring from inside the house.

Wheeler pulled a temperature gun from his pocket and moved closer to the structure. He returned with a reading that seemed absurdly high considering the distance from the flames that he recorded it. Typical house fires reach temperatures of just over a thousand degrees. The temperature on his device registered over three thousand degrees. What I mistook for lava was probably just a bathtub with an iron core melting, something which would never happen in a normal fire.

"Ever seen anything like this before?" Wheeler asked. I could tell by his expression that this was something he had never experienced before.

"Thermite is the only thing that comes to mind."

"That's what I was thinking, but who sets a fire with thermite? And who sets four of them?"

Thermite is a combination of iron oxide, aluminum, and sometimes sulphur. It is capable of burning at temperatures approaching four thousand degrees. These ingredients are readily, and legally, available on eBay, and a pound of thermite would cost under fifty dollars to blend. Thermite does require a very hot trigger to ignite, such as burning strips of magnesium. That is the same chemical burning on a child's sparkler on the Fourth of July and explained why the neighbors thought they smelled fireworks.

"Even if we agree that was the accelerant, why start the fire in the bathtub?" I saw no reason to start such a hot fire in such a controlled environment. Wheeler ordered the fire hoses to avoid spraying the bathroom because spraying water on the bathtub would cause a steam explosion.

"I have no idea what someone wanted to burn, but I'll tell you this, whatever was in that bathroom is long gone now." Wheeler sounded more frustrated than confused. His job was to decide if a fire was accidental or intentional and then to sort out how it was started. Those questions were likely resolved, but neither of us liked the answers.

One of the local TV correspondents arrived in time to videotape the roof caving in for their station's morning broadcast. The young man spotted the State Fire Marshal and understood that Wheeler's presence meant the blaze was not a normal house fire. The reporter shoved a microphone in the Fire Marshal's face and asked Wheeler for a comment about the fire.

I tried to stay out of the camera frame but the Fire Marshal pulled me close to his side and proceeded to divulge just enough information to encourage people to call the State Police with their tips. I said absolutely nothing and Wheeler made no disclosures regarding the use of thermite or heat that could melt bathtubs. Wheeler made a point of not linking this fire to any of the previous fires. I liked his way of sounding very helpful without actually disclosing anything to a suspect who might be watching his interview.

Chapter 8

One of the most important details Wheeler did not divulge was our mutual suspicion that someone was going to show up to haul the house away once the sun came up. He lost the evidence from the previous fires, but we might link this fire to the others if the accelerant was what someone was going to great lengths to conceal. The motive was also likely identical for all four fires. We were certain enough of there being a pattern that we decided to remain on the scene to confirm our suspicions, which a disposal crew from the incinerator crew would certainly do. We also wanted to confront whoever showed up to shoo us away and learn who was responsible for the carefully orchestrated cover-up.

We filled our time until dawn going door to door on the block, cajoling statements from the few neighbors who were still awake and willing to answer our questions. They lost a little of their instinctive reluctance to speak with us when Wheeler informed them that we were actively tracking a serial arsonist. Saving their own homes loosened their lips.

I had more to work with by the time we were finished than the Fire Marshal did. He was able to establish a very rough time for when the fire started and how fast it burned. Two separate witnesses arrived home between midnight and twelve thirty and had not smelled smoke or seen fire, but the fire department was on the scene by one o'clock. It was now three in the morning and the fire department was cooling a pile of ashes and roofing tin.

I came away with confirmation that four men in their thirties were renting the house. The neighbors all believed the men were from Mexico and that they claimed to own a food truck. Nobody recalled ever actually seeing this truck, but the neighbors remembered seeing the men drive a Ford pickup truck that was notably absent from the scene.

I saw no reason for the four men to set fire to their rental unit in the middle of the night and drive away in a two-passenger vehicle. Any neighbors who arrived home just before the fire would have noticed the Mexicans loading belongings into the truck unless they also burned everything they owned. We both doubted the men the neighbors described possessed the skills it took to mix and ignite the thermite. It is an accelerant few people would consider utilizing unless they were already experienced in handling it.

The neighbor whose house abutted the white-hot bathroom fire repeated the Vietnamese neighbor's statement about hearing metallic popping sounds. This neighbor compared it to a paintball gun, and offered to demonstrate this with their own paintball gun. I realized then that both witnesses had no idea what they really heard, but were telling me what came closest to a sound they did recognize. There was no reason to believe either witness was accurate in their choice of what made the sounds. It was doubtful either household decided to use a nail gun or have a paintball gun shootout in the dead of night before setting their rental homes on fire.

"What do you make of these fires?" Wheeler asked as we walked back to his vehicle from our last interview.

"I hope it doesn't turn out to be a gang war. I'm sure every one of these fires was meant to burn down a stash house."

"That's going to be your problem, not mine." Wheeler was grinning about the turnabout that took place since our first meeting. He was well on his way to determining the ignition source for the string of arson fires, while I was now the one with almost no clues to pursue.

The tenants in all three of the rental units were missing and unlikely to turn up at a police station to file a complaint. All I knew for sure was that an arsonist was targeting the worst possible choice of victims. These fires were going to be avenged one way or another.

Chapter 9

We needed to kill some time while we waited for a demolition crew to arrive, so we drove to the IHOP on the I-10 service road for coffee and something to eat. The fire department was still cooling down the embers of what was left of the house when we left, and would do so for another few hours.

"Charlie!" I spotted a young Seventh District narcotics detective at a long table near the kitchen and led Wheeler to meet him.

"Can you tell me anything about the house that just burned down over on Gannon?"

"It was a stash house for a Mexican cartel called the El Caminos. We staked it out a couple of times, but we never could get enough for a search warrant. I thought the Baghdad Brotherhood might have torched the place, but my sources are all saying they had nothing to do with it."

"The Baghdad Brotherhood?" I thought I knew the names of all the local gangs, but this one sounded too much like an Iraqi insurgent group for my comfort.

"They're a bunch of Black veterans who started a gang when they came home from Iraq. They've been using a paintball place over by Shell Beach as a cover for their operation for the last year or so. The Brotherhood and the El Caminos share this part of town right now, but we expect them to fight it out sooner or later."

"Any idea where the guys living in the house might have headed?"

"The El Caminos have half a dozen houses in the East, so they likely just went to one of their other places. The El Caminos opened shop here because it is right off of I-10. Their mules can pull off the highway, deliver their goods, and be gone again in no time. These guys are strictly heroin wholesalers, so good luck catching them dealing."

Chief of Detectives Avery and I exchange any information we have about the city's resurgent gang activity. I have better eyes and ears on the streets than he does, but NOPD has far better intelligence sources overall. The cartel called the El Caminos took their name from the days when their leadership transported cocaine and marijuana in 1970s and '80s era Chevrolet El Caminos. Older cars and trucks offer more space to make hidden compartments than newer vehicles. They subcontracted to infamous outfits like the Medellin and Sinaloa cartels until they felt strong enough to compete against them. They now controlled part of northeastern Mexico, from where they could walk their shipments across the border into Arizona. They also smuggled them in go-fast boats into Houston, and into Alabama using shipping containers packed with produce. New Orleans sat in the middle of their distribution network, with Interstate 55 providing a northbound artery feeding the robust heroin trade in America's heartland.

"Do you think someone wants to burn them out?" I asked Charlie.

"A person would be suicidal to pick a fight with the El Caminos. Even the Brotherhood seems to have decided to ignore them rather than get into it with them."

"New Orleans isn't noted for having the brightest criminals." I was neither making a joke nor telling Charlie anything he did not already know.

"The Mexicans will start leaving body parts around town if they ever catch the guys who burned their place," Charlie predicted.

"Just in time for Mardi Gras," Wheeler pointed out as he took his first bite from his omelet.

This was a bad time for a gang war. The city was barely four days away from the start of Carnival season and not much farther away from an election to choose a new mayor to lead the city's stalled recovery. On top of that, the New Orleans Saints were in the playoffs for only the second Super Bowl they ever stood a real chance of competing in during the team's forty-three-year history.

I ordered a Lumberjack Slam breakfast to go with my coffee. I wanted to keep my strength up for what was to come.

Chapter 10

The fire department rolled up their hoses and left the scene of the fire just before the sun cleared the horizon. This left Clyde Wheeler and me alone in his Acadia to await either the arrival of someone with higher authority or a demolition crew. We agreed that the arrival of either one would connect this fire to the thread leading back to the first fire. I suggested to Wheeler that we surveil the fire scene from a vacant driveway about a block away. Parking in front of the scene might provoke or scare away anyone else with an interest in the property.

It was going to take considerable bluster on both of our parts to derail our anticipated adversaries. Members of the State Police lack the rank to refuse an order to desist when issued by any Federal Agent and Wheeler and I did not have any authority over a demolition crew holding a demolition permit approved by the New Orleans City Council.

We watched the neighborhood slowly come to life. Grade school kids boarded their busses. Parents herded the older kids into cars to head to schools or jobs. The parents drove off in separate cars and directions because it takes two incomes to raise a family, especially in a poor neighborhood. The entire block was empty by nine o'clock.

A dark sedan pulled to a stop in front of the smoldering pile of bricks just after ten o'clock. Two men in suits got out and seemed to be looking for the NOPD detail they expected to find securing the crime scene. They drove away just as a demolition crew from the incinerator in Mississippi arrived.

I did not share my opinion with Wheeler on who the well-dressed advance crew might have been. I would have liked to know what badge those agents carried, but was relieved that my day would not begin with a jurisdictional wrestling match. We headed to the crime scene and looked for the person in a hard hat doing the most arm waving to show our own badges. We weren't Feds, but they were good enough to bring everything to a standstill for the moment.

"This is a crime scene. You'll need to reschedule." Wheeler went so far as to hand one of his Fire Marshal business cards to the supervisor.

"I don't know about this being any crime scene. All I know is that we have a demolition permit and it's only good for today." The foreman was not arguing with us. He wanted it on the record that we were putting a huge wrench into his operation. Stopping now would require re-starting the bureaucratic process to get a new permit.

"Give me a minute." I interrupted. "If he'd be willing to move some things around for us, we'd be on our way."

"We can do that." The company these men worked for made no money until the lot was cleared, and this guy's boss was not going to be happy about having his men stand idle.

"There's really just one section we need to investigate," the Fire Marshal decided.

Our focus was on the hottest part of the fire, specifically the bathroom on the right-hand side of the house. We would look at other sections as the crane removed them but did not expect to find anything significant anywhere else. The intensity of the fire was thorough in destroying the interior and contents of the house.

The first bucket of material moved the collapsed roof off the section of the house we were there to investigate. We climbed into the dump truck when the front-end loader deposited the second load of material atop the charred roof. This pile contained what was left of the bathroom's walls. Wheeler scraped some char and bagged a few other evidence samples while I looked for anything I believed was inconsistent with a charred and soaked bathroom. The amount of water used to cool down the structure made a mush of the drywall. The third load of material from the bulldozer bucket included the grotesquely disfigured bathroom fixtures.

The sink and toilet looked partially melted like candles left in the summer sun. Wheeler told me that porcelain would not melt below thirty-two hundred degrees, so this evidence validated the absurdly high temperature readings taken the night before. I asked a couple of the workers to rummage around until they found the kitchen sink and discovered that it, as well as a second bathroom, suffered only normal amounts of heat and damage. Someone wanted something in that one bathroom to cease to exist. They were intent enough upon doing so that they contracted to have the house pulverized and burnt a second time.

"We aren't going to find anything else here." Wheeler finally concluded what we both feared all along.

He led me around the exterior of the house to collect samples of the now hardened ooze, which had trickled through the wall onto the lawn. There was enough material to test for thermite.

"I just wish I knew what was in that bathtub," Wheeler complained.

"You might look in the drain pipes," the demolition supervisor said almost offhandedly. We both looked at him for a moment before we realized he was stating something obvious. "Maybe whatever they tried to burn made it down the drain a ways and didn't get burnt up."

"Yes, indeed." Wheeler was ecstatic at the prospect of coming away with viable evidence for a change.

The foreman shared a quick word with his backhoe operator and the big bucket on the rear of his tractor began digging up the drain pipe. The crew marked the utility and sewer lines before they unloaded their heavy equipment, so finding what we needed was not a problem.

The sewer pipe was cast iron, but it snapped just as easily as PVC from the force of the backhoe's bucket. Wheeler approached the broken drainpipe with a handful of empty evidence collection tubes and turned his flashlight on to peer inside. He gave a brief shrill cry and then waved me to have a look at what he had just discovered.

I anticipated the sickly sweet stench, but did not imagine I would be looking at a river of recently clotted blood. Someone must have poured a couple of gallons of blood down the drain before destroying the tub they used as a catch basin. I do not imagine slaughtering a cow would have left this much blood. Whoever carried out this ghastly deed went to a lot of work to hide their tracks, only to forget to do the simplest of things. They should have been running water in the tub while they did their dirty work.

Wheeler and I carried the evidence bags back to his vehicle and spread them out on the hood to do an inventory. I laid claim to all of the collected blood evidence, arguing that they were part of my new murder investigation. We agreed to share any findings that would help one another's search for an answer to what was really happening in these houses.

I am not sure whether Wheeler noticed the pair of black Chevrolet Suburbans that passed us as we left the scene. I counted four occupants in the first one and focused my attention on watching it in my rear view mirror rather than count how many passengers rode in the second one. The vehicles had Arizona plates, which made them stand out all the more in this neighborhood. They turned around to follow us. One of them parked in a loading zone after Wheeler dropped me at the bistro, but the other one trailed behind Wheeler's SUV towards the westbound interstate.

Chapter 11

"What the hell have you done now?"

"By the tone of your voice, I can tell you right now that your guess is as good as mine." I wondered who chewed a piece out of NOPD's Chief of Detectives rear end so early in the morning. Avery seemed intent on replacing his loss with a chunk of me, and it was barely eleven o'clock.

"How do you know Bradford Kinkaid?"

"Strictly by reputation." I wondered why the Chief of Detectives was asking me about someone way above either of our pay grades.

"Well, he wants to have lunch with the two of us and Captain Hammond. Wear a suit and meet us at your door at noon. Set places for five in a private room and be on your best behavior."

Hypothesizing why the Deputy Director of Homeland Security was having lunch at my bistro left me little time to wonder about the fifth person on the guest list. State Police Captain Ken Hammond is my boss, but he is just a mid-level administrator. NOPD's Chief of Detectives is not the sort of lowly municipal employee normally invited to eat at the table of the man tasked with keeping everyone along Interstate 10 safe from real and imaginary threats. I was at a loss to understand how I caught the attention of such a high-level operator in the dark world I once occupied. I was also clueless as to why Kinkaid would know I owned a restaurant, but I assumed the man knew everything about everyone with whom he deigned to share his company.

Captain Hammond's glossy white Chevrolet SUV stopped in

front of Strada Ammazarre exactly one hour after I hung up the phone. A Lincoln Town Car limousine followed the SUV. Two men and one woman exited that vehicle, while another young woman and three more men rode with Chief Avery and Captain Hammond. I was wearing my favorite blue Hugo Boss suit as instructed. Chief of Detectives Avery and Captain Hammond wore their dress uniforms. Chief Avery seemed especially uncomfortable in his because his pants size was not keeping up with his waistline.

Juaquin arranged for our meal service in one of the private dining rooms on the mezzanine level. The maître d led our group past the bar, where Chef Tony arranged to be using the telephone, and up the wide flight of stairs. Kinkaid's security detail closed the door behind the invited guests and we all took seats at the large round table. The imposing security detail blocked the top of the stairs while the administrative staff milled about outside the room.

I asked Belinda to be our waitress because she knows how to keep what she hears to herself while missing nothing. She has served at some of the South's finest private clubs and restaurants; places where secrets flow with the bourbon. The fiery redhead could have retired long ago on the investments she has made using her decades' worth of insider tips, but chose instead to continue pouring sweet tea while she kept her ears open and her opinions to herself.

Bradford Kinkaid's svelte blonde aide asked for my cell phone. She placed it beside my bosses' phones in the aluminum briefcase from which she then removed three non-disclosure forms. She passed copies to Chief Avery, Captain Hammond, and me. I did not bother reading mine before I signed it and slid the form across the table to her. She retrieved the paperwork and left the room. Avery flashed me a nervous glance.

I studied Kinkaid while he waited for these formalities to conclude. He was much older than I expected. His handle bar moustache made him look more like a retired Texas rancher than the man running domestic intelligence and counter-terrorism operations from El Paso to Atlanta.

"Do any of you gentlemen know why I invited you here today?" Kinkaid grinned slightly when the three of us shook our heads. "Good. I don't want to have to fire the man in charge of security. The lady here to my left is Jill Bledsoe. She represents the private contractor hired to lead our project here in New Orleans."

My ears perked up at this. My last intelligence mission in Iraq was to identify and locate anyone targeting Coalition forces, and to eliminate their ability to carry out their attacks. I recruited and led the trigger-friendly operatives paid to accomplish this mission, but we all drew our salaries from a private contractor called D-Tech. The company's unofficial motto at the time was "We don't make the drones. We make the drones scarier," and their technologies and software programs made far more than drones scary. They developed technology capable of covertly turning personal electronic devices, such as phones and computers, into tools for surveillance and targeting. They could take any telephone number and use its metadata to develop an accurate chain of command based on the numbers an individual called and who called them. D-Tech remotely accessed the microphones and cameras on electronic devices to sit in on meetings in real time, and then use a targeted individual's phone to track their exact location. My job was gather as many electronic devices as possible, in any manner necessary, to provide their technicians with the metadata they used to decide the threat level individuals posed. I added the names of anyone posing an imminent threat to the list kept by the wet-works team led by the chef presently cooking our meal. We were not interested in taking prisoners or conducting drawn out interrogations. We assumed everyone was guilty. I could imagine no legal domestic applications for anything D-Tech used in that operation. D-Tech never struck me as a company interested in developing any domestic applications, either. Foreign contracts received less oversight and most likely generated far greater income as well. I shuddered to think they might be involved.

Belinda interrupted the meeting when she returned with our Caesar salad course and took our entrée orders. Kinkaid asked Belinda if the chef objected to special orders, and then described the seafood dish he wanted in precise detail before she could answer his question.

Kinkaid resumed the meeting as soon as Belinda left.

"Jill, please explain to these men why they have been asked here."

"The stand-down of our nation's military in Afghanistan and Iraq endangers the ability of private contractors to sustain their readiness for future deployment. Homeland Security has agreed to utilize their capacities and lessons developed in fighting jihadists to target domestic situations. Gang activity has risen dramatically in New Orleans in the wake of Hurricane Katrina, so we have brought an operation to town to address this situation, as it seems local law enforcement has proven itself unable to contain it. Our mission in New Orleans is to combine the technical capacities of our private contractor with the interdictions of former Special Forces operators, such as Detective Holland. Detective Holland was part of a very similar operation in Iraq. Seeing Detectives Holland and Wheeler on the morning news is what made it necessary to read you in on the basics of this operation. Maintaining the cover story for our activities is critical. " Bledsoe made it all sound so reasonable, and legal.

"I'm sure this is another outstanding example of my tax dollars at work, but how will any evidence your operation collects stand up in court?" I resisted the urge to question how Jill Bledsoe was familiar with the mission that nearly got me killed. Kinkaid and I were the only ones I believed had the security clearance to fully understand what I did in Baghdad, or how hiding behind a private contractor to cover my tracks in that mission allowed my team to operate far outside of the Geneva Conventions or international law. I watched Jill's facial expression change to one of imagining painful ways of having me killed if I said another word.

"The man in charge of security on this operation told me I wasn't going to like you. I am surprised you could even find work after the fiasco you caused in Baghdad. You came close to singlehandedly derailing our government's relationship with the new Iraqi government, and did cost your employer their other contracts. He suggested we involve you rather than risk your interference," Kinkaid interrupted to snarl at me.

"I just want it on the record that I am not going to get on any wagon with a private contractor providing the asses that pull it." I formally objected to the role I was assigned.

Kinkaid turned a few shades of red before he abruptly burst out laughing and gave my bosses time to catch a breath of air. It remained obvious that he still wanted to drop me into a dark hole until Bledsoe's men completed their dubious mission. He was merely laughing at my notion that I had a choice in this matter.

Bledsoe waited a moment before picking up where she left off. "The antiquated War on Drugs changed dramatically in the post-9/11 landscape. Our concern became preventing terrorist organizations and the drug cartels from banding together. There is increasing evidence that the two groups share arms dealers, smuggling routes, and even use the same bankers. The Mexican cartels have begun dealing increasing amounts of heroin since our draw down from Afghanistan. The work we intend to do here is, in some ways, just a variation of the type of classified intelligence work we have taken part in elsewhere."

She looked at me as if to dare me to speak up.

"So, you're here to combine the War on Drugs with the War on Terror?" I ignored the troubled looks in the room. "Or are you just trying to rebrand the War on Crime?"

Deputy Director Kinkaid frowned at both my question and my attitude and took over the sales pitch. "Our operation will disrupt the heroin traffic into New Orleans from Mexico by interdicting the supply chain and create tension between the cartels and their local distribution partners. Drying up the heroin supply will create chaos that will enable the DEA and Justice Department to bring serious criminal charges against targeted individuals high on the cartel ladders."

"Are you here to start a gang war?" I wanted his answer on the record. The operation I ran in Iraq passed off many of its victims as being part of that country's civil war. It was easy to hide our dead bodies in the thousands of others.

"My latest briefing indicates there have already been instances of violence and destruction between the factions in question." The Deputy Director's statement did not answer my question, and raised some of its own.

"Is the private contractor responsible for the violence?" Captain Hammond has problems seeing other people's big pictures, but he seldom missed even the finest detail. The Deputy Director decided it was time to spell a few things out for all of us. Hammond's question remained unanswered.

"Private contractors are not as constricted by the rule of law as NOPD or the State Police. Our contractor has hired men Detective Holland once described as 'coming out the shadows to leave ghosts in their wake' to goad two potential adversaries into action against one another. The fires Holland investigated are a by-product of that operation." My own words began echoing too loudly in my ears for me to focus clearly. He had just quoted my supposedly still classified Delta Force exit interview. "We're here because the operation requires your detective's services. To be clear, any case involving either the El Caminos or a local gang called the Pistol Peetes will be assigned to him."

"And who do I report whatever I findings to?" I rhetorically wondered aloud.

"Miss Bledsoe, on a weekly basis, or not. I really do not care. She will let you know when her task here is completed, and she will provide you with a report you can use to explain everything to the public's satisfaction. Your record shows that you have experience with sweeping things under the carpet, and that's what I expect all of you to help Miss Bledsoe complete her mission." Kinkaid all but ignored the astonished looks on Hammond and Avery's faces. The three of us took a moment to digest our dubious orders from the Deputy Director and his partner from the dark world of clandestine private contractors. My bosses were utterly flabbergasted that Captain Hammond was supposed to stop Wheeler's arson investigation and Avery was to assign me any cases related to the Pistol Peetes or El Caminos so I could park their investigation in a blind alley. All the same, neither of them raised an objection to what they realized was unnegotiable and unstoppable. Our careers would end before Kinkaid ordered Jill Bledsoe to stand down from countering whatever threat he was convinced existed.

Belinda returned with five covered dishes on a serving tray. She presented Jill with ravioli stuffed with crawfish and lobster bathed in a three-cheese cream sauce tinged with Tabasco and sherry. Hammond savored a plate of Veal Picatta, fragrant with lemon and garlic. Chief Avery dug into his lasagna. I chose an herb and spice-rich pasta dish called Puttanesca.

Jill Bledsoe's smirk told me she caught my ordering a dish named after Italian prostitutes as being the statement on my situation I dared not say aloud.

All of our attention shifted to the middle of the pasta bowl Belinda now set before Deputy Director Kinkaid. We could smell the delicious seafood medley swimming in its broth of white wine and marinara, just as he ordered it. He did not request the raw catfish head rising above the center of his meal. The fish's twin whiskers drooped over either side of the shallow pasta bowl in a perfect imitation of his own moustache. Kinkaid used his fork and spoon to set the severed head to one side. He grinned at a nervous Belinda before he winked across the table at me.

"I see your chef isn't a big fan of taking orders, either."

Chapter 12

I silently assessed the situation while I ate my lunch. Kinkaid asked Chief Avery very specific questions about NOPD's manpower levels. New Orleans' police force was already seriously understrength before Hurricane Katrina hit town. It dropped by over a third in the first year following the storm, and it was still below that inadequate level five years after the storm. The ongoing decimation of NOPD was due as much to burnout and low morale as it was to demotions and terminations related to malfeasance during the city's darkest hours. I was barely able to keep Chief Avery out of the FBI's line of fire in their investigation into his department's cover-up of nearly a dozen storm-related shootings by NOPD officers. The State Police pulled their own officers from New Orleans during the investigation, and still harbored distrust of the department.

Deputy Director Kinkaid questioned Captain Hammond about the State Police's slowly diminishing role in supplementing NOPD's numbers. He seemed unusually pleased to hear that the State Police now limited its assistance to New Orleans' police force to festivals like Mardi Gras. Hammond felt NOPD was still woefully understaffed and I was troubled that a Deputy Director of Homeland Security seemed to like hearing Hammond's negative report on my city's overwhelmed police force. It never occurred to me, until now, that someone like Kinkaid might have played a role in the FBI opening their investigation to distract NOPD, and to drive a wedge between the local and state police so D-Tech would have an open city in which to operate.

The Deputy Director and Jill Bledsoe headed to their waiting vehicle once Belinda cleared our entree dishes. There was no suggestion made of having coffee or dessert. The attractive aide with the metal briefcase met my bosses and me at the bar and handed us back our telephones. She raised an eyebrow and cracked a small smile when I handed the phone she gave me to Hannah, the daytime bartender, in exchange for my own phone.

"So much for your investigation," Captain Hammond reiterated, just in case I was not paying attention or planned to ignore the Deputy Director.

"Don't you want to know what I've already learned?"

"No. I also suggest you forget whatever you think you know." Hammond never was one to push back against a higher authority. He likes being part of a chain of command and is content with his place on it.

Chief Avery gave me similar instructions, but then drug his feet about leaving. The valet brought Hammond's SUV to the curb moments after Kinkaid and Bledsoe departed. Captain Hammond was no fan of New Orleans on a good day, and today was not a very good day for him. He headed back to Baton Rouge, uncomfortable with what was going on, but satisfied that he stopped my interference with an operation conducted in the interest of national security. Wheeler's curiosity about the cause of the fires was already satisfied, so he would raise no objection to closing his part in our joint investigation.

Hannah opened and passed cold beers to the Chief of Detectives and me as soon as Captain Hammond left the building. We went to the kitchen and took our usual seats at the Chef's Table.

"You aren't about to give this up, are you?" Avery caught the tension between Jill Bledsoe and myself in the dining room. He also wasn't happy with the expectation he felt was being placed upon himself to ignore serious crimes.

"Of course not." There was no reason to tell him a lie. "Do you want to know what Wheeler and I found at the latest fire scene?"

"It would be good to know that you are committing professional suicide over something more than just not liking private contractors handling police work."

"I only have an issue with any private security contractors working here." I didn't bother to elaborate.

"So I gathered from what Kinkaid let slip about what you did in Iraq." Avery's face showed more of the same terror it held when

Tony and I explained how our friendship pre-dated the ambush that nearly took my life.

"Someone has been setting super-hot fires to destroy evidence related to taking down stash houses. So far, they have torched two connected to the Pistol Peetes and two I believe belonged to the El Camino cartel. I don't think there is a gang war. I think someone is making it look like there is one. In fact, I would say that the exact opposite of what we were told is happening is what that woman is here to do."

"Do you really believe Kinkaid approved her doing that?" Avery was bracing himself for the other shoe to drop.

"If it was just a matter of burning stash houses, I would stand down, but there's a lot of killing already going on as well. Wheeler and I found evidence that someone poured a lot of blood down the drain of the last house before torching it with thermite. I'm pretty sure we would have found similar evidence at one or two of the other houses as well if they weren't bulldozed."

"How much blood are you talking about?"

"I have no idea how much blood it takes to reach from a bathtub to the main drain at the street, but I'd say it must have looked like a slaughterhouse in that bathroom. There were four men living in the house and they are all unaccounted for." I let the implication settle into Avery's thought process before we continued.

"And you still have the samples?" Avery's eyes narrowed as he thought things through for himself. I could tell that Kinkaid's orders were simmering inside him, and his temper would boil over eventually.

"Yes. I was going to drop them off at the Crime Lab after lunch. Wheeler has probably already dropped his samples at the State's lab."

"Don't turn yours in. Not yet." Avery held up his hand. "Kinkaid will probably do a search for anything you may have submitted. They might be satisfied with destroying the Fire Marshal's evidence."

"Hopefully."

"You can't appear to be investigating the fires. Is there anything you can you look into that could run parallel to the arson investigation?" Avery was surprising me with this odd determination to defy the orders of someone so high above him.

"You're not afraid of losing your job? Kinkaid was clear that you were to close down my investigation."

"I heard him," Avery growled. "It seems real important that we not interfere with whatever they are really doing here. I think that Jill woman lied when she said she discovered you were investigating the fires when she saw you on the news. That would mean that the soonest Kinkaid knew about your investigation was eight o'clock this morning."

"So?" It was rare that Avery saw something I missed.

"The Deputy Director flew down here from Washington. He called me from his jet right before I called you, and he had just called Captain Hammond in Baton Rouge. He had to already be on his way here by the time you would have been on the news this morning."

"That's probably right. What's your point?" I failed to make the connection he was waving in my face.

"Who's the dog and who is the tail wagging the dog? D-Tech already knew you were on the case. That Bledsoe woman needed Kinkaid to give them an official cover so you would stop looking at this."

I was impressed with Avery's assessment of the dynamics at play. It made perfect sense that the Deputy Director would personally intervene in my investigation because Homeland Security wanted to be sure their legally dubious operation stayed hidden. It was not worth violating secrecy laws to tell Avery what I knew of companies like D-Tech because he already sensed Kinkaid's choice was shady.

I nodded quietly at his theory that the operation originated with someone higher up the ladder than Bradford Kinkaid. What Avery did not understand was that this possibility was another good reason to let the whole thing drop. I was not likely to stop whatever was going on, because Kinkaid wrapped his operation in a heavy national security blanket. We could never tell anyone what I uncovered, even if we found anything illegal.

"You do know that disobeying Kinkaid is a bad career move, right?" It was friendly advice I knew he would ignore when I gave it.

"I don't care. I want you to get to the bottom of this. The Feds cannot keep coming to town and doing whatever they want because they think NOPD is too weak to notice or to stop them. We're not going to be the place Uncle Sam keeps sending his dirty laundry." Avery pounded a meaty fist on the table.

"You go, now!" I found myself nearly laughing at Chief Avery's tirade. Such emotional outbursts were uncharacteristic behavior for him, but Avery was devoted to defending NOPD against outside criticism.

"Tell me how you can do this and keep us both out of jail," Avery demanded in a much calmer voice and wiped the grin off my face.

"I can start by investigating one of the Peetes as a missing person's case."

"Then do that. I'm asking you to ignore your orders, but you're on your own if you decide to do so. Are you okay with that?" Avery was already apologizing for the most likely outcome of what he was asking me to do.

"I've been thrown under buses by the best of them." I tipped my beer bottle to him in an unspoken toast to keeping our city safe.

Chapter 13

I drove Chief Avery back to his office at the Headquarters Building on Broad Street. We used my Cadillac CTS-V wagon because he is too big to climb in or out of the XLR convertible's low-slung frame. The wagon is a tiger on four wheels. It is easy to dismiss anything with a station wagon body as being harmless, but this beast's 556 horsepower supercharged engine would top 116 miles an hour in a quarter mile. I have surprised suspects who were convinced a Mustang or Camaro could leave me in their dust.

"Rides nice," was the closest Avery would come towards admitting he liked the Cadillac.

"You're just lucky my nickname isn't Beetle." I grinned at him as I nudged the gas pedal and burst through the traffic light at Tulane and La Salle. Avery waved at an officer driving an NOPD squad car we passed at a speed that would warrant a ticket. I parked in one of the spots in front of the courthouse reserved for police officers and tossed my State Police placard on the dashboard. The expensive Cadillac stuck out like a black eye in the row of marked patrol cars.

We went to Avery's office and he sent an officer for the file on Richie Franklin of the Pistol Peetes. I took the file to an empty desk in the detectives' squad room and made notes for a missing person case. Franklin's juvenile record was in the file as well. I looked up his father's name in the database and found he died in a drive-by shooting when Richard was just fourteen years old. Richard's first scrape with the cops came less than a year later.

His mother's drug possession record extended years before

Richard was even born. There were a couple of misdemeanor theft and shoplifting charges as well and, looking at the records of the entire Franklin family, I saw an all-too-familiar story. Richie's father supplied the dope for his mother's drug habit and made enough money that she could sit around the house high for days at a time. Four children were born into this household. Two died as infants and Richard took over supporting his mother and his kid sister when his father died. It was likely he took over his father's piece of the local trade, but lacked any real street smarts until he evacuated after Katrina and fell in with the dealers and thugs that became the Pistol Peetes.

The Pistol Peetes were the result of one of the many missteps FEMA made in the wake of the storm. Someone in FEMA thought handing each of New Orleans' poorest displaced citizens ten thousand dollars would encourage the evacuees to resettle wherever they received their checks. The plan failed to take into account that the only place the evacuees knew as home was New Orleans and ten grand was more than enough money to take them home. Street gangs pooled their money to buy cars, guns, and enough dope to get back into business in New Orleans. The Pistol Peetes banded together under a name that paid homage to their lives and neighborhood before the storm.

I wrote down the address Richard Franklin gave at the time of a handful of arrests prior to the now burned-out house off Louisiana. I crosschecked it with his mother's last known address and caught a match. She was living in the remodeled C J Peete Projects, rebranded as Harmony Oaks, with her daughter.

The government waited for over a year after the storm before tearing down the flood-damaged projects and dumping millions of dollars into a new method of warehousing poor people, but they did not spent a dime on changing the lives of anyone living here. Families still needed to eat, and the storm washed away more low-paying jobs than rebuilding the city created. The new housing in Harmony Oaks was a far cry from the brick dormitory-style buildings of the old projects. HANO's new buildings were a hodge-podge of designs that at least tried to blend into the neighborhood architecturally. The newly paved streets twisted and turned to make drive-by shootings and high-speed pursuits intentionally difficult. The new units each had an individual lawn instead of the central green space that previously served as a killing field.

Residents were enjoying one of the month's rare warm days

while talking with their neighbors on their balconies and porches. Everyone silently took notice when a patrol car stopped in front of the Franklin house.

I would only make things difficult for the Chief of Detectives if I personally initiated a missing person case for Richard Franklin. Assigning me to the case after Ritchie's mother filed a formal complaint did not technically violate Kinkaid's instructions to either of us. I needed to drag along a rookie officer to file the report once I convinced Richard's mother to declare him missing. Kinkaid could not blame Avery if I chose to investigate Ritchie's disappearance rather than bury it.

"What y'all want?" Mrs. Franklin demanded through her locked screen door. She was a tall woman, rail-thin and probably not much over forty years of age. She may have been pretty once upon a time, but her years-long drug habit ruined her looks along with her health.

"We're hoping you might want to help your son." I tried to reassure her and showed her my State Police badge.

"What's Richie got himself into now?" I could not decide if her question was a sign that she was not aware of her son's abduction or if she was trying to cover for his absence. It was unlikely she did not know his house burned down.

"We know he's missing. Can we come in and discuss this?"

She hesitated for a moment, but then allowed us in. I could tell my State Police badge unnerved her. She sized up the NOPD rookie behind me and summarily dismissed his presence entirely.

"How do you know my boy is missing? Why do you even care that Richie be in trouble?" It was the second question that betrayed her knowledge of her son's activities.

"Because I'm afraid something very bad may have happened to your son. Someone is setting fires, and I think they may be doing so to hide a lot of murders." I tried to be as dramatic with this as I could. It was going to take a lot to convince the mother of "Richie Rich" that the police held any real concern for a drug dealer's welfare. "The fire at your son's place fits the pattern in those fires."

"Why would anybody be doing that?" She sat down at the green Formica-topped kitchen table. I motioned the officer onto the sofa in the living room and then I sat on the arm of the sofa. I did not want to seem to be towering above her once she sat down. She liked having her distance and I still had not earned the trust that would allow me to sit across from her at her kitchen table.

"That's what I would like to know. I need you to file a missing person's report on your son so I can try to find out. Unless you already know where your son is hiding, that is." It was not going to hurt to ask her if she could just direct me to where he was staying.

She took a moment to consider her limited options. She had to believe I was trying to trap her into filing a false report if she actually knew where her son was hiding. She would also have to admit to herself that I was the best way she of finding her son if she genuinely did not know his whereabouts. I told her the arsonists were cremating their murder victims to judge her reaction.

"I don't know where he is," she said, and the tears started. This was no act for our benefit. She was truly concerned about her son. "Do you really think someone burned up my boy?"

"I hope not." This was true. I needed her son to answer questions that his abduction might make him more open to discussing than were his fellow gang-members. I slowly approached her and handed her a paper towel from the roll on the counter to wipe her tears. I also waved the officer into the seat at the table across from her. "It's better for all of us if I can look for your son as a missing person rather than a suspect. I know he's in a gang, but that's not why I want to find him."

"What are you going to do with my boy when you catch him?" She was always going to want to protect him. Ritchie was probably her only source of income and, sadly, drugs.

"I only want to find him, not arrest him." She did not understand legal semantics, but it was important that she feel I was helping and not hunting her son. "I hope he can help me find who is starting these fires. You never know where someone like that will strike next."

This line was working wonders for me so far. Who wants a serial arsonist on the loose? She gave the NOPD rookie what he needed for his report. It was not much, but I already knew his criminal record and a few things about the fires. I also knew another woman nearby to speak with about Richie. I still had her number in my cell phone's call log. I didn't want to add her to my phone contacts in case someone took my phone and mistook her for an informant.

I stepped out on the porch and dialed the number of the woman across the street from Richie's house. I did not want to drag the rookie to see her, and she absolutely would not want an NOPD patrol car and a State Police Detective rolling up on her doorstep in broad daylight.

She answered on the fifth ring. That is a long time for somebody with nothing to do all day.

"Remember me? I'm the detective that called you a couple of days ago."

"I remember you. What you want now?" I detected more reluctance to speak than impatience about whatever I might have interrupted.

"I'm over here at Richie's mom's place having her fill out a missing person's report on her son."

"What are you doing that for?"

"So I can start looking for Richie as a missing person instead of a suspect in the arson fire at his house. I think you might know some of his friends and I would like you to pass along that I want the arsonist, not Richie."

"What makes you think I know any of those people?" Now she was sounding defensive, even offended by my accusation. She was good.

"You live in the neighborhood. It is hard not to. Just pass my number along to anyone that might get it to Richie, if he's still alive."

"Yeah. Okay." She hung up on me. I went back inside and waited for the rookie officer to finish taking the report. He was a white rookie with the flat accent of a Midwesterner. This was probably his first time in Harmony Oaks, and maybe the last time he would ever be remotely welcome. There was a long learning curve ahead of him about handling, and avoiding getting handled by, the city's life-long residents. I only hoped he would take the time to understand his assigned district and did not become another newcomer who viewed the city through his patrol car windshield as if it were just a bad movie.

Chapter 14

The first break in Richie's missing person case came two days later. There was a call to the Fifth District about an abandoned car in the parking lot of the Crescent City Casino on Chef Menteur Highway. The place is a casino in much the same way a convenience store is a grocery store. This was a casino in name only; there were rows of video poker machines under its roof but no live games of chance like roulette. They didn't even have a buffet. All the same, the place did a lively business and the parking lot was usually packed anytime I drove past.

I arrived to find NOPD's forensic technicians making a thorough photo record of a battered Ford F-150 pickup truck bearing Louisiana plates. A pile of black trash bags in the bed of the truck held the chopped up remains of something fleshy. My first thought was how glad I was that it was January and not July. Decomposition has a unique odor and smelling it left no doubt about what those plastic bags contained. The techs stoically took their blood and fiber samples from each of the bags before transferring the goo- filled black bags to the coroner's waiting van.

I went looking for the unlucky officers who first responded to the call and was only a little surprised to find it was the two police officers I spoke with about the house fire, which occurred only a few blocks away.

"Looks like you guys keep getting the good stuff." I tried to joke with them. They seemed unnerved by what they discovered in the truck.

"Sorry, it's my first real crime scene like this," the younger of the pair said as he began dry heaving.

"They said there are no heads in there with those bodies," his partner explained. I patted his partner on the back.

"What else can you tell me?" Focusing on my questions might take the rookie's mind off the images in his horrified mind's eye.

"One of the bartenders called it in during the casino's shift change," the older cop said. "He's inside if you want to talk to him, but he's a mess as well."

"And I'll bet the video footage doesn't have a clear image of the parking lot, right?"

"It does, actually. We're waiting on a subpoena for the video, but the manager already showed it to the detectives. A Black kid drove it here and then left in a white Hummer someone else was driving." The officer gave me a curious look when I reacted to the information about the Hummer. "There's a BOLO out on a white Hummer. Is this connected?"

"Probably more than we imagine. Whoever dumped the bodies here wanted to be sure the Hummer was associated with the truck and the bodies. It's why they picked a place with good cameras." I could not tell them my real theory about this, so I turned and walked away from them at that point.

I spoke to the forensic team and told them about the missing Mexicans who owned a truck matching the description of this one. I needed to tip Avery off to the Hummer connection so he would not bother assigning an NOPD detective to investigate the case. I seriously doubted Richie Rich made this delivery, despite the intention and effort to implicate him.

It was intriguing, though, that Richie Franklin's SUV magically reappeared less than a week after Kinkaid ordered me to ignore the fire at Richie's house, and just days after the missing person report from Richie's mother appeared in NOPD's computer system. Someone was trying hard to make Richie appear to be alive, and to be feuding with the cartel supplying his gang with its heroin. There were no good reasons to do this. The first bad reason that came to mind was it that it was a perfect way to get people upset.

I realized too late that coming here meant I swallowed the bait in a trap Kinkaid's mission leader set in place for me. I scanned the small crowd gathered by the sight of so much police activity. I did not know whose face to look for in the crowd, but I was sure that at least one of the bystanders was there to take my picture and report on whether I showed up at the crime scene.

Chapter 15

The next afternoon provided a brief distraction from trying to determine what Kinkaid was getting me into and how it connected to four house fires and a truckload of headless bodies. Frankly, I needed the break. I could not imagine a single scenario that explained the crime scene that did not spell trouble for somebody.

My sister and I learned how to handle difficult people by having a control freak for a mother. Camille Devereaux Holland was much more of a force to reckon with when I was growing up than anyone I have encountered as an adult. It is established fact that she married my father in a moment of spite towards her parents. She spent the next thirty years trying to mold him into the prominent man she should have married. Apparently, my father decided to spend his last years living in peace and quiet because my parents separated shortly before he vanished.

Katie and I drove to my mother's house off Highway 90 in the Rigolets to attend a rally in support of Lionel Batiste's bid for a seat on the City Council. We enjoyed a leisurely lunch of softshell crabs at a seafood joint on the way. The Rigolets is a razor-thin strip of high ground in the wetlands bordering Lake Catherine and Lake Ponchartrain and extending from New Orleans all the way to the Mississippi border. Katrina's storm surge scoured away every camp, bar, and diner flanking the highway and I try to give the handful of businesses that reopened any patronage I can.

"What are you doing here?" Tulip demanded of me seconds after I parked the station wagon. I knew she was mad about something the minute I pulled into the driveway and saw her headed our way.

"We're here to show our support for Lionel. I even brought my checkbook." I did not believe I needed to defend my presence. Lionel Batiste is the son of my bistro's sous chef so I felt obligated to make an appearance. Lionel was the presumptive winner of the City Council seat despite entering the race as a publicity stunt for a book he was writing about his experiences at the Convention Center in the wake of Hurricane Katrina. He did not take the odds of his campaign's success seriously until the incumbent candidate's arrest. "You can't get someone indicted and then show up to support the candidate favored to take their job. Do not give him money, either. It would look bad for both of you," Tulip fully explained her distress. I should have seen what she was talking about myself before I ever drove out there.

"Fine, I'll leave. But tell me again how you talked Mother into this." I was curious how anyone, even her daughter, convinced the matriarch of the politically connected Devereaux clan to allow the angry nephew of a former member of the Black Panther Party to campaign under her roof. My sister jokes that the Devereaux family is so old money they still own the first seashell they took in trade.

Katie and I trailed behind Tulip as she approved the caterer's final preparations for the informal event. It was going to be difficult to juxtapose a poor African-American kid and this setting in media coverage and not make Lionel look like a lackey. The Modern-style house my father financed with the royalties from his first successful novel is an anomaly in an area of homes built high up on pillars in hopes of avoiding destruction by the next thirty-foot storm surge. The house sits defiantly on a slab foundation; repairing the place in 2009 cost twice what it did to build in 1982. Then again, my mother's tastes grew more expensive in the interim as well.

"Roger was the one who figured out how to do it. This is now a fund-raiser for the ASPCA and Lionel is just going to happen to stop by for a photo op." Tulip touched a finger to her temple to show me how smart she thought this was.

"And our Mother doesn't have to look like she supports Lionel."

"That reminds me. Mother insists that you talk to Roger about the dog," Tulip said. Our mother refused to call Roux anything but "the dog."

"What about Roux?"

"Am I Roger?"

I saw her point and excused myself to find Roger. Katie and Tulip began a different conversation as I wandered off.

I found Roger on the slate patio that stretches between the house and the in-ground saltwater pool. He was sporting a new haircut, one without his Grateful Dead roadie's ponytail of gray hair. The patio bartender was still setting up, but I talked him out of a bottle of donated Abita Amber and stood in Roger's line of sight until he noticed me and disengaged from his conversation with what I assumed were ASPCA volunteers.

"Tulip says we have a problem with Roux," I said to open the conversation. Roger seemed nervous about talking with me so I did not start our conversation with his conformist haircut.

"Roux chewed up another set of cushions. Your mother wants him gone." Roger seemed genuinely embarrassed that an animal under his personal care was responsible for the destruction of multiple sets of patio furniture cushions.

"Mother will make you move back into the boathouse." I meant it as a joke but he blushed immediately. "Does my Mother think we don't know your razor is in her bathroom? Tulip and I are just happy you're here to keep her occupied. Now we don't have to have dinner with her every month so she can lecture us. Thank you. Really."

"Well, don't tell her you've figured us out." Roger knew enough not to rock that boat. "I've been working with the canine unit in Slidell to train Roux to sniff out explosives, narcotics, and bodies, but they don't need another dog. Do you know anyone in the NOPD that might want him?"

"I could ask around. I can tell you right now that nobody will want a dog that's going to chew up their vehicle if he's left alone." I felt somewhat responsible to help relocate Roux. He was living there because of me.

"Roux's just acting out. He will stop chewing if someone spends more time with him. I guess I let myself get too distracted." He was beating himself up for paying attention to the wrong beast, to put it nicely. I could tell by Roger's expression that Roux was destined for the dog pound.

"Katie and I came here in the wagon. Load up his kennel and I will get him out of your hair when we leave today. It's the least I can do to show my gratitude for giving Mother someone new to pick on." I sighed and walked him over to the bartender for a fresh beer. "Then you two will have to find another excuse to explain why you're still living here."

We went to the boathouse and I spent a few minutes renewing my tenuous connection to Roux. The thickly muscled male pit bull arrived here as a murder suspect named Taz. One of the conspirators dyed his fur a deep blue in an effort to conceal the fact they had switched dogs in order to kill a man in as cold-blooded and brutal of a manner as I have seen in civilian life. The murder plot involved substituting Taz for the victim's comparatively benign pet because of Taz's winning record as a fighting dog. Roger and I sorted what triggered Taz to make the fatal attack and then Roger desensitized the pit bull to that cue.

I put a leash on Roux and practiced leading him along the gravel driveway while Roger loaded the dog's kennel, chew toys, and food into my station wagon before I could change my mind. It took only a few minutes on the front lawn with Roger to learn the proper way to command Roux with the cues he trained the dog to follow when it was working. I was amused that the dog sniffed every car he passed and laughed aloud at Roger's mortification when Roux sniffed around the tires on my mother's Mercedes.

I waited until Lionel Batiste's motorcade arrived and then shared a discreet moment with the candidate to wish him luck, something I did not think he needed. Tulip and her political hack friends were still working behind the scenes to replace themselves with a capable campaign staff from among Lionel's neighbors in the Lower Ninth Ward. Nobody in our family wanted Lionel to look like our puppet, especially me.

"Did you win the door prize?" Katie asked when she finally realized I was not simply watching Roux for my mother's boyfriend. Katie had seen Roux before, but this was the first time she was close enough to either pet the dog, or for it to bite her.

"Um, no." I was at a loss for how to explain my situation. Roux was how Katie and I re-connected. She was the prosecutor who dealt with the couple that used this pit bull as a murder weapon.

"You're a bit old to be getting your first dog," she laughed.

"Your backyard is fenced, right?" There was no good way to hint at what I had in mind.

"Yes, it is. To keep dogs out." Katie reminded me. "Keep him at your place. You have so much in common anyway. You're both trained killers learning to be the good guys. I'm always afraid you're going to hurt me in one of your nightmares. Maybe the dog can protect me when you're sleeping and you can keep me safe from him when you're awake."

I had obviously underestimated Katie's concerns about sleeping next to me. Her attempt at making a joke out of it actually offered a valid excuse for me to adopt Roux. She was also entirely correct about both of our natures.

"Roger trained Roux for use as a police canine, maybe with a narcotics or bomb squad." I was still trying to sell her on something she already seemed to have resigned herself to accept into our life together.

"Great. Now I get to date two cops for the price of one." Katie seemed more amused than agitated with Roux's arrival in our lives. "He'll probably eat more than you do."

"So, I can keep him?"

"You walk him and pick up his messes." Katie was rubbing his ears a lot more than she would have if she really hated dogs.

I loaded Roux into his kennel and grabbed one of his chew toys from the back seat. He needed to understand immediately that the Cadillac's expensive leather upholstery was never going to be on the menu.

"And he sleeps on the floor when we're at my house. Not the bed," Katie added as I started to back out of the driveway.

"That's how I spent our first night together." Katie was unamused by the comparison. This comment, true as it was, earned me a punch in the shoulder. I did not mind in the least that Katie was giving the dog more attention than me by the time we reached her house off Nashville. She went inside to see what she could put together as supper for three while I walked Roux the short distance to Audubon Park and gave him two laps on the hiking path. He made two new dog friends and gave three frat boys from Tulane smoking pot on the golf course the scare of their lives, which was a story I would enjoy telling every chance I found.

Chapter 16

C hief Avery called me just ahead of noon on Wednesday to have me join him at the scene of a shooting on Saint Charles Avenue. We needed to determine if it was part of what we were supposed to be ignoring. It was impossible to overlook that this happened on what would be a parade route in a matter of weeks. Avery was already displeased about having to keep his detectives from investigating the first string of violent crimes and fires. The most he was supposed to do was to let his detectives create incident reports that I was supposed to pretend to investigate. The situation had not yet reached a point where his own men detected a pattern or questioned their commander's decision to pass cases my way. Allowing his investigators to believe the State Police were stealing their thunder provided the Chief a way to handle his conundrum.

The nineteen-year-old African-American murder victim died from a single gunshot to the back of his head. He probably never saw his killer. His brains coated the parking lot of a Wendy's two blocks off Lee's Circle. The gang tattoo of a revolver laid over a basketball on the kid's right arm probably had something to do with his death. The restaurant fell inside the area the Pistol Peetes' claimed as their territory.

"Tell me the story," I asked the NOPD Homicide Detective who should have lead the investigation. He looked at Chief Avery before he said a word to me. The Chief did not look any happier about transferring the case than he did about there being a murder on St. Charles Avenue.

"Jimmy Washington came out of Wendy's with his kid brother and headed towards the streetcar. Some Mexican got out of a car and clipped him from behind. A second shooter wounded the brother and winged a tourist in front of the hotel who was filming the whole thing as it went down. EMS took him and the brother to get patched up."

"Can we use the video to make an ID on the car or shooter?" It would normally be fortuitous to have a video tape of the crime. Evidence was going to be a lot less handy when I was not supposed to solve the crime.

"It's pretty good. He didn't get the license plate but we know it's an older El Camino. He did get a pretty good shot of both Mexicans' faces."

"Great." I forced a smile. Avery and I exchanged unhappy looks about a circumstantial link to the El Caminos.

The NOPD Detective ripped his notes about the injured tourist from his notebook and handed me the pages. It was his unnecessarily polite way of telling me to kiss off for having taken his case.

"I'm not sure I can keep doing this," I admitted to Chief Avery.

"I'm pretty sure I won't make you." Avery was frowning. "By the way, the coroner confirmed that the bodies in those trash bags were all decapitated."

"I figured as much. I'm used to seeing the cartels chop up their victims, but I don't think I've heard of gangs around here doing so. I'd hate to referee a gang war between any two gangs willing to fight that rough." It would be a very bad thing indeed.

"My narcotics guys and the DEA say the El Caminos are suppliers to the local heroin trade. Everything I have says the El Caminos are the only ones the Pistol Peetes could be getting their dope from. Maybe there actually is some sort of beef between them that we don't know about." Avery was trying to give me everything he knew even though there was nothing I was supposed to do with the information.

Beheading enemies is an act of intimidation the cartels picked up from the jihadists they began doing business with when the heroin trade shifted back to Afghanistan from the Turks and Pakistanis. I doubted the Pistol Peetes had the stomach for decapitating their victims, but it also made no sense for the cartel to have executed and decapitated their own men. My mind reeled with scenarios and suspects until I took a deep breath and reminded myself I was not even supposed to solve the crime.

Chapter 17

The wounded tourist was a sixty-something-year-old white male named Mike Grainger. Mike looked and talked like the retired Marine he claimed to be. He showed off the bullet wounds to his abdomen he brought home from Vietnam and made a point of refusing the offer of pain meds for what he called the "scratch" on his upper arm. It was one of those scratches where a few millimeters to the left might have cost him the arm, and a few inches to the right would have cost him his life. One thing I certainly had in common with the aging jarhead was a personal understanding that dwelling on things that did not happen is a useless way to spend one's time.

"Where are you from, Mike?" I asked just to make conversation until the intern finished wrapping a bandage over some butterfly bandages.

"Blytheville, Arkansas." He said this as if he was proud of the fact. It was probably his hometown and a place where he felt well respected.

"Really," I chuckled. "My family is from Cooter."

"I'm not familiar with it." This was an incredibly careless admission. Cooter, Missouri is where my father was born and raised. The family still runs a farm set back from the Mississippi River levee a few miles east of town. I've only been there a couple of times in my entire life, and never by my own choice. The town of Cooter is also less than ten miles from Blytheville. It isn't much of a town, but anyone Mike's age should have had stumbled upon it at some point in their life.

"How long have you lived in Blytheville?" I asked, hoping I didn't react too strongly to his previous answer.

"My whole life, except when I was in the Corps," Mike went right on spinning his story.

"So, you're a big fan of the Weevils," I suggested. I have no idea what Blytheville High School calls their teams. I'm more than sure it has nothing to do with boll weevils, which are the scourge of the local cotton crops. "There's nothing like small-town high school football, right?"

"So, I guess you want to see the video." Mike wisely changed the subject. He pointed to a camera bag beside his neatly folded clothes on one of the chairs. The one thing I did not doubt was that he spent some time in the military.

He cued up the footage of the shooting. He filmed one of the streetcars passing the hotel, and swept the camera in its wake just as the shooting occurred. He caught the shooting in amazingly stable footage and even filmed the passenger in the vehicle shooting him.

This little movie would have been something to show off in a bar wherever Mike actually lived. That was never going to happen and Mike was about to face very different questions than any his practiced answers covered. There would be no big pat on the back from NOPD for being in the right place at the right time.

I viewed the tape in an entirely different light now that I felt Mike was lying about something as basic as where he lived. I was sure someone hired him to record Jimmy Washington's execution. They slipped up by failing to give Mike enough backstory on his fake identity.

The shooting occurred at about one o'clock in the afternoon. Hotel checkout was at eleven o'clock, and the NOPD detective's notes said Mike claimed to have been doing exactly that when the shooting happened. That would need explaining. Why Mike felt he needed to waste video footage on a streetcar was a question that I have wanted to ask every tourist I have ever seen filming one. The quality of his footage was near cinematic in its clarity and focus. This might have been the product of a quality camera, but my bet was that it was because a retired Marine would not flinch when the bullets started flying. There was no camera shake when it became obvious on the screen that a young man was about to be, and then was, shot in cold blood at point-blank range. Mike filmed the crime and caught a perfect image of the shooter looking directly at him.

Mike did not attempt to catch the license plate on the shooter's car. The Marine did do an excellent job of catching his own wounding on tape. I thought it more than mere coincidence that, while he was left handed, the one bullet he took was in his right arm.

"Are you planning on being in town long, Mister Grainger?"

"I was checking out and heading home when this happened."

"Yeah, that's what the NOPD detective has in his notes." I made a charade of looking at the NOPD detective's notes. "The thing is, Mikey, there's a lot we're going to have to go over before I'm comfortable letting you out of my sight."

The grizzled veteran dropped his jovial disposition and gave me a very hard stare. This NCO glare probably broke down more than a few of the Marines who served under him. He did not know what to make of my ignoring this well-practiced expression.

"What are you saying?"

"I'm saying that right now you're a material witness to a homicide," I informed him and then truly upset him. "But, once I figure out who you really are, you'll be booked as an accessory to murder."

"I want a lawyer and I need to make a phone call." There was no defensive argument, just an automatic raising of his defenses.

"I'm sure you do." I promised him neither opportunity.

I placed the camera back in its bag and pulled his cell phone and wallet from his pants before I handed him his stack of neatly folded clothing. I allowed him to pull the curtain closed to get dressed. I also kept an eye on his legs in case he decided to run.

Chapter 18

I handcuffed Mike Grainger and drove him to the State Police headquarters in Metairie. The building still smelled new. It took barely a year for FEMA to replace the one the storm wiped out, while FEMA's negotiations with New Orleans were holding a new building for NOPD's Fifth District in limbo. I did not take him to Central Lockup because I would catch hell if another prisoner shanked him before the order came to release him. I was able to hold him in an interview room at the State Police headquarters without creating a paper trail that I would have to burn later.

I let Mike use his own phone to make a call before placing him in a holding cell. I found an empty computer station and used a reverse directory to check the number he dialed. The telephone number was in the phone's directory of favorite numbers. The area code of the number was the right one for Blytheville, but the number came up without a match. I had some time, so I began to play with the contents of his wallet to see what other questions I would never have answered. I ran his driver's license through the interstate DMV database and it came back as a valid license, with his photograph. That would satisfy our standard check for any outstanding warrants. The officers running those checks are not former intelligence operatives who have carried false identity papers in their own past. I put the address into a Google Earth search and came up with a match for Grainger's home address. Whoever was behind Grainger's fake identity took the time to be sure anyone checking his home address would not find it was an empty lot. I called the library in Blytheville and asked if they had a current Haines Criss+Cross. All libraries used to carry a copy of this annual directory anyone could use to learn who occupied a given address. They have fallen out of use in the digital age, and people creating false backgrounds have reason to hope nobody thinks to check one. A Federal Marshal doing witness protection relocations told me about this vulnerability.

There are intangible benefits to speaking with a bored librarian. They tend to know everybody and everything and just need someone with whom to share their knowledge. Louise, the librarian, had a cousin who worked with the young man named Dan Sullivan who lived at the address Mike was using. Dan was a member of her Baptist church and was married to his high-school sweetheart. They were raising twins, Emma and Grace, in the house his daddy left him when he passed away from "the cancer" just last year. I did not need all this information to know that Mike Grainger was lying about living at the address occupied by the Sullivan family.

I used a fingerprint kit to pull prints from other cards in the wallet I had not touched. I would lose any fingerprint records I took directly from my suspect when whomever he called came to retrieve him. I did not even log Mike Grainger into holding. He would disappear when he left this building.

"Damn it, Holland." I glanced up from the computer screen I was working on when I heard Dan Logan's voice. I instinctively closed every open folder and browser window on the computer in front of me.

"What?" I asked with obviously feigned innocence.

The city's most notorious defense attorney pointed to an empty office and I followed him inside. I had no idea whose office it was and Logan did not seem to care. Patrol officers and detectives in the squad room began finding reasons to leave the squad room.

"You were told to sit on anything related to the El Caminos and the Pistol Peetes, right?" Logan went on talking but I was busy trying to figure out the extent of his role in what Kinkaid was trying to hide. It was becoming obvious that the real puppet master liked using local assets to hide their shadowy out-of-town operatives like Fake Mike.

"I was told to 'bury things' if I remember correctly. I'm not sure if that is the correct legal term for obstructing justice at the behest of a Deputy Director of the Department of Homeland Security."

"Don't get cute about this." Logan almost never laughs at my jokes. I only wanted to see if he knew who his boss was. The involuntary wrinkling of his eyebrows told me No.

"I took a nineteen-year-old boy's murder investigation from NOPD, just like I was ordered. How was I to know their phony witness couldn't hold a basic cover identity together? Why in the world did they make him say he was from Blytheville anyway?"

"Who do you know in Blytheville?" Logan was already exasperated, and became even more so when he discovered something so trivial was causing his client so much trouble.

"It's ten miles from where my dad grew up."

"Good grief." Logan sighed deeply. "Where's Mike Grainger?"

"He's in an interview room. I'll have him brought up front."

"Good enough. Any paperwork needing shredded?"

"I didn't waste the time." I gave a little shrug and then I sat down behind the desk. "But, he isn't going anywhere until you have someone explain to me how Grainger knew to be standing outside that hotel at that precise moment."

"Give it a rest," Logan said and started for the door. "Sources and methods are not something either one of us are cleared to know."

"Well, from where I'm sitting, it looks like the people you represent executed a young man and wanted it videotaped."

"What makes you say that?" Logan stopped and turned around. The bluster he brought into the office was gone.

"If I was going to send this to the grand jury my girlfriend runs, I'd point out that Mike Grainger doesn't exist. Then I'd share the statement he gave in which he claimed to cap off his weeklong vacation in New Orleans by videotaping a streetcar. It's the only footage on the entire tape and I'll bet it's the only video footage he shot all week."

"Go on."

"Jimmy Washington was shot with a handgun, but Mike was struck with a single round from a nine-millimeter carbine. It's not a rifle I associate with street gangs. It is a lot easier to aim and doesn't cause as much damage as an AK or AR-15. In addition, nobody on a New Orleans grand jury would believe a member of any gang would only fire one round. What do you imagine the natural odds are of a left-handed man being grazed in his right arm at fifty yards by the typical Mexican cartel gunman firing only one shot?"

"Okay." Logan motioned for me to shut up. The questions I posed were harder for him to listen to than any client's confession. "Here's what I was told. Sources tipped my client off that the cartel was looking for the kid and subsequently learned the Mexicans were going to ambush him at the Wendy's. My client sent Mike to prove they did it."

"What was so important about the kid?"

"Jimmy was the main enforcer for the Pistol Peetes. There are a dozen shooting arrests on his record, half of them as a juvenile, but not a single conviction. The El Caminos believe the Pistol Peetes have been knocking over their stash houses to supply their own heroin dealers."

"Dan, do you really believe a gang of African-American kids from New Orleans up and decided to take on one of the meanest Mexican cartels? I am also refusing to believe they decapitated their own men and left them in the back of a pickup truck. Your sources are full of crap. Who are your sources anyway?"

"That's the part of things you need to stay away from, Holland. They told me they are running an operation very similar to one used successfully in Baghdad. It involves a lot of surveillance and electronic monitoring that would need a court order if they were not the ones doing it. Take this free advice and just play your part."

"Tell me again why it is your clients don't need court orders."

"They're private security contractors here to test new surveillance devices and methods for the United States Government. They are not looking for evidence but, if they happen to overhear or witness any criminal activity, they're legally obligated to turn that information over to the proper authorities." It was an impressively razor-thin line to tread. Few defendants would be able to afford an expensive defense attorney, such as Dan Logan, who might think to question the legality of any evidence clearly showing their client's criminal misdeeds. Someone picked their attorney much more wisely than Logan had chosen his client.

"And why aren't the State Police and NOPD considered to be the proper authorities?"

"This is all being done way above your head. Homeland Security is interested in the Mexican cartel connection to the Afghan heroin trade. The Department of Justice wants to break a big case here to show Uncle Sam really does give a crap about New Orleans. The people that I work for are bridging the distance between those two objectives."

"It also makes the locals look weak, ineffective, and stupid." I had seen this scenario more than once. "I gotta tell you the truth. You can have their guy back, but you need to tell them I'm done with this."

"These are powerful enemies to be making," Logan warned.

"And dangerous friends to have. How did you get this gig?"

"Someone approached me right after the grand jury looking at my clients in the Pistol Peetes was shut down."

"Let me guess, it was a dark haired woman named Jill." I relished the mildly confused look on the attorney's face when I described his client. "I think she hired everyone in New Orleans that hates me."

I made sure Mike Grainger had all of his belongings, including his camera and videotape, before he left. He did not laugh when I told him the name of the Blytheville high-school teams is the Chickasaws.

Logan took hold of the video camera case. Exposing Grainger's role ruined any chance of the video being evidence in a future trial. Jill Bledsoe and Deputy Director Kinkaid made two mistakes that day. The first was choosing Daniel Logan to retrieve their agent. The second was expecting me to play the role they handed me when the stakes for New Orleans were so high.

Chapter 19

There were no additional fires or shootings in the immediate aftermath of Jimmy Washington's murder. I hate to say it, but there should have been. Revenge is a dish never served cold on the streets of New Orleans. We like it dished up hot off the grill.

One of the many advantages of belonging to an influential family, or to being a silent partner in a successful French Quarter bistro, is that everyone wants to be your friend. All of them want something, and most of them believe giving you something creates a debt they can collect on down the line. Very few people approach me about using my mother's family name or her connections for business or personal gain because I am very mindful of appearances, and working for the State Police tends to creates situations that look a lot like influence peddling and bribery. My partner and I receive opportunities and gifts from vendors and patrons of the bistro we occasionally accept as business owners This lagniappe occasionally includes tickets to Saints' games.

Chef Tony complained to our meat purveyor that he was not receiving the quality of beef and lamb he expected and that he was shopping other vendors. This was not true. What was true is that the current vendor's owner has a skybox in the Superdome. Tony timed his complaint just right and came away with four tickets to the first divisional playoff game. The Saints had won previous playoff games, but never advanced to the Super Bowl. I grew up when even loyal fans wore a paper sack on their head out of embarrassment for the team's performance. Seeing them in serious contention for the championship was a welcome change.

"Nicely played, my friend," I congratulated the chef for the tickets he obtained in such a clever and underhanded fashion. "I would have settled for club level seats."

"We are not club level people, Cooter," Tony said and used his index finger to raise the tip of his nose skyward.

"Christ, you're starting to sound like my mother," I laughed.

We hovered over the lavish buffet of hand-carved meats and steaming pans of jambalaya, gumbo, and crawfish Monica while our dates joined the wives and other women on the balcony to hoot and holler during the team introductions. The men in the room were content to be in the Dome watching the game on one of the many television sets hanging from the paneled walls. This is a feature unique to large social gatherings in New Orleans. The men will eventually gravitate to the kitchen and judge their host by his spice rack or exchange recipes while our better halves sit in the parlor discussing the Saints players' statistics, coaching staff and any recent player trades.

I handed Katie a bowl of crawfish Monica. It's a spicy cream sauce packed with hot sauce and peeled crawfish tails tossed with rotini pasta. She set her beer on a nearby bar table and began devouring the bowl of food while Kermit Ruffins used his trombone to warm the local crowd before the game. Katie seemed especially happy to be dating me just then.

The playoff game went astoundingly well, but the Saints dominated their division the entire season by winning most of their games by at least fifteen points. New Orleans fans are accustomed to winning or losing regular season games by a field goal or miracle play in the final seconds. They are less certain how to react to decisive victories, but they were not shy about expressing their opinion of Coach Peyton intentionally letting the team's undefeated season slip away by holding key players out of the final games of the regular season. Now he was beginning to look like a genius.

Everyone was healthy and ready to play. That was what put an all too familiar chill through the stadium when the Arizona Cardinals scored first with a seventy-yard run by Tim Hightower. Even the most loyal fans held their breath until Drew Brees answered with a one-yard step-over touchdown by Lynell Hamilton.

Someone in the skybox turned down the volume of the TV

network broadcasters on the television sets and cranked up a radio to use the play-by-play by Jim Henderson and the always colorful commentary of Hokey Gajan on WWL Radio. This was how I grew up watching Saints games. Our local sports commentators always brought more insight and energy to the games than anyone else ever would. I had even learned to accept the disjointed time lag between the radio and the TV.

The Saints put up a defensive wall against the Cardinals' running game and stacked two more touchdowns on our side of the scoreboard by the end of the first quarter. Fans of just about any other team in the NFL would have begun celebrating, but Saints fans knew to fear their team's repeatedly demonstrated ability to squander a lead. My dad once decried them as being a soccer team because they only seemed to play for three periods, not four.

The offense added to our team's lead with two more passing touchdowns in the second quarter. The Cardinals responded with a single successful scoring drive. The skybox crowd spent the half-time break in a muted celebration, fearful of jinxing our team's fragile luck.

"What are you doing?" I asked Tony when I saw him on his cellphone in the hallway. It was the quietest place he could find to make a phone call on that level of the stadium.

"I'm calling my bookie to make sure he's still in town." I could have lectured my partner about illegal gambling, but I chose instead to applaud his foresight. This was going to be an expensive night for a lot of betting parlors. Betting on the Saints to follow tradition was just too tempting for people who still had not quite grasped that ever since The Storm, as Katrina would forever be known, you were now betting against an entire city and not just its team.

The third quarter went our way, as well. We entered the fourth quarter with a thirty-point lead on the Cardinals. Even the Saints could not blow this lead. The coaches gave the second and third-string players' time on the field after they carefully packed away the team's most expensive assets for use in the next game. It meant that every member of the team could look their grandchildren in the eye one day and honestly say they played in the Saints' first championship season, if the team made it through the next game.

Tony and Tulip made our appreciation known to the owner of the box. I sat at the mini-bar and watched the post-game and locker room banter on one of the TVs. Katie held onto my arm, but she used her free hand to grab a pair of beers from one of the porters breaking down the bar. She surprised a number of people in the skybox who had never seen the prosecutor in jeans and a team jersey, with her lush brown hair hanging loose halfway down her back.

I felt a brief flush of emotion when Coach Peyton began handing out the game balls. The first one he gave away was to the man who gave him his first coaching job. It was an emotional moment for both grown men.

"What's wrong?" Katie whispered in my ear.

She had caught the shudder in my arm and heard the little hitch in my breath as I found myself wanting to cry at that demonstration of male bonding. My visceral reaction came as a surprise even to me.

"I was just thinking how my dad really should be here. All those years, the bad years, that he was a loyal fan and then he dies right before the season when they finally do so well." I had not thought about my dad, or his death, in nearly a month. I still missed him as much as ever, but knowing his murder had been avenged let his memory settle deeper into my thoughts.

"Well, he's either making this happen in Heaven, or he's getting bad satellite reception in Hell." It is not often that Katie lets her sense of humor come out, but it is usually good for a laugh or two when she does. "Either way, he loves you and knows you're keeping the faith for the two of you."

I nodded at this but she saw the expression that still drew my face so tight. It obviously did not have a thing to do with football.

"What aren't you telling me?" Katie took my hand in hers.

"It's work related, not about us. It's also very hush-hush."

"You can hush-hush yourself tonight if that's how it's going to be," Katie said with barely enough humor to make it sound like more of a joke than a threat.

"I can't drag you into this because I signed a nondisclosure agreement with Homeland Security. They are running an operation here and my job is to keep it under wraps," I gave her hand a squeeze and managed to force a smile out of her.

Katie could not have cared less about the confidentiality agreements. "It's obviously got you messed up, and I'm not going to stand by and let that happen."

"I'm supposed to run interference with NOPD so they don't stumble over what Homeland Security is doing."

"Which is?" I couldn't fully explain my task without referencing my covert work. We had agreed never to delve into the lives either of us led before we began dating.

"I'm supposed to cover up anything they do that gets noticed."

"Such as?"

"I'm doing my job if you haven't seen or heard anything." I needed this to be a joke between us and Katie reluctantly smiled and let it pass.

"It sounds like a crappy job to me." Katie sensed it was time to let the matter drop, if only until we were somewhere private.

I really hoped I was not becoming more trouble than I was worth in her life. She'd been divorced only a couple of months when we went on our first date and was not at all interested in getting involved with anyone. Katie and I had not spoken aloud of our love for one another until she let her feelings slip out on New Year's Eve. This did not mean she was suddenly enthusiastic about dating a disavowed intelligence operative with a pit bull and PTSD. I needed to be a better partner than just being a guy who could get her Italian food and free Saints tickets whenever she wanted.

Chapter 20

C hief Avery called me two days later to respond to a call from someone at a junkyard on Almonaster Avenue, the industrial road running parallel to the Gulf Intercoastal Waterway. This man-made inland waterway intersects what the locals call the Mr. GO near Chalmette and the eastern boundary of New Orleans. Unlike the Intercoastal, which runs from Florida to Texas, the Mr. GO was nothing but an aquatic superhighway from the Gulf of Mexico pointing straight into the heart of the low-lying city. It performed exactly as the Corps of Engineers designed it to when Katrina's winds funneled dozens of feet of water unchecked from the Gulf of Mexico into Chalmette and New Orleans East. The businesses along Almonaster were devastated and few of them received large enough insurance settlements to reopen. Fewer still could afford the higher flood insurance premiums they faced if they did reopen. There were still dozens of abandoned buildings, junk yards, and disposal sites flanking the road as I looked for a street number. Avery must have told the man who called 911 what I was driving. The old man was standing on the side of the road waving at me.

"You the State Police detective they said was comin' here?" The old man wanted reassurance that I was actually a cop. I was wearing jeans, a button-down shirt, and a jacket with the State Police emblem on it. My license plates even said I was driving a COP CAR. I showed him my badge and gave him my business card. "You any relation to Ralph Holland?"

"He's my dad. Did you know him?"

"He ran me in a few times for possession of stolen goods. Nice guy, your dad. He really was." This was not the sort of recollection I usually heard, but it is always nice to hear my dad was not a total jerk on the job.

"The Chief of Detectives didn't tell me what you found."

"Your dog bite?" The man still had not identified himself and seemed anxious about extending any part of his body in my direction, even for a handshake, until he was a little more comfortable about Roux.

"Not lately." I shook his hand to show Roux we were not enemies.

The man's name was Scott and he made his living by picking up metal scrap from the side of the road, or anywhere else, he could snatch it to sell to one of the recycling centers. He was little concerned about permission or provenance, and admitted he was cherry picking scrap out of the junk left in the abandoned businesses along this stretch of Almonaster. It was all going to waste, at least in his expert opinion. I decided to overlook the legal issues to find out what he had to say.

"I was pulling copper wire when I smelled something awful." Scott brushed past his euphemism for stealing the flood-damaged wiring from one of the vacant buildings.

There is only one 'awful' odor that will make a criminal call the police. I grabbed a fistful of latex gloves from the trunk of my car and followed Scott behind the long cinder block building. I caught the unmistakable odor of decomposing flesh as we approached the levee.

"I've got this, Scott. Thank you for calling it in. You'll probably want to be gone before I call in the reinforcements."

Mostly, I was the one who wanted Scott to leave. He did not need to be anything more than an anonymous tip if this was a drowning victim or the body of someone killed by anyone other than the El Caminos or Pistol Peetes. Finding drowning victims is more likely in the industrial canals than it is over on the river, where the current eventually carries everything lost in America to the Gulf of Mexico. I doubted I would stumble upon a present from the Pistol Peetes, because a gang from Central City has plenty of vacant lots and abandoned houses where they can dump the bodies of their victims rather than haul them this far east.

I was very much afraid Roux and I were about to walk up on another murder scene left by the El Caminos. I found the body thirty yards downwind of the spot where Roux and I first crested the levee. Roux led the way and took me to a small pile of driftwood and trash caught in the saplings growing at the water's edge. I recognized the shirt before I even determined I was looking at a body.

This was a fresher body than many I have seen. The last time I saw this shirt, and the now barely identifiable man wearing it, was on the videotape I watched at the hospital. I had located Jimmy Washington's executioner, but his presence here was quite disturbing.

I was not the least bit upset to find a dead murderer. What bothered me were the conditions under which we met. It was a bad thing to find an El Camino gang member's body dumped in his own neighborhood. The Pistol Peetes were not bright enough to lure this particular victim into a trap far from their own home turf. I still found it hard to imagine the cartel drowned their own man. No member of either criminal gang dies without someone gaining some sort of advantage. Eliminating the enforcer for the Pistol Peetes was an obvious strategic move. The gunman who pulled the trigger on that hit should have been elevated in the ranks of the El Caminos, not executed in turn. Killing button men is something I would expect more from a Mafia family than a drug cartel. I am entirely comfortable with bad people dying, the more painful the better. I will never be comfortable with anyone dying for reasons I do not fully understand.

Roux and I approached the body. I did not want to have to go in the water, and the corpse was too heavy to drag out of the water on my own. I checked his back and found no evidence of blood or wounds. It only meant he was not running away from his killer. I surmised he died in a face-to-face confrontation. That meant he knew, or at least trusted, his killer.

I pulled on a double thickness of gloves and turned the body most of the way over without having to get wet. I tapped at his pockets but found no wallet or a set of keys. There were no signs of trauma on the victim's front or flanks. I was prepared to believe the man drowned. It did not matter whether it was by accident or if someone assisted the process. I was surprised to find the large caliber revolver he likely used to murder Jimmy Washington in a holster on the waistband of his pants. The snap on the holster was why the handgun did not wind up buried in the mud wherever he went into the canal.

My job normally would have been to step away from the body and call for a forensic team and the Chief of Detectives to formally declare this a crime scene. There would be pictures taken and his autopsy would probably confirm drowning as the cause of death. There might be news coverage and a small effort made to identify the victim. Most likely, he would wind up as another number on the year's death tally, but calling this an accidental drowning made it easier to forget. NOPD and the State Police were not going to make a major investment of time in figuring out precisely how or why this bad man drowned. They would use his death to close Jimmy Washington's murder investigation.

My job here was to clean up someone's mess. Losing the victim in the water likely complicated his killer's larger plan. I took the belt from the corpse and removed his weapon. I then said a short prayer and used the longest stick I could find to push the Mexican back into the canal for someone else to find.

I hoped the pistol might hold the answers to a few other questions. The serial number on the pistol could tell me whether the El Caminos were buying their weapons locally or elsewhere. A drug cartel has a huge appetite for firepower that taking weapons in home burglaries and by breaking into parked cars cannot fill. Every member of a drug cartel's army carries two or three firearms, including pistols and some sort of rifle such as an AR-style carbine or a pump shotgun. Even a small cartel would need hundreds of armed men, and something the size of the Medellin or Sinaloa cartels would own more firepower than is issued to an infantry brigade. I checked the cylinder on the revolver and found two more rounds fired than Kinkaid's phony tourist caught on his videotape. There may have been a very brief firefight before he chose to take his chances swimming rather than battle against the final odds he faced. I tucked the pistol into my jacket pocket and picked up Roux's leash.

"Let's go for a walk." Roux was glad to be out of the cramped passenger-side floorboard of my XLR. Apparently, the dog did not like my driving and felt safer on the floorboard than in the seat.

I guided Roux along the canal side of the levee with no clear idea of what I might find. It was a nice day for a walk, with dry warm air and a sunny sky. January weather in New Orleans can be very capricious. I know people with vast experience in the Arctic who have a hard time coping with Louisiana's winters. A thermometer reading of forty under clear skies has less meaning than the fact it has arrived with eighty percent humidity. Live south of I-10 for a year and you will never own or wear dry clothes again. The moisture here gradually wicks into you nearly as insidiously as the culture does.

This was an unusually warm day, and the heat was probably what ripened the crop of drowned Mexicans. Those words ran through my thoughts and I immediately knew I could never repeat them aloud. I was mad at myself for letting the callousness towards life and death I needed to survive in Iraq undo the humanity I rediscovered after coming home. Katie was worried about how poorly I began sleeping after my lunch with Kinkaid, but I did not burden her with the images dominating my mind lately. They were not just bad dreams, but rather a flood of bad memories.

I pulled Roux to an abrupt halt. The sudden tension on his leash signaled him to walk back to where I was standing. He sat down, but his nose twitched as he caught a scent from the anomaly below us that caught my own attention.

I had spotted a shiny rear quarter panel in a row of very rusty cars. The other cars were relics from the time when brackish floodwater covered this flat ground for nearly a month. FEMA had thousands of privately owned vehicles towed away once the floodwaters receded five years earlier, but final disposition of the vehicles in the abandoned salvage yards along Almonaster involved lawsuits between business owners and the EPA or insurance companies.

Roux and I entered the salvage yard through a hole in the metal fence large enough to step through. I took a moment to check the ground before we went any further. I could make out a couple of relatively fresh heel marks in the packed earth. I thought on set matched the boots on the dead man's feet, but I would never know because this was never going to be a crime scene. Roux tugged me towards the recently discarded automobile.

What was left of the El Camino's sheet metal was the same color as the one used in Jimmy's shooting. The front half of the vehicle was gone, melted in a lumpy mess that was undoubtedly the result of more thermite. Any identification numbers from the engine or VIN on the dashboard were gone, as was the rear license plate. I saw only one set of tire marks in the rear salvage yard, and the next hard rain would eliminate those tracks and start rusting this abandoned vehicle to match its surroundings. I looked at what remained of the vehicle and saw no evidence of the bones of the second shooter or otherwise useful material. I let Roux have a good sniff and used the teaching technique Roger taught me to add thermite to Roux's scent vocabulary.

Roux and I followed the driveway around the building towards Almonaster Avenue. There were two more sets of tire tracks in the parking lot. I was not going to be able to call in an expert to tell me anything about the vehicles that made the sets of wide tire tracks so I used my phone to take pictures of the tread marks for possible future reference. There was no point interviewing the sales people at the specialized RV rental place across the street. I was not going to chase down any clues they might be able to provide. The only thing I really wanted them to tell me was who would come to such a crappy location to rent one of those tricked out Greyhound buses musicians travel in between concerts. If your business generates that kind of rental income, you should not need to set up shop on Almonaster.

Someone used a rotary cutter to slice open the lock on the front gate rather than use bolt cutters. The thinner cut left the lock appearing undisturbed. Locks are usually the only thing the owner or their security guard would check. Someone crimped the hasp back together and rubbed it with dirt to hide the damage as they were leaving. There was a little shine where the metal wasn't properly smudged. It would rust soon enough, like the torched car out back, and then nobody would ever know the difference.

I learned this technique many years ago and it told me more about the crime scene than anything else I saw all day. Jill's field operatives might as well have signed their names in the crushed shell pavement with their piss. This crime scene just rubbed my nose in the bloody handiwork of Kinkaid's mysterious private contractor.

Chapter 21

C hief Avery accepted my lunch invitation with much less enthusiasm than usual. The last invitation resulted in my telling him about the suspicious house fires. This invitation came a day after he sent me to check out a report of a suspicious odor behind an abandoned business. He was beginning to understand I was using pasta as a cushion for the blows I needed to deliver.

He barely settled into his seat at the Chef's Table before I handed him the unloaded pistol in its evidence bag. He recognized the pistol as a probable match for the murder weapon in Jimmy Washington's execution. Avery was not pleased about the three spent cartridges in the bag. We both hoped there were not two more bodies awaiting discovery. I asked Avery to run the pistol through the ATF database. He stood a better chance of finding a way to tuck it into a stack of requests or otherwise hide the origin of the request than I did. He was better off not knowing the circumstances under which I found it. Chief Avery would wind up looking at the drowning victim eventually. It was best to let him be genuinely surprised when the time came.

"Did you find anything else I should know about?" my boss wondered.

"Semantically, there is nothing you *should* know about. There are a couple of things I think you *need* to know."

"Oh, boy." Avery sighed and pushed his unfinished plate of pasta away. He leaned back in his chair until he was more comfortable and braced himself.

"Whoever Kinkaid hired has some very well-trained operatives backing up their technical guys. I keep stumbling across bits of tradecraft that tell me the company's doing a lot more than trying out a bunch of new surveillance toys on Homeland Security's dime."

"Such as?" He was curious, but he knew not to ask too many questions.

"The tourist who conveniently videotaped the Washington shooting works for them. His ID didn't hold up and someone sent Dan Logan to pull him out of the State Police headquarters on Veterans after he made just one phone call. Logan gave me a story about how Kinkaid's secret surveillance operation overheard the El Caminos talk about killing Washington in time for them to have someone in place to document it. The tape would have been great in court, but I think it was really intended to remove any doubts you and I have about the El Caminos being in a war with the Pistol Peetes." I could tell by Avery's look that he was going to like the next piece in the puzzle even less than this one. "I also found the shooter's burned-out El Camino in an abandoned salvage yard a mile or so from where I found that gun."

"So the shooters burned their car. There's nothing new in that." Avery seemed relieved to have something turn out to be a standard criminal act.

"Except they used thermite, the same military-grade incendiary used to torch the four houses Wheeler was curious about. They also gained access to the lot by cutting through the lock on the car lot's gate using a method they teach Intelligence and Special Forces operators. Keep in mind that the Deputy Director of Homeland Security admitted the purpose of his pet project is to instigate a gang war."

"What you are insinuating would be bad." Avery understood that much if nothing else.

"Kinkaid said they're trying to interrupt the flow of heroin into the city ahead of a major sweep of arrests. Katie told me a couple of weeks ago that the DOJ asked the local DA to suspend his own investigation into heroin dealing, but her contacts in the Federal building say there are no indictments being prepared at that level. Maybe you should talk to her boss."

"I need to, anyway. It would be a big feather in my cap if we could get his grand jury going again." Avery likes to frame his view of any given Big Picture in terms of any advantage or disadvantage to NOPD. I have learned to frame my own needs and the justifications for my actions in those same terms when he comes crashing down on me.

Avery set his napkin beside his plate and stood up to leave. He waved the bagged pistol at me as he headed out the kitchen door.

"I'll get back to you on this."

Chapter 22

Chief Avery sent a text message to my burner phone to arrange our next meeting. It was a one-word text using his personal identifier of 'Brees.' It was barely twelve hours after we last parted company. Apparently, he could not wait to share whatever he had uncovered.

Avery hates that I carry a second phone. He hates it even more that Tony calls it my Bat Phone. Still, there have been a few times over the years that my boss has realized it would be best if there were no record of our having spoken. Avery may have borrowed one of his detective's phones to text me this time. I never answer any voice calls to the telephone and I only use the letter K to answer any texts. My contacts can let me know they are in immediate danger by texting me anything other than their one word identifier. These one-word personal identifiers tell me who to meet, and when and where to do so.

My rally point with Avery is a bar next door to the William Faulkner museum in Pirate's Alley. We chose this place because it is not usually busy at the time we have set to meet. Spotting tourists is easy in a place that usually only serves regulars at three in the morning. Anyone still hunkered over their drinks at that hour are not paying much attention to anyone or anything else. The bartenders know I am a cop, but only a couple of them are familiar with the local Chief of Detectives. My professional identity alone is reason enough for them to turn a blind eye.

Avery paid for two bourbons on the rocks and led me to a table in the dim alleyway overlooking the garden behind Saint Louis

Cathedral. The illuminated statue of Jesus is referred to as 'Touchdown Jesus' because of the way the light shining on the statue casts a shadow on the back of the historic cathedral that looks like a football referee signaling a touchdown. It is why Avery's code word to meet here is the last name of the Saints' current quarterback.

"Well, this hasn't happened for a while."

"Consider that for a second." Avery said. He may have been trying to impart special importance to what he needed to tell me. His wearing a non-departmental issue revolver off-duty, in a shoulder holster, and drinking hard liquor had already caught my attention.

"What's so important that you need tell it to me here?"

"Nothing. Absolutely nothing." Avery declared this and then chewed on a piece of ice from his glass. He has sworn off hard liquor because of his inability to be a fun drunk. His wife still allows him to get tipsy on beer, but she has promised to leave him if he ever goes back to being the mean drunk he was when they first met. Tonight was apparently a special occasion. "The ATF wants to know where I got the gun but they won't tell me why."

"What else?" An uncooperative Federal agency was not enough to bring us together like this. It takes a lot to spook Bill Avery.

"The prints you gave me from the guy calling himself Mike Grainger came up in a database that must have rung bells. Deputy Director Kinkaid called me at home tonight and ordered me to suspend you immediately. He said he'll be calling the Commandant of the State Police in the morning to recommend that you be terminated for disobeying his direct orders."

"So, I guess we're onto something." I forced a grin but could not get him to smile back at me.

"What the hell am I supposed to do?" Avery's face flushed from emotion and not the small amount of liquor in his system.

"That decision has been taken out of your hands. You have to suspend me. I will not be the reason *you* get fired. Don't worry. I can retire and run the bistro." I tried to sound casual, but I was furious.

"What about Kinkaid's pet project?" Avery's deep concerns about what was happening behind his back explained why he used our emergency contact arrangement.

"That's still my problem, not yours. Kinkaid's problem is that he doesn't understand pulling my badge means I can now pursue this as a private citizen. A citizen the military and government spent a lot of time and money training to operate alone. So what if I cannot access to your resources anymore? Apparently they're not doing you any good right now, either."

"Is there anything I can do?" Avery probably hoped I knew a different way to handle this situation than slipping off the leash I accepted when I joined his department.

"You should see if Hammond can get me suspended instead of fired. I really would like to come back to work someday."

"I mean anything besides that." Avery hoped my comment was a joke and forced a smile with his weary response.

"Turn your back and avert your eyes." I suggested and shook his hand as I left the bar. I left my badge and State Police issued sidearm on the table. I was going to need a lot more than a badge and a gun to survive what lay ahead.

Chapter 23

There was definitely one phone call I should have made when I woke up the next morning. My girlfriend was understandably displeased to learn of my suspension from someone besides myself. She dispersed the heat in her anger upon the defendants and witnesses she confronted in court all day, so her level of aggravation downgraded from "livid" to "visibly annoyed" by the time she confronted me that evening.

I was speaking with Ryan Kennedy and a couple of other regulars at the street-end of Strada Ammazarre's zinc-topped cypress bar when I spotted Katie crossing the street. I immediately grasped the failure in my priorities when I saw her expression. She was still dressed in the dark skirt and jacket she wore to work. Her taste in pencil skirts shows off her long firm legs, which makes most male defendants and witnesses underestimate her. Katie is just a female lawyer in the same way Roux is just a large dog.

"Is there anything you should have let me know this morning?" Katie asked with exaggerated patience.

"Nothing I wanted you to spend your day worrying about." It was the best I could come up with in the seconds I had to make up an excuse.

"In the future, let me decide what to be worried about. I'm a big girl, in case you haven't noticed."

Jason, the evening bartender, silently offered her a glass of Marquis de Perlade champagne from the bottle Ryan had been working his way through for the past hour. He usually drinks an entire bottle of champagne each evening. Jason is willing to endure the fat man's sexual innuendos, and much less subtle offers, because Ryan tips him very well. Jason also feels there is no harm in allowing Ryan to spend what time the older man's long list of terminal ailments and afflictions has left him to chase unicorns.

"Something I can spread a rumor about, my dear boy?" Ryan asked after overhearing our conversation.

"NOPD has seen fit to give me some unanticipated time off."

"He got himself suspended. That's what he means, Ryan," Katie told him. Ryan's considerable girth began slowly convulsing with laughter.

"Damn. I placed my bet in that pool on two o'clock next Thursday afternoon." He wisely moved to his usual seat at the hostess' end of the bar when he gauged our reaction to his taunt. He likes sitting at that end of the bar because it affords him the opportunity to torment our hostess, Marie. Ryan greets unsuspecting guests if she is away from her podium just a moment too long. Ryan and Joaquin have an ongoing argument over his behavior.

"What did you do? I called Bill and he said he couldn't tell me." She took a calming sip of her champagne and gave me a consoling hug.

Katie's calling my boss to find out what I should have been the one to tell her added to my regret about my oversight. It must seem to her that I place too little faith in trust and relationships. She does grasp that I am not that long out of a career where trust and relationships nearly got me killed.

"He really can't." I wanted her to know that the Chief of Detectives was not stone-walling her to protect me in some fashion. "We both signed the agreements I told you about. I've decided I'm not going to continue being a part of it. Bill was ordered to suspend me until the operation is complete. The people behind this have the dumb idea that suspending me is going to make me go away."

"But you aren't? You could get fired." This possibility seemed to upset Katie far more than it did me.

I waved an arm at the interior of the bistro. "I'm not going to end up broke or homeless if that happens."

"I'm a lot more worried you'll get yourself killed poking your nose where it doesn't belong." Katie clarified her concerns. That very real possibility worried me just as much, maybe more.

"Where doesn't a good cop's nose belong?"

"Since when have you been a good cop?"

"Fair enough. I'm still on the side of the good guys."

Katie nodded her agreement to this self-assessment. I should have changed the subject, but a question suddenly popped into my mind.

"If Bill didn't tell you I was suspended, then who did?" Suspending me was not something my boss was happy about, nor proud of allowing himself to be forced to do.

"Ray called me while I was headed to work. He was laughing about you losing your job. I acted like I already knew." Returning to the subject of my poor judgement sparked a bit of her initial anger again. "I thought divorcing Ray meant I was through with the men in my life making a mess of their careers."

"I think I need to ask your ex-husband how he knew about this." There was no good answer to this question. Katie immediately grasped that her ex-husband was involved in something way over his head.

"Let me ask him." Katie knew she would be wise to keep me from questioning Ray in person in my present mood.

"I won't leave a mark on him." I held up my hand as if giving a sacred oath. I don't think she realized I know multiple ways to kill a man without leaving a single mark.

Chapter 24

The question of how Ray Reilly learned of my suspension so soon after it happened began to run in a continuous loop through my thoughts. I wondered if he might have known about it even before it happened. Mostly I was just concerned that Ray knew anything about it at all. Far too many of the pawns in Kinkaid's covert operation seemed to have direct connections to me.

Katie understood the implications of her ex-husband's call. It was why she insisted on being with me when I talked with him. She very reasonably wanted to keep her boyfriend out of jail and her first husband out of the hospital.

Katie called Ray on her cell phone Saturday morning to arrange a meeting between the two of us. She set the phone on speaker for my benefit. Ray told her no. He then called back a few minutes later, from a phone number she did not recognize, and agreed to the meeting. He insisted we meet somewhere well outside of New Orleans. He said he would text Katie with the time and location for the meeting. The man is not as dumb as the things he does sometimes make him appear to be.

The text came through half an hour later, from the same unknown phone number. The message was short: Annie's at two. Annie's was the name of the supper club in Pass Christian, Mississippi where my father proposed to my mother. It is on my list of places lost to the storm surge that scoured the Gulf Coast. Hurricane Katrina's unprecedented flooding also demolished the shorefront blocks across the water in the town of Bay St. Louis. It destroyed the tourist shops, cafes, and art galleries that supported the town's economy. It is easier to rebuild structures and businesses than to restore pieces of history.

I kicked myself yet again for not having come home more often when I was in the military. I assumed everything would be the way I last remembered it whenever I finally decided to return for good. The hurricane's ferocity taught everyone a cruel lesson about making such assumptions.

I could not drive my convertible coupe with its COP CAR license plates and I still did not trust the pit bull with the leather upholstery in my Cadillac station wagon. Katie and I loaded Roux and the picnic basket Tony prepared for us into the living room-sized interior of the bistro's Raptor pickup truck. The beast of a truck is useless as a business vehicle, but Tony and I both admired the Ford's power and off-road capabilities and bought it anyway.

It took an hour to get to Bay St. Louis. I used Highway 90 to get there, and tried to convince Katie my reason for doing so was that it was a more scenic route. She caught me watching my mirrors for anyone following us, but she didn't make a fuss because she grasped that there must be a reason Ray were being so cautious.

I pulled off the far end of the new bridge spanning Bay St. Louis, the old one being yet another victim of the hurricane, and drove past the vacant lot where Annie's stood for half a century. The dining room floor and the remains of a circular staircase were all that remained of the restaurant, bar, and motel. I parked by the water's edge and let Roux off his leash. He sprinted for the beach and wasted no time submerging neck deep in the brackish water. I opened the metal toolbox spanning the width of the truck bed and pulled out a nylon tarp Katie and I could spread over the sand and salt grass. Katie kept an eye out for her ex-husband's arrival. Ray gave us a specific time to be there, but punctuality is not his strong suit.

Tony had Miss J pack our picnic basket with two small Caprese salads and a full-sized muffaletta to share. The sandwich, a round bun stuffed with olive salad and a variety of salamis, was large enough to feed a family. Roux caught the scent of the sandwich and trotted up to see if Tony packed anything for him to eat. He shook himself dry just short of the tarp and barely avoided hitting either of us with the spray. I handed him one of the sandwich quarters, which he swallowed in six noisy bites. I made a water dish from an empty salad bowl for him and he took a slobbery drink before stretching out to work on his tan. It was a sunny day, but the mid-day temperature was a bit brisk for those of us not wearing fur coats.

"Your dog needs to be on a leash," an amplified voice advised me. I turned around and saw a Harrison County Sheriff's car parked beside our truck.

I waved the leash in the air and motioned for Roux to let me snap the leash onto his harness. The patrol car did not leave so I led Roux in that direction. Katie stayed on the tarp. I figured the deputy was writing me a ticket for some sort of ordinance violation I should have anticipated. I had hoped the absence of houses and other beachcombers made it acceptable to let the big dog run free.

"Sorry, deputy, I didn't see anyone else around. Roux doesn't get nearly enough exercise so I thought I'd let him wear himself out." I tossed the dog's name into my apology just to make him sound less menacing. The deputy kept a nervous eye on the sizeable pit bull sitting beside his car door. He may have regretted rolling his window down to speak with me.

"I understand that." He was not writing anything.

"Unit seven, this is dispatch." The volume on the deputy's car radio was set low. He held the microphone in the hand on his lap.

"Go ahead."

"No wants or warrants," the dispatcher advised him. Apparently, he was just waiting to see what the truck's license plate would tell him about me. The deputy glanced at me and then looked at Katie and the truck.

"Are you two here alone?"

"Yes, sir, it's just us and the dog. Is that a problem?"

The deputy seemed to give this some thought, but he did not have an immediate follow-up question. His last question was a strange thing to have asked me anyway. The number of people here was inconsequential if the problem was an unleashed dog. It was becoming obvious that the dog was not the real reason for his stopping by.

"No. The complaint said there were more people here. I thought it might be a bunch of teenagers making a mess. You know how they are." I know a bad lie when I hear one.

"Well you can report back that it's just two love birds and their puppy dog. I know how nosy people can mess things up, too." The deputy looked at me, and I just stared back as blankly as I could.

"Keep the dog leashed," he said and rolled up his window. He backed away and then drove back onto the highway. I did not see him cross the bridge and I did not think he had gone very far the other way.

I walked back to the tarp and sat down next to Katie before I unhooked Roux's leash and watched him run back into the water. There was almost certainly an ordinance against allowing Roux to run loose, but violating it seemed to have nothing to do with the deputy's visit. I was about to say something about it to Katie when she motioned towards a man who had just appeared under the bridge. It was Ray and he looked like he was fishing with a lightweight rod and reel. Katie recognized the shirt he was wearing as a birthday present she gave him.

I took Roux's leash and walked along the water's edge as though I was retrieving him. I rolled up the legs on my jeans and waded out into the seventy-degree water. It felt good, and was actually a bit warmer than the air temperature. I maneuvered Roux towards Ray while trying to make it look like I was chasing after the dog. I dropped the charade as soon as I stepped beneath the bridge structure.

"This is all a bit cloak and dagger, even for you, Ray."

"Well, it needs to be." He still didn't turn to face me. He was wearing a Saints ball cap and dark sunglasses. I started looking at the far shore he was so intent on scanning. There were a few people there, but they seemed preoccupied with other things. The deputy wasn't among them and I saw nobody sitting in a parked car with binoculars. "What did you want to meet me about?"

"You called Katie about my suspension."

"I just wanted to show her that you didn't do any better with NOPD than I did." I hadn't driven this far just to hear Ray try to gloat.

"Well that's hardly a secret." I laughed just to see him frown. "I'd like to know how you found out about my suspension."

"Suspension? I thought you were fired." Calling Katie with the news of my suspension was the first shovelful of dirt in the hole Ray was digging. This was the second.

"Did someone tell you I was fired?"

"Not in so many words."

"Well what words did they use?" I was losing patience, but I tried to hold my tone in check. His being here was a favor to Katie, not to me.

"They just said you wouldn't be wasting any more taxpayer

dollars." The phrase struck me like a thunderbolt.

"And that someone was a guy named Jack, right?"

Ray began to reel in the line he had cast into the channel, and said nothing until he'd retrieved all of it. He was casting a small lead weight all this time. There was neither bait nor lure on the line.

"I don't know anyone named Jack. It was a scary bitch named Jill."

"Scary how?" There were far too many ways this might be possible. The mystery man I was afraid gave him the news scares people by just showing up.

"There's some weird stuff going on. I had no idea what I was getting into with these people." Ray clearly was genuinely terrified.

"How'd you get mixed up with the woman that told you about me?"

"A woman named Jill Bledsoe hired me as a local liaison about three months ago. She works for a government security contractor, but she never said which one. I didn't know those kind of companies could even work in this country. Did you?" I was not about to share anything I knew about such companies with Ray. "She offered me a signing bonus and a year's contract doing some easy leg work for her company. All they wanted, at first, was pictures on a list of addresses she gave me. They were mostly in the East and Central City. Then she started asking about you."

"What about me, Ray?"

"She wanted all of your phone numbers and anything I could tell her about who you know and where you hang out, that kind of stuff."

"Personal stuff." I said this with an inflection meant to let Ray know he had crossed a line when he started handing over that kind of information. "What did you give her?"

"I told her about your restaurant and who you report to at the State Police and at NOPD. I told her about Tulip and all of the things she's into, like her war crimes group and helping that Black kid in the election."

"And telling her all of that didn't bother you?" It was dumb of me to expect my girlfriend's ex-husband to respect my privacy if he thought for a second not doing so might drive a wedge between us.

"Things about you? Not at all." At least he was being honest.

"What are you doing for Jill Bledsoe now?"

"Not much. I get a call to run errands a couple of times a week."

"How many of the houses that you photographed have burned down?" I was finally getting a clear idea of what was going on.

"Six." That was more than even Wheeler knew about. "I went to see my contact about the fires after the third one and that's when I got a good look at their operation. I've tried to stay away from them ever since."

"What did you see, Ray?"

"They had this place set up to track people using their cell phones and the GPS in their cars. They were flying small drones over people's houses. There were a dozen men walking around with some heavy firepower, and they had these boards with pictures of a Mexican gang and some gang with a bunch of Black kids. There were big marks across some of the faces, like something bad happened to those people." Ray had seen more than he realized, and I was now sure that his reaction to the inner sanctum put him on a short list for his employer's attention. "Do you have any idea what any of this is all about?"

"Some. I've seen operations like it before." Ray's eyes widened just a bit at this disclosure on my part. I had not meant to scare him with it.

"Anyway, I've been staying away from those people as much as I can. It's occurred me that she's probably tracking all those phone numbers I gave her, including Katie's." Now I understood both his paranoia about meeting me, and his willingness to do so.

"Where did you see Jill's operation?"

"It was in a warehouse on Tchoupitoulas, but I know she's moved at least twice since then. The last time I spoke with Jill was a week or so ago and I met her at a new site she was already packing to leave. I do not know where she's working out of now. I doubt she's going to invite me back."

"Thank you for telling me all of this." I was genuinely appreciative. Ray's disclosures validated my anxieties about Jill's real purpose in New Orleans. These are not the sort of people you want taking any interest in your life.

"I'm worried about Katie being safe."

"You should be." I was not going to let him feel better for having shared his secrets. "You've put all of our lives in danger. Take my advice and stay away from both of us and avoid your new friends all you can."

"What are you going to do? You're not even a cop anymore."

"People keep telling me that like it's a bad thing," I grumbled.

"It just means I can play by the same rules as the people Kinkaid sent here to make trouble. You don't want to be near either of us when this comes crashing down."

"I understand." Ray was going to leave this meeting as scared of me as he was of his client. Any reassurance he came looking to me about Katie's, or his own, safety was gone. "Just remember I'm on your side now."

"Keep telling yourself that, Ray."

I snapped the leash onto Roux's collar and walked him back to Katie. She saw the look on my face and chose to wait for me to tell her about the short conversation I had with her ex-husband. Ray cast his weighted line into the water a couple of more times and then began moving away from us. Katie and I continued our picnic lunch until he was out of sight, and then we packed up and headed back to New Orleans.

Chapter 25

I parked the truck in our garage on Chartres Street and then led Katie by the hand around the block to Café Ammazarre. I played music on the radio the entire way between the beach and the garage and placed my fingers against my lips the three times Katie tried to start a conversation. I could not very well tell her aloud that I was afraid someone was listening. We returned the picnic basket to Tony and took the elevator to my apartment, which I know is secure against electronic eavesdropping.

"What's going on, Cooter?" Katie demanded the instant I closed the wood-paneled steel door behind us.

"Ray says we're under surveillance. I'm assuming our phones are compromised and the GPS in the truck has been hacked. That's just the start." She did not take this explanation for my silence well. She started to speak twice, but stopped in mid-sentence each time. She eventually curled up on one of the large chairs in the living room. I went to the bar and made a gin and tonic for her. I also poured four ounces of straight bourbon into a glass for myself. I handed Katie the tumbler with her cocktail and then sat on the edge of the coffee table to be able to look her in the eye when she finally calmed down.

"I should have suspected as much when Kinkaid singled me out." I sighed.

"Why me, though?" Katie was so concerned about her safety that she missed what I just said. She may not have known the name of the local head of Homeland Security.

"Because you link Ray, who works for the company he sent

here, to me, a guy who they suspect is working against them. That's why Ray told you he wouldn't meet with you when you called him. He probably called you back on a line they don't know to watch. Jill Bledsoe's outfit isn't likely to be listening in on your calls. They'd need to have a court order to monitor your phone." I tried to make it sound as routine and casual as I could, and that Bledsoe cared about court orders.

"So there is a court order to monitor my phone?" Katie very obviously did not like being in a position where she placed other people, all of whom were suspected of offenses far greater than dating me.

"It may not end there." I hated to tell her that. "You'll need to move in with me for a while. This place is more secure than your house. I'll give you a phone to use to reach me and I'll teach you some tricks to use if you're being followed. Try to think of it as being a game, can you do that?"

"No," she immediately decided. "It's illegal and it scares the crap out of me. Doesn't it scare you to know someone is watching you?"

"It's how I lived for about twenty years of my life."

The only way for me to make Katie comfortable in her changed surroundings was to remind her that I was familiar with the dark world we were about to share. We had consciously avoided discussing my work as an intelligence operative or any details about her divorce from Ray. It was time for all of that to change. I extended my left hand and Katie reluctantly surrendered the refuge she found in the chair and cocktail. I led her to my office. She had never seen the windowless room until that moment. The door was always locked during her few previous visits.

I had done some remodeling since my last case. The left and right walls were nine feet long and the wall opposite the door is twelve feet wide. Dark green magnetic chalkboards began about three feet above the floor and extended six feet up, nearly touching the crown molding on the three walls. Floor to ceiling bookcases covered the wall with the doorway. These shelves included a formidable gun rack. The room had no desk. The only furniture was a low, dark leather sofa ordered from a Modern-style furniture catalogue along with the metal coffee table. I did not want there to be anything I might be tempted to toss when I become frustrated working on a case. The floor was the building's original thick heart-pine, and I could manipulate the overhead track lights to shine anywhere on the boards.

Katie sat down on the bench and looked around. Her first impression was unexpected. "This explains a lot."

"How so?"

"This room is like being inside your head. Everything has its own little compartment so you don't have to deal with more than you want to at any given moment. The gun safe there represents the huge capacity for violence you try to keep locked away. Moreover, there isn't anything the least bit sentimental in here. Do you realize there isn't a single picture of your life before you came back to New Orleans anywhere in your entire apartment?" She patted the sofa and I sat down next to her.

"There are no pictures because I'm not the same guy. I don't even look the same." This was true. I needed facial reconstructive surgery because of the injuries I suffered in the ambush that sent me home. I was also trying hard to be a much different human being now than I was as a warrior.

The left hand chalkboard was labeled with WHO and WHERE. The WHO column divided into thirds, with Jill Bledsoe and Deputy Director Kinkaid's names at the top of the WHO section. Richie and Jimmy's names were in the bottom third of that section. They were the only names I knew. A laminated map of New Orleans filled most of the WHERE workspace. The map bore magnets marking the addresses of the fires and the scene of both Jimmy's murder and where I'd found his killer's body. I did not elaborate on this particular magnet to Katie.

I still needed the addresses of the remaining stash houses and the residences of every member of the Pistol Peetes and the El Caminos. I especially wanted to know where Jill Bledsoe was basing her operation.

I assigned the right hand chalkboard to handle HOW and WHEN. The HOW column consisted of the few newspaper articles about Jimmy's shooting and about each of the fires, but otherwise HOW and WHEN were in limbo. There had not been another arson fire since Wheeler and I discovered the blood evidence at the scene of the last fire. Deputy Director Kinkaid shutting me down let me know he was aware of the fires and by extension was aware of the murders. There was an important part to WHEN that I needed to keep in mind, as well. I needed to figure everything out before Jill Bledsoe was able to finish whatever she was sent to do and left town. The contractor would cover its tracks far too well for me to follow their trail when it went cold.

The WHAT and WHY columns on the center chalkboard were nearly blank. This is always the slowest piece of the puzzle to fill with notes because it is where I record the connections between the two other boards. I had written a simplified paraphrase of Kinkaid's justification for his dark operation under the WHY column:

To disrupt the flow of heroin into New Orleans.
To create opportunities for criminal prosecutions of those dealing heroin.

I underlined the phrase, because these were the only false things I knowingly wrote on the wall. I knew for certain that this was not the contractor's purpose in New Orleans. I needed to find the exact opposite of the phrases on the board to know what they were really doing. I could not let myself speculate on the WHAT and WHY. I doubted I would find anything positive behind Kinkiad's actual motives. There were far too many possible bad reasons to let myself pick an early favorite.

Roux had followed us into the room and stretched out on the long sofa. Katie was cradling his square head in her lap and quietly petting him while she considered my handiwork. Most of what Katie and I were confronted with here was wide-open space under some short words which were far more complicated than they seemed.

"I take it you're determined to get to the bottom of whatever is really going on here." Katie was not smiling about this prospect. I was the cop who disrupted the City Council election over an entirely legal offer to buy Miss J's home in the Lower Ninth Ward.

"I pretty much have to. The State Police and NOPD are unable to do anything because they have their hands tied by Homeland Security. I can only do so much publicly without ending up in prison for violating my secrecy agreement. I can't even tell you the lie we were told about what's happening."

"Is there anything I can do?" Katie asked and released my hand.

"Not legally, no."

"That's not what I asked." She stood up and walked around the room. She glanced at the newspaper articles and then looked at me. "I'm not going to be stalked like some rabbit and do absolutely nothing about it. I'm also not going to let you take all of the risks, or all the heat."

"I need information from Avery. I need addresses for the members of the Pistol Peetes. I need whatever he has on the El Caminos. I need to know what is going on that he isn't telling the newspapers. Someone must still be keeping a lid on things, and I'm afraid Kinkaid has dumped that job on the Chief of Detectives. He isn't up to it." I was sure it would give my obese and ethically minded boss a heart attack or stroke.

"I'll get it for you." Katie had to know she was risking her career and law license. Kinkaid would make her life miserable for decades if she crossed him or the Department of Justice. "Tell me what we need to do."

That was a very long conversation to have. We started with bringing three large suitcases of her clothes to my apartment and securing her house. I also gave her an old flip-phone with no camera and no built-in GPS.

I saw it bothered her that I had a collection of burner phones in my gun safe. The arsenal in the gun safe probably worried her more than she let on, as well. It contained an unreasonable amount of firepower, so I chose not to tell her about the even larger number of far more specialized weapons I kept stored elsewhere.

The last thing we went over was assigning her a unique distress code like the one Avery used to summon me for our last meeting. Her code word was going to be 'Jackson.' Anyone intercepting it would most likely interpret that word to mean Jackson Square, or maybe even extrapolate it to mean the battlefield all the way out in Chalmette. It actually meant to meet on the patio of Napoleon House, which is across the street from the building where Andrew Jackson and the pirate Jean Lafitte met to make their battle plans. The landmark tavern was easy to reach from either my apartment or her place of work, was well away from Jackson Square and was perpetually full of people.

We had a quiet dinner in the restaurant. I think the staff believed we argued all afternoon. Katie was visibly tense and angry. I was fatigued and more humorless than usual. Neither of us deserved the lives we were about to live, but Katie was being subjected to this stress simply for having fallen in love with me. There are ways to test the strength of a relationship that do not involve crossing Homeland Security.

I held Katie while she cried herself to sleep on my bare shoulder. Her tears dampened the puckered, circular scars from the three bullet wounds that nearly cost me my life. Roux was up all night, prowling about the apartment in an effort to find what had the two of us so upset. I slipped out of bed in the middle of the night and sat in the office for a few hours to stare at the vast blank spaces in my knowledge.

Chapter 26

I took Roux for his morning run on the Esplanade Avenue neutral ground just after sunrise Sunday morning. Katie was finally sleeping without a frown on her face and I didn't want to start her day any sooner than was necessary. The day before required adjustments she probably would not have made if she didn't love or trust me.

I was looking at my world differently as well. I spent nearly five years losing the paranoia and the comfort with the violence required of me while doing what civilians like to call black-ops. I still battled with symptoms of hyper-vigilance related to my PTSD associated with those dirty deeds. I risked scaring away everyone I knew or loved if I chose to weaponize my anger in this fragile mental state.

I began taking note of every vehicle and pedestrian I did not recognize on our normal path. I mentally inventoried the cars parked along Decatur Street and Esplanade Avenue to begin isolating any surveillance teams set in place to follow me whenever I drove past. I told Katie nothing about this new part of my morning routine with Roux.

I called the bar downstairs and had breakfast delivered as room service. Sunday brunch at Strada Ammazarre was busier than usual. New Orleans was full of people in town for the first Carnival parades and for the NFC Championship game in the Superdome that evening. I was glad the Saints were drawing so much attention that people were missing the other things going on around them. The local TV and radio stations were pandering to an audience that wanted to know about the hometown football team, not arson fires in poor parts of town or the latest gang violence. It was something Jill Bledsoe's operatives were probably counting on.

Katie and I spent the afternoon refining the office chalkboards. I added Ray and Dan Logan's names under the WHO heading. Ray's lamentations aside, he was still involved and was probably still being paid by Bledsoe. Adding his name did not surprise or upset Katie. She believed he genuinely wanted to keep her safe. She was just as certain he would let others do me grave bodily harm.

We compiled a list of the police files and records I needed from Chief Avery to update the boards. Most of it was database material, such as lists of all known members of the Pistol Peetes and their last known addresses. Suspended detectives cannot request those files.

Katie was feeling cooped up by the time we finished the updates so we both walked Roux before having supper. My limited conversation and the way I moved my eyes betrayed what I was doing as we moved about the neighborhood. I was able to make Katie a bit more comfortable with our new situation by giving her a lesson in counter-intelligence. I pointed out three parking spaces. Only two cars occupied those spaces during the last ten hours, and people sat in the cars the entire time. One of the cars was a silver BMW that looked identical to one I felt was following me even before I knew about Jill Bledsoe's operation. The problem for anyone running a stakeout in the French Quarter is that parking is so scarce that their vehicles must swap out parking spots. Rotating the same vehicles risks making their purpose glaringly obvious. We returned to the apartment and stood on my third floor balcony with its great view of the Old Mint, French Market, Marigny Neighborhood, and the wharves along the Mississippi River. I pointed out windows in the Old Mint where someone could be watching us. There were tall plants and sheer drapes in an apartment near the French Market that had not been in place a week earlier. Anyone in the Market taking pictures might genuinely like the architecture, but they were just as likely taking our picture.

We enjoyed dinner while sitting at the bar just after six o'clock. The restaurant was not going to do much business because kickoff for the Saints playoff game was set for just after seven o'clock. We sat at the bar to hoot and holler with everyone else in the place as the Saints pulled off a last minute interception and field goal to win their first trip to the Super Bowl. I wanted to be a proud and happy fan, but I was still a cop at heart and knew that the impending influx of tourists and residents still living in exile who'd make a point to be in town on Super Bowl Sunday was going to complicate my situation. I had a large enough haystack to look through to find Jill Bledsoe's needle before the pile grew any bigger. I was also becoming concerned that any civilian casualties in the gang-war being encouraged Homeland Security's Southeast Regional Deputy Director seemed to be something the man was far too prepared to explain away as collateral damage. I was beginning to wonder if Kinkaid planned to use a contrived cartel terrorism or gang-related incident during Mardi Gras to bolster his personal influence over the region.

Chapter 27

I called a United Cab for Katie to use to get to work on Monday morning with the promise that I would pick her up from work. I got in beside her and the driver took my cue to pull away from Strada Ammazarre at the right moment to put a Metro bus between anyone on our tail and the two of us. I handed Katie my iPhone as we passed Jackson Square.

"What's this for?" She put the phone in her purse and waited for an answer. She had begun to accept that I would not answer all of her questions.

"It will take anyone tracking me by my phone a while to figure out that I'm not with you." Katie shrugged at the day's first bit of intrigue. "I'm going to meet someone to arrange a sit-down with the Pistol Peetes."

"And if I need to call you?"

"I transferred my calls to this number." I showed her the basic flip-style phone I activated while she was in the shower. I got out of the cab at the second Uptown-bound streetcar stop on St. Charles and blended into the waiting knot of people. Most of the passengers were service industry workers heading home after spending all night, and all their tips, to continue celebrating the Saints' victory. The regular riders were more like the woman on her way to clean one of the huge houses along the St. Charles streetcar route, because nobody buys a mansion to clean it themselves.

I rode the streetcar as far as Louisiana Avenue and then walked under the massive canopy of live oaks to my destination. I patrolled this neighborhood following Katrina. It took months before being here after dark stopped reminding me of night patrols in cities like Fallujah. New Orleans was still fighting its own Gulf War of a different kind, an economic gulf. The only thing the "haves" to one side of the streetcar line and the "have nots" on the other side share equally is a zip code. The City Council seemed to be at a loss on how to address the income gap and resulting crime wave.

Anyone following me here had to be doing so at Jill Bledsoe's direction. I made a point to wave at any of the petty crooks and felons I had dealt with in the past. I did not want them thinking I was a walking ATM, the new term for an easy person to rob, or that this was the day to seek revenge. I turned to my left at the post office and headed down a less traveled street to see the person I was here to question.

I had waited as long as I could for the woman who witnessed Richie's abduction to contact me voluntarily. I called her once I was within sight of her building to say I was on my way to speak with her.

I watched the apartment building for a few minutes to see if she would choose to flee. I also wanted to get a better look at the cars parked on the street and in the building's small lot. I did not think anyone else was fully aware of this woman's importance, but I was certain that NOPD lacked the money to keep her under surveillance.

I rapped on her door and put a thumb over the view hole. I could hear someone approaching the door, and then heard their confused tone when they could not see me.

"Who's out there?" the woman's familiar voice asked. I listened for whispers or the sound of anyone else moving around inside.

"Your telephone buddy." I hoped she understood my simple code. It would do neither one of us much good for me to declare to the apartment building's other tenants that a detective with the State Police was visiting her. Even so, there was still a long pause before she responded.

"What do you want?"

"We need to talk. Open the door. I'm alone." I was going to give her thirty seconds before I developed a Plan B. She opened the door barely enough for me to step past her as I counted to fifteen.

"I don't have nothing to tell you." She did not tell me this defiantly. She also did not sound like she was refusing to talk with me. She understood by now that I was convinced she was involved with the Pistol Peetes and would keep showing up on her doorstep until she answered my questions.

"Start with the easy stuff. What's your name?"

"Jasmine." She did not give me her last name and I did not press her on something so meaningless. She was younger than I thought, probably in her late twenties. She was no great Creole beauty, but she was not unattractive. She was also shorter than she looked on the balcony.

"A lot of people need your help, Jasmine." I sat down in a chair facing into the apartment, with its back to the door she had re-locked. "Someone wants to start something between Richie's gang and the Mexicans they've been buying their heroin from."

"What do you know about all that?" Jasmine did not deny the connection I had just declared existed.

"What you need to know is that heroin is not why I'm here. Think what happens if two gangs start a war right now, during Mardi Gras. A lot of innocent people are going to get hurt that have nothing to do with those gangs."

"What can I do about that?" The images I planted in her mind obviously unsettled her.

"You can put me in touch with the Pistol Peetes. Let them know I want to help them solve whatever their problem is with the El Caminos."

"Why would you do that?" Jasmine knew there had to be a hidden reason for me to show up in person to make such a suspicious offer.

"To keep the peace around here. I also need for you to tell me more about the night Richie Rich disappeared." I motioned for her to take a seat on the sofa across from me. Her constant pacing made it hard for me to keep part of my attention focused on the rest of her apartment.

She paused. I could not really tell if she was dredging up bad memories or editing what she was about to say. I assumed her version of things would include attempting to minimize her own role with the Peetes.

"I was watching TV when I heard cars stop in front of the place where Richie was staying by, there across the street. I looked out and two men was dragging him to a van. One of the other guys took his car."

"Describe the men who took him. Were they white guys, Black guys, Mexican guys? What did the van look like?"

"They was wearing black masks over their heads. They was dressed up all in black, too. They looked like cops, not like no gang I ever saw. They had pretty fancy guns, too. Not no AKs. The van was old. It had some sort of writing on the side, like it was from some business or something." She knew more about guns than automobiles. That was not so strange for a girl who grew up in this neighborhood. "Then another car pulled up about an hour later. Two white men went inside with a backpack and come out with a couple more bags of stuff. Then the house caught fire."

"You couldn't identify the ones who took Richie but you know these two guys were white? What were they wearing?"

"Jeans and t-shirts, and bullet proof vests."

"Did you see badges on either set of men?" This was doubtful at best. Nobody involved felt a need for any subterfuge to abduct Richie Franklin.

"No. Those first guys were real smooth, though. They had plenty of guns, but they never fired no shots. Richie got pulled out of that house with a bag over his head and his hands behind his back. They tossed him in that van with no problems."

"So there were two separate visits to the house?"

"That's what I done told you." She did not like thinking about what happened to her friend and did not appreciate me questioning her story.

"Who did you call after Richie was taken?" It was a loaded question and I anticipated getting my first lie. She surprised me.

"His momma."

"Not the police?"

"I hoped the police was who had him. I called his momma so she'd know to call someone to put up his bail." Her actions made perfect sense.

"When did you figure out Richie was taken by somebody else?"

"When them other guys come and burnt down his house."

I was not certain that she was being completely honest, but her story sounded entirely credible. Who else was likely to have raided a drug dealer's house in the middle of the night without shooting the place up? A normal police arrest does not end in an arson fire, though.

"When did you tell all of this to the Pistol Peetes?" I was fishing. It was time to find out how connected the young woman was to the gang.

"Why do you think I done that?"

"Just answer the question, Jasmine, okay?"

She considered the position answering this question placed her in long and hard before she spoke again. I was asking her to implicate herself in whatever the gang was doing, before and after Richie's disappearance. Answering me truthfully could open the door to some questions about her knowledge of the gang that she really did not want to answer. It came down to trust, and I tried very hard to look trustworthy while she stared at me deciding what she should do.

"I called 'em right after I called his momma."

"Are they paying your rent?" This was definitely not a question she wanted to answer.

"No." Her tone and inflection made this one word into an entire statement.

"But someone in the gang is, right?"

"I'm not going to tell you who." I had pushed a bit too hard.

"It don't care who it is, Jasmine." I made a point of using her name to try to reconnect. "I just need you to put me in touch with him, or someone else in the Peetes. That's all I came here to ask you to do."

"That's really all you come here for?" She sounded roughly equal parts relieved and suspicious.

"Well, no. I wanted to check out your apartment."

"You lookin' to move Uptown?" Making jokes was a good sign.

I shook my head and stood up. She watched in silence as I passed her dining room table and moved into the kitchen. I counted the dishes in her sink and opened her small refrigerator and a couple of the cabinets. The refrigerator contained more liquor than condiments or food. I left the bathroom and bedrooms alone, but noted she kept both doors closed. Most people leave those doors open. I had already seen what I needed to see.

"Who's here with you?"

"Nobody."

"Well your imaginary friend leaves his plates as dirty as you do, and you've stocked quite a bit of beer along with your wine coolers." I leaned against the kitchen doorframe and cocked my head towards the pair of dirty plates still on the table from breakfast. My right hand was strategically close to the Glock holstered on my hip.

"My uncle come by to fix my sink." Her alibi only explained the dirty dishes, not the stockpile of cold beer.

"I wrote the number someone needs to call on the back of this card. Let's make this the last time I drop by, okay?" I handed her one of my State Police business cards. I would be in quite a bit of trouble if she called any of the numbers printed on the front of the card.

Jasmine remained mute about her roommate situation. She flicked the card with her long fingernails to let me know she understood what I wanted, and what I was threatening to do if nobody called me.

We both looked out the window to be sure nobody seemed interested in my visit before Jasmine pushed me out the door and locked it behind me.

Chapter 28

Chief Avery sent Katie home with a thick envelope of material for me. She said Avery also wanted me to know that the bloated corpse of Jimmy Washington's killer washed ashore in the Industrial Canal overnight. I felt proven right in my assumption that NOPD would use the body to close the open homicide case.

The envelope's contents included a roster of every known member of the Pistol Peetes and an organizational chart that NOPD's narcotics squad put together for a previous task force. There had been distressingly few felony convictions of any of the names on the chart in the three years since that task force disbanded. The gang's membership knew one another since childhood and their loyalty was absolute. It takes RICO Act prosecutions to dismantle gangs that base their membership recruiting on shared histories. Usually their rivals exterminate them before the legal system can take them off the street peacefully.

The information on the El Caminos was comparatively thin. The DEA provided most of the material about them. There was also a memo from the ATF about their smuggling lots of guns into Mexico across the Arizona border. The majority of the intelligence material in the envelope on the El Camino cartel from NOPD was little more than speculation based upon second-hand rumors from unreliable street sources.

"I checked with the Attorney General's office and they said they haven't brought a single prosecution against the local El Caminos.

They know the cartel is here, but the Justice Department takes away any cases they want to file. I asked around in the Federal court building and the general assumption is that the DEA and FBI won't pursue any cases unless someone will testify against the people above them in the cartel." I already knew what Katie was telling me. I had seen enough news stories and read enough briefings and memos on the spread of the violent Mexican cartels to grasp the difficulty in making cases. The government found itself stymied by witnesses unwilling to testify against a drug cartel prepared to make them fear the gang's retribution more than prison time.

"Kinkaid sent a private contractor to town to shake things up so the Feds can make cases of their own. I was so focused on that part that I totally blanked on his also saying they were testing new surveillance equipment and techniques."

"What sort of surveillance are we talking about?"

"My last work in Iraq involved a government contractor, not an agency directly. The mission involved using their technology and programs to pull huge amounts of metadata from cell towers in order to link known cell phone numbers to the people those callers were in contact with the most. They could triangulate the addresses where suspects used the phones and then send up drones or have someone track a subject's movements. Eventually the minor players led us to senior players and we worked our way up the leadership ladder. This company could remotely activate any phone or computer's microphone and camera we chose to use as a bug. It was like sitting in the room with the plotters as they made their plans. I think this company has the same technology and that it was how they knew about the El Caminos' plan to kill Jimmy Washington."

"What did you do to the people you singled out in Iraq?" Katie was bright enough to look past the whiz-bang technology to see the ethical and legal issues with what I had just described.

"My mandate was to eliminate threats to Coalition forces and the transition to a new Iraqi government. We were to isolate resistance and jihadist networks and then neutralize any viable threat before anyone inflicted casualties or cause more chaos." I was necessarily vague about my specific activities, but I did not sound in any way conflicted about what I had done.

"I assume due process wasn't part of your mission statement." Katie was choosing to let sarcasm stand for her criticism. We were both acutely aware of Tulip's involvement with an activist group intent on seeing war crimes charges brought against those involved in exactly the sort of covert activities I just described.

"To say the least." I let the sudden tension in the room dissipate a bit before I brought up what I wanted her to consider. "It's entirely possible that Kinkaid is using the cover story of a defense contractor testing new surveillance methods and equipment as a means of gathering actionable intelligence on the gangs. I think his plan is to draw the El Caminos and Pistol Peetes into a contrived war to get them to kill as many of each other's members as possible. Anyone left standing on either side of the fight would go to prison. I am supposed to hide the use of outside agitators by DHS."

"How is any of that legal?" Katie demanded. It appalled her that anyone could conceive of such a plan and, worse yet, that a deputy director of the agency tasked with protecting the nation was who unleashed it upon New Orleans.

"It's not legal, but none of that matters if nobody knows it happened." Which brought us back to my dilemma.

"It doesn't make any sense. I doubt the Justice Department would have approved any such thing."

"They don't have to. Homeland Security can do almost anything they want by stamping it as being to fight terrorists. They are convinced the cartels are getting cozy with the Islamic militants, so it is no stretch to think they would take the step of designating the cartels as terrorists. Plus, weakened gangs would be ripe pickings for the Justice Department, and Americans would be so happy to see drug dealers in prison that nobody would care how it happened."

"I really don't like how your mind works sometimes," Katie sighed and sat down on the office's long bench. I stopped writing the names and dates Avery had provided into the squares on the massive chalkboards.

"I don't either." This was no joke. "But I'm sure Homeland Security has given a green light to something close to what I just said."

"You're taking on a bit more than City Hall this time." Katie took my hand. "I don't think I'm the sort of partner you need in this fight, but I'll be your attorney when you finish whatever you have to do."

I had shaken the foundations of how she believed either of our worlds actually work. Katie's desire to abide by what is legal and my search for balanced justice is what originally brought us together, but the unholy terror of what I suspected Kinkaid was up to was at the opposite end of both of our spectrums.

"It's better that I partner with someone used to playing dirty anyway." I said and sat down next to her. We both looked at what I added to the office's workspace. This information would give me many new leads to develop.

"Anyone I know?" Katie asked this with a slight smile.

"Not as well as you think." My response was not at all funny to her.

Katie wrapped an arm around me and I kissed her. She was trembling. We sat quietly for a moment, each of us lost in our thoughts. Mine focused on what lay ahead of me, but I could see in my lover's eyes that her concern was on my past. I felt the shadows in my own eyes that always bothered her begin to darken once again.

Chapter 29

My phone remained silent well into the next day. I did not expect the Pistol Peetes to welcome any offer to mediate their gang dispute with the Mexicans, especially not mine. Still, they knew they were in a tight spot with amazingly dangerous people. The only reason any of them were still alive was that the El Caminos still needed the gang as business partners. The Petes likely saw killing Jimmy Washington as the cartel's way of making a point or extracting some sort of toll from the Pistol Peetes. The Mexicans were not going to whittle the Peetes down one by one if they decided to scorch the earth of the gang. Wiping their local distributor out would mean something very bad had happened between them, but I'd found nothing in Avery's notes to indicate a betrayal or double cross that would incite the El Caminos to make any such move. I had to believe that Bledsoe was behind any of the turmoil, intent upon sparking the gang war Kinkaid wanted. I could not wait around for a call that might never come, so I turned my attention to approaching the Mexicans with my offer.

One of the cornerstones of my Green Beret pre-mission prep was familiarization with the culture and traditions of whatever violent corner of the planet I was going to be dropped into next. It might seem like a long shot to get the Mexican cartel to agree to use me as a mediator, unless you understand the culture and traditions unique to drug cartels. Cartels own entire police departments and politicians by the score in Latin and South America. They intimidate or eliminate anyone they cannot bribe.

Those who will not kiss the ring on the velvet fist wind up slaughtered and replaced with someone who will. Having a state police detective offer his services to their benefit would seem perfectly natural to them, even if it were an American law enforcement officer.

The best person to help me locate the El Caminos was also the man least likely to want to get involved. Ray Reilly had already admitted to seeing a list of home addresses tied to members of both gangs. I watched his building most of the morning and spotted no foot traffic that looked like they worked for a private security contractor. Everyone fit the profile of the clientele of the gallery on the floor below his. I had no trouble seeing why Ray had located his office on Julia Street. It is in an area full of art galleries filled with starving artists and their models. The forty-year old man is still Irish-handsome enough to be able to exploit his newly re-instated bachelorhood in such company. I was a little disappointed with how surprised he was when I stepped in line behind him at the coffee shop a couple of blocks from his office. He should have anticipated my approaching him about those addresses.

"I need something from you," I whispered in his ear. I could see an actual shudder roll down his neck and stiffen his spine.

"What are you doing here?" Ray did not turn around.

"I need to get that list of addresses your client had you photograph." I did not want to get into a long conversation here. I had been in the coffee shop for ten minutes when he arrived and I absolutely did not want it to appear as though this was a pre-arranged meeting.

"What for?" He surely did not expect me to explain my uses for the list of addresses. He was buying time, and he took a while ordering his convoluted cup of coffee as well. I ordered a small cup of black coffee and the girl on the counter mouthed the words "Thank you."

"You won't be tied to anything I do with the list, so don't start acting like you care why I am asking you for it."

"Fine. Can I email it to you?" He just wanted to be done with this.

"Not unless you want your client to know you handed it over. You're the one who was sure we were all being watched, so act like it." Ray can be staggeringly naïve and ignorant of his situation and surroundings. "Put it in the pages of this magazine and have your office girl leave it in the gallery downstairs. I'll pick it up and we'll be done."

I pressed a copy of New Orleans Magazine into the crook of his arm and paid for my coffee. He headed to his office and I walked around the block, tossing the coffee into a trashcan as I rounded the corner. I made it back around the block just as Ray's secretary entered the art gallery.

She took her time looking at the current exhibit. It was a lot of color with very little theme or style, but sometimes you just need something colorful to hang over your sofa. I saw where the secretary dropped the magazine and then waited for her to leave before I went inside and picked it up. The rail-thin sales girl paid neither of us the least bit of attention.

I took the list, which was longer than I anticipated, and added color-coded magnets to the map in my office. The Pistol Peetes went on it as blue pins and the red pins represented the El Caminos. Jill Bledsoe's operatives were marked with black magnets, but the only locations I had for them were crime scenes where the trail was already cold. The addresses of active El Camino stash houses and their residences were all near exits and entrances to Interstate 10 on the eastern side of the city. The farthest address from the interstate still placed it halfway between I-10 and the bypass of I-510 leading into Chalmette. It had the most escape routes, as it also offered an escape route on Highway 90 to Mississippi. This was the most promising address I had for the El Caminos, but it was almost certain to be under the highest surveillance.

I chose one of the other places at random. It was neither the first nor the last house in the string, and it did not fall into the middle. I chose it just because it was the closest to a police station. The house was a brick and stucco ranch-style house on a corner lot in a neighborhood of homes that could all have used a little paint or repair. In short, it did not look like a place most people would believe members of a drug cartel might be living.

I rang the doorbell, and stepped back and to one side from the door. I did not want to take a burst of gunfire or a shotgun blast to the chest if that was how the residents decided to answer the door. I absolutely looked like trouble to anyone sizing me up. I was a well-groomed forty-two year old white male in very good physical shape driving an expensive pickup truck. I did not need to wear a badge to look too official to be the local Welcome Wagon representative.

The door opened and a young Hispanic woman peered through the screen door at me. I smiled as engagingly as I could and pressed one of my business cards against the screen. The change in her expression told me I was close to my quarry. I dusted off my Spanish. "I would like to speak with one of the men in your house, Senorita."

"I am alone, Detective," she said in English. I knew better, and the way her eyes flicked to her right towards the thick wooden door she was shielding herself with betrayed the lie even further.

"It would be best for them to speak with me now. I won't return alone." I said this in what I call a 'dog tone.' Dogs respond to the tone in their master's voice more than they do to any spoken words. I wanted the tone in my voice heard by whoever was listening from behind the door.

The young woman said nothing but continued looking very hard at the card I still held at eye level in the screen door. I needed to have both of my hands free. I listened for whispers or the sound of the back door opening, but only a heavy silence filled the air between us. I did not excuse myself and leave. She did not move to close the door.

The smile that suddenly began twitching at the corners of her mouth told me it was time to move.

I reached to pull the Glock from its holster as I spun and jumped from the porch to hide behind the overgrown bushes beside the porch. A pair of young men with AK-47s had managed to close to within fifty feet of me from behind. They froze in their tracks when I vanished. The one I chose to point the green dot of my laser sight on pulled his finger from the trigger of his weapon, but his partner now knew where to aim.

"I'm just here to talk." I shouted at them in Spanish, loud enough for anyone inside the house to hear me as well. The majority of the nearby neighbors did not speak Spanish, and were trying hard to ignore us.

"About what?" I glanced to the open doorway where the male voice came from, but I kept my attention on the only men in a good position to shoot me.

"Someone's trying to start a war you don't want." I took my finger off the laser's trigger and stood up before I made a deliberate show of holstering my pistol. I was taking a stupid chance, but it was unlikely I could have shot both men without one of them shooting me, anyway. Dumb as I act at times, I really don't ever want to get shot again.

"You have my attention." The Mexican spoke surprisingly good English. His elaborate tattoos and ponytail of coal-black hair made him look like the gunmen he waved away. His men crossed the street and disappeared into the open garage of a house I should have checked before I rang the doorbell. We had sufficiently impressed one another with our maneuvers and calm, but the cartel's gunmen surprised me and I could not let that happen twice and expect to live.

"So, tell me who is trying to start this war."

"May I come inside?"

"Of course not. Let's take a ride in your truck." I was sure there would be nothing incriminating left in the home by the time we returned. "My name is Fernando Rodriguez."

"Mine's Cooter Holland, but people call me 'Cadillac'. I'm a detective with the State Police. What do your friends call you?"

"I have no friends, Detective Holland." He opened the passenger door of the Ford Raptor and climbed in as I did the same. Two nondescript sedans pulled in line behind us as I started driving towards Interstate 10.

According to the DEA files I had been studying, Fernando Rodriguez was one of the main lieutenants the cartel dispatched to New Orleans when they decided to expand their distribution network. He was college educated and was once a respected military officer. His annual pay in the military was likely to have been less than he now spent on bullets in a month. Fernando was in his thirties and either Katie or Tulip would tell me he was handsome, in that dark swarthy way they swoon over Tony. His hair was dark, but his skin looked more tanned than Hispanic, as if one parent might have been from north of the border. He was probably not the man responsible for running the cartel's operation in New Orleans, but whatever I said to Fernando would reach the right man's ears the same day.

"I believe there's a plan to provoke a gang war between you and the Pistol Peetes. Someone is killing people on both sides and trying to make it appear to be something between the two of you. I'll bet you've both been trying to deny killing one another and to keep your ranks in line." I was trying to sell my personal theories as fact. What I wanted in response were real facts.

"I believe what you are saying is true."

"What doesn't make sense to me is why anyone would go to so

much effort. It's easier to handle two dogs that aren't fighting each other." I was trying to make an analogy, but he heard an insult.

"So, we're just dogs to you, Detective?" My comment cost me whatever goodwill my visit created.

"A bad choice of words," I needed to rebuild the already tense rapport. "I only meant that it's easier to build a drug dealing case against each of you if you're distracted by killing one another."

"Nobody is building a drug case against us, Detective. The El Caminos have a deal about that," Fernando informed me. This was interesting news to me, but all I could do was file it away for the moment.

"Really? What sort of deal do you think you have to keep that from happening?" Skepticism is a hard thing to keep out of your tone of voice.

"An understanding then. Believe me; we have no reason to fear being prosecuted in your courts for anything we are doing here."

"Does that agreement include murder?" I was going to assume he was lying about everything if he said he had such license.

"We have killed nobody in New Orleans and do not wish to do so."

"What about Jimmy Washington? That wasn't you?"

"No. He was a good man and we liked him." Fernando did not sound like he was lying. This verified my very worst suspicions about the killing. It also confirmed for me what Kinkaid's private contractor was up to on my home turf.

"What happens if someone tricks you into doing so? What happens to that deal of yours then?" I was pulling into traffic on eastbound I-10 towards Slidell and could not read his face for a reaction to my scenario. The highway passes through miles of swamp at the eastern edge of the city. I pointed out the remains of an abandoned amusement park that was now a backdrop for movies using the last remnants of Katrina's destruction as a stand-in for the apocalypse.

"I do not believe murder would be forgiven. Are you saying you have been killing my men and burning our homes to make us fight one another?"

"Oh, it's not me, Fernando." I realized he thought I was there to shake him down. "I'm just trying to keep the peace. It will be bad for everyone's business if you or the Pistol Peetes start a shooting war."

"Revenge is more important than any deal someone killing my

men thinks we have." Fernando did not need to explain what he meant by this.

"Tell me who made this deal with you and I'll talk to them." Fernando was forthcoming so far. I did not think I was pushing him.

"You're not the person to speak for me if you don't know who that man is."

"I may not know everything, Fernando, but ask yourself this. How did I know where to find you this afternoon?" I certainly was not going to admit that stumbling upon Fernando was nothing but dumb luck. This was the best place for me to end the conversation and I could sense he felt no need to add anything. I rattled him by knocking on his door as though I knew where he lived. He shook me far more with his talk about having some sort of blanket immunity deal, and his willingness to risk it to exact revenge.

I pulled off the highway at the foot of the Twin Spans Bridge to turn the truck around. I watched anxiously as Fernando's security team pulled to a stop on either side of us in a classic crossfire position.

"How *did* you know where to find me?" Fernando rolled his window down and gestured to the driver of the car on his side. We certainly did not trust one another, but he felt I had not lured him here to kill him.

"The men attacking you know everything about your operation in New Orleans. I believe their plan is to disrupt your dealings with the locals in such a way that you can all be taken down, and that will enhance their own position."

"That is an ambitious plan. You should let the men you suspect of this know we will no longer die without a fight." I could tell Fernando relished the thought of a fight.

"I would tell them if I knew them. I will tell you this, Fernando. I cannot let a fight hurt my city. This is not your hometown, it's mine."

"I like your city. I would protect it, too, if I were you." He extended his right hand and we shook hands. This did not make us friends. It only meant neither of us wanted to have the other for an enemy.

Chapter 30

J asmine called me later that same afternoon. She wanted to relay a message from the Pistol Peetes, but did not want to give it to me over the phone. I agreed to meet her in an hour. I let Chef Tony know Jasmine's name and address before I left the bistro, just in case.

I believed I could identify each of the surveillance teams tracking me. Whoever was paying for constant coverage of my activities was not getting their money's worth of details about what I was doing. Their teams were spread so thin that eluding them was easier than it should have been, and I'd patrolled the French Quarter long enough to know how and where I could disappear.

I walked through the Quarter and towards the office buildings in the CBD. I abruptly jumped into a cab dropping its passengers in front of the Monteleone Hotel on Royal Street and gave the driver a winding route to a gas station at the corner of Claiborne and Washington Street. Getting out of the taxi there gave anyone who might have tracked the vehicle very little to work with in finding me. I walked the last three blocks.

Jasmine was standing with two other women by the stairs leading to her apartment. It was the first time I saw her outside of her apartment and I found it very suspicious that she was being secretive with me about our meeting, but stood in the open for the entire world to see us together.

"Good afternoon, ladies." I did not want to betray Jasmine as being the reason I was approaching them. She had less of a problem with this.

"Y'all step inside. I'll be up in a minute or two." She gestured to the partially open door at the top of the stairs. It was too cool of a day to have left her front door open. My dad used to accuse my sister and me of trying to heat the neighborhood when we did this as kids. It looked like a clumsy trap, but I was going to have to step into it to move the investigation along.

"On the floor!" A teenaged boy hiding behind the front door jabbed the barrel of a shotgun behind my left ear as I stepped inside.

I had not completely cleared the door. My weight was still on my back foot, which was about even with the middle of the door. I counted two additional masked gang members sitting at the dining room table and a fourth assailant standing outside of the hallway bathroom. The one behind the door continued holding his shotgun close to my head while the rest of his pals aimed their own pistols at me. They were all wearing masks from Halloween costumes.

"Not going to happen." I said and stopped walking. The shotgun nudged against the side of my head was a powerful inducement to follow orders, but nobody could shoot at me and not hit this kid as well.

I waited as the gunman to my right approached and extended his hand to take the pistol from the holster on my hip. I ducked and took a step backwards as I shoved my weight into the door. This knocked the one holding what proved to be a Russian-made Saiga shotgun off balance. I used my left hand to grab the barrel and wrested the weapon from the boy holding it. My maneuver also positioned the kid reaching for my pistol into a perfect position for me to drive the stock of the shotgun into his belly. I pivoted the shotgun in my hands and aimed it, rather than pointed it, at the last two members of the Pistol Peetes' welcoming committee. I waited for them to lower their weapons before ejecting the shotgun's magazine and tossing it, and the shotgun, on the Formica tabletop between the stunned pair.

I extended a hand to help the embarrassed youths to their feet. "I'm obviously not here to kill any of you."

"Jasmine said you wanted to talk to us. We're here, so start talking." The quartet leader's voice was much deeper than I expected. Avery's intel led me to believe the oldest of the Pistol Peetes were in their early twenties. He was also taller and heavier than his peers were, and was either mature for his age or older than the others were. I passed very close to him as I moved to sit at the table and saw crows' feet at the corners of the brown eyes glaring at me behind his mask.

"Take off the masks. They've got to be getting hot by now." I said this as casually as possible and avoided doing anything to imply I was in control. I would get more cooperation by pretending to be their prisoner.

I recognized the three younger members from the files Avery sent home with Katie. The one doing the talking did not remove his mask. I extended my right hand in his direction. He reluctantly snapped his Beretta pistol into its leather shoulder holster before shaking my hand.

"Cooter Holland. I'm from the State Police." I tried to draw his name out of him by making him be polite.

"We know who you are, Detective." So, that idea did not work.

"If you aren't going to introduce yourselves, what can I do for you? I get the feeling that you don't really want to talk with me."

"I hear you are looking for Richie Franklin," the stranger said.

"That's why I told Jasmine I wanted to talk with you. I've been hoping you had some leads to share." I could see this was not going to satisfy them. "Jasmine told me Richie was abducted by some white guys in a van and hasn't been seen since. The timing is odd because someone began leaving dead El Caminos all over town right after Richie was abducted."

"We had nothing to do with any of that." The leader sounded adamant. "We know where Richie is. You need to stop looking for him."

"No, I can't. Ritchie seems to be the key to everything that is going on right now." I wanted to sound like I knew there was a larger picture than a kidnapping. "The El Caminos killed Jimmy Washington, right?"

"They say they didn't." I looked in the leader's eyes and saw nothing to indicate he doubted the El Caminos.

"So, you're taking the word of the only gang with a reason to kidnap Richie and shoot Jimmy?""

"Whoever has Ritchie wants the Peetes go to war with the El Caminos because they're too afraid to fight a Mexican drug cartel themselves."

"Who would want a war?" I tucked away that he just said "they" and not "we" in reference to going to war with the cartel. I stood up and moved to the sofa. The gang members moved as well to be sure I was constantly surrounded.

"Don't worry about who. You should be looking at why. If you figure that out, you answer both questions. Meantime, leave off looking for Ritchie. You're putting his life in more danger than you know." It was obvious that the leader was not going to take off his steamy plastic mask. I began looking for any distinguishing features in the small amount of face left exposed and anything revealed by the clothes he wore.

"Does all of this have to do with your Mexican pals and an immunity deal they have worked out? Care to share what you know about that?" I could only hope that Fernando bragged about the arrangement to them at some point.

"We don't know anything about any deals," the leader insisted, but not very convincingly. "I still don't think you give a rat's ass about what happens between us anyway."

"I do care about the possibility of two gangs shooting up Mardi Gras parade routes and about tourists being sent home in body bags." I had one other thing that was driving me forward. "And I want to find whoever is responsible for the fires and murders."

"But you don't care that we're selling heroin?" This came from one of the younger gang members. The leader turned towards the kid and gave a faint shake of his head to let his minions know to stay silent.

"Oh, I care. It's just that my job today is to try to keep you alive."

I looked for gold teeth and fillings when the masked leader broke into a big grin and started laughing at my response. One of his incisors had a diamond-studded gold cap on it. The leader also wore no jewelry; except for a wristwatch that I recognized as a replica Army Ranger timepiece.

"How do you propose to find who is responsible?" The leader, who I named Gold Tooth on the spot, leaned forward to get his face close to mine. It stretched his neck out of his long sleeved shirt and exposed a piece of tattoo on the right side of his neck. I also noted that he was wearing military surplus boots and carried a Beretta 92 pistol. The other Peetes brandished Ruger and Glock handguns.

"I'm looking for Ritchie's car. When I find it, I find my man. It is good to know there isn't going to be a gang war. Still, it will be a very bad thing if the answer to why all of this is happening isn't because of one."

I stood up and noted that the heavyset leader and I were the only ones in the room who were wearing boots. Winter weather in

New Orleans seldom gets cold or wet enough to worry about winter footwear. I wear boots because I am a military veteran and am used to wearing them. I could not ask my mysterious host his reason for doing so. I slowly reached for my wallet and pulled out a business card to hand to the gang leader. He handed the card back.

"Why are you giving me a card for some sales guy from SYSCO?"

I acted embarrassed by my mistake and traded the card for a State Police business card with my private contact numbers printed on it. "I hope you'll let me know if you see or hear anything."

"Don't wait up." The leader was just being straightforward with me. One of the other gang members opened the door and I stepped into the bright afternoon sunlight. Jasmine said nothing to me as I walked past.

I began walking towards the streetcar. I briefly considered walking out of my way to get a snack at Pascal's Manale on Napoleon Avenue. A cold beer and a half dozen barbecued shrimp would have been more enjoyable than having to sort through everything that was beginning to bother me after speaking with the leadership of the two gangs.

Chapter 31

Chief Avery could stay away from Strada Ammazarre for only so long. We had not had breakfast together since he suspended me, and neither of us knew how much longer Deputy Director Kinkaid intended to keep me sidelined. It was Katie's idea to use carpooling with the Chief of Detectives as a way to arrange for the Chief and I to confer without either of us openly arranging a meeting. The idea offered the secondary benefit of giving Katie a secure means of getting to and from work.

"I've lost ten pounds since you were suspended," Avery complained.

Miss J, the bistro's daytime sous chef, had presented him with a breakfast that was certain to stop, if not reverse, that weight loss. Avery's breakfast included buttermilk biscuits topped with sausage gravy, buttery grits, scrambled eggs doused in hot sauce, fresh beignets, and a plateful of thick-sliced bacon. Avery kept his mug full of chicory coffee from the carafe Miss J set in the middle of the table. Roux sat beside Avery in hopes he might drop a bite of food.

Katie tapped my arm to get my attention and then whispered in my right ear. "Does he always eat this much?"

The noise in the kitchen made it hard to hear the question. I tapped the powdered sugar off my third beignet and answered with a shrug and a nod. Katie shuddered slightly and returned to cutting the wedge of melon in front of her with the spoon she used to eat each piece.

"Did you ever hear anything from the DEA about the house fires?" I had reviewed my notes from the fire investigations the night before and saw a note that he intended to speak with the agency.

"Their lead agent tried to make it sound like the fires are tied into some sort of active investigation. His response sounded like he was reading from a script someone handed him." We both sensed the agent was lying.

"I have a new question for him. I sat down with the Pistol Peetes yesterday. I'm sure the guy doing their talking was a military veteran in his mid-thirties. He did not fit the Peetes' profile. Can you ID him?"

"You met with the Pistol Peetes?" Avery nearly spat out a mouthful of grits.

"Yeah. I met with a guy from the El Caminos, too." I ignored the distressed expressions on both of my dining companions' faces. "They both swear they're absolutely not at war, and that they haven't been targeting one another."

My companions paused in mid-bite at this news.

"You can't be doing things like that. You're suspended. You have no authority." Avery was not telling me anything I did not already know. I saw no reason to argue that I could do whatever I want as a private citizen.

"Are you hearing what I'm telling you? They aren't the ones burning down the houses or shooting one another."

"They could have killed you." Katie's objections were far more personal, but no less on point than Avery's.

I chose not to mention the armed receptions I received during both visits. "I tracked their leaders down and offered them an opportunity to set the record straight about what's going on. Everyone seems upset about what's been happening, but they also share a conviction that someone is trying to pit them against one another. I also need you to run the prints on this so I can ID one of the guys I spoke with yesterday." Avery reached out to take the SYSCO business card I tricked Gold Tooth into handling.

"And you believe them?"

"I do. I spoke with a witness that said two men took Ritchie from his house in the middle of the night. They claim different men came back to set the house on fire an hour after Richie's abduction. I can't decide if this means we are looking for one or two sets of suspects, but it's telling that the Peetes are certain that Richie is still alive."

"*We* aren't looking for anything at all, remember?" Chief Avery raised his voice and shifted into the tone he uses when he wants no response to his rhetorical questions. "You can't poke your nose into things where it might get noticed. It's fine to analyze those files you requested, which I was more than happy to pass along. I cannot protect you if you start going out in public."

Katie gave me a look that showed she completely agreed with Avery.

"Kinkaid has already figured I'm not prepared to ignore what's going on. I know he's put surveillance teams on me. At least I think they're his. I'm convinced he realizes I am not going to help him cover-up trying to start a gang war."

"Why would Homeland Security want to start a major gang war?" Avery sounded a lot more curious about than dismissive of my suspicions.

"Because a gang war can be used to hide a lot of nasty things. Kinkaid implied Jill Bledsoe is basing her operation here on the one I was part of in Iraq. We used a civil war to hide things that would have otherwise looked like the work of outsiders to the locals. Everyone in New Orleans is so used to people dying in gang wars they are just happy when they don't get caught in the cross fire."

"Do you really think this Kinkaid guy hired someone to kill people and burn down stash houses and then expected you call it a gang war?" Katie was more than skeptical of my theory. I did not want to debate the integrity of the Federal government, especially its more ambitious bureaucrats.

"Crazier things have been done with taxpayer dollars." I did not care how far-fetched it sounded. I was sure I was close to the truth. "Think about it. If something terrible happened during Mardi Gras which Homeland Security could label as terrorism or gangland violence, Kinkaid might use it as an opportunity to take over NOPD by arguing that NOPD is unable to protect the city. At the very least, he would get a huge budget increase and a mandate to expand his agency's authority in this region. "

"I can't believe that is his plan." Katie did not want to believe me, but she had spent as much time staring at the same information I was basing my conclusion on and had yet to come up with a better theory.

"It's certainly somebody's. I'm also not convinced that Kinkaid is the person in charge."

"I thought we'd already decided someone was pulling his

strings." Avery was warming to my theory. He had also stopped eating because he lost his appetite thinking about all of this. "Who could be behind such a thing?"

"All I can do is reverse engineer what I did in Iraq and hope it leads me to whoever is behind everything. We're getting closer and closer to the first big Mardi Gras parades."

"Don't remind me. We're already stretched thin." Avery picked at his eggs and then wrapped the last few pieces of bacon in a napkin as he stood up. "Keep me posted and don't get shot. You're the only guy I have available to investigate your murder if somebody turns on you."

The Chief of Detectives led my now deeply worried girlfriend through the empty bistro. Joaquin opened the front door for them and then held it open again for Roux and me. I glanced around for the morning surveillance teams and then took my dog and our nameless shadows on a three mile run through the Marigny while I worked out a plan in my head.

Chapter 32

My meetings the day before confirmed for me that there was no feud between the gangs. The solid relationship that existed between the two criminal enterprises offered an uneasy comfort. Someone was intent upon creating the illusion of a rift until a real one developed. I had my suspicions about who, but no easy way to confirm them.

I suspected Jill Bledsoe worked for D-Tech for no better reason than my personal experience with the company. Deputy Director Kinkaid merely provided a rubber stamp of legitimacy to their black-ops mission. The company Jill Bledsoe fronted for was supposedly only here to test some sort of new surveillance equipment. They were being passed off as being nothing more than the eyes and ears of whatever else Kinkaid had going in New Orleans. That was D-Tech's cover story in Iraq as well, but they were also in charge of the men at the point of their very bloody spear.

It made perfect sense that the covert operatives tailing me were reporting directly to Jill Bledsoe and not to the Deputy Director. Kinkaid might be called to testify before Congress if his mission were exposed. Bledsoe was his alibi when he claimed to have no direct knowledge of what went wrong. My unexpected refusal to play the part Kinkaid needed me to fill posed an immediate risk to his private contractor's ability to operate in the shadows. Based on my own experience, this sort of covert operations tend to be legally fragile and collapse under the least public scrutiny.

My mission for the day was to find the location of the

additional fires Ray said occurred. I wanted to look closer at those sites to find how they had slipped past the fire marshal. I left Roux on the living room sofa watching Morning Joe while I took a shower and put on jeans and a sweater. I could hear him growling at one of Joe's guests. I wrapped a towel around myself before I went to my office and placed Ray's list in my messenger bag. The two unaccounted for burnt houses were somewhere on the list of thirty-four addresses. Removing addresses I had already visited reduced the list of possibilities to less than thirty. I was relieved to find that Jasmine's address was not on the list.

I walked Roux to the garage and let him get comfortable on the station wagon's front floorboard before I started the engine. I could have shaken off the cars that began tailing me as soon as I left the garage, but I needed certain pieces of my activities reported. I was familiar with the four cars constantly rotating their positions on Esplanade Avenue. They never moved, but they served as spotters for the cars running routes parallel to mine on side streets. It probably seemed like I was out on an aimless drive through bad parts of town to the operatives following me, and to anyone tracking me with electronic or aerial surveillance. Only someone familiar with the list Ray gave me might be able to make sense of my route. My task was simply to check the condition of the addresses on the list. I glanced down the intersections at cross streets and looked through yards as I cruised parallel streets to avoid actually passing in front of any of the addresses.

Both of the crime scenes I was looking for turned out to be on the El Caminos' turf. I hypothesized that both places served as stash houses and the plan was to make it look like the Pistol Peetes were double-crossing their heroin supplier. I could not imagine the El Caminos allowed this to happen, twice no less, without having exacted some sort of retribution.

I spoke with the captains at the fire station closest to each of the fires and learned that both occurred in September, well before the fires that attracted the attention of Fire Marshal Wheeler. Concerned neighbors reported both fires, and in both cases, the homes were already fully involved before the fire trucks arrived. The firefighters focused on keeping the embers from spreading the fire to the adjoining homes. The fire department only found bodies in the rubble of the very first fire.

I noticed that the owner of both properties was the realty company in Arizona that also owned the burnt-out house Wheeler and I investigated in Plum Orchard. I do not accept that level of coincidence as being a coincidence.

I intentionally parked in front of the first fire scene. The Pontiac Bonneville tailing me parked a block away, behind another car parked on the street. The fire destroyed a century-old two-bedroom shotgun-style house that was rebuilt in the aftermath of Hurricane Katrina's flooding of the neighborhood.

The char on the new wooden fence between the house and the neighbors' home attested to the level of heat from the fire. The demolition and debris removal of this house involved far less precision than the later fires. The vacant lot received no blanket of new dirt leveled and compacted over any stray evidence. There were still sections of old lead pipe and charred roof shingles in the weeds.

I put a leash to Roux's harness and let him walk around the weed-covered lot. The records listed the official cause of the first house fire as being "likely arson to cover evidence of criminal activity." The neighbors claimed they heard and saw nothing until one of them saw a glow through their bedroom window and realized the house less than ten feet from their own was on fire. The fire investigator's report mentioned multiple bodies found in the incinerated bathroom.

Roux and I walked a zigzag pattern through the over-grown back yard. He stopped when he came upon a dulled brass shell casing behind the back gate. I crawled around on my hands and knees to move grass out of the way and came up with two more pistol cartridge-sized shell casings. I would not criticize the crime scene technicians, but they had very obviously stopped their search for evidence before they opened the back gate. It is human nature to stop looking when you find what you expect to find.

The markings on the Remington nine-millimeter casings indicated that all three were jacketed hollow point rounds, designed to inflict the most damage possible to their targets. I was less surprised than reassured by the additional markings on each casing indicating the rounds were subsonic loads.

Pistols loaded with subsonic ammunition sound more like an air rifle, or a nail gun, than a firearm. Subsonic nine-millimeter rounds fired through a suppressor make less noise than a pastor's fart in church. Civilians can legally buy subsonic ammunition, but the regulation of sound suppressors is considerably tighter. These particular casings were evidence left by the same team of paramilitary operatives I was now certain were responsible for the later fires.

The operators who attacked this house would have slipped between the two houses behind it before leaning over the fence to shoot whoever was guarding the back gate that night. The security guard would have taken two rounds in his chest and one in his head. The team would have then split up and crashed through the front and back doors simultaneously, shooting their way to the center of the house and killing everyone in their path before they could react to the intrusion. A team of trained shooters would have secured the house in under ten seconds. I wondered how much time passed between the gunfire and the house fire. The team would have tossed the gate guard's body into the stack along with everyone else they killed before mutilating the bodies and torching the place. Jasmine's account of the fire at Richie's house placed two distinct teams at that scene, one team shooting and another setting fire behind them. I was at a loss for why the arsonists used different methods to erase evidence at this location and the fires that caught Fire Marshal Wheeler's attention.

It might have been because these murders were open cases for Chief Avery's homicide detectives. The attempt to sell the murders as a gang war must have failed, even though the autopsies would have concluded homicide was the cause of the occupants' deaths.

I doubt NOPD's coroner noticed the few anomalies in the deaths. Any bullets in the burnt bodies melted beyond recognition. Entry wounds from subsonic rounds tend to be less ragged or deep because there is substantially less force behind the projectile, but only a handful of military coroners see many of that sort of wound. Fatal bullet wounds provided an obvious cause of death, and that was the extent of what the coroner needed to determine. It was up to NOPD's homicide detectives to learn the identity of the victims' killer or killers, and the autopsies were not going to suggest they look for trained assassins with military backgrounds rather than amateur shooters from violent gangs.

NOPD's continued interest in this case could eventually have led a smart detective to connect the later deaths and fires to this one. Now I understood why Kinkaid brought me into the situation to intercept any such interest by NOPD, but the number of shootings was becoming hard to ignore.

The fire investigators called the second house fire a "probable electrical short" related to the quality of the wiring done during post-K rebuilding. This was becoming a leading cause of fires in the city. Out-of-town electricians rewired most of the homes rebuilt after Katrina. The electricians certified the quality of their own work because the city laid off most of its building inspectors when it ran out of money. I sensed that choosing this cause allowed the owner to collect an insurance settlement on their loss. The absence of bodies at this fire indicated the first change in the perpetrators' plan. They must have hauled the bodies away rather than risk another homicide investigation. The burden of packing bodies and finding a place to dump them may have been what led to the introduction of thermite and burial of the crime scenes to the later assaults.

The fire-damaged structure that once stood there was gone as well. As with the first scene, nobody covered this scene with fresh dirt. The brick piers of the home's foundation marked where the house once stood and the ragged ends of pipes marked where the sewer and water lines still ran. Roux and I picked our way through the pieces of wood spiked with rusted nails and the shards of broken glass left from the home's demolition to find the bathroom.

I picked up a piece of lead pipe that carried water to the kitchen. I wiped one end of the pipe on my pant leg to get it clean of dirt and soot and then wiggled the pipe as deep into the larger sewer pipe as I could. I was not in the least bit surprised to find caked material in a shade of dark red on the end of the pipe when I brought it back to the surface. Rust is a lot lighter than dried blood, and this was a very dark crimson. It was curious that murdering members of the El Caminos and burning the house down around them failed to spark a response from the cartel. The El Caminos lack patience, so their inaction told me they knew the Pistol Peetes lacked either the intent or the cajones to start a war.

The refinements in the second fire were likely not a reaction to the cartel's failure to respond, but rather to the growing interest of NOPD detectives. Any subsequent fires needed to look like the work of an unrelated serial arsonist. That was what brought Wheeler into play, and my involvement was an entirely unforeseen consequence. Forcing me to play a central role in covering up Kinkaid's conspiracy was the easiest way to shut me up about it.

I was beginning to sense the presence of an unexpected and unseen intermediary keeping the peace. This phantom did more to disrupt Kinkaid's secret operation than I might accomplish by exposing it. I realized I was no longer trying to stop a war between the El Caminos and the Pistol Peetes. I was being pulled into a fight between enemies so strong that the Devil himself was placing bets.

Chapter 33

C hef Tony and I were standing at the bar discussing my day's findings and extrapolating scenarios to explain them when Katie and Avery returned to the bistro about six o'clock that evening. I extended a hand holding my girlfriend's now customary glass of champagne when she met me at the end of the bar. Jason spotted the pair coming through the door and set Avery's favorite beer in front of the portly chief detective before the man even thought to ask for one. The chef made a polite excuse to return to the kitchen, leaving me to offer the best explanation that Tony and I had managed to think up to my boss.

"Who did you tangle with this afternoon?" Avery asked before I even mentioned anything about my day's activities. There was no anger or frustration in his voice. He sounded amused if anything.

"Nobody. What's up?"

"Deputy Director Kinkaid called this afternoon to confirm that you are still suspended. He didn't offer me any reason for having asked." Avery still wanted an explanation.

"Nice to know he's thinking of me," I chuckled.

"Kinkaid wasn't pleased when I reminded him that I stopped being your keeper when you went on suspension." Katie had her back to us but I could tell she was giving our conversation her full attention.

"Did he have anything else to say?" Kinkaid would not have given Avery the last word in such a conversation.

"Just that he was going to have to find something else for you to worry about."

Avery and I looked at one another as though one of us held the punchline to a half-told joke. It was an odd, and troubling, comment for a man in Kinkaid's position to have made. Katie now turned to face us.

"So, what *did* you do today?" Katie always sounds like she is cross-examining someone, even in a casual or polite conversation.

"I stopped by two addresses that are likely part of that string of fires I started investigating with Wheeler."

"Bingo." Avery now understood Kinkaid's phone call.

"Both of the fires occurred back in September. That was months before the state fire marshal took any notice. Someone demolished the houses, but they were not nearly as thorough as they were with the later ones. Nobody bothered to carry off every board and nail, or to spread two feet of new dirt over the crime scenes. The first one may still be one of your open cases."

"How so?" Kinkaid's call made Avery anxious about my inability to conceal my continued pursuit of answers. He was already on his second beer by the time we got this far.

I gave him the address of the first fire and he flinched a bit. The fire was indeed still an open case on his homicide detectives' wall. They had no leads, suspects or witnesses, and the case file was already boxed and ready for cold case limbo with Avery's blessing. I asked Avery to fill me in on what the homicide detectives found. He did not want to be guilty of discussing an open case with a suspended officer, but there was very little to share.

The autopsies showed all five men suffered gunshots to the chest and decapitation. This alone was baffling to the homicide detectives. They had never encountered a crime scene involving such deliberate mutilation of multiple corpses. They were more accustomed to assailants emptying a magazine's worth of ammunition into a body. Avery's detectives found no firearms or narcotics in the rubble, not even any shell casings from the killings. The blood trails indicated that the victims died elsewhere in the house before their killers dragged them to the bathroom. Someone with a strong stomach decapitated all five men in the claw foot tub. Whoever staged the fire tried to make it look like a grease fire on the kitchen stove, but the bodies made the fire inconsequential.

I reached into my pants pocket for the baggie containing the three shell casings I found at the scene and set them on the bar in front of Avery. He opened the bag and studied one of the shells, then looked at me in an admission that he was missing what I hoped he would see.

"These are Remington sub-sonic rounds. The shooters probably used MP-5s with suppressors instead of handguns. The neighbors wouldn't have heard much from these rounds, even if they didn't use silencers." I did not need to explain how I knew any of this. The mess we were in was giving Avery a crash course in black ops.

"Then the murders weren't gang related?" Avery needed me to spell this out a bit more. "The Pistol Peetes really aren't involved?"

"The cartel was targeted, but definitely not by those amateurs."

"Why target only the El Caminos?" Katie could no longer ignore our conversation.

"That's the sixty-four-thousand-dollar question." I took a sip of bourbon and then tried to walk them through the scenario Tony and I believed gave the best explanation for what we knew. "I think Kinkaid hired a private contractor called D-Tech to run the El Caminos out of New Orleans. He hired a succession of former black-ops operators to use their old bags of tricks on an entirely new situation. They meant the first attacks to shut down the El Caminos' stash houses and implicate the Pistol Peetes for double-crossing their heroin supplier. The El Caminos didn't take the bait and the attack certainly didn't scare a cartel used to seeing far worse carnage. The attacks that caught Wheeler's attention may be the work of a new team. These assaults were more vicious, and the end game seems to be to force the cartel to defend itself. These latest attacks still involve multiple executions, but whoever carried them out covered their tracks a lot better. Any evidence wound up at an incinerator within hours of the attacks and they buried the crime scenes under two feet of fresh dirt to hide any evidence their clean-up team missed. This smacks of being a D-Tech operation. They have done this sort of work elsewhere." I could have been more specific about where, but Katie seemed rattled enough for one day. "I think now they're just trying to drive the cartel out of town and have given up on selling their being a gang war as either a distraction or a cover for the operation."

"You're positive that there are no gangs behind any of the attacks?" Katie sounded a lot more surprised than I expected after the hours she had spent with me in my office. Jimmy Washington's murder was the closest thing I had seen to revenge, but the El Caminos convinced me they had nothing to do with killing him.

"I think the cartel knows who is responsible and is just biding its time before retaliating." I could not say much more around

Katie.

"Against who?" Avery wanted me to finish my thought.

"Whoever they believe is responsible. If it isn't a rival gang then they'll likely blame law enforcement, either local or Federal. That's who comes after them in Mexico, so they may believe that's who's coming after them here." It was a terrible prospect to throw onto Avery's crowded plate.

"You think they'll attack NOPD or the Feds?" Avery's hands shook as he set his beer on the bar top.

"Unless they can find any better target. The parades always stretch NOPD to its breaking point. The State Police and Feds will send additional officers and agents to help out, so the city will be a target-rich environment with ample opportunities for killing cops when they strike. They like car bombs and mass shootings. We've never seen either of those styles of killings at Mardi Gras, and I seriously doubt you're prepared for them."

"Do you think Kinkaid sees that his operation might cause that?"

"Like I told you yesterday, that would be better than Christmas for DHS if it did happen. They would label the attacks as terrorism and then begin to militarize every metropolitan police force in the country. The DEA and FBI could ramp up their counter-cartel operations, and the ATF will go crazy on gun control. Meanwhile, New Orleans will lose millions of tourist dollars."

"I don't think that's what Kinkaid's trying to do here. Do you?" Katie challenged my gloom and doom scenario, but then hid her face behind her champagne flute.

"I know for a fact that he isn't trying to keep it from happening. It's likely that someone higher than the Deputy Director decided to pick a fight with the El Caminos in New Orleans during Carnival and put him in charge of containing things. I just can't figure out why here or why now."

"You don't have to. You're suspended, right?" I realized she might actually be pleading with me. We both knew I was going to keep pushing forward.

Chapter 34

The Chinese are famous for their proverbs, but their curses can be equally apropos. My favorites are the phrases that serve both purposes: "May you live in interesting times," "May you come to the attention of powerful men," and "May you get all that you deserve." It took less than a day for Deputy Director Kinkaid to make good on the first two. I needed to avoid the third at all costs.

Taking Roux for a long walk through the Quarter after Katie goes to work replaced my usual three mile-run every morning. He needed the exercise as much as I did. Katie and Avery left the bistro at their usual time after breakfast and I was more than a little surprised to receive an email from her barely five minutes later. The email heading read "We're Okay", which is never a good sign. She wrote a short note about how two separate hit and run drivers struck Avery's SUV as his driver entered Canal Street. The photos she sent with the email showed the first vehicle struck them across the left front fender and then the delivery truck clipped their right rear panel and spun them onto the streetcar tracks in the neutral ground. It was likely that the driver of the truck bearing a company logo left the scene of the accident because he stole the truck that was reported missing over the police band just moments after the accident.

I received a text message with a photo attachment from my mother barely three hours later as I was sitting down to an early lunch with Chef Tony. My mother sent the message to thank me for an orchid floral arrangement she believed I sent her. The flower delivery disturbed me for two reasons. First, I had not sent my mother flowers of any description in at least six months. The second, and by far more troubling reason, was that orchids are her favorite flower but almost nobody outside of our family knows this. Roger or my sister would have taken the credit for having sent the flowers if they sent them.

"I do not know what you were thinking, but the orchids are beautiful," my mother gushed uncharacteristically when I called her. "There are so many. This must have cost you a lot of money. What's the occasion?"

"Happy Mardi Gras." This was the only upcoming occasion that came to mind.

"Well, thank you."

"Is Roger around? I have a quick question for him." I listened as she either crossed a room or walked down the hall to hand the phone to Roger Kline and told him I asked to speak with him.

"Nice flowers," he said with a touch of mirth. "How guilty are you and what did you do?"

"I didn't send the flowers, Roger."

"Then who did? The card says they came from you."

"Is the flower shop's name on the card by any chance?"

It was difficult to not sound concerned about strangers delivering flowers to my mother's isolated home.

"Nope. A gray van pulled in and a delivery person about your age dropped them off an hour ago. I didn't even have to sign for them. I thought that was a little strange." Roger gave me a better description of the deliveryman and the van, but neither description made me feel any better. The plates on the van were not commercial ones. The delivery person was about six-foot tall, very lean with what Roger described as a military-style haircut. He also wore sunglasses that he never removed. The man's uniform was gray trousers and a uniform-style shirt with a nametag bearing no company logo of any sort. Roger could not remember the name on the tag. It was unlikely to have been the deliveryman's name, anyway.

The next message I received about the flowers was an email with a large video attachment. The time stamp on the email showed there were barely three minutes between my mother's call and when someone sent the email. The jokers sent their warning in the fashion of a confirmation email from a company called Safe-and-Sound Florists. I did not bother searching for their website or business profile. The name and their opening message made the point of the email clear enough before I even scanned the attachment for viruses and spyware. The message's heading was the first words out of my mother's mouth when I called her; I Do Not Know What You Were Thinking.

The attachment was a series of high definition video clips of my mother and Roger going about their daily lives in a house that was nearly an hour away, and isolated except for a few vacation homes that were unoccupied most of the time. They made at least half of the videos by activating the camera and microphone on my mother's personal computers. They filmed the remaining ones through a high-powered riflescope, which overlaid unmistakable crosshairs on the subjects. The message lacked any subtlety.

The El Caminos do not use cyber-terrorism as a weapon and the Pistol Peetes were unworthy suspects to have carried out the flower delivery or the emailed video. Someone using the very lowest end of D-Tech's capabilities sent this direct warning. It was time for me to find a safer place for everyone I cared about and to switch phones again.

The only other person I was worried about, besides Tony, was my sister. I immediately began dialing her office phone number on my cell phone. Tulip called me as I was dialing her number.

"What are you doing right now?" my sister demanded. It was an unusually brusque way for her to start a telephone conversation.

"I was about to call my sister. Apparently, the body snatchers got to her first. What's got you upset?" It was not like Tulip to let anything that was bothering her show through her practiced toughness.

"Have you ever heard of Operation Stoplight?"

I spent half of the past decade afraid of the day she did.

"No. Why do you ask?" I lied. I wished she had not mentioned it on the phone, but could not say so without revealing I knew details of the operation.

"I received an email this morning containing a PDF file on what the sender claims was an unauthorized intelligence operation in Iraq."

"Did this come to your lawyer email or to that war criminal thing you keep working on?" Being dismissive of a decade's worth of my sister's work was not my brightest move just then.

"The offer was made to one of the Tribunal's researchers late last night. He says he only responded that he was interested in learning more about the operation and that he did not give anyone my private email address." I wanted to reach through the phone and strangle everyone in her circle of well-meaning associates. Tulip was part of a group of attorneys and reporters calling themselves The Taxpayers' War Crimes Tribunal. The Tribunal's amateur researchers comb through the internet's ramblings, declassified reports of shady provenance, photo-shopped images, and dark-web rumors for anything that might substantiate their convictions that intelligence operatives like myself committed criminal acts waging the War on Terror. Tulip was sure I was one of the few with clean hands and pure hearts and I did everything in my power to let her believe this.

"I'd say your guy actually did ask them to send the file and they sent it to you personally as a way to show how much they already know about your group." Tulip fell silent, but I knew she was still on the line. "You've probably managed to download a highly classified document to your computer and now realize you've broken serious Federal laws. Your researcher is in trouble just for soliciting the classified file, and now you are in trouble for receiving it. Is that about right?"

"Can we meet?" I knew my assessment was right without her own legal opinion, but she put up a fight. "We've received classified documents before."

"Which you received through Freedom of Information requests and were rendered useless with redactions. Was this file redacted?" I seriously hoped the document in her inbox was full of blacked-out material. I was far more concerned that she would read the classified report than I was that she had it in the first place.

"I'll meet you at that coffee place you hate," Tulip said and hung up. I abandoned a plate of freshly made shrimp etouffee to race Uptown.

The coffee shop in question is in a remodeled Queen Anne-style home near Audubon Park. I believe the owner tries too hard to be trendy. The places serves even plain black coffee in an awkward shaped cup and gives it a cute name. Tulip was sitting at a small table out of the traffic pattern. She wore one of her crisp pinstriped suits and looked as though she came straight from court.

I stepped behind her and saw the downloaded PDF file on her open laptop computer screen.

"How much of this have you read?" I motioned to the eager-faced server headed my direction to turn around and wait on someone else.

"I didn't go past this page. I stopped when I saw the cover page with the words Secret and Sensitive Compartmentalized Information. What's that?"

"Never mind about that. Delete the file and over-write your hard drive. You can't wipe the email off the server but you can make sure you aren't caught with the file and you need to be sure you genuinely have no idea what's in it when the men in suits start to water board you." I realized that I was nearly screaming at my sister. The manager was debating whether to approach us.

"You're overreacting," she scoffed. The look I gave Tulip made her flinch.

"I'm overreacting to your rolling yourself up in the barbed wire of the Espionage Act? You will not be near as pretty when you get out of prison as you are right now. Downloading that file may have dropped everyone in your little group into a dark hole for the next twenty years."

"How do you know? You haven't read the file, either." Tulip asked.

"That level of secret classification is way beyond anything you've ever dealt with. You would get a ream of black paper if you received this with a Freedom of Information Act request. Whoever offered your researcher this file intended to poison the Tribunal. Did either of you forward it to anyone else in your knitting circle?"

"No." Tulip remained defiant but her response sounded honest. "What should I do? Really, I don't want just your big brother advice."

"Delete the file, shred the trash folder, and clean your hard drive." I watched as she did what I demanded. She did not argue with my instructions because she immediately grasped that the situation must be extremely serious if I was this tense and adamant. "Now you should prepare your story for when the FBI comes for that computer."

The person who sent the report on that particular interdiction program in Iraq to Tulip's personal email did so for a reason. My sister faced certain investigation simply for receiving the email. She faced charges if they found any evidence that she solicited the file. They might try to implicate me as the person who gave it to her because my name would appear in it, prominently so. Printing just one page of the document was enough to send her to a maximum-security Federal prison. Explaining my adamancy about distancing herself from the file to Tulip would require admitting familiarity with the operation. I managed to get my sister to see the larger picture by telling her that the offer of the file came from the same person who sent orchids to our mother and orchestrated Chief Avery and Katie's hit-and-run collision to scare me off a case I refused to drop despite being suspended.

I returned to the bistro in time to sign the form a very apologetic inspector from the health department handed me as I walked through the door. She said her department received a complaint from one of our guests about cockroach odor in the bathrooms. The inspector and I were both curious to know what scent a cockroach gives off. The city ordinance required her to do a full inspection, but she found only a couple of minor food handling issues that Chef Tony immediately corrected. The health inspector repeated her statement to the Tony that she believed he made a point of operating a clean and healthy foodservice operation. It did nothing to wipe the scowl from his face. Tony takes any questioning of our code compliance as a personal affront to his honor and answering to a contrived complaint was especially offensive to him.

"Trust me, partner. This had nothing to do with you or the restaurant. It's just another reminder that I have things to lose if I don't stop putting my nose in whatever Kinkaid's got going. Let's have a beer and I'll tell you about my day." I wanted Tony to understand that the health department's visit was only one small part of a series of things thrown at me in the course of a day that was barely half over.

We rode the elevator to the third floor in awkward silence. He could tell that I was upset about more than the health inspector's visit. I could tell that he was upset that someone questioned his dedication to running a clean restaurant in a part of town that made doing so difficult.

"What's going on?" Tony asked as soon as I closed my apartment door behind us. We sat down in the living room, him in a chair and me on the sofa with Roux.

I had surrendered to the inevitable and thrown a cheap blanket on the leather sofa for Roux to lie on. He stopped sleeping on the wood floor once he learned how soft the sofa was. I would have done the same in his place.

"Katie and Chief Avery were involved in a minor collision on their way to work this morning. They're okay. My mother called barely two hours later to thank me for orchids I never sent. Then I received a video right after she called to let me know that she and Roger are under constant surveillance. Then Tulip called for advice after someone emailed her a copy of the final report on Operation Stoplight."

"You're sure it was Operation Stoplight?" Tony hoped I was mistaken as much as I had when I heard the name.

"I saw the report cover. Tulip claims she did not open the file after she saw the level of classification. We both know my sister wouldn't have been nearly so calm had she read the un-redacted version of that report."

"Someone's really trying to brush you off the case, am I right?" English had been Tony's first language for barely five years. He learned a lot of slang from our kitchen and service staff in that short amount of time.

"Someone is making a point of letting me know that they can make bad things happen to people I care about. They've killed I don't know how many of the El Caminos and burned a half dozen houses to the ground. They want me to know they are prepared to murder my mother and my girlfriend, and to throw my sister in prison just to make me stand down while they slaughter the rest of the El Caminos."

"What's the plan then? Your mother can move into my place," Tony offered. It was a temporary solution, but a practical one worth considering.

"Oh, so you'll have an excuse to stay with my sister?"

"I'd need somewhere to stay. I can maybe keep her safe." Tony grinned and even made a feeble shrug. I just shook my head.

"No, I think we need to get very serious. I'll get Joaquin to line up some Super Bowl tickets. We'll close the restaurant for Carnival so you can take Tulip, Katie, my mother, and Roger to Miami for the Super Bowl. It's the only reason any of them would agree to leave town at Mardi Gras."

"No." Tony said and stood up to pace. "We were partners before we came here, right? We must handle these men together, like always before."

"I'd still need someone to protect my family. Getting them out of town is not going to be enough."

"Send your fat cop friend with them. He's too big of a target to help us in a gunfight, anyway."

Tony's argument made sense. Chief Avery's hands were tied by the very people who were allowing, maybe even encouraging, others to try to intimidate me by threatening my family. Avery could lose his job if he chose to help me and defy Kinkaid. The Chief was woefully physically unprepared for the fight he would be facing if he chose to stand at our side, but I could trust him to protect my family and that was proving to be true of few people around me.

"Okay, so we send the Chief and his wife to Florida with Tulip, Katie, my mother, and Roger. That will only give us a few days to settle this before they come home. I have no idea who we're fighting or where they are. I do know that D-Tech, or whoever Kinkaid hired, is on the other side this time, not ours."

"Good. I never liked those guys anyway."

We went back downstairs and the cooks were relieved to see the chef in a much better mood than when he left the kitchen. I went into the dining room and talked to Marie about the evening's handful of reservations while I waited for Joaquin to finish his pre-shift meeting with the service staff. He brings the servers and cooks together at the start of each shift to pass around plates of the dinner-service food specials and to name a couple of wine selections to push so we can rotate our inventory.

I motioned for the grinning Cuban to join me on the patio once the staff scattered to inspect their stations and practice their sales pitches on the specials.

"Can you get your hands on any Super Bowl tickets?" Joaquin came to New Orleans from Miami and I hoped he might still have some connections to call upon for a favor this large.

"How many?" This was all he needed to know. He did not want to know why I needed tickets on short notice and I knew there would be no price negotiations if he found them.

"I think six will be enough. I'll need hotel rooms, too. Please don't use the house phone to make your calls." I assumed the line was tapped.

"This could get expensive," Joaquin warned me, but he was already dialing a number into his own cell phone.

"Price isn't a problem."

"It never is until you have to pay it," Joaquin said and laughed.

The price Joaquin quoted me later that evening sounded like the GDP of a small nation, but the plan was falling apart by then, anyway. Tulip and Katie flatly refused to leave. Tulip turned my own argument against me and said it would look like she was fleeing prosecution if she left town after having illegally received classified documents. Katie used the argument that she had court cases pending. My mother and Roger hate football. She felt deeply perturbed about the latest inconvenience my job brought to her life, but she agreed to move into her family's ancestral home on Audubon Place and to let me pay for a private security detail. Avery and Katie returned to the bistro with a pair of bodyguards the Chief of Police assigned them after Avery conceded that the hit and run incident may have targeted either NOPD's Chief of Detectives or an Assistant State's Attorney. Katie offered no argument about moving into my apartment. My sister moved in with Tony rather than join our mother and Roger on Audubon Place. I put up only token resistance to this idea, as I would not have accepted my Mother's invitation either.

The chef and Joaquin decided to begin closing the restaurant until dinner service. Eliminating lunch would allow Tony to help me with my investigation. It would also keep the place busy and less of a target at night than it would be if it were empty except for our apartments.

Chapter 35

The previous day's incidents were meant to illustrate the range of potential serious consequences for persisting with my investigation. I felt morally obliged to respond to that message. The first part of my response involved disrupting the surveillance teams to establish that my team held the home field advantage in any game of cat-and-mouse.

This was when establishing a precise pattern to my routine would pay off. I walked Roux at the exact same time every day and followed a set loop through the Quarter until I identified every operative following me. I used my network of informants to watch them in turn and learned when and where they made their transitions in coverage. This gradually lulled them into a pattern of their own, whether they saw it or not.

The first break in my routine came when I opened the bistro's front door and herded Tony, Tulip, and Katie through the door ahead of me an hour before I usually took Roux for his walk. They headed in different directions while I locked the door.

Tony set off at a brisk pace towards the French Market. His route would circle the Old Mint Building. He would help me with my first disruption before moving on to his second assignment. The multiple unexpected departures sent too many people in different directions for the person in charge of keeping me under surveillance to process. I wanted to see if they could be distracted from their primary mission, but I trusted the team's default plan to kick in because that plan should ignore everyone but me.

I walked Katie to the corner of Decatur and Esplanade, kissed her on the cheek for luck, and turned towards the river. Katie crossed Esplanade to wait inside the corner bar named Checkpoint Charlie's until Tony and I finished our first takedown. Tulip was supposed to walk around the block and then meet Katie inside the bar before they both returned to the bistro and locked themselves inside.

I made a quick glance to confirm a silver Volkswagen Jetta was in its usual space a block away, at the corner of Esplanade and Elysian Fields. The surveillance team should have used a greater variety of cars.

I had assigned each member of the surveillance team names based on their cover stories. A woman I called Joan was responsible for alerting the crew to the start of each day's walk and for tracking my progress until I stepped through the floodwall at the far end of the French Market. The driver in the VW was Jetta. The couple in the BMW facing the opposite direction two blocks away were The Lovers. Jetta always pretended to be asleep when I passed his position, but was clumsy about keeping one eye open to watch me. Jetta's concentration on me left him unaware that Tony crossed the street in front of him before doubling back in his blind spot. Tony smashed the driver's side window and shoved a 1911 Colt .45 hard against Jetta's left temple. Tony had taken the pistol from a street punk four months ago and it would not trace back to either of us if he pulled the trigger.

I ordered Jetta to get out of his car on the passenger side and hastily patted him down. I snatched his radio and earpiece. He wore a Beretta pistol in a shoulder holster but carried no ID. I pocketed his cell phone and pulled two large plastic zip-ties from my hoodie to secure his hands to the tall iron fence circling the museum. I continued on my way while Tony dropped a lit fireworks sparkler into the car's gas tank. The gasoline immediately burst into flames and engulfed the entire car within seconds. The fire station less than a block away arrived on the scene in under two minutes. We left the still-armed driver in a very awkward predicament to explain. I was counting on The Twins to notify the watch supervisor of the situation and for this to baffle the team about their next move in the game I was suddenly winning. My name for the surveillance supervisor was Den Mother despite having no knowledge of their actual gender. All the same, she and her cubs were about to have a very bad start to their day.

Tony sprinted down Frenchman Street while The Lovers

worried about Jetta. Tony needed to circle the pair of operatives without them spotting him as he double-backed into the Quarter to rendezvous with me on Royal Street.

My normal routine led me through the French Market as it began stirring to life. Trucks loaded with fresh produce were leaving to make deliveries while vendors in the market opened their re-stocked stalls with fresh fruit and vegetables. I always greeted the ones I knew. It was important that they were aware of the last time they saw me each day, just in case I ever disappeared.

Joan was enjoying her usual cup of coffee beneath the gilded statue of Joan of Arc in a small courtyard at the end of St. Peter Street. I did as she expected me to, and walked through the gap in the floodwall across the street from her to follow the tracks for the riverfront trolley towards the Moonwalk across from Jackson Square. She would have picked up the pursuit if my path ever changed. I called the next link in their chain Top Gun, because he was the best of the bunch at what he did. His surveillance began when Roux and I reached the trolley tracks.

Top Gun thought he was blending into the homeless veterans camped around the Moonwalk's concrete steps that lead from the tracks to an observation platform overlooking the river and Jackson Square. In fact, those men were the ones who tipped me off to the surveillance in the first place. Top Gun would leave his position as soon as I approached the riverside steps. He would turn his reversible jacket inside out and don a ball cap to change his appearance before I might notice him again on Royal Street.

The fourth link in their chain was Beignet. He would watch me leave the observation deck to buy one order of beignets and a tall café au lait at Café du Monde before crossing the street. This was why we called him Beignet. He would watch me eat the hot pastries as I walked beneath the porches of the Pontalba Apartments towards Saint Louis Cathedral. His last task was to alert Top Gun to which side of the Cathedral I walked past on my way to Royal Street.

I did not stop for my usual beignets, but I did walk away with a large cup of coffee one of the Vietnamese waiters microwaved for me. My not buying donuts did not alarm the man watching me as much as it should have. He probably did not notice I was wearing Jetta's earbud, either. Den Mother was unaware that I could listen to her cubs chattering about my walk through the Quarter. She had a nice voice, which meant Jill Bledsoe was not Den Mother.

My normal route was between Saint Louis Cathedral and the Presbytere Museum. This took me past the quaint garden behind the church and put me directly across the street from Rodrique's Gallery on Royal Street. I altered my course this morning to pass along the opposite side of the church. Den Mother now had to make a big decision because of my very small one.

Den Mother ordered Beignet to follow his normal routine and sprint down Chartres Street and position himself on Barracks Street with the last members of the team. They would wait there to confirm I turned right from Royal Street and headed home. Den Mother kept a bullpen of operatives there to chase me down if I chose to go anywhere but home at the end of my dog walk.

I changed this part of my morning's path to make Den Mother decide whether I was changing the entire route. Top Gun was due to step out of his usual doorway and follow me down Royal Street. Tony and I were about to throw him a wrinkle. Tony was still catching his breath as I approached the doorway he was standing in opposite of the Cathedral. We swapped hoodies and I handed him Roux's leash before I sprinted back the way I had just come. Tony counted to ten and then proceeded towards Royal Street. Those precious seconds allowed me to get around the church and follow my usual path.

I was relieved to see that our plan was working almost perfectly. Top Gun was a skilled operative but he still saw what Den Mother told him to expect to see. Today that was a man walking a pit bull coming from behind the far side of the well-lit Cathedral. This was farther from him than normal and Top Gun waited until Tony was already walking away from him before he stepped out of his hiding spot in a shop doorway. He failed to notice the hooded figure who slipped around the corner a dozen yards behind him.

Tony made the final change to my practiced routine. He started walking down Orleans towards Bourbon Street instead of heading down Royal Street to Barracks Street. Top Gun made his first mistake by waiting to report this change until he was sure it was not a feint. I let the operative commit to following Tony before I closed the distance between us. Top Gun walked along the opposite side of the street from his target. It lacked shop windows that could have tipped him off to my presence. Tony gave him a moment to become fixated on himself before he abruptly reversed course.

Top Gun hastily followed suit. He should have walked slower and given Tony a longer than normal lead as my body double fell back into the routine our marks expected. He would have done that if I did not throw a pint of nearly scalding hot coffee in his face the instant he turned around. The operative fell like a stone and screamed like a small child. Tony and Roux sprinted to where I now towered over the stricken man. Anyone looking out their window would see two passerby trying to help the poor man to his feet.

I kicked Top Gun in the diaphragm with the rubber sole of the walking shoe I was wearing for good measure and went to work patting him down as we picked him up off the slate walkway. I handed Tony the operative's radio before I pocketed his cell phone and a small-caliber Walther pistol.

Tony and I each held the operative by one arm and dragged him between two buildings in the middle of the block. The pseudo-voodoo store kept a trash dumpster on a concrete pad that did double duty as a patio for the apartments upstairs. A brick wall blocked the building from behind and long windowless walls on the adjacent buildings formed the boundaries of the courtyard where we had hauled the discombobulated operative. I knew the tenant above the shop would not be home for a couple of hours.

I finally took a good look at the shadow who had been following me. Top Gun was nearly perfect for surveillance work. He was slightly less than a full head shorter than my six feet. He was lean, but of proportionate weight. There was nothing remarkable about his facial features or his haircut. His barber left just enough length to hide his earbud. I would not have remembered his face in six months' time if I did not already know who he was.

I held him in place while Tony bound his wrists to a wooden railing with the same plastic bindings I used on Jetta. I then cinched zip-ties snug just above his elbows. The wrist bindings would hold him in place while Tony used the larger ones to encourage his cooperation. He could already feel a slight constriction in the blood flow to his lower arms and hands.

I pulled a chair in front of our prisoner and sat down. "What in the hell are you doing here, Paul?"

"Long time no see. That was quite a nice move out there." Paul Lancaster was doing private security work at the American embassy in Kabul the last time we spoke.

"Sorry, I forgot to pack my water board. You know how this goes. Tony will tighten the zip-ties anytime you refuse to answer a question. It will take EMS five minutes to find you, *after* they're called, so be sure to keep that in mind when you refuse to answer."

"Let's just do this," Paul sighed.

"Who hired you?" Tony put a hand on each of the plastic bindings. I counted to five and nodded to Tony to notch the ties half an inch tighter. There was very little slack in this pair of plastic bands and I had lots of questions to ask.

"We'll come back to that one. Here's an easy one. Does the shadow of the statue behind the Cathedral remind you of a referee signaling a touchdown? It does me." I watched the confusion wash over his well-tanned face. If this was a trick question, it was diabolical.

"Yeah, sort of."

"So, you *can* answer questions." I mocked him.

"Screw you." He hissed.

"Where are you guys working out of?"

"Next question."

"That was another easy one. Your loss." Tony closed the bindings a fraction of an inch and we watched him instinctively flex his fingers. "Let's go back to who hired you."

"Go to hell." I reached out and cinched the zip-ties half an inch. The sound of the zip-tie tightening had the desired psychological effect. "Damn it! You know I'm not going to tell you anyone's name."

"Then just tell us why you were following me."

"Our team was assigned to watch you in the Quarter." He sounded like he hoped this response might stop me from hurting him again.

"So your part in all of this didn't involve any of the killings or fires at the El Caminos stash houses?" I only asked this to see his reaction to the question.

Even an amateur would know not to admit to being involved in any sort of felonious activities. The point I wanted to remind him of was that being part of the overall operation implicated him in its worst elements.

"I told you, my job was just to watch you." Paul's voice grew strained as the numbing pain in his hands increased.

I reached for the bindings. "Tell me something I can use about the guy who hired you."

"Come on, you and I became government surplus the minute we hung up our uniforms. Now we are both lucky to have jobs that let us go on carrying a gun. Stop for a minute and think of who you know with the right connections to hire men for a domestic intelligence operation like this. He recruited each of us individually. He didn't just put out a want ad." Paul's description of the man who hired him was vague, but I had a sinking feeling that I knew exactly who he meant.

"But it's D-Tech is who paid you to follow me around." I was hoping I could trick him into confirming their role by acting as though it were common knowledge.

"They're even using your playbook from Iraq. Think of it as getting the band back together. You could be on the winning side this time when they are done," Paul said and tried not to whimper as his hands began growing a very dark shade of red. Purple was next, followed by blue, and then the very real risk amputation.

Paul may not have realized he had done more than confirm that D-Tech was the private contractor Kinkaid hired to do this dirty work for Homeland Security. I had what I needed to know to reverse engineer my own plan to cost D-Tech yet another lucrative contract.

"You were recruited? Someone finally hired some out-of-work veterans. Well, it's about time."

"Screw you. I was a Seal." His earning the right to wear that trident would have impressed any other audience. He certainly deserved a better job than the one that came after blowing this assignment.

"And I was Delta. That was a long time ago for both of us." We were not here to enjoy old-home week and swap war stories. "So, what else is D-Tech doing besides having you walk behind me?"

"No comment." I was too close to the answers he refused to give me to leave without trying my best to get them.

"That makes sense, though, right? D-Tech lost their contract in Iraq so they shopped around a combination of the best operators they could hire and a proven technology they designed to fight terrorists until Homeland Security took the bait and slapped a national security tag on whatever it is Kinkaid has cooked up to do here. That keeps it under the radar so the civil liberties-types don't get wind. Any of this sound familiar?" I wanted to see Paul's reaction to see how much of this he knew from the inside, and to be sure he repeated it word-for-word to Jill Bledsoe in his debriefing. He gave me much less reaction than I knew would come from D-Tech when they realized I had pieced together exactly how they were spending my hard-earned tax dollars. We were out of time, but it was hard to tell if what I needed him to confirm was on the tip of his tongue or locked in his increasingly numb fingertips.

"Why do they have you following him?" Tony interrupted.

"I was told to take pictures of anyone you meet." Paul knew how to keep his responses vague and knew how to drag out giving me any answers. Time was still on his side.

"Why do that?" Tony seemed to have hit on a subject Paul was prepared to discuss. Our friend was aware of Tony's other interrogation techniques, but he may have just been looking for a way to keep any circulation in his hands.

"They think you're going to go public about Operation Stoplight. Does that name sound familiar?" Paul was taunting me, but I seriously doubted that he knew he was part of its new incarnation.

"It does, but you can rest assured I'm the last guy to want that story out in the open." I was tired of being haunted by my past. I had not thought of the particulars of the mission that nearly cost me my life in years, but it was beginning to seem like it was following me like a curse.

"We were told you were responsible for D-Tech losing a lucrative contract for an intelligence operation by that name in Iraq. They say you nearly got them kicked out of the country." There was no point in letting him know how much of an understatement "losing a contract" was.

"Last chance to give me a reason to cut you free." The zip-ties were within less than an eighth of an inch of cutting off the remaining blood flow to Paul's arms. His fingertips were beginning to turn purple.

"Just do it," he said and lowered his head.

"No hard feelings, Paul. You ought to consider getting out of town while there is still time," I advised him before I watched Tony tighten the zip-ties. He did so without the slightest hesitation or visible emotion. We warned Paul of the consequences and Tony believed he was just keeping our promise. The operator's forearm and hands, which must have tingled as if he had frostbite, were going numb. It would be merciful if the mercenary passed out from the excruciating pain that would come with the restoration of the blood flow to his hands when the zip-ties were removed.

Paul did not bother screaming for help as we walked away. The tenant upstairs would be home him soon, but not soon enough to save Paul's hands. I surrendered any element of surprise when I used Paul's own phone to call 911 for an ambulance.

It was a foolish act of kindness. Den Mother surely began considering her options when Paul failed to check in and Beignet notified her that I had not yet appeared at the corner of Royal and Barracks Street. I was certain she would make a connection to her missing man and the 911 call from his phone in my voice. We had only a couple of minutes to finish before she pulled everyone else out of the Quarter.

I sent Tony down Royal Street with Roux, to continue playing the role of being me, before I wrapped my hoodie around my waist and pulled Paul's hat low on my forehead. I backtracked to Jackson Square before sprinting down Chartres Street.

I spotted Beignet and Joan at the corner of Chartres and Barracks with what I assumed were The Lovers. I wanted them to mistake me for an early-morning jogger if they glanced in my direction. They kept their full attention focused up Barracks Street, towards Royal. I assumed they were awaiting Den Mother's decision on what to do next.

Tony and I made the decision for her. Tony unsnapped the leash from Roux's collar when he was less than a block from the gathered operatives. Roux took off like a rocket towards the corner as if Tony aimed him at the foursome. Tony picked up his own pace because he no longer needed to maintain the illusion of being me. I ambushed the operatives only a few seconds ahead of Roux. He snarled at the startled operatives as he closed the last few yards between them.

The two men drew their pistols and took aim at Roux, but lacked any rules for engagement with my pit bull. They knew shooting Roux would cause big problems. The others chose to back away and raise their arms into defensive positions. This made it much easier for me to establish control of the situation. The beam from the laser sight on my Glock made it clear that I was not as worried about killing any of them as they were about shooting Roux. I spoke a couple of words in Dutch and Roux sat in the street while Tony helped me zip-tie the foursome to the metal security doors of a house on the corner.

Tony stripped them of the semi-automatic Walther pistols tucked into holsters in the small of their backs. I also tossed their cell phones and two-way radios into the hood of my sweater before we left them for someone else to find.

Chapter 36

I anticipated Chief Avery having a verbal reaction to a group of uncooperative robbery victims found bound with plastic cuffs in the French Quarter at sunrise. His call came about five hours after Tony and I headed home to bed. Katie and Tulip rode to their offices in the company of uniformed officers sent by Avery. It is hard to sit in the back seat of a police car and not feel guilty of something, and our early morning activities provided both women with a good reason to ponder their actions.

"You need to come see this. We're at the landfill by the NASA center on Chef Menteur." Chief Avery did not mention the operatives, but he still sounded unhappy. I noted that he was at the edge of his jurisdiction and spoke in the plural.

It took me nearly twenty minutes to get to his location in my Cadillac wagon, even with the dash-mounted police lights I had no authority to use. I stashed them behind the passenger seat before I pulled in behind Avery's NOPD vehicle, which was in a row of marked and unmarked State Police vehicles and dark sedans with Federal plates.

This landfill closed shortly after the bulk of the material from homes and businesses damaged in Katrina's floodwaters wound up there. Lawsuits and indictments about the management of the dumpsite were on multiple court dockets. Everything about the landfill was a mess, and now someone was adding a new chapter to its troubled story.

Captain Hammond motioned for the uniformed State Police officers at the gate to let me enter the crime scene. He and Avery were standing with two State Police detectives from gang task-force operations. I looked around and realized whatever occurred here was serious enough to catch the attention of FBI and DEA agents from the New Orleans and Baton Rouge offices.

The focus of everyone's attention was a seriously bullet-riddled panel van. The van was a murky dark green with faded lettering from its past life as the work vehicle for a local electrician. It was also a nice match for the van Jasmine claimed Richie Franklin's abductors drove.

"So, what happened here?" I asked the Chief.

"We're trying to sort that out. We have a van full of bullet holes and blood, but no bodies. The van is still registered to a retired electrician who claims he sold the van six months ago, but he can't find the sales paperwork."

"No bodies? How much blood are we talking about?" Most people aren't killed in a shootout. The van's occupants may have limped away.

"A heck of a lot. Most of it's in the back and according to the forensic guys not all of it's new," Hammond informed me. "I only said there were no bodies in the van. We have bodies. We have lots of those."

"That can't be a good thing." I held off sharing what I knew about the van as I followed my two bosses past the gory scene to a series of holes that were being excavated by hand in the rear of the landfill.

There were six spots marked so far. Each hole opened a patch of ground that seemed to have been disturbed fairly recently. The first hole held a number of burned corpses. It was hard to tell how many, but I could see the corpses were headless and someone used thermite or another high-temperature accelerant to cremate the bodies after they were dumped in the hole. It seemed reasonable to believe the five remaining spots would contribute to the body count.

"The patrolmen who found this say a white Humvee left the scene as they approached." Hammond really hates this sort of thing. "Any thoughts?"

"It sounds like there's a good chance this is part of that thing we already don't understand. What's the DEA and FBI have to say?"

"Whatever they're saying they seem to be yelling into their phones." Avery answered my question because Hammond was already walking away from us. My captain has a very hard time dealing with murder and mayhem, and situations that strike him as being off-kilter annoy him the most. He likes to live in a world with black and white situations and yes and no answers. He is ill suited to be in charge of detectives who encounter a lot of grays and maybes trying to solve crimes in Louisiana. "We're hoping you might have some insights. I hear you've been looking for that van while you've been suspended."

"I've been calling that a vacation. Why am I really here?" There was no way Avery called me to this crime scene just to look at a bloody van and offer my opinion about burnt, headless bodies buried in the ground.

"You're being reinstated."

"Why? Did the Deputy Director change his mind?"

Avery's jaw went a bit tight and his wide nostrils flared even wider. "This wasn't his decision. I filled Ken in on your theory that someone wants to ignite a shooting war during Mardi Gras. We can't afford even the possibility of your being right. The election's next Saturday, the Super Bowl that Sunday, and Fat Tuesday's in two weeks. I need you to put a stop to this. I probably won't want to know how you do it, but please don't let the Deputy Director blow up our city."

Avery and I walked down the hill. I followed him to his SUV, where he opened the glovebox and returned my detective shield and sidearm. The badge felt much heavier than I remembered it. It now included the weight of the responsibility Avery and Hammond were placing on me. I dropped the handgun in my satchel and set the badge in place on my belt before I buckled myself into my car.

"I'll give you any help I can, but keep this low key if possible," Avery said through the window of my car. I was barely on the job and going to add to his day's problems.

"I'm glad you said that. I need the metadata off some cell phones."

"How many phones are we talking about?"

"Six. It might be hard to get because they're also encrypted." I reached into my satchel and handed him the cell phones Tony and I harvested that morning. I was keeping the weapons and walkie-talkies.

"It's funny that you have so many phones. Exactly that many were stolen this morning in your neighborhood." Avery looked at me for a long moment, maybe hoping I would share some details. I kept my mouth shut and he moved on to other matters. "Oh, I got a hit on the prints from that card you gave me. You were speaking with a former Army Ranger named William Hawkins. He received a dishonorable discharge for violating rules of engagement in a firefight in Mosul. Apparently, he ordered a tank to blow up a house without making sure it was clear of civilians."

"I'd say he was taking fire from the place and got pinned down." I could not say I would not have done the exact same thing.

"Well, Willie Hawkins is running the Baghdad Brotherhood these days. They sell guns to the gangs out in the East and the gang task force says they are also working with the El Caminos." Avery had no idea how many connections this information made for me. Willie was my new candidate for being the mysterious keeper of the peace between the Pistol Peetes and the El Caminos.

Chapter 37

I was not expecting a lot from Avery's effort with the cell phones. It was unlikely he would discover a list of contacts with real names in even one of those phones. He was also unlikely to discover any stored messages or texts or helpful photographs. All I wanted, and the best I could hope for, was a list of numbers used and the locations of the cellular towers each phone pinged off of most often.

Tony was awake when I returned to my apartment. I found him sitting in my office trying to familiarize himself with the various moving pieces in my investigation. There were multiple players, but at least they all seemed to have teams. Everything that was happening, including the shootings, had something to do with movements by these teams and not by individuals apart from any given team.

"What have you come up with?" It felt good to know that Tony and my bosses were on my team. We were outnumbered, but were still formidable opposition.

"Nothing from your notes. The connections don't really line up." Tony pulled one of the radio handsets from the pile of things taken from Paul and the other operatives. "How much range does this have in the Quarter?"

"Less than a mile. It needs good line of sight to work and all the brick and cast iron would mess with the signal." This is a big problem for police and EMS radios, and theirs are far better than what Tony held in his hand.

"What if they used a repeater tower?"

"There's no way anyone got permission from the Vieux Carre Commission to erect a radio tower anywhere in the Quarter. The VCC wouldn't care what national security excuse Kinkaid tried to use." The Vieux Carre Commission has final approval of alterations or improvements to any structure in the French Quarter, down to the front door knob on a million-dollar condominium. They are like a homeowner's association with OCD.

"So, their transmitter must be within six or seven blocks of the Quarter." Tony had something in mind. "The transmitter is probably close to wherever the men following you stayed."

"I don't think they used an office building or a suite way up in the Marriott or Ritz-Carlton."

It would have been difficult to keep hotel maids from being curious about why they could never clean a room for weeks on end. It was also hard to imagine the operation was able to secure enough hotel rooms because hotels book their rooms for Mardi Gras years in advance. We were looking for a house or converted commercial space at the edge of the Quarter. It made logistical sense to operate out of a space close to the bistro, but that meant running the risk of my stumbling over it on a walk or that I might follow one of their operatives home. It was more likely that the command center was in a quiet commercial area. They could not work out of any of the office towers in the CBD at night without attracting attention from a security guard who would blab about them. There was no place in the Marigny Neighborhood they might hole up un-noticed. That is a tight-knit and mostly residential community where I have some reliable informants. The only other place to consider was along the Rampart Street corridor, forming the lakeside boundary to the Quarter.

Rampart Street itself is a mix of well-established private businesses and storefront nightclubs and cafes that constantly change hands. The street passes Armstrong Park, the First District's new police station, a historic chapel and cemetery, and the former Lafitte Projects. It is an ideal part of town to hide in because everyone living there makes a point of ignoring what is going on there. The surveillance team we effectively dismantled would have been justifiably confident believing they were able to leave and return to their secret lair unnoticed.

I was happy to be back in my XLR coupe, with its COP CAR license plates, as I drove the handful of blocks from our garage to the First District police station. It felt good to know Den Mother's chase cars were gone. I parked the Cadillac in one of the open spots on the street and showed Tony that I had my shiny gold badge. The chef was happy that I was happy, but he also understood that my reinstatement meant we were both back in the line of fire. This was my job, and involving Tony meant a new set of problems. I did not want the chef to put aside his new career to go back to the no-survivors mentality he perfected in Iraq.

We walked the length of Rampart Street in both directions. We were looking either for antennas that seemed new or out of place. We found nothing strikingly amiss. Our next step was to chat up the daytime bartenders and usual street corner panhandlers. The bartenders wanted bribes and the bums would have told us any story we wanted for a buck.

"Did you check out the RV lot?" Loki, a tour guide working for Two Chicks Tours, asked when I spoke him near St. Louis Cemetery. Loki grew up with the Garden District and French Quarter as his playgrounds and knew both parts of the city like the back of his hand. I should have already thought of the nearby recreational camper park, so I tried to pass off a shrug as an answer before leading Tony to the campground.

I passed the place hundreds of times and never gave it a moment's thought. It backed up to Claiborne Avenue and the ancient St. Patrick Cemetery. The RV lot looked filled to its maximum, but there were only three dozen spaces to lease inside its fenced compound.

I flashed my badge at the lone security guard at the gate. He looked at Tony as though the chef would produce one as well. The young man backed off when Tony used his nastiest glare in place of a badge. There was no point questioning a guard unwilling to challenge anything suspicious.

The first thing I looked for was a white H-2 Humvee. It was a long shot, but so was someone spotting it at a crime scene, and that happened. We eliminated any of the motor homes that could not hold at least eight people, the bare minimum necessary to service the surveillance team we dismembered and a small communications team. We next ignored those with no external antennas of any sort. We had hoped to find at least two very large motor homes with far too many antennas parked in a corner of the lot.

We found the next best thing. There were two empty spots at the farthest corner of the lot. There were covers on the tires of the motorhomes parked nearby and varying amounts of outdoor furniture and grills outside of each of them. These were good signs that they had been there a while. This was an ideal place to park a motorhome during Carnival season. The lot is within sight of the French Quarter. It is also within walking distance of the major parade route on Canal Street. I found it suspicious that there should be two adjoining spaces still available so close to Fat Tuesday.

Tony began talking to a few of the renters while I headed into the office to speak with the middle-aged woman standing behind the counter. I was not sure how to approach the matter of the open spaces. I considered asking the clerk if she remembered seeing a pair of EM-50 Urban Assault Vehicles. That might have sounded like an insult to the RVs she made her living from if she had never seen the movie Stripes.

"I see you have two spaces available."

"Are you interested in renting one?" She reached for the paperwork.

"I was just curious why they're even available. Is there something wrong with the pads?"

"Oh, no. Those people left real early this morning. I heard they both had some sort of emergency."

"Were they here long?"

"You're not here to rent the space are you? Are you a cop?" She was more disappointed about not renting a space than about a detective questioning her.

"State Police." I showed her my badge and stopped sounding quite so nice with my questioning. "I need to see your rental records."

"What do you think they did?" Her tone betrayed fear, not interest.

"That's all a Federal matter. I'm just trying to locate the suspects."

She handed the two rental forms over without any argument. She could have insisted on my getting a search warrant. I find most people are quick to surrender their rights and privileges to avoid looking guilty or complicit. It makes my job easier and lets them feel like they helped.

She provided copies of the driver's licenses used by the men that rented the spaces. One was from Ohio and the other was from Utah. They just happened to arrive on the same day and both suffered family emergencies at the exact same moment. She told me to take the agreements and photocopies if they were of any use, and began assuring me that her bosses operated a very safe and honest campground. I thanked her for her help and promised their name would not show up in any news about the investigation.

Tony learned that the two missing, and very expensive looking, self-contained motorhomes were already parked in the lot when the other campers arrived.

I told him the rental agreements dated to late October. I should have noticed being watched a lot sooner if they had begun their surveillance on me four months earlier. I wondered how many times I convinced myself Ray was stalking his ex-wife when it was really this band shadowing me. I also wondered where the vehicles were. Ohio and Utah were definitely not their actual destinations.

One of the other RV owners shared their pictures of the motorhomes with us. I looked at the pictures and recognized the type of motorhome as being the luxurious Greyhound bus-sized travel buses that bands and celebrities use while on tour.

A thought came into my head as we walked through Armstrong Park towards my car. "It's a long shot, but let's take a ride. There was a company renting this sort of motorhome near one of the crime scenes. I thought it strange at the time, but maybe it makes perfect sense."

"You've never believed in coincidence," Tony needlessly reminded me. I have never encountered a genuine coincidence. There would be no science in the study of probability if related things occurred independently of one another.

I drove around the police station and followed Basin Street towards the interstate ramp on Claiborne Avenue. It was only a five-minute drive to Chef Menteur Highway. I took the exit and then turned from the highway onto Almonaster. I pointed out where I met the scrap metal thief and where I found the partially destroyed car. I glanced out my side of the car as we passed that vacant lot to sneak a peek at the motorhome dealer.

I parked my conspicuous vehicle behind a row of empty semi-trailers two blocks away. I took a fifty power spotting scope out of the trunk and led Tony towards the levee. We stayed below the crest of the levee to retrace our route and then set up the spotting scope behind a piece of brush I eased onto the edge of the earthworks. There were video cameras monitoring the supposed sales lot. Three more cameras were monitoring any traffic on

Almonaster. One of these pointed directly towards us. I was only a little worried that anyone watching might have noticed that a tree branch suddenly appeared on the crest of the levee fifty yards away. I knew they would panic if the sun flickered off the lens of my spotting scope as we peered into the lot.

There were half a dozen motor homes parked in the lot. They were all nearly fifty feet in length and had their multiple pop-outs extended. I noticed sewer and electric hookups ran to each motor coach as well. These were in use, not merely on display. As best we could tell, all of the vehicles bore the logo of the same manufacturer. It was odd, then, that the business did not list itself as a dealer of that specific brand on any of its limited signage. The main sign on the street was not particularly enticing. This struck us as a company going out of its way to send people looking elsewhere for its product. Tarpaulins lined the chain-link fence, even the double-width gate, and concertina wire topped it. The two office windows facing the street were tinted and there was little reason to believe the OPEN sign in the office window. We resisted the urge to have Tony step inside to try to rent one of the RVs.

We watched the lot for half an hour. It did not take that long to map the layout and find three vulnerable places in their camera coverage. I focused on establishing the specific use for each trailer. The two used for communications were easy to isolate because of the heavy cable running to the impressive antenna tower in the rear of the lot. There would have been very clear communications between this location and the campground off Rampart Street. We could see the hotels lining Canal Street from our own position. I also waited patiently to see if the gray-haired man that the NOPD officers and Paul Lancaster described showed his face. I found something unsettling about the generic description everyone gave to describe him. I hoped they were not talking about the man I had in mind. It was worth it to me to lie on the riverbank indefinitely just to be sure Jack Rickman and I were not breathing the same air.

The mystery man did not make an appearance, but my patience still bore fruit.

I wrote down descriptions of every vehicle we saw and the license numbers of any we could read without changing our position. It would be nearly impossible to run this many vehicle registrations through the DMV records without alerting anyone monitoring that database. I needed to decide if there was any benefit to even trying. I was confident that Jill Bledsoe's company owned the buses on the lot. It was also reasonable to believe the passenger vehicle registrations would trace back to the people who sold the company's straw buyers their family cars, just like the bullet-riddled panel van. It was better for me to be able to recognize these vehicles the next time I saw them than it was to make the operation buy new ones.

Chapter 38

Our after-work cocktail hour conclave moved upstairs after Katie moved in with me. It was not because I did not want to share my friends' company, or because I suddenly realized how vulnerable we were standing by the front door. The topics I discussed with the Chief, Katie, and Tulip were now too sensitive to share with the rest of New Orleans, particularly Ryan Kennedy.

Tulip started our nightly round-table by telling us about her visit from Michael Conroy, the local FBI Special-Agent-In-Charge. He arrived unannounced, flanked by two agents, and stood over her desk while his men began putting all of her electronic devices and computers into boxes. She had already taken the precaution of copying her electronic files so she sat and read the search warrant rather than protest their actions. It wiped the smug look off Conroy's face.

My mother's family is the sort of politically connected old-money family that make men in appointed positions tread carefully. Tulip and I try not to trade on that any more than necessary, but Tulip's situation was one of those times.

Tulip surprised the SAC by saying she had been expecting his visit for a while. She handed Conroy a notarized statement that detailed how she received and handled the classified file. She included my instructions to delete the file without reading it. Conroy read the statement and asked only a couple of questions before leaving her with the FBI's standard warning not to leave town and to be available for further questioning. He probably left the office understanding that he needed to rethink how to handle my sister.

"Sounds like you got off pretty easy," Katie commented. Everyone in the room knew how such interviews normally transpire. Tulip might have been hauled off to a windowless interrogation room. The research assistant who initially expressed interest in the file might still be sitting in one.

Tulip was lucky SAC Conroy filed no charges. She could have spent quite some time waiting for an arraignment hearing because so many judges were already on their way to Miami for the Super Bowl. The courts normally close during the last week of Mardi Gras anyway, when so many plaintiffs and defendants would rather risk contempt citations than miss the party. Any revelers arrested during the last weekend of parades and revelry are stuck in jail until the Orleans criminal court judges receive their holy ashes the day after Mardi Gras ends, on Ash Wednesday morning.

I refilled everyone's drinks and then turned towards Chief Avery. I was proud of what Tony and I accomplished and wanted to share the news. "I think Tony and I found where Jill Bledsoe has D-Tech's communications center."

Avery raised one hand. "Is that something we should be discussing? Isn't it bad enough that Tulip is accused of receiving one highly classified file without our actually discussing a classified operation in front of her?"

"Could you ladies go powder your noses or something?" I asked.

Katie kissed my head and followed Tulip to the elevator. The women began a conversation of their own at the bar while the chef headed to the cooks' line to prepare for the evening meal service. Our business was about to drop way off. Strada Ammazarre is too far from the parade routes and too formal and expensive for the thousands of tourists who only bring beer money and live out of their cars for the last four days of Mardi Gras. Our targeted trade are locals and the comparatively genteel tourists who come to town for the annual French Quarter and Jazz and Heritage Festivals.

"Okay, you found the communications center. What next?" Avery asked once we were alone in the apartment with Roux curled up in his kennel at the end of the hallway. The kennel's door was open if he cared to join us.

"Nothing. An operation like this has to be very compartmentalized. The surveillance teams should never have any contact with the team taking direct action against the Pistol Peete's and the El Caminos. They, in turn, would never meet the clean-up crews coming in behind them, but what we learned this morning indicates everyone knows there is a wet team in their mix. Disrupting the surveillance team following me would have no effect on the other teams. At most, they decided to ramp up their security measures."

"Does it help you to know that the Fifth District reported a case of road rage? They found a pickup truck full of bullet holes and blood less than two miles from where we found the van. Oh, and our crime lab found a faulty canister of thermite inside that van from this morning." This now firmly linked the van to the string of arson fires. "The DOD claimed the canister is sitting on a shelf in Saudi Arabia. A case was missing from inventory and nobody knew."

"Imagine that." I did not accept another coincidence. "How about the dig sites?"

"None of them had intact bodies. They pulled two dozen torsos out of the holes, but the coroner already said he would not be able to make any IDs. Two other holes were full of guns someone tried very hard to melt. The lab identified sixty different gun barrels, a lot of them from AK-47s and knock-off AR-15s. It is hard to say how many weapons they completely melted down, but I am glad as hell that they are all off the street. It's interesting that the lab hasn't recovered a single serial number, though."

"It explains where the bodies went after the first fires. One team came through and shot the Mexicans. Another team decapitated the bodies in the bathtubs and hauled them out here to try to cremate the bodies. One or the other team also grabbed any guns they found at the scene."

"So where are the heads?" This question must have nagged at my boss since ever he learned about the first headless bodies in a trash bag.

"My bet is they were gift wrapped and delivered to the El Caminos' local guy or shipped to Mexico. Either way they were supposed to get a specific reaction out of the cartel. I think the hope was that the Mexicans would feel intimidated enough to leave town. Whoever thought up that scenario doesn't know much about Mexican cartels. The El Caminos are not very sentimental about the people they lose, but they are tactical about avenging deaths. They're waiting for whoever's attacking them to make one small mistake before retaliating."

"What sort of retaliation should we expect?"

"It will be big and bloody. The cartels use car bombs and massacres as billboards to send their messages.

"You've got a handle on this, right? You said you spoke to their guy and they know it's not really a gang thing." Avery was more anxious than I had ever seen him. Visions of exploding carnival floats and the cartel's gunman strafing throngs of tourists lining Canal Street ran through his mind.

"That doesn't mean I can stop them. It just means we know they are prepared to wait until they find the people actually responsible. Right now, they consider you and me to be better suspects than the Pistol Peetes. They kill cops in their own country, so they won't have any qualms about doing so here if that's what they think they have to do to get their point across."

"What do you need from me or from Captain Hammond?"

"Confidence and patience. Tony and I had a good day today. We compromised a major piece of the surveillance element behind Bledsoe's operation. I got confirmation that D-Tech *is* who Kinkaid sent here, and I know what their game plan is. Tony and I are working out how to counter their mission. Our knowing all of this makes it harder for D-Tech to carry out their mission, but not impossible."

"What's it going to take to stop the action teams?"

"You know the answer to that. Isn't that why you and Ken brought me back?" I did not really know that Avery or Hammond fully understood that the only way to stop what Kinkaid wanted to do was either to stop the operation itself, or to lure them into an environment where I could confront them on my terms rather than theirs. They came to New Orleans on a do-or-die mission. Those were the only options they were putting on the table for me to stop them.

"We don't expect you to pick a fight with a bunch of mercenaries." Avery seemed appalled at the prospect.

"This war is already on our doorstep, whether or not we chose to fight in it. Neither of you can stop it, now can you?" I stood up and set our glasses on the kitchen counter. It was time for dinner and much lighter conversation.

Chief Avery politely excused himself to go home. It was strange seeing him in the company of bodyguards. He has never had trouble fighting his own battles. This was the last opportunity for the Chief to spend time with his family before his work schedule during Mardi Gras would absorb every waking minute of his days and nights. He would be on duty for over one hundred hours between Friday noon and Wednesday noon. His fears now included waiting for radio calls about car bombs or mass shootings along one of the parade routes.

I was about to begin putting in some long, and strange, hours as well. I needed to be sure my family and Katie were safe before I did anything. I needed to carve out some time Friday evening to attend Lionel Batiste's pre-election bash. It would be easy to attend because Tony gave Miss J a very bargain rate so her nephew's campaign could use the bistro for the occasion. I also intended to vote on Saturday, and to be close to a television for the Super Bowl on Sunday. I was going to devote the rest of my time to hunting my quarry, being ever mindful that the biggest risk in hunting large and deadly predators is that they find you first.

Chapter 39

Katie and I were in bed by ten o'clock that night. She found me standing in my office at three o'clock the next morning. I had opened my locked closet to remove a pair of ballistic vests, which I placed in the zippered bag on the bench. Katie focused her attention on the handgun and rifle case lying on the other end of the bench. She picked up one of the suppressed .22 caliber pistols in the bag and frowned. I did not tell her there was one in my satchel bag for the Springfield Armory M1A rifle as well.

"You and Tony going hunting?"

"Sort of." I continued getting dressed and placed one of the pistols in a leather shoulder holster. "I need to shake some things up."

"Well, this ought to do the trick. What are you up to, Cooter?" Katie sat down on the bench and put her hand on my arm. I sighed a little too loudly and took a seat next to her, holding her hand in mine.

"We weren't the ultimate target of those men Tony and I handled yesterday. They were just supposed to keep an eye on me while their darker half did some very bad things to the men they are really after. We found out the same company we worked for in Iraq is running the show, using the exact same plan Tony and I came up with over there. I cannot tell you how we know that, but it is a fact and it helps us plan our way to stop them. We think we have tracked down their base of operations. Now we need to make them think the men they're here to get have tracked them down."

"You're telling me the two of you are waging a psychological battle in the middle of a shooting war?" A familiar tone of exasperation was creeping into her voice. "I just don't want you to get shot trying to outsmart a thug.

"I let that happen once before. I won't let it happen again." I said this a bit too glibly and leaned over to start lacing up my flat-soled, dark leather boots.

"Then find another way to do whatever it is you're trying to do."

"This is the only way we're left with, and Tony and I are the only ones able to do this. At least we're very good at it."

"Why is Tony even involved? He's just a chef."

"He wasn't always a chef. Can we leave it at that for now?"

"Maybe we all need to talk." Katie obviously meant to hold me to our pact about which secrets about my past I could keep from her.

"I love you. I promise to be careful and to be back soon."

"Never promise me that. Just leave me with the 'I love you' part." She kissed me on the lips. I could feel the warmth of her naked skin under the thin tuxedo shirt of mine she had adopted for a nightgown.

"I love you." I picked up the gun case and headed towards the elevator. Tony was waiting for me when I stepped into the small vestibule between the doors to our apartments and the elevator. He did not look Katie in the eye before we both turned towards the elevator and waited for the doors to open.

"You're slipping. I got here without waking Tulip," he chided me.

"She'll be awake when we get back." He did not like the way I said it, but he focused on our immediate task. Our personal lives were now on hold.

We drove back to Almonaster Avenue in the company's Ford pickup truck. It seemed like the best vehicle because people expect to see a pickup truck in a commercial area. This one also had the horsepower necessary to get out of the area quickly if things went wrong.

I drove behind the RV dealership on Chef Menteur and then doubled back on Almonaster to park the truck three blocks away, next to a building that backed onto the levee. We waited in the truck for ten minutes to see if any vehicles drove past to check us out. We unloaded our gear and headed over the steep levee bank behind us once we were sure our arrival went unchallenged. We were not able to see our target after we crested the levee and gambled that our subjects were unaware of our presence.

The cameras we spotted the previous day looked like they had night vision capability. Few surveillance systems have infrared images that show much more than hazy green figures with weird eyes. Small movements are hard to see, and a monitoring screen with those sickly green images is hard to watch for any length of time. I'd planned on being in position by three thirty in the morning, a time I figured would have placed anyone doing the monitoring on the job long enough to have grown lax. We were running late and our concern was that a shift change would bring a fresh set of eyes that might catch our movements and initiate an effective response.

The tree branch was still in place at the levee's edge. I set a bulky night vision scope on the semi-automatic rifle and scanned our side of the levee for any sign of additional cameras or human patrols lurking in the shadows. I took a chance changing the static appearance of the levee with the tree branch, and leaving it in place when we left gave D-Tech's the security element enough time to set a trap for our return. I arranged the heavy rifle on its bipod while Tony scanned the parking lot with the fifty-power spotting scope. The lot was dark except for where a halogen light hung from a pole near the office. Light leaked from behind the drawn blinds in the vehicles we agreed were their communications center. The shop was dark, as were the remaining RVs we believed to be living quarters.

Tony and I turned our attention to the radios we took from the surveillance team. We knew there would have been a change in frequencies because of the loss of the radios. I remained convinced every member of the operation carried the same model of radio. Tony and I began scanning the sixty available frequencies, he from the top of the scale and me from the bottom. It was four in the morning and there was going to be little radio traffic on these frequencies at that hour. It took us under a minute to meet in the middle and begin again. We made three passes before we found an active conversation. There were two ways to find out who was speaking. The first was to listen to what they said. The second was to see if we could change the topic of their conversation. The latter option was the quickest one.

I fired three rounds. The sub-sonic .308 caliber rounds left the suppressor on my rifle with an audible cough, but did not raise enough dust on the levee or cause the leaves on the branch to give away our position. My training said to shoot the center camera first, as it was pointing straight at me, and then the other two. I also knew that the men who would chase us learned the exact same tactic. I shot the cameras in a left to right maneuver because I wanted any reaction to the shooting to focus on a spot to our left, away from our escape route. We waited for a reaction through our respective scopes. I held my finger off the trigger, but rested it close enough that I could begin firing at human targets if it became necessary to shoot our way to the truck.

The lights went out in the communications vehicles. Nobody left the relative safety of the other RVs. The only ways to leave one was through a single door, which faced our direction, or by pushing out heavy windows on the far side of each RV. It was suicidal to go through the door into a known line of fire, and illogical to open up the interior of a defensible position by smashing its windows. Everyone seemed to choose to stay in their respective vehicles.

The conversation immediately changed topics when a familiar female voice reported our gunshots. I was pleased that Joan had not lost her job because of the other morning. A male voice informed her that help was on the way. I noted the time on my watch and went back to watching the lot. My plan was to pin down anyone inside the perimeter trying to either shoot back or drive off the lot. It was not necessary to kill anyone to do what we'd come here to accomplish.

The response team was five minutes away. This seemed like a very long time to me. Jill Bledsoe, or whoever was in charge of security, must have felt better hidden than they were.

I handed Tony the rifle and took over the spotting scope once a pair of Chevy Suburban SUVs roared up to the gate from the direction of the Quarter to block the lone entry point to the compound. Each vehicle held six gunmen, who slid out of the vehicles on the far side and established a basic perimeter. Two of the men waited for the front door to the office to open from the inside and then dashed the few yards from the safety of the Suburbans to get inside the cinder block building. Shooting them, or even firing in their direction, would have given away our position.

I wanted to identify as many of the team members as I could, and the actions these two took established that they held command positions within the security element of the operation. They might be part of the team tasked with destroying evidence, but I would have designated men already prepared to kill people to fill the dual role as the security element. They reappeared leaving a side door with a third male in about twenty seconds and headed directly to the left hand communications trailer. It took less than ten minutes to identify men responsible for the slaughter of members of the El Caminos, to pick out at least two of their senior commanders, and to learn the purpose of each vehicle on the lot.

I gathered the spent cartridges and led Tony to our waiting truck. Armed men from inside the compound took over at the gate. We watched as the security team made their way to the levee in pairs. We made it over the levee a few yards downriver of where the closest team made its approach on our shooting position. We crept to the truck and then sat and watched the search teams try to find us.

None of the flashlight beams working their way methodically along the top and far side of the levee seemed to linger on the spot we used. The season's cool weather meant there was no dew to have disturbed, and it was not quite cold enough to have produced any frost. One of the men kicked our tree branch in frustration.

Tony monitored the channel the operatives were using while I scanned for any others that might have come to life. I thought the leader might report the situation to someone higher in the operation on a channel designated for his part of the operation. It was unlikely that the shooting teams that killed the Mexicans spoke openly of killing so many people on unencrypted radios in an urban setting full of radio scanners.

Tony started the engine in the Raptor pickup once four of the men climbed back into one of the Suburbans. It was unlikely anyone standing by the gate would hear our engine turn over as far away as we parked, but Tony tried to time starting the truck to the driver of the other vehicle starting his engine. We drove away from the scene before the other vehicle departed. Tony retraced our steps and pulled onto Chef Menteur nearly two miles from where the Suburban was likely appear ahead of us. He drove down the highway at nearly a hundred miles an hour and ignored every stoplight we encountered until we approached the intersection where we expected to see the Chevy leave Almonaster. They would move a lot slower, looking for any vehicles or pedestrians they might connect to the shooting. Tony kept a few blocks between the Suburban and ourselves as we tailed it towards town on Chef Menteur in distressingly light traffic.

I watched our rear view mirror for the other vehicle. We did not stay at the scene long enough to see if they split up or if one remained on the scene for the time being. I was sure nobody called 911. The absence of patrol cars to stop Tony's racing on the empty divided street was a good indication of how much police presence there was in the area.

We followed the Suburban after it entered the interstate. Tailing the big SUV in an oversized pickup truck when there was practically no traffic was tricky. It meant putting far more distance between us than we wanted to allow. The other driver could lose us in a flash just by taking the next exit and hiding behind the nearest building or by turning off his lights and racing in one direction or the other. He would be blocks away by the time we even reached the exit.

Conducting the team's preliminary debriefing in the vehicle may have distracted the occupants of the Suburban on their way home. The response team would compare notes on what each saw or heard to arrive at a consensus on what transpired. They would use that to determine how the team should reinforce the lot's security perimeter. We followed them at a discreet distance as they turned onto Paris Road and headed towards the river. I was more than a little surprised to be driving through the largely vacant Lower Ninth Ward at such an early hour of the morning. This was the time of day the place belonged to the drug dealers and other denizens of the dark. The Lower Ninth Ward was the last place one could still get a good look at Katrina's aftermath. It looked like a ghost town, and this one had real ghosts.

The Chevy paused for a worrisome length of time at a stop sign on St. Claude Avenue. Tony was on a parallel route three blocks to the driver's left and we needed to decide whether to cross the street or risk someone in the Suburban noticing us while we waited to see what their driver did next. I told Tony to cross the street and park four blocks down the street. It was a very risky calculation. The truck would be gone if they turned on St. Claude and headed into a more populated part of New Orleans. I played a hunch that they would head all the way to the Mississippi River levee and enter the Holy Cross Neighborhood.

The Suburban did continue into Holy Cross. We kept pace just behind it and then let the driver get five blocks ahead of us before we turned onto the same street. The driver pulled into a driveway and we turned left at the next intersection. I jumped out of the truck as Tony barely slowed down. He would turn around on St. Claude and meet me two blocks on the other side of the Suburban.

I ran through the neighborhood and then snaked my way through backyards, being mindful of any pets left outside that would give away my presence. I located the Suburban parked beside one of four houses I knew to be rentals units owned by a house flipper named Alex Boudreaux. I headed to my rendezvous point after I watched the second Suburban pull into a driveway three doors down.

Chapter 40

The handful of people Tony and I encountered as we walked home from the garage in the last of the pre-dawn murkiness all tried to ignore our appearance. Tony was carrying the heavy shoulder bag with our vests and pistols inside. The rifle was stowed in its case, but nobody was imagining that I was carrying a guitar in the black plastic case with the words Springfield Armory prominently embossed on its side. I was so used to carrying weapons in public during my life before New Orleans that it never occurred to me we were probably scaring people half to death.

"Go take a shower and come down for breakfast so we can talk," Katie instructed us when we encountered her in the restaurant's kitchen with Tulip. Something that smelled delicious was in the oven and the women were well ahead of us on the day's mimosa count. Roux was paying more attention to their cooking than to our return from battle.

Tony headed to his apartment and I returned to mine. I had intended to go back to bed and wake up to Katie's lecture on my behavior. The only thing she absolutely insisted upon from me when we began dating was to be honest with her. The years of classified work I did before returning to New Orleans were the only secrets she allowed between us, but I swore to answer any questions. This morning's greeting in the kitchen certainly indicated that she and Tulip intended to lower the threshold on their need to know.

Tony and I rode the elevator to the kitchen together. We had reached the point that the curtain around our past lives was wearing thin and we were going have to decide whether to keep our secrets or to find a way to answer Tulip and Katie's questions without losing their affections. Total honesty was unlikely to prove to be the best policy.

Tulip portioned out the breakfast casserole they had concocted while Katie passed around a plate of piping hot calas, a rice-filled version of a beignet. I was already pouring mimosa refills for Tony and myself by the time my sister opened the discussion.

"We think it's time you just ripped off the bandage and told us everything." It was an apropos way of phrasing their demands.

"Everything?" Tony asked. We knew what "everything" was, but they had no clue.

"Go back six years as a start." Katie's suggestion did not sound like an arbitrary point in time.

"Six years would put me in Iraq." I wanted to remind her that doing what they asked meant opening a door she and I previously agreed to keep locked.

"We know that," my sister insisted.

I was beginning to grasp that Tulip sought a different path into the file that brought the FBI to her office. I looked at both of the women. Tulip may have put Katie up to this.

"You're in enough trouble over the Operation Stoplight file as it is. To have me divulge even more things covered under the Secrets Act will only get us both in trouble." This was the argument I thought might deter the two lawyers. I immediately saw that it would not, and I raised a hand before Tulip could tell me how little that concerned her. "Let's finish breakfast and head back upstairs to our apartments. Tony will answer your questions and I will figure out a way to answer Katie's. He is not bound to the agreements I am."

The two women were visibly frustrated, but agreed. My suggestion made some sense to them and allowed us to enjoy a delicious meal without everyone losing their appetite over what we told them. Tony and I made sure to drink less of the champagne cocktail than did our girlfriends. I helped him carry Tulip into his apartment. Katie paced her own drinking better and was fully into her prosecutor persona by the time the door to my apartment closed behind us.

"Start with Tony's story. I need to be prepared for what I hear from your sister later." Katie was prepared to use my living room as an improvised grand jury room. She made herself comfortable on the amount of the sofa Roux was not occupying. I sat in one of the heavy oak and leather Stickley chairs across from her.

"I don't want to tell you anything he doesn't tell her."

"I won't tell her anything you tell me that he doesn't tell her." She must have been practicing her own arguments.

"Say that three times really quickly and I will," I tried to joke. She was clearly intoxicated, but she was still able to recite the tricky mouthful three times in a row.

"Tony's full name is Antonio Vento al-Majid. His father was an agent of the Mukhabarat stationed in Italy."

"Isn't that Iraq's secret police?" Katie was proving to be well enough informed. I would not have to explain every small detail, or be able to hide very much from her.

"His father was recalled after he impregnated and married a woman from Sicily. Saddam executed him in a purge and deported Tony and his mother back to Sicily when he was only ten. The Mukhabarat approached Tony when he was in his mid-twenties. They threatened to kill his mother if he did not do what they wanted, so he did their bidding for a decade. What he did for them is his story to tell. He returned to Iraq right after Baghdad fell and tracked down every man who'd either killed his father or threatened his family." She did not ask what Tony did when he found these men. Their fate was obvious, and well deserved.

Katie's face drained of its alcohol-induced rosiness. She was considering the damage control it was going to take to keep Tulip from losing her mind after hearing everything her suddenly-not-Italian boyfriend confessed to her.

"How did you meet him?" Katie's chin was on her raised knees.

"He stayed in Iraq to help organize resistance to our invasion of Iraq. He shared the view of the military and the Mukhabarat that we were invading his father's country. Eventually he realized occupation was Iraq's opportunity to purge its past and start over. He also knew the only way to get the troops to leave Iraq was to make our government believe America restored democracy to a place that never had any such thing."

"That's not an answer to the question."

"He recruited a team that began tracking down foreign jihadists and Iraqi dissidents trying to keep the chaos going to make it politically impossible for the occupation to end. I recruited Tony and his pals to help with an operation I believed the State

Department had sanctioned. I later learned a private contractor named D-Tech was pulling its strings. I needed Iraqis for our public interface. We systematically eliminated threats to Coalition troops and the process of rebuilding a viable Iraqi government by combining D-Tech's electronic intelligence gathering with the firepower of Tony's crew." I could not count the number of crimes I had just admitted to covering up for nearly a decade.

"Operation Stoplight." Katie may have been guessing but she sounded confident in her answer. I was relieved she chose to confirm this rather than condemn my actions.

"I can neither confirm nor deny your assumption. I will say that the operation ended right after the ambush where I nearly died. Tony somehow spirited me from Iraq to a hospital in Rome. Tony's mother raised him using her last name, so he went back to being Antonio Vento when we landed in Italy. He also went back to using his Mukhabarat cover as a chef. The CIA and State Department knew his family history and involvement with the Mukhabarat. They only approved his visa application after he and I threatened to go public about Operation Stoplight." I satisfied Katie's curiosity after stretching my non-disclosure agreement as thin as it could go. I would have told her anything she wanted to know, but she did not seem to want to know as much as I was sure Tulip might. Maybe she just wanted to keep what she would need to keep to herself to a minimum.

"But, now you're saying there's an identical operation being run here." I was relieved to find Katie was also juggling the law and her desire to know.

"I think there's a way we can talk about this. Come with me." I was relieved that she did not hesitate to take my extended hand.

I led her into my office and sat down beside her on the bench. All of my collected evidence and case notes were on the board. While some of this overlapped what I needed to keep secret, the events themselves were public knowledge. Katie's face showed how much she regretted demanding full disclosure. It was a lot to process, and little of it was positive or redemptive.

"I'm going to have talk in broad strokes and theoretical terms on some of this, but I'll get into specifics when I can, alright?" Katie nodded, but she already saw the legal hurdles ahead. "You know the saying about character being who you are when you're alone? Stoplights are a prime example. Law-abiding drivers stop at a stoplight on an empty street early in the morning. Running stoplights means you don't care about laws or disrupting society."

"I'm with you so far."

"The Geneva Convention was ratified when wars were still fought between actual nations. The war on terror pits us against ideologies that know no such niceties, but the Geneva Convention codes of conduct bind our military and intelligence agencies fighting these new styles of conflict. If we classify a terrorist organization as a criminal enterprise, the judicial rules for dealing with them are more restrictive and cumbersome. The only enemy our military has faced with a fierce ideology was the Japanese in the Second World War. Look what it took to defeat them. Nobody wants that."

"And how did this Operation Stoplight plan on fighting these new wars?" The question was too direct for me to answer. She frowned at her own inability to frame it more obliquely.

"The DOJ handed down a legal opinion stating intelligence agencies and our military were free to use intelligence provided by sources not tied to any government body, like cops use informants. It opened a narrow path to get around the Geneva Convention, and human rights advocates like my sister. It placed the responsibility of using legal and ethical means to acquire the information on the informant, but nobody was required to actually verify the intelligence was gathered legally to use it."

"That's some murky water," Katie tossed in her personal opinion along with a free legal opinion.

"There were hidden reasons behind the way the invasion of Iraq was conducted. The air strikes intentionally wiped out the country's entire communications infrastructure just to necessitate its rebuilding. A company by the name of D-Tech received a no-bid contract to do so. They build some of the finest telecommunications equipment around, but they also develop a lot of telecommunications surveillance equipment and software. D-Tech created a virtual spy network within the cellular and wired telephone networks they rebuilt. They could now track an individual's movements, monitor and record their calls, and use metadata to create a phone tree of their contacts. Isolate one known terrorist and track his call patterns, use those to listen to specific conversations, and you can wipe out his entire cell."

"That's a huge kick in the head to that entire country's rights to any privacy. Not everybody is a terrorist. You'd never get to use that sort of blanket technology in this country."

"Unless, perhaps, the cover story is that D-Tech was in town simply conducting field trials on some sort of brand new surveillance technology they are not yet marketing. They'd be obligated, of course, to report if they learned of anything illegal about to happen to the law enforcement authority of their own choosing."

"Such as Homeland Security?" Katie and I were past the hardest dots for her to connect. I touched my nose and began again.

"Now imagine you're someone like Tony, an intelligence asset with a nasty past, who really wanted to provide information to the Coalition. You would not want anyone you betrayed to the Americans to know it was you, or even where or how you found out. You might be given your own detention and interrogation facilities, but you could not release any prisoners because now they know who you are, and what they had told you. If you chose to kill any suspects you questioned, you would need to make it look like somebody else was responsible. What are a few more bodies in the middle of a combined civil war and military occupation? Maybe you could even use those bodies to start fights between groups you were already fighting. Let them do your work for you."

"Tell me you're kidding." My ruse of making veiled theories and scenarios out of actual, but classified, events was not making it any easier for my girlfriend to hear thinly veiled accounts of what Tony and I did in the past. She had begun to understand why I built such a thick wall around my own history. I turned towards the material on my walls rather than look her in the eye.

"Lately I've been called to crime scenes involving the decapitated bodies of Hispanic males. The victims were low ranking members of the El Camino drug cartel. Someone abducted a member of a Mid-City gang called the Pistol Peetes just before a Hispanic gunman executed one of the gang's members in an effort to point to the El Camino gang killing him as an act of retaliation. A tourist who lied about his identity and subsequently vanished even conveniently videotaped that shooting. Jill Bledsoe hired Ray and gave him a list of houses to photograph. She did not ask Ray to locate where specific gang members lived because she already knew. They were already on the list she handed him. Captain Hammond did not know what he was dropping me into when he sent me to look at an arson fire at an address I found on Ray's list. There were a half dozen other fires, and the young man's abduction, at other addresses on that list. Every address had some connection to either the El Caminos or the Pistol Peetes. I am satisfied that neither gang is involved in any of these attacks. It means a third party must be responsible, and all signs point back to why D-Tech is really in town. I was suspended when I refused to stop investigating the fires or deaths and to help hide the shady operation Deputy Director Kinkaid sent here."

"You believe Kinkaid gave his blessing to an operation identical to the one you and Tony pulled off while in Iraq?" Katie looked like she wanted to vomit.

"It definitely can't be the exact same operation. That one ended when Tony and I had to run for our lives to get out of Iraq. Someone handed the names of every member of our team over to the newly elected Iraqi government. Their new secret police executed any of the Iraqis they could find."

"Why were they executed? They were trying to stop the attacks against the new government."

"The operation also exposed members of the new government had financial ties to the insurrection, even family ties. It was potentially embarrassing to both the Iraqis and the Americans if those names ever got out."

"Can I just say this? I am stunned that you have such a long history of making a mess out of things. I thought maybe that you were just having a hard time adjusting to civilian life, but you really do have a big problem balancing authority with your own sense of justice, don't you?" Katie sighed, but then showed the closest thing to a smile she had cracked all day. "Back to what's going on here. What are you two going to do?"

"Avery gave me my badge back, but he can't really do anything else because of the agreement we both signed with Kinkaid. I can't let either of them know I told you what is probably going on, but Tony and I can certainly try to throw a wrench or two into the plan. I have already ruined any chance of their passing off any future killings as being gang related. I am afraid, though, that none of this has to do with wiping out the heroin trade or taking either of the gangs into court. I am afraid this has to do with some weird agreement the El Caminos think they have with our government. I spoke with one of their lieutenants and he told me in as many words that they can do whatever they want. The key to stopping this is learning what the agreement is all about."

"That might explain why our grand jury investigation into the El Caminos was shut down."

I forgot that Katie told me about the Department of Justice summarily quashing her boss' own investigation into drug trafficking by the El Camino cartel. The two of us kicked around any explanations we could imagine and came up with only two plausible reasons for the DOJ to have not only ordered an end to pursuing indictments, but to have taken the investigatory files as well.

The Department of Justice might be shielding the cartel because they were bait in larger trap, or they were shielding them because of something a defendant linked to the cartel might reveal in open court. I was willing to bet it was the latter and that the cartel was blackmailing someone at DHS or DOJ into giving them a pass. Kinkaid must have asked D-Tech to wipe out the cartel in a way that made someone other than our government look responsible.

I was done telling Katie what she'd insisted on knowing. Very few of the things she heard said good things about my past or me. I took it as a good sign that she was not packing her bags. I sat down next to her and she grasped my hand.

"I assume this is why you have tried to keep your sister and Tony apart all this time," Katie sighed.

"I knew today would come eventually and I didn't want her to get as hurt by this as she is probably going to be."

"You have no idea," Katie frowned and moved to sit on my lap. "I may even hate you by the time she's done crying."

"I'm just glad you don't right now," I sighed and placed my head on her breasts as she stroked my hair.

Chapter 41

The morning's positive side was locating two of the houses where D-Tech's security team were living. I estimated that there were at least two additional houses for them and one for the command staff, which would likely double as the staging area. This residence was likely away from the others, but all of the locations would have a line of sight to one another for security reasons. The command center needed to be separate from the RV store. It would accommodate at least a dozen people in one space for briefings and debriefings. A finished basement would be ideal, but with the near absence of basements in New Orleans, they were most likely using a two-car garage. Any house with a two-car garage would be in a newer part of town. Tony and I agreed that this hypothetical house was likely to be closer to D-Tech's base on Almonaster than the one in Holy Cross.

I left Katie with Roux and headed out to speak with Alex Boudreaux about his rental properties. Katie wanted to stay close to Tulip. Tony would relieve his tension through work.

Boudreaux was at his latest job site. The last time we spoke, he was under investigation by the FBI because of the evidence I handed them related to Boudreaux's influencing the upcoming election. Alex graduated from Tulane ahead of my sister. She was intent upon bankrupting him with a civil suit on Lionel Batiste's behalf for having framed the City Council candidate on drug charges to better his own man's chances in the coming election. I doubted that he was going to be very cooperative under the circumstances.

"You just keeping creeping along, don't you?" I asked him. The house we were standing in was only eight blocks from the fire scene where I met Fire Marshal Wheeler.

"I'll still let you invest, detective. I could use the money. Your sister is doing her best to put me out of business." Boudreaux chuckled at my indifferent shrug and turned to finish the instructions he was giving to one of his tile men.

"Well, you did slander Lionel Batiste pretty badly when you framed him for selling meth," I reminded him. He had done far worse than this in the past few months, but his crimes were harder to prove than a civil action required.

"I'll survive. I'm not about to let a lawsuit keep me from rebuilding New Orleans," he assured me.

"Meanwhile, people still trying to return to New Orleans can't afford to buy a house thanks to the gentrification you've brought to town."

"Other people can. You don't think it's a good thing that people with real money want to live here?"

"You're awfully ignorant of the French Revolution for a guy with a French name." We both had better things to do than rehash our arguments about free market economies and income disparity. "I wanted to ask you about a couple of your rental properties in Holy Cross."

"What do you want to know?" Boudreaux was paying attention to me, but his eyes continued to watch his crew of work-release ex-cons.

"You have two units rented to the same company. I was wondering if they rented any other places from you as well." I gave him the addresses I knew for a fact were occupied by men connected to D-Tech. Boudreaux took a moment to go through the index in his mind and then gave me a very curious look. A robin gets the same look when hunting earthworms.

"What's your interest in those places?"

"Professional. Do I need a warrant so we can discuss this in a more formal setting?" I had never needed to do either thing to get his cooperation in the past.

"It's just that the guy who rented the places said to let him know if you ever asked. He said you two knew each other, but that you have lost touch. I never gave it that much thought until you showed up just now. What's up with you two?" Boudreaux probably knew at the time that this had nothing to do with friends losing touch.

There is also only one reason police detectives ever ask Alex Boudreaux about any of his properties.

"The guy have a name?"

"I've got it somewhere. He was about your height, short gray hair, and a real weird face. I didn't like being around him very much."

"Jack something?"

"Sounds about right. I'll look it up and let you know. What do you want to know about those units?"

"When were they rented?"

"I figured the guy was moving his company here from somewhere out west. They started in September and he is renting them month to month. He told they'd be gone right after the Super Bowl." I hated that every D-Tech timetable I encountered was about to end.

"Why do you say they moved here from somewhere out west?"

"He was driving a new Chevy Suburban with Arizona plates."

"Did he tell you the name of his supposed company?"

"Nope. He just said they worked in telecommunications and he needed to be able to put up some antennas. He paid cash for everything and hasn't been a problem since. That's pretty rare in a tenant."

"How many places did he rent?" I rephrased my earlier question because Boudreaux managed to leave an answer out of his intentionally rambling conversation.

"Four that I can recall." He was quick to give me the two additional addresses. I was not in a mood to play semantical games with him, though.

"And how many others might you have forgotten?" Boudreaux broke into a big grin and brushed a hand through his thick black hair. It was a casual gesture, but one I had come to recognize as one of his tells.

"Hey, boss, can you look at this?" It took only a few seconds for one of Boudreaux's workers to need him after he signaled them to brush me off. I recognized the pair of heavy-set construction workers on the porch as part of his long-time supervisors. They would not mind risking their parole if he decided to have them beat me into pulp.

"Again, I'll check my records and give you a call. There may be one or two other places. What should I tell your friend when I call him?" It was a trick question. I would owe him a favor if I asked him not to say a word. I was beginning to feel that I was running out of time to stop whatever was happening, or what was about to get worse. I needed to upset that timetable.

"Tell him he's blown. He'll know what I'm talking about."

That call was likely going to cost me knowing where the teams were staying. They would close up the four houses Boudreaux told me about and be in their backup locations by the end of the day. I could stake them out and see where they went. I chose to do no such thing.

Tony and I were a fly in their ointment. The raid on their RV lot proved to both of us how easily we could disrupt their entire operation.

I was sure they would choose to tighten their security rather than move this late in whatever their plan of action was. Boudreaux would let his mysterious renter know I had finally tracked him down. It was not going to be seriously disruptive to do so because Alex undoubtedly had other properties at the ready, but I held out the hope that it would bother the men to know I was this close to either of them. They would not appreciate feeling like cockroaches when the kitchen light goes on.

I was sure D-Tech made sure Kinkaid was aware of my meeting with Fernando Rodriquez by now. They may or may not have known about the meeting with the Pistol Peetes. That meeting was not the one anyone needed to worry about, anyway. I now realized that Rodriquez was the one who could expose what Deputy Director Kinkaid was trying to hide. Now someone was bound to come to me to learn what I knew about both sides.

Chapter 42

I took a nap after Tony and I ate lunch together on the patio. He looked drained, but said he was immensely relieved for Tulip to finally know the secrets about him that the two of us kept from her for so long.

I was standing at the bistro's bar when Tulip and Katie came through the front door. They had spent their afternoon at their own places to water their plants and change out their wardrobes. Katie stepped up and gave me a kiss on the cheek when she saw me speaking with Ryan Kennedy.

"How was your afternoon?" I asked both of the women. Tulip remained unsettled by Tony's disclosures and stared vacantly out the window rather than at Katie or me.

"It was fine. I took Tulip to her spa after we changed out our suitcases. I took over a little more of your closet by the way." Katie was making an effort at polite conversation, but she was as concerned by my sister's mood as I was.

I tapped my sister's shoulder. "You okay?"

"Probably not." She admitted. She was willing to look me in the eye, but it was with a harsh look. "It's like everything I ever knew was wrong. You two never should have kept me in the dark like that unless you could do so forever."

"No good was going to, or has, come from telling you. Tony and I are entirely different people than we were then or there."

"Maybe you, and maybe you really aren't. I don't know about Tony, either. You don't get to act out your aggression in public anymore, but you can still shoot people. Tony just carve on meat and vegetables instead of human beings." I could tell how honest my partner's confession was by her statement.

"I think we're going to take this opportunity to go freshen up for dinner," Katie declared and poured their drinks into plastic cups before leading my sister towards the elevator in the bustling kitchen.

"Something I can spread a rumor about, my dear boy?" Ryan asked after overhearing our conversation.

"Afraid not, Ryan. It's all pillow talk from here on." Telling him anything was the same as announcing it to the entire French Quarter. Ryan excused himself and moved down the bar to be closer to Jason.

Chief Avery arrived and filled Ryan's vacant spot next to me a few minutes later. Jason saw him coming and made sure a cold draft Abita beer was waiting for the Chief when he squared himself at the bar.

"Anything new to report from your end?" His asking me this meant he brought news of his own.

"Just that Tony and I finally came clean to the girls about Iraq."

"Holy Jesus." Avery's eyes blinked and he let loose of the cold beer stein he was twisting on its coaster. He turned to face me but did not ask how or why this transpired. "No wonder you're here by yourself."

"It's going to be okay. I think. Katie and Tulip just went upstairs. Neither of them has moved out yet. Katie took my version pretty well, but Tony may have confessed way more than Tulip can handle at once."

"What did he tell her?"

"Apparently damn near everything. He told her his real name and confessed that he and his father were both Iraqi assassins in Europe. He also told her a lot more about the work we did in Baghdad together than I told Katie, but he isn't bound by the same confidentiality agreement I am. I have to assume Tulip and Katie are still comparing notes."

"You've got to feel a little bit relieved," Avery suggested. "Keeping everything from your sister has been hanging over your head for a long time."

"We'll see. It can't be great finding out Tony and I are exactly the sort of war criminals she's been trying to find." Avery hid behind his beer because there was no good response to this.

"What's your big news?"

"Kinkaid said he's coming to town to talk with you. I won't use the exact words he said. Just understand you're in his sights."

Kinkaid giving notice about chewing my ass intrigued me far less than his obvious interest in my active opposition to D-Tech's presence in New Orleans.

"He's pretty upset that you keep putting your nose where he doesn't think it belongs anymore."

"Where doesn't a good cop's nose belong?"

"Since when have you been a good cop?" Avery was finally able to start joking about my situation.

"Let me clarify. I'm on the side of the good guys." My boss barely nodded his agreement to my self-assessment and tapped the rim of his glass against my tumbler of Elijah Craig bourbon.

Tulip and Katie came back and stood beside us at the bar. They were dressed in clothes suited to an evening of parade watching. Tulip seemed to be in better spirits. They exchanged greetings with Avery and Tulip gave him her usual hug.

"Care to join us for dinner?" I asked my boss.

"Nope. I just came by to give you the head's up. I want to sit down with Janell and the family before they lose me to Carnival season." Policing the evening parades and daytime ones on the weekends, plus the tourist hordes, is an annual test of NOPD's capacities.

I motioned to Marie and she led us to a small table in the rear of the bistro. It gave me a good view of the place so I could monitor our busy Friday night. I could see the bar, hostess stand, and kitchen door from my seat. Katie realized this as well. She smiled and took my hand when I asked for a different table.

Trying to be a good boyfriend cost me a tactical advantage that I should not have surrendered. The purpose of everything done in the last two days was to disrupt D-Tech's operation and force them to waste time and energy reassessing their defensive posture and surveillance of me. I knew they would have to find a way to keep me in some sort of disadvantaged position. Their obvious choice was the use of intimidation, such as being more their surveillance of the bistro and myself more overt. I expected a few more veiled threats against my family, but my mother was well protected in her enclave on Audubon Place and Tulip and Katie were even safer here. Avery had also reversed the decision to take away my badge and the Health Department was unlikely to let themselves be used to embarrass or harass the bistro again.

What I absolutely did not believe would happen was for the mystery man running the operation to suddenly appear at our hostess stand with a party of twelve. My back was to the door when Jill Bledsoe came in with five men and some hired dates. I knew the dates were hired because I'd been in two of the ladies' company myself at a time when I'd been more prepared to pay for intimacy than to nurture it.

"We might have trouble up front, boss man," the young African-American back-waiter clearing our dishes whispered in my ear. I turned my attention towards the bar.

I recognized Jill Bledsoe immediately. It took only a moment to realize that the others in her party consisted of the members of Paul's six-person surveillance team I tangled with two days earlier. The other man in the group, standing next to Jill, had his back to me, but I recognized him all the same. I was still in a moment of fight-or-flight decision making when he abruptly faced towards me.

Tony and I were already convinced that Jack Rickman was involved in D-Tech's nefarious operation. It had to do with the way suspects kept hinting that their boss knew one or both of us and that the operation was tied to an operation I'd run in Iraq. Mostly we believed the only person who would dare to bring such a deadly circus to town was Jack. His presence here with Jill Bledsoe and the blown surveillance team should have been less of a surprise. It was classic Jack to want to rub my nose in his own failure. He was signaling that the gloves were off and he was willing to blow up both of our lives to win in the end.

Jack clearly intended to cause stress to our business by bringing such a large group to dinner without a reservation. He precisely timed their arrival to the hour when our strongest walk-in dinner business would begin streaming in from the street. It was also when the bulk of our reservations were scheduled to be honored. This evening was crazier than most because most of the people coming to eat hoped to be finished eating in time to catch the first evening parade of Mardi Gras. The Krewe du Vieux was not yet on the move, but it would pass directly in front of the restaurant when it did. The satirical marching parade, and its revelry, would last until long after midnight.

Marie and Joaquin were patiently trying to explain why they refused to accommodate Jack and his guests. I knew Jack wanted to draw me into a confrontation. There are few things worse than when an owner loses their cool when their restaurant is full. That's not true: The only thing worse is losing control of their restaurant by allowing a guest to dictate policy or to allow menu substitutions with a slammed kitchen. Tony and I hired Joaquin, and every manager before him, just to avoid those moments by keeping us from being the ones to tell people No. Either of our angriest expressions could scare even the most self-entitled guest from ever eating in public again. My sister and Katie silently followed me to the end of the bar so I could monitor the situation.

"Don't you have a table in the kitchen?" Jack pressed Joaquin.

Our barely smiling manager was unaware of the actual dynamic before him. Joaquin glanced past Jack when the idea of sacrificing our Chef's Table came up. Jack probably interpreted this as Joaquin considering that option. What the wily Cuban actually did was nonverbally ask permission to use that option. I gave him an unmistakably negative frown. Putting Jack and his party anywhere near Chef Tony would have been a disaster. My career choice requires self-restraint while Tony feels free of any conflicts about acting on his instincts in his kitchen. I made a gesture with one finger to remind Joaquin that the private dining rooms upstairs were open. It would mean shuffling servers about.

"We do have a private dining room open on the mezzanine. I'd be more than happy to provide it for your party." It was Joaquin's final offer. He was still trying to treat Jack as a welcome visitor and did not want to lose his business in the future, but he ran the restaurant and our guests were treated like guests only so long as they acted like guests.

"I demand to speak to the owner." Jack raised his voice enough to be heard over the jazz combo playing nearby.

"That's your right, sir," Joaquin readily acknowledged. "I will warn you, though, that he'll be most impolite when he tells you to leave. I'm offering you a table."

"Then I suppose it will have to do."

Jack was able to create a little drama but no chaos. He was not going to bully his way past an experienced French Quarter maître d. He also failed to pull me into the conversation. Jack's only options now were to take Joaquin's offer or to leave hungry. He was out of ways to disturb the restaurant without being the one who looked uncooperative. He would still have opportunities to complain loudly about the food, the service, and having to pay the hefty gratuity Joaquin was undoubtedly going to add to his bill.

Jack acquiesced, but he made one final jab. "Just don't give us a faggot for a waiter."

"You'll need to be prepared to starve while dining in the French Quarter with that attitude." Joaquin informed his obviously out-of-town guest. Jack was not happy that his companions were laughing at this sage advice.

"Well, that was certainly ugly." Katie was clutching my right elbow.

"You don't know the half of it, dear." My expression was still dark when I turned away from the stairwell to face her. "That was "Casper" Jack Rickman."

"Jack? Your boss from Iraq? I should have let you kick his butt."

"Let's just get out of here."

Jason handed us go-cup cocktails before I led the two women out into the festive night air. We turned to our left and headed towards the start of the parade route on Frenchman Street. I needed to find a means of shutting out that my personal bogeyman had just re-emerged from the shadows. The only way that worked for me right then was to put on a smile for my companions, while I silently imagined ways to kill the beast.

Chapter 43

Video surveillance recorded a Ford Econoline van pulling into the Iberville Parish Tourist Information Center just west of Baton Rouge at about three o'clock the following Wednesday morning. The Arizona plates on the van suggested the van's driver had been on the road for nearly twenty hours. The van remained outside the closed center until a Mercedes SUV and an identical van entered the parking lot ten minutes later. Nobody stretched their legs or got out to find a place to take a piss. The three automobiles immediately left in the direction of the interstate as a convoy, with the Mercedes cradled between the pair of windowless vans.

The vehicles followed Interstate 10 through Baton Rouge and were roughly equidistant between Baton Rouge and New Orleans when a sheriff's deputy from Ascension Parish decided to stop the Mercedes.

Interstate 10 is the main west to east path for drug and human traffickers crossing the southern states. Parish-level law enforcement pride themselves on making major drug and human trafficking arrests each year from traffic stops. A pair of vans with Arizona plates crossing the state late at night would have been a strong magnet for the deputy. The vans were profiling bait, but the owner of the expensive Mercedes SUV might be carrying unexplainable cash a parish could legally seize to reap a sizeable reward for itself.

The deputy never had a chance to congratulate himself on getting the Mercedes to pull over. The luxury car pulled off the highway and headed a mile further to the visitor center just outside of Sorrento. The deputy probably did not notice one of the vans trailed behind him. The Mercedes stopped at the parking lot's entrance. The driver stopped at a right angle to the deputy's pursuit vehicle. The driver tried to park outside of the view of the surveillance cameras, but a maintenance worker had bumped one weeks ago and nobody repositioned it.

The van boxed the deputy in from behind and at least three people opened fire on the Dodge cruiser from behind after the van's sliding door rolled open. The van then made a wide turn and started back towards the interstate. The driver of the Mercedes slowly drove past the riddled cruiser. They probably wanted to confirm the deputy was dead.

A witness statement by a trucker parked near the on-ramp detailed what happened next. The vehicles encountered two other cruisers bearing the State Police logo as they left the tourist center. The van tried to block the two patrol cars as they gave chase to the Mercedes. They roared past the trucker at close to ninety miles an hour. The second van waited at the top of the ramp to resume its escort duties. A gun battle ensued as soon as the cruisers pulled even with this van.

The cruisers found themselves boxed into a rolling ambush between the two vans as the Mercedes escaped in the direction of New Orleans. Bullets filled the air for the next five miles along the interstate. The few cars and trucks traveling at that hour all pulled to the shoulder at the sight and sound of the gunfire and the troopers' flashing blue lights approaching them at a high rate of speed. They watched as the gunfight rolled past before they could raise a camera to record the spectacle or call 911.

The State Police have very strict rules related to both high-speed pursuits and firing at moving vehicles. The rules are simple. We have to avoid doing either one. The cruisers should have taken evasive action and let the vans pass. They could then safely radio their situation and call for a roadblock to be set up somewhere down the highway.

Neither patrol car stopped their pursuit. Neither of them made a single radio call about their situation. They did finally manage to shoot out the tires on the leading van, but the men in the vans pockmarked both patrol cars with high velocity rounds fired from AK-47 and AR-15 style assault rifles. Blood trails indicated that at least one officer in each patrol car was struck. Witnesses also reported that at least six men dressed in State Police uniforms were firing from the two cruisers. That would put three officers, including the drivers, in each of the sedans, and we never do that.

The trailing van blasted its way past the troopers as the occupants of the lead van set the damaged vehicle on fire. The shooters jumped into the second van and made their escape. About the only identifiable thing on the charred van were its Arizona license plates. The few witness reports saying anything about the occupants of the vans claimed they were all Hispanic-looking males.

I was blissfully unaware of all of this until Captain Hammond called me to the scene about seven o'clock in the morning. Eastbound traffic on the interstate remained rerouted from I-10 onto US 61. The rubbernecking in the open westbound lanes meant traffic leaving New Orleans slowed to a crawl. I was on the causeway to La Place before I realized I trapped myself in this traffic.

The two patrol cars were loaded onto flatbed trailers along with the burned wreckage of the van by the time I arrived at the scene. Forensic teams needed to document the scene before the State Police reopened both lanes of traffic.

I gave Captain Hammond's recitation of the events only passing interest until he reached the part where multiple witnesses claimed the State Police officers involved abandoned their vehicles and left the scene. They did so in a pair of black Chevrolet Suburbans that came from the direction of New Orleans and arrived within a few minutes of the van escaping. The Suburbans bore license plate numbers stolen in New Orleans in the past week.

"Let me guess the rest." I interrupted my boss because I was sure I knew the story. "These cruisers aren't really ours. The patrol car that should have been covering this stretch of road answered a call miles from here that turned out to be a false report."

"They responded to a traffic accident on Highway Twenty-Two. Nothing was at the scene when they arrived." Hammond did not sound pleased. "These patrol cars were bought at one of our auctions back in October. The decals are fake and the lights aren't even the model we use."

"I'm sure the suspects noticed. It's probably why they started shooting."

Hammond was in no mood for my sarcasm. He said the veteran parish deputy had the presence of mind to drop to the floorboards when the shooting began. The deputy still received some minor wounds, but his boss would not have to knock on a home's front door with a new widow and fatherless kids behind it.

"Just tell me if this is connected to that BS we got signed up for with Homeland Security." Finding the answer to that one question was the only reason Captain Hammond called me all the way out there.

"Of course it is, Captain."

Hammond started to say something a dozen times before he was able to formulate a measured response. Captain Kenneth Hammond has never liked me. My captain has never fully understood the shadowy world I came from before becoming a police officer. He bridles at my casual approach to uniforms, such as the denim jeans and sweatshirt with the State Police logo I was wearing. He deeply resented my leap frogging through the ranks because of my family's political connections in Baton Rouge. He wasted no time before assigning me to assist NOPD's Chief of Detectives the very same day he handed me a detective's badge. I was only part of Hammond's world because I was still technically a State Police Detective and not an NOPD one. This morning, however, he put a hand on my shoulder and looked me in the eye.

"Chief Avery says you're trying to shut down whatever they have us mixed up in. You need to work faster for all of our sakes."

"I'm working on it, sir. Did the sheriff's deputy put out a call for help when the shooting started?"

"His radio was shot to hell. He called for help on his cell phone."

"But the two fake patrol cars approached the Mexicans as they left the second rest area and headed towards the interstate, right?"

"That's right. I can't tell you how the fake cops knew where to find their target." Hammond sounded as if he also believed the timing of those cars' arrival was just a little too convenient.

"How did you know to look at the footage of the other tourist center?"

"We pulled people out of bed to check all of them. I figured that if the Mexicans knew where this one was that they may have used some others getting here. I was hoping we might get a better timeline on their path across the state as well. It turned out that these two centers were the only ones any of those three vehicles stopped at in the entire state yesterday. Does that make any sense to you?" Hammond was not asking a rhetorical question. The ambush would bother him until someone provided an answer to what happened here.

I shook my head because I could not tell Captain Hammond that D-Tech was probably monitoring cellular traffic along Interstate 10. That mean they knew exactly where we were standing at that very moment.

They likely trapped a call from a phone number they associated with an occupant of the Mercedes. The pair of fake cruisers headed to the tourist center while D-Tech made the 911 call to pull the actual State Police unit in the area away from the interstate. The Mexicans anticipated an ambush, and the sheriff's deputy had the great misfortune to encounter the convoy before D-Tech's shooting team did.

"Nothing makes a lot of sense, but I'll let you know when it does." I thought it was better to leave Captain Hammond frustrated and ignorant than it would be for him to be well informed and feeling powerless to stop it, like me.

We moved to the flatbed trailers holding the three autos abandoned in the aftermath of the gunfight. I looked inside the very thoroughly torched Ford van. There was a shallow carpet of spent shell casings in rifle and pistol calibers on the floor of the van. There were the remains of two sofas as well, which would have been more comfortable than sitting on the floor of the windowless work vehicle. The discarded fake patrol cars had a slightly more interesting story to tell. I spotted pools of oil beneath each vehicle and clambered onto the trailer holding them. I popped the engine hoods and confirmed my worst suspicions about the oil leaks. I suspected rounds from a fifty-caliber rifle destroyed the engines in the fake cruisers. The heavy bullets would have split a human being in two. I went back to the van and poked around in the spent shell casings. The ones I was looking for were magnitudes larger than anything I found.

"Has anyone recovered any fifty-caliber shell casings?" I asked Hammond as I hopped off the low trailer.

"No. Do you think someone actually used a fifty-caliber rifle here?"

"I'll bet you find the shards of a couple of rounds in the engines on those Chargers. With firepower like that, it won't be good if whoever has that gun thinks the State Police was responsible for what happened here."

"You're a real ray of sunshine, Holland. Go find these guys. Call if you need help with anything."

Hammond did not wait for a salute that I was never going to give and did not offer a handshake before he turned and left me standing beside my Cadillac XLR. I saw no reason not to take advantage of the miles of closed highway stretching before me. I stepped on the gas and sped to the end of the roadblock with the speedometer buried in the triple digits.

Chapter 44

I wasn't joking about the potential menace of a sharpshooter with both a rifle capable of hitting a target a mile away and the conviction that the State Police tried to kill him. The occupants of the Mercedes were not going to be very receptive to anyone from the State Police, but I needed to make an effort to keep the peace. I left Hammond and headed directly to the house where I stumbled upon Fernando Rodriguez a few days earlier.

I removed the electronic fuse to my car's GPS the same day I shared lunch with Deputy Director Kinkaid on the chance that D-Tech was tracking me. I turned my phone off before I exited the interstate and approached Fernando's house. I kept a burner phone in my messenger bag in case I needed to make any emergency phone calls, or if Avery needed to reach me without NOPD logging our conversation. The point was to keep D-Tech from capturing any metadata, as they had done with the ambushed convoy.

I saw no vehicles or other signs of life at the house. I honked my car horn three times before stepping out of the convertible and making an elaborate show of locking my pistol in the car. I walked towards the house with my hands holding my shirt up to expose my beltline and waist. I rang the doorbell and stood on the front porch. I dropped my hands to let them hang loose at my side. There was no response, so I rang a second time and continued to wait.

I accepted the folly of what I was doing and gave up after half an hour. I started walking back to my car and tried to recall other addresses on the list Ray gave me. I was prepared to spend my afternoon visiting each address until I found someone to put me in touch with the passengers in the Mercedes.

A maroon Chrysler 300 with tinted windows and oversized wheels trapped me between the two automobiles as I unlocked my car door. The front passenger window slowly lowered and a familiar face gave me a very hard stare. I was looking at the same gold-toothed man I spoke with when I went to see the Pistol Peetes about their role in what was now an obviously non-existent gang-war.

"What'cha doing here, po-po?" Willie Hawkins asked with an exaggerated grin.

"I'd ask you the same thing if I didn't think you belonged here." I wanted to convey that I remembered his link to the El Caminos.

"You got business with someone in there?" Willie turned this around on me by implying he knew who it was that I came to see. It was time to drop this little charade.

"I wanted to talk with Fernando about a shooting that happened last night the other side of La Place." I was not about to provide any further details. Willie should know exactly who and what I was referring to if he was the one who could put me in touch with my El Camino contact.

"I think I know that guy. I know he'd love to talk at you all about that."

"So, do you know where I can find him?"

"I think he'd rather come find you." The man's golden tooth shone in the late-morning sunlight when he broke into another smile. "You could say there are trust issues."

"Let him know the men that ambushed his boss' Mercedes last night weren't real State Police. Someone bought the cars at auction and dressed them to look like ours. Odds are the men behind last night's attack are behind the other attacks on the cartel. Tell him he's being tracked by his cell phone. That should be worth an audience with his boss."

"What makes you think Fernando's boss was in the Mercedes?" The smile was still on Willie's face. He thought he was toying with me, but I had already memorized the car's license plate number and taken a good look at two of the three other people in the car with him.

"Fernando isn't driving any Mercedes or traveling with near so much firepower. Someone important is in town, and I doubt they are here for Mardi Gras. Just have him call me. You've still got my number, right?"

He reached inside his wallet and produced my business card. He waved it at me and then placed it back in the wallet.

"Don't wait by the phone," Willie laughed and raised his window. I waited to get into my car until I watched the Chrysler sedan turn left at the corner and speed off.

Chapter 45

I kicked myself for not questioning how the El Camino cartel was able to operate on the Brotherhood's turf without there being any problem. New Orleans saw daily gunfights and bloody retaliation shootings over turf no larger than a street corner. The operations at play here were magnitudes larger than that of corner-boys. I should have been figuring out how Willie Hawkins and his military veterans fit into a three-way relationship with the Peetes and El Caminos. It was certain that Ritchie played a very big part in this and now Willie's very clear instructions to stop looking for the kid were beginning to echo and make me wonder what was going on.

I stopped by NOPD Headquarters and had Avery run the plates on the Chrysler. He was no happier to learn of my latest visit to the El Caminos than he was about the first one. The car was registered to a corporation called Brotherhood Enterprises. I was as much bemused as I was surprised to discover Willie and his band of merry men were trying to appear legitimate. I took my DMV information and walked down the hall to see the gang-task force detectives. There were four detectives in the squad room when I stepped through the open door.

"Anyone know a guy in the Baghdad Brotherhood named Willie Hawkins? He's got a big gold incisor." I pointed to the place on my own jaw to show which tooth I meant. "Guy's about six two and weighs maybe two seventy or eighty?"

"Well, if it isn't Detective Holland. We heard you were suspended. Something about not following orders. Not you, right?

We couldn't believe it," Detective Steve Kramer spoke up. The last time we crossed paths was after Councilwoman Delia Adams' brothers tried to frame Lionel Batiste for drug dealing. We had not parted on the best of terms.

"Don't believe everything you hear," I grinned and showed them my newly reinstated badge.

"Whataya got on him?" one of the other detectives tried to bring us back on track so I could ask my questions and leave them to whatever they were doing before I walked into their office.

"I am working on a jigsaw puzzle and keep finding more and more pieces that don't seem to connect. I've been looking for a missing gang banger named Ritchie Franklin and this Hawkins guy keeps trying to wave me off. He seems to be what connects the Pistol Peetes and the Baghdad Brotherhood to the El Camino cartel, so it makes no sense that he doesn't want me to find a missing member of one of those outfits. I also can't figure out what the Baghdad Brotherhood is getting out of letting the Mexicans move dope through their turf to the Pistol Peetes."

"What do you think is going on?" My inquiries pulled Kramer's partner, Troy Frontenac, into the discussion.

"The Brotherhood is the cartel's middle-man with the Peetes. But, why use the Peetes and not someone closer to the Brotherhood's own turf? For that matter, why not just move it themselves?" I came to them for answers, not more questions.

"The Brotherhood won't touch heroin. They saw enough poppies when they did a tour in Afghanistan before shipping out to Iraq. You need to think of another reason that they'd get involved."

"The Brotherhood is getting something else from the Mexicans than heroin." The two detectives looked at each other and laughed.

"You don't really need our help," the former narcotics officer chuckled. "The Brotherhood arranges the meets between Richie's gang and the Mexicans, but they keep their hands out of it. I don't think they are taking a cut from the local kids. The Mexicans are selling them the guns they turn around and resell to the local gangs."

"I heard the Brotherhood is into guns, but I never considered where they got them." I had never even heard of the Baghdad Brotherhood until this case, and I pride myself on being up on such things.

"They run a paintball course out by Shell Beach as a cover. Their real thing is an open-air shooting range where they teach kids how to shoot better with the guns they sell them. Now we get fewer kids wounded, and a lot more kids killed." Frontenac said and went back to reading the file on his desk. "Knock yourself out trying to build a case, though."

"How so?"

"Every single gun we seize that we think will tie back to the Brotherhood is swallowed up by the ATF. They take the guns and tell us to forget about them. We thought they were building a case of their own, but they've made no arrests."

"That's pretty weird," I agreed. I didn't want to interrupt him, but I did want to express my interest.

"We think the ATF screwed up and let some guns get on the market that they are still trying to collect. We are happy with a stack of favors we can call in from them for all the guns we turn over without making any fuss," Frontenac shrugged. It was an odd fashion of turning lemons into lemonade, but it seemed to be working fine for both sides. NOPD could always use a favor now and then and the detectives seemed fine with just getting the guns off the street.

Selling guns is a much easier way to make an illegal living than running a narcotics racket. There is a substantial mark-up on their product and a place as violent as New Orleans steadily turned over their inventory. Taking the time to toss in some skilled product familiarization, and maybe some upselling, meant a gang like the Baghdad Brotherhood probably made at least as much as the Pistol Peetes on a monthly basis with far less risk.

"Well, that's interesting. Any idea why Willie doesn't want me looking for the kid?" This what I really came there to get some help figuring out. The story about the ATF sounded like it might be a tiny piece of my puzzle as well.

"Nope, but I do agree that's pretty weird. Ritchie Hawkins is his nephew." Frontenac had no idea how many pieces of my puzzle this slid into place.

"I don't suppose Ritchie has an aunt named Jasmine," I wondered. It was less of a long shot than it seemed just a few minutes earlier.

"No, but Willie Hawkins used to be married to a chick named Jasmine Flores. That help you, detective?" Kramer and his partner seemed to be having some fun feeding me this information in spoonfuls. It was nothing much to them, but knowing these connections tied things together for me.

It also deepened the mystery of why Willie Hawkins did not want me looking for his nephew. The way the kid's fellow gang members sat through that meeting without raising an objection to his telling me to ignore their friend's disappearance didn't sit right with me either. It occurred to me that I might not know why Willie wanted me to stop looking for Ritchie until I found the kid and asked him myself.

Chapter 46

"**I**s this really the best use of your time?" Avery demanded when he spotted me standing with Katie and Tulip on the Krewe of Cork parade route Friday afternoon. Katie coaxed me into leaving the bistro to watch the krewe do its afternoon march down Bourbon Street. This was a small parade, and one of the few allowed within the French Quarter. Most krewes stage parades with tractor-pulled floats too wide for the Quarter's streets. The two women must have been waiting all year to put on these Mardi Gras outfits involving tutus and high-top sneakers.

"You heard about the shooting up on I-10 a couple of days ago?"

"It sounded like a scene out of a bad movie." Avery stuffed his mouth with the Lucky Dog one of the passing NOPD police officers handed him.

"It wasn't the State Police. Somebody went to a lot of trouble to make it look like we did it, though. They were trying to ambush a caravan driving here from Arizona in the middle of the night." I knew telling him this much was enough for him to fill in the rest. His eyes widened noticeably at the mention of the word Arizona.

"So what are you going to do about it?"

"I'm still waiting on someone to arrange a meet with whoever the El Caminos sent to town in that Mercedes."

Avery snarled around the half-chewed bite of hot dog. "What do you expect to accomplish?"

"At the very least I hope to keep them from retaliating against real State Police troopers. They brought some very serious firepower to town with them. The fake squad cars were taken out with a fifty caliber rifle."

"Oh, that's just great. Do you have any idea what one of those could do out here? They could kill a dozen people with every round." This was only a minor exaggeration of the weapon's capacity to wreak havoc on a parade route.

"What are you two talking about now?" Katie demanded when she realized I was paying more attention to the Chief than to the parade. She and Tulip were amassing impressive collections of plastic necklace throws.

"The weather." I waited for her to turn around before finishing my debriefing with the Chief of Detectives. "I believe the El Caminos brought more than that to town last night. They used a pair of heavily armed vans to escort a late model Mercedes SUV. I think someone high up in the El Caminos is in town to find out what happened to their people and their stash houses. We know they stopped to make a phone call at the tourist center west of Baton Rouge and that a parish deputy tried to stop them outside of Sorrento."

"Why stop to make a call so close to where they were headed?"

"The way Captain Hammond described things, I think the vehicles got separated west of Baton Rouge and regrouped at the pull off. Someone made a telephone call and D-Tech's web caught the metadata. D-Tech was likely monitoring whoever took the call in New Orleans and rolled the cruisers to intercept the convoy." It was all just a theory, but everything fit and Tony and I were able to set up ambushes using D-Tech's phone monitoring in exactly the same way.

"You've got to find that rifle, Cooter." Avery did not need to tell me anything this obvious. He was just talking because what I told him made him nervous.

"I'm working on it."

"Come on, you," Katie walked over and grabbed my arm. She pulled me beside her in the tightly packed throng lining the parade route. It took me a long moment to transition from being a detective to being her boyfriend. I glanced behind us a moment later, but Chief Avery had already left to return to his patrol duties.

Chapter 47

I realized we might not make it to Strada Ammazarre from the parade as we followed the dispersing crowd along Orleans Street. Our path would take us past the courtyard where Tony and I questioned Top Gun. There were a half dozen rough-looking Mexicans following us in the boisterous crowd. I never noticed any of them standing close to us during the parade.

The Mexicans were trying to herd us rather than intercept us. There was only this single block's distance between the parade route on Bourbon Street and the back of the Cathedral at Royal Street. Four additional Mexicans appeared ahead of us in the drunken throng and blocked any chance of turning either direction on Royal Street. The other six kept ten paces behind us. I assumed they were all armed. I was carrying my Glock, but starting a gunfight in this crowd was out of the question.

"Are you carrying your pistol?" I whispered into Katie's ear. Katie's ex-husband bought her a .38 caliber handgun as a present shortly before their divorce, but never taught her to use it. Ill-considered presents like this played a big part in their separation and divorce. I had taken her to the police firing range until we were both satisfied she could use it.

"Of course I am. Why?" Katie's ability to keep her composure when I popped questions like this had improved since our first date.

"We're about to be kidnapped. I'll try to get them to take just me." I pointed out the men blocking Royal Street.

"Why do they want you?" Katie and I managed to keep our

conversation from my sister. It was going to be hard to keep what was about to happen a secret much longer.

"I sent a message asking to meet my contact with the El Camino cartel. I need to convince them that the State Police had nothing to do with the shooting on I-10." Katie knew she did not have time to berate me for having placed any of us in danger. Her expression made her opinion of my habit of placing my head into the mouths of lions clear.

"Take Tulip into the gallery and I'll let them grab me at Pirate's Alley." We were now at the corner and Katie abruptly grabbed my sister's elbow to pull her towards Rodrigues's gallery. I immediately crossed the street and headed towards the slate-paved alleyway leading to Jackson Square. I offered no resistance when the two Mexicans positioned there grabbed either arm and started fast walking me up Royal Street towards Canal Street.

"Easy, mis amigos." I kept pace and did not attempt to pull free or show any other sign of resistance.

The thugs dispatched to round up Tulip and Katie were the ones who encountered resistance. Tulip screamed at the top of her lungs until one of the Mexicans clamped a sweaty palm over her mouth. Even then, she repeatedly bit her assailant's palm. One of the others ripped the phone cord out of the wall when the woman behind the counter tried to dial 911. It took two of the men to subdue Katie, in part because of the self-defense moves I practiced with her. She stomped the first guy's foot and knee with all her might and sent him howling out of the gallery. She fumbled for the pistol in her purse rather than gouge at the face of her second assailant, and he swatted the purse out of her hand before wrapping her in a bear hug and dragging her out of the gallery while his limping partner snatched up her purse.

I spotted a Chevy delivery van with commercial plates idling at the next corner. One of my burly escorts opened the rear door of the vehicle and shoved me inside. His partner did a quick search and relieved me of my pistol and phone. I watched the frustrated Mexicans pulling Katie and Tulip towards the vehicle before someone pulled a black hood over my head and hastily zip-tied my hands. Katie was cooperating, but I could tell how angry she was. Tulip was trying to pull her arm free and would have still been screaming if her abductor removed the hand clamped over her mouth. I was chagrined that they snatched us in broad daylight two blocks from NOPD's French Quarter substation. It was just one more thing about New Orleans, and the case I was working, that reminded me of being in Baghdad.

"You don't need them," I shouted to the unseen men around me.

"I hate to break up a set, Senor Detective." I recognized Fernando's voice. "Let them know they are safe."

I heard the side cargo door open and the sound of someone binding the two women after tossing them inside the now crowded van. I assumed hoods followed the bindings.

"It's going to be okay. Tulip, relax." I doubt my sister found the words I spoke from inside my own black hood very comforting.

"I hate you for this," Katie declared after she accepted the futility of resisting our captors and was sure she was speaking in my direction. "I wouldn't want to die without making that clear."

"I like your women," Fernando laughed. I was able to wiggle around until I could grasp Katie's hand. Tulip eventually stopped hyperventilating.

The drive was surprisingly short. Our captors hauled me from the side door of the van first. My eyes easily adjusted to the light once the hood came off my head because the van driver parked inside an old warehouse. I was less surprised to be looking at Willie Hawkins than he expected me to be. He served as my messenger to the cartel, so it made sense that he would be at this meeting.

I mouthed a request to Fernando to have the men dragging the women from the van keep the black bags over their heads. Leaving the pair literally in the dark seemed like a good idea. Tulip was going to be terrified whether she wore the hood or not. I was more concerned Willie might have previously encountered Katie in her state's attorney role. The henchman that frisked me patted down the women as well. They took both of their purses, but did not look inside either of them. Their failure meant I should be able to reach Katie's automatic, if I could free my hands.

The concrete walls and faintly musky odor gave me an approximate age for the building. It also helped me narrow our location. We were probably in one of the industrial areas still recovering from Katrina's flooding. I did not remember Ray's list of addresses including any warehouses. The short drive time likely placed us at the edge of the Pistol Peete's turf so the warehouse might have been theirs.

"Quick question?" I aimed my query at Willie and not Fernando.

"We have time." Willie's attention focused on the metal door leading further into the building from the loading dock.

"Have you heard anything from your nephew?"

"I told you I know he is safe and to drop it." Willie did not seem surprised I had finally found their connection. We followed Fernando through a doorway and headed deeper into the abandoned warehouse. I took comfort in these two men being part of what was about to happen. They could easily have delivered us to the slaughter and left the scene if killing me, or the three of us, was why they grabbed us.

We walked into the former shipping clerk's windowless office in the middle of the cavernous building. One of Fernando's other tattooed stacks of muscle standing just inside the room pressed each of us onto wooden chairs. Willie positioned himself behind the two women while Fernando's henchmen took up positions outside the office.

"You cost me twenty dollars, Detective." Fernando was laughing about this, so I didn't worry too much about my costing him money. He walked around me and stood a couple of feet away with a tight smile on his face. "Senor Hawkins said you would try to find me after the State police ambushed my men. I believed you were smarter."

"I'll pay the bet if I can talk to your boss."

"What makes you think I am not the boss here?" Fernando acted like my comment hurt his feelings, but he was toying with me.

"Even bosses have a boss. Someone higher up your chain must own the Mercedes that got ambushed."

"You'll pay the bet anyway." Fernando laughed and took all the cash from my wallet. "What do you know about the ambush?"

"It wasn't the State Police that ambushed the Mercedes. I have seen the patrol cars they used and they are not ours. Whoever attacked your boss bought them at an auction and dressed them up."

"Why should I believe you?" Fernando seemed to believe questioning me was important for appearances sake in front of the women and Willie Hawkins.

"Why not believe me? It makes more sense that your boss was lured into a trap than it does that a half dozen highway patrolmen found him purely by chance."

"It *could* have been genuine police officers. They do these things in my country."

"You have my word it wasn't." I did not want to keep arguing with him. I had not come here to speak with Fernando anyway. "Maybe your boss will believe me."

Fernando greeted this comment with a shrug. "Maybe we should find out."

Another door to the office opened and two bodyguards entered the crowded office. There was no mistaking that the man who entered was in charge. He was older than his men were, and his face looked as tough as I imagined his soul to be. My companions would not have found him handsome under other circumstances. His shiny black hair hung loose past his shoulders. He wore a tailored suit on his muscular frame that did nothing to make him look any less fierce. He had a negative presence about him that had nothing to do with his size or appearance.

"This is the one who wants to talk to me?" The man stood in front of me and looked down to study my face. "What makes you think I am not going to kill you?"

"Killing any of us doesn't serve any useful purpose. The State Police didn't ambush you, so killing me won't send them any message. I'm not one of the men who attacked you, so there's no revenge to take. You also don't have to hurt these women to get me to cooperate with you."

"Maybe it would make me happy just to see a gringo die." The way he said this made me suddenly very concerned for our safety. He might well kill us for no reason.

"Wouldn't you be happier killing the gringos who attacked you?"

The man looked at me long and hard. "Do you know those men?"

"Not personally, but I'm pretty sure I can point you in the right direction to find them." I could see Katie out of the corner of my eye and the way she turned her head let me know I was better off not seeing her expression. She might forgive me for getting her into this situation. She would be far less forgiving about my telling this man where to find his enemies so he could kill them. "But first I'd really like to know why you're in town. Fernando has been doing a good job, hasn't he? Your drugs are still getting on the street despite the losses you've taken. I don't see any reason to expose yourself this way."

"I am here on other business." I *really* did not like the sound of that.

He glanced at Fernando. I could not tell if he was concerned that I was acting like I knew everything about his business or if he was looking for an indication of whether or not I could be trusted. I could not see Fernando so I have no idea what signs he gave the man before he continued.

"It seems I must renegotiate a deal your government doesn't wish to honor."

The mystery man sounded aggravated about having to do this. I held my tongue about my government's incapacity to honor most of its agreements once the men who made them left office.

"What deal could you possibly have with my government?" Katie put herself into the conversation in the worst possible way. Her tone was too harsh and the question she asked was far too direct.

"Let's all play nice." I spoke up to bring his attention back towards me. The Mexican stranger was not going to let any woman interrogate him. We were still far from being out of danger. The man could still decide to have the three of us killed. "Maybe introductions are in order. You already know me, but this is my girlfriend Katie and the lady next to her is my sister Tulip."

"I am Stephan. My friends call me El Carnicero."

Having a last name that translated into English as "butcher" strongly suggested Carnicero was not actually the man's real last name. It also suggested to me that very few people who ever met Stephan face to face lived to tell about it. His idea of friends was also undoubtedly different from what I considered my own companions. Most importantly, it told me he was not a leader in the El Camino cartel. His presence in New Orleans could only mean he came to spill blood. I hoped Katie did not blurt out something else that would betray her professional life. It was best that this man view her only as the mouthy woman sharing my bed.

"Could I persuade you to tell me more about the agreement you're renegotiating? It might explain why someone thought it was better to kill you than to agree to whatever new terms you've brought." I tried to relax in the chair. My hands were getting a little numb and my shoulders were stiff. I was slowly losing the strength to snap the plastic zip-ties by flexing my wrists outwards.

"I will tell you about my deal with your government and you will tell me where to find the men who tried to kill me. I can tell you this because there is nothing a police detective can do about the deals made by the men far above him." I become less certain that Carnicero would allow us to leave once he had the information he wanted. Disclosing secrets hardly mattered if we were dead.

"Fair enough." Assuming we were going to survive, having Stephan explain the El Camino cartel's alleged deal to Katie and Tulip was better than my trying to explain it to them later. Alternatively, at least we would know why he had us killed. I was hoping for a quick death when it came.

"The men who began the El Camino cartel saw an opportunity after the terrorists collapsed your World Trade Towers. They told agents from your Homeland Security that they would betray other drug cartels who might smuggle terrorists into your country in the future for a price. In exchange, your Homeland Security Agency agreed to make your DEA return any of our people they arrest in your country to Mexico instead of putting them in prison. They also allow us to buy guns to fight the cartels we warned them about, which we have traded to Senor Hawkins for protecting our people and product in New Orleans. There are no Arab terrorists in Mexico, but your government helped us to become the biggest cartel in Mexico. They let us bring our drugs into your country and to use your DEA to arrest our competition and take away their business."

"So why are you here making a new deal if you already have such a great deal?" Katie asked. I shrugged to try to imply that she was just a nosy girl who posed no threat. Stephan smiled when I stomped on Katie's foot as a non-verbal way to tell her it was best that she stop talking.

"Now your man from Homeland Security says they will only honor our arrangement in Arizona. They will put my men in prison if they catch them anywhere else. This man is also making it hard for us to buy guns. They say they are worried someone will find out about our arrangement."

"Well, anybody that could prove that government agencies tasked with protecting us helped a Mexican drug cartel smuggle drugs into this country and guns into Mexico would certainly have a story to tell. I can also see where having my government backing out of the deal you made could really cramp your business." I said all of this for Tulip's benefit. Verifying this man's story should be a far more palatable thing for her to pursue than looking into probable war crimes by her brother and her new boyfriend.

"I have been sent to explain the consequences if they do not honor the deal we have made." This threat sounded like the end of his story. I could have pressed him for the name of whom he was in town to meet, but he would have either stone walled me or shot me. "Now, tell me where to find the men who attacked me last night."

"I'm very sorry if I made you think I know where those men are." I watched his face for his reaction to my failure to make good on the deal he offered. He disclosed much more than I was going to offer in exchange. I was prepared to trade our lives for those of Jack's men, but only if that was absolutely necessary. I did not want to initiate the very gang war I was still trying to avoid.

"That is not what we agreed to." El Carnicero said. I was not hearing any anger behind his words. Then again, he did not have to waste time on sharing his emotions with people in our precarious position.

"It's what I have at the moment. I promise to find the address you want and give it to Fernando before you conclude your business." I am sure this sounded like an empty promise. "I have a much better idea where to look now that I know why you're here. I am also sure that the men who tried to kill you work for the man you came to New Orleans to meet. Give me a chance to prove this to you."

El Carnicero stared me in the eyes for a long moment. Neither of us blinked, but I made sure to be the one who broke contact once I believed I had convinced him I was not lying or bluffing. He walked past me and stood behind the still-hooded women. He rested a hand firmly on each of their shoulders. I watched the two women silently squirm beneath his touch.

"Perhaps I should hold one of these ladies until you fulfill your promise to me, Senor Detective." He moved his left hand and patted the top of Tulip's head. She let out a surprised yelp in response. He walked back to stand in front of me with a smile on his face. Apparently terrifying women was one of his favorite forms of torment.

"You don't need a pet." My comment did not diminish his Cheshire-cat smile. I doubt many of this man's prisoners bantered with him quite the way I was making an effort. I heard his threat to take a hostage as a sign that we were all going to survive being in his company.

"Perhaps you are right. My men know where to find you if you make it necessary." It is not really a threat when you know the other party looks forward to making good on their promise of dire consequences.

"It won't be."

The cartel's enforcer and his men left the room. Willie pulled the dark bags from Katie and Tulip's heads and proceeded to cut our bindings. He set my badge and pistol next to my wallet on the desktop. Tulip and Katie glanced in their purses to see if anything was missing. Katie opened her purse to let me know her pistol was still available.

"Y'all can drive yourselves back to the Quarter in that van. It's stolen so you don't want to get too attached to it." Hawkins laughed at his own joke. We needed something, anything, to break the tension still hanging in the room. "And the man didn't tell ya' this, but he's not going to be here real long. So, you best find those dudes real quick."

I kept Katie and Tulip in the office with me until Hawkins left. I listened for the sound of his car leaving the building. I took Tulip's hand as we walked out of the office and headed towards the loading dock. I did not know what to tell her and she was quite obviously deep in her own thoughts. Katie was also unusually quiet. I knew I would eventually hear plenty from both of them.

The stolen van belonged to a local bakery. It was how the cartel managed to get a vehicle into the heart of the French Quarter during Mardi Gras. NOPD blocks everything but commercial and resident traffic from the area because of the massively increased foot traffic. I backed the van out of the building and looked around to get my bearings. The loading dock was part of a condiment factory off Earhart Boulevard that flooded during Katrina and never reopened. It was doubtful that it was any part of the Pistol Peetes' or El Camino's operation. Neither of them would use the location again after today.

Chapter 48

The bistro's kitchen was busy preparing for Lionel's pre-election party in our absence. His election night victory party was booked for a storefront preacher's church in his own neighborhood. This party thanked his supporters from Uptown who would not go to the Ninth Ward after dark for any reason. His victory was all but assured after Councilwoman Adams' arrest, but his campaign was still one of the election's focal points. He would be in the national spotlight if voters in the Ninth Ward elected him on Saturday. Tulip should have been ecstatic that the candidate she helped enter the race and helped get through his legal difficulties was about to win. I was responsible for those legal difficulties, but Lionel had forgiven me.

I was not surprised in the least that she was withdrawn and edgy after what she experienced. I was not nearly as calm about our abduction as I seemed. I trained to survive such interrogations, but I recalled being an emotional wreck for weeks after enduring what I knew was a simulation. I worried that dating me was untenable for Katie, but she gave me a brief reaffirming smile as she led Tulip to the elevator.

"What's wrong with Tulip?" Tony tried to hug my sister as she and Katie passed through the kitchen, but she squirmed away without saying a word.

"The three of us were snatched by the El Camino cartel. I asked Willie Hawkins to arrange a meeting and they decided to grab all of us instead of just taking me. I imagine both of them are pretty shaken up."

"You let your sister get kidnapped by those Mexicans?" Tony's tone of voice was one that had not passed between us in a very long time. We moved our conversation into the walk-in cooler for privacy.

"Nobody 'lets' anyone get abducted by a drug cartel. If they decide to take you, you are gone. I wasn't going to start a gunfight to protect Tulip or Katie when I didn't have any reason to believe they meant to harm us. They drove us to a place off Earhart to meet the cartel's enforcer. We were there about an hour and they let us go." My explanation would not have calmed me down any more than it did Tony if I was the one hearing it from him. Even leaving out a few things, like the dark hoods and El Carnicero's particularly evocative nickname, did little to make the meeting sound sociable. I also left out the deal I struck to keep us alive.

"You've grabbed enough people to know the whole point is to scare them. It's going to take a long time for her to get over this." Tony was not going to let me off the hook for endangering the woman he loved since he now viewed her as his girlfriend first and my sister second.

Tony and I went to my apartment to piece together an action plan. I hoped that Katie would invite me to join the conversation in Tony's apartment when she felt I would not just add to Tulip's stress level. I filled a pair of tumblers with good bourbon, let Roux out of his kennel, and sat beside Tony on the bench in my office to see if we could bring what we knew into better focus.

I began to explain what the last few days, especially the last few hours, brought to light. "I realized today that this case began years ago, and well out of my jurisdiction. An overly ambitious bunch of drug smugglers managed to dupe somebody right after 9/11. The cartel used Washington's paranoia about terrorists to strike a deal with the ATF to arm them and the DEA to destroy their rivals."

"How did they do that?"

"They tipped off the DEA about other cartels' smuggling operations and then used their own get-out-of-jail-free card to take over those territories. They managed to pull all of this off because somebody in D.C. had a bigger fear of terrorists sneaking into the country than they did of creating the very real danger the El Caminos now pose. Apparently, Kinkaid is trying to lure the cartel's leadership to New Orleans to either force a new deal or kill whoever they have to in order to cover up the mistake of making the first one."

"I thought your government was a bunch of idiots in Iraq, but I guess they mess up anything they do. Every time your President tries to make your country safer they make it more dangerous." I offered Tony no counter-argument.

"Anyway, Homeland Security must have felt the cartel reneged on their deal when they started expanding beyond Arizona. I think they thought saw a window of opportunity to stop the El Caminos when they set up shop here after the storm. NOPD is understaffed and everything is still a big jumble as new gangs have begun replacing the old gangs. I imagine D-Tech and Jack Rickman thought they'd have an easy time taking out the cartel while everyone was focused on Mardi Gras and the election. The Super Bowl is a just a cherry on their sundae." I was convinced this was true. I remembered Kinkaid grilled Chief Avery and Captain Hammond about NOPD's shortage of officers and about the State Police pulling their patrolmen out of New Orleans when he staged that lunch meeting. I also remembered the local head of the FBI claiming someone meant to distract Avery by forcing him to defend his department's investigations into nearly a dozen police-involved shootings after Katrina. He admitted his agency's investigation was mostly about distracting NOPD. I was beginning to wonder how long this attack on the cartel had been building.

"And they had the perfect plan to do this." Tony's anger was beginning to surface. He'd come to love his adopted city as much as he did the village in Sicily where he'd grown up, and he felt no less of an obligation to protect New Orleans than he'd felt about defending his father's country.

"Just be glad ours is the plan they're using. We know how it works and know where to throw wrenches to grind it to a halt." Tony gave me one of the looks he adopts when my analogies become too oblique. "We know how to stop Operation Stoplight."

Tony nodded and tucked the phrase away to study later. "It will be dirty."

"Messy. I don't think Avery or Hammond care about that now."

"Then what do we need to do?" Tony was finished with his drink. I barely touched mine because I did so much of the talking.

"We have to disrupt their communications before we can do anything else. That means we have to find a way to shut down D-Tech, but I'm sure they've increased security around those trailers."

"And then what?"

"Then we need to find a place where Jack and his men and the cartel can kill one another off. Jack began trying to convince the cartel that either NOPD or the State Police were behind the attacks on their operation after the cartel stopped buying the idea that the Pistol Peetes were double-crossing them. He knows where this puts me, and that may have as much to do with his new plan as anything else. I think the cartel's man accepts the cops aren't the bad guys. He expects me to help him get his hands on Jack so he can kill the men responsible for making him drive this far."

"It's okay with me if you give him Jack." Tony grinned. It was fine with both of us, but I needed to be sure doing so was enough to satisfy all of the Mexican's taste for revenge.

"I need to get rid of the cartel, too. That is going to be the hard part. They have an army of their own, and two local gangs, to use against the two of us."

"What's that thing you used to tell me? We just need to turn the dogs on each other?" Tony was getting better about using the slang and phrases I tormented him with in Iraq, when his English was not much better than my Italian is.

We stopped talking when we heard the apartment door open. I put a hand on my pistol and stood up to approach the office doorway. Tony backed against the wall behind the door. I did not remember whether I locked the front door when I came home or not, but the only other person with a reason to be in my apartment was Katie.

"I thought I'd find you in here," Katie said when she spotted my head poking out of the office doorway. Luckily, she did not also see me slide my pistol back into its holster or Tony step from behind the door he was ready to slam on anyone coming into the office without permission. Katie entered the office before she realized I was not alone.

"Does any of this make sense to you?" she asked Tony.

"I leave that to the police." Tony used the break Katie's laughter provided to leave. Lionel's party would start in a few hours and there was still a lot of work needing done.

"It's never going to be reasonable to any of us, but at least I think I finally understand what's going on. My old boss is here to force the cartel to head back to Arizona and to cover up the agreement someone made with the El Caminos before Homeland Security was created to handle the threat of more terrorist attacks. Kinkaid and Jack contrived a way to hide their dirty work behind the rescue of a city the Feds left to die after Katrina. I believe

Kinkaid thinks he's going to come out of this as some sort of a hero."

"Like any of that is ever going to happen." Katie had far less understanding of the dynamics and specifics at play than I did, but she still came up with the same conclusion. "He's just going to piss the off the Mexicans. They have no incentive to negotiate a lousier deal."

"They would not have sent Stephan if they were happy."

Katie took a drink from my glass and let the dark amber-colored liquor trickle down her throat. There was no ice to chill the sensation of the alcohol warming her from the inside out. Katie was embarrassed by her facial expressions, but not so much that she did not take another drink.

"You should be glad that your sister's Spanish is rusty. She doesn't realize Stephan's last name isn't a name." Katie said this without a trace of humor. "Things are going to get very bad now, aren't they?"

"Nobody sends a guy named The Butcher on an errand to make peace. Things are going to get very bloody, and will do so very soon. I think the cartel plans to expose their deal with Homeland Security in sixty-foot tall letters written in blood. That's their negotiating style."

"Can you stop them?" Katie claimed my glass as her own. She took another drink and grimaced a bit. Her taste buds will always prefer wine.

"I need to stop both sides. I think Tony and I can do it, but it won't be easy and how we do it probably won't be any more legal than what they've been doing to each other." She did not say a word about my including the chef in my plans. I was being as honest with her as possible because now was the moment she would give up on me if she ever would.

"I guess nobody's one of the Good Guys anymore." She set the glass down and grabbed my face in her hands to kiss me. There were tears in her eyes when we broke the kiss but she stayed with me.

Chapter 49

Tulip appeared in the dining room just before nine o'clock, wearing a simple cocktail dress, a colorful necklace, and a stylish up-do courtesy of Katie. Katie stood beside her in one of her work outfits. It wasn't nearly as formal as she might have liked, but we did not have time to go to her house for anything nicer. Tulip must have taken a turn at hairdressing as well because Katie's long, brown hair was French-braided from her neck down. I wore the tailored jacket and slacks I keep in my closet for formal occasions.

My sister started a little each time someone bumped or spoke to her from behind, which happened far too often in the crowded environment of Lionel's celebration. I whispered to Katie that they should take seats at one of the tables along the walls. Joaquin had tables removed from the dining room to create an open space for dancing. Sitting at a table also meant servers kept their champagne glasses full and hors d'ouvre at their fingertips.

Tony stayed busy supervising his cooks in the kitchen. He put one of the senior cooks in charge about ten o'clock and joined Tulip at the table. This allowed Katie to come find me at the bar.

"How's she doing?" I asked as Katie snuggled against me. I gradually moved through the crowd to take my usual position between the front doors and the end of the bar. It allowed me to monitor traffic through the front door as well as anything happening at the bar or the dining room. I kept a clear line of sight to the hostess stand and monitored the house phone in case Tony needed me in the kitchen. This position also affords me a good view through the front windows to the sidewalk and the street, with an unobstructed view all the way to the French Market.

""I think she'll be better in the next day or two, if you don't give her any more reasons to fear for her life." Katie was back to babysitting Tulip.

"And how are you doing?"

"I keep telling myself it was a good experience to have. The next time one of my cases involves an abduction I'll be better about handling the victim." I could not tell if this was her way of compartmentalizing her own emotions or if she could process things with my own capacity for detachment. "I also think it's time you teach me how to live with shooting somebody."

"I hope you never have to do that." I gave her a peck on the side of her forehead and she squeezed my arm.

Hannah, the evening's bartender, leaned over the bar in her platform-soled black leather thigh boots to give Katie a fresh glass of chardonnay and to replace my Manhattan. She pulled the cherry from the cocktail and set it next to the four others on the bar. She winked at me to let me know my liquor service was now suspended.

I was not nearly as drunk as I should have been. I finally realized I was also still reeling from our run-in with El Carnicero. Stephan turned us loose, but on very short leashes. I needed to find a way to threaten the Mexican in a way that would make him forget all about carrying out his threats against us. The man was very obviously capable of being incredibly single-minded, but I was drawing a blank on ideas.

Negotiation held the key. He was sent to New Orleans to speak with a representative of my government about an ill-considered deal made in the aftermath of an unconscionable act of terror. There were plenty of deals made with devils around the globe in the aftermath of 9/11. People who felt they failed to protect us believed it was necessary to do whatever it took to keep the country from suffering such an attack ever again. I was one of them. I protected CIA agents sent into Afghanistan's mountainous border region to buy the loyalty of warlords. I helped abduct people suspected of little more than knowing the name of a person who might know the name of a person that played a small role in the attack on the towers on 9/11, using tactics I experienced first-hand earlier that day. I tracked down men with our blood on their hands and made sure the last thing their eyes saw was their own blood on mine. Even so, I never made any long-term bargains with devils like the El Caminos.

I needed to find whom it was that El Carnicero came to town to meet, and where they were meeting. I would then have to figure out a means of cancelling the deal from both ends, and of containing the consequences that would come in the wake of my having done so.

Lionel's party provided a distraction from the very ugly thoughts running non-stop through my head. The guest of honor arrived just after ten thirty, with his mother and his aunt, Miss J. The women both gave Katie and me big hugs before trailing behind their pride and joy as he made his way through the room. Someone took Lionel to a good tailor and had him dressed to look like the prominent minority politician he was about to become. It was strange to see him in anything but a t-shirt, baggy-assed jeans, and sneakers. He did not seem entirely at ease with his changed circumstances, but he had very nearly perfected a good politician's ability to fake it.

Lionel worked the room, shaking every extended hand and stopping to thank anyone who had written a check or given their time to help put him in a seat on the City Council. It was a challenging district, but also the place he called home. He lived in a house the Make It Right Foundation built on the lot where his family's home stood until the walls to the Industrial Canal gave way and surging water washed away that house and the lives of five family members. Now the low-income neighborhood was finally coming back, but in large part because of gentrification by people like Alex Boudreaux. What was once a tight-knit Black community was now a neighborhood in racial and financial transition. Lionel was going to have his hands full satisfying both the established families and brand new upscale residents with very different ideas about that part of town's future.

I turned to look at the second entourage coming through the front doors. This one had no business there with anyone but me. This was a very private party and one where Deputy Director Kinkaid was going to stand out more than usual. I was one of a dozen white faces in the crowd. The handful of others played much more positive roles in the election of Lionel than my arresting him had.

"May I see your invitation?" It was only marginally a joke to ask Kinkaid for his invitation to such an event.

"Where can we go to talk?" Kinkaid was not here to mingle or to make small talk. He traveled halfway across the country to deliver a message he already suspected I would ignore. I remembered now that Chief Avery said something about Kinkaid wanting to see me, but I had no appointment with the Deputy Director and received no prior call from his office verifying Avery's heads up. Now here he was, complete with his security detail in their dark suits that barely concealed their side arms. I could tell they were beginning to draw unwanted attention.

"We can use the same room we used the last time we met." I wanted to spirit him as far away from Lionel and the media here to see the candidate, as possible. I lead the Deputy Director and his minions to the small dining room on the mezzanine.

I took a seat on the far side of the table, facing the doorway that Kinkaid and his four-man security team came through close on my heels. Two of the men positioned themselves at the top of the stairway and the other pair stood to either side of the doors they closed behind their boss. Kinkaid sat in a chair that allowed him to face me directly, and went through an elaborate process of straightening his jacket and checking his cellphone before addressing me. I was supposed to grow nervous, but I was done being nervous about things I could not control. I could barely control my emotions and my patience.

"You have intentionally ignored the agreement you signed. You have continued to pursue details about the operation you are not cleared to know. You have endangered the lives of members of the operational teams. You have hindered their efforts, and you have made direct contact with people the operation views as targets. Now I hear that the cartel has even threatened your own family." Kinkaid overplayed his hand with this last comment. He only had two ways to know about my meeting with El Carnicero and my telling him was not how he knew this. The fool also betrayed that angering him loosened his tongue.

"You're right. I have conducted an independent investigation into the nature of your operation. I believe I now have a clear understanding of the purpose of the operation, and the idiotic agreement that precipitated its necessity." I expected at least a minimal defense against my description of the deal that gave ascendency to the El Camino cartel.

"Why have you done so?"

I leaned well across the table to invade his comfort zone.

"Because I live here. D-Tech's operation has threatened to

place this city at considerable risk for loss of innocent life and property. Attacking the cartel woke a bear you thought you could catch napping. Sir."

Kinkaid studied me from across the table. We were sizing one another up like a pair of high-stakes poker players. He said nothing for a long moment, but I could see his lips quivering as he mumbled a number of unpleasant things to himself that he wanted to say to me.

"Would you care to explain that statement?"

"You wanted to draw the cartel to the negotiating table by shutting down their expansion efforts. Instead, the El Camino cartel sent a small army to New Orleans to find the people responsible for the damage done to their operation. They will not care who those people work for when they find them. The cartel only has one way of handling anything it perceives as an attack and it doesn't involve negotiating." I was assuming a lot, but the way Kinkaid's agitation grew convinced me I was right to believe he approved the full breadth of D-Tech's activities. I abruptly understood that this meeting was not the main reason the Deputy Director came to town. I saw no reason to advise him that the cartel's "Butcher" was not the negotiator Deputy Director Kinkaid expected the cartel to send. "The cartel has no intention of giving up whatever deal you two cooked up and your fake gang war idea created a situation you can only escape by plowing straight ahead at full steam. I cannot let you do that. No, I will not let you."

"You're not going to let me? What are you going to do about it?" Kinkaid was on his feet and seemed prepared to throw a chair at me.

"I promise it will not involve breaking the agreement I signed nor using the press or any other cops to clean up your mess. Honestly, I do not care whether your operation succeeds or fails. My only concern is that my city doesn't get destroyed."

"Well, let's not waste any more time." Kinkaid set his fists on the far side of the table and leaned nearly halfway across the table to explain his final position. "I am going to destroy the El Camino cartel and anyone else that gets in my way. I will not take the time to worry about what you might try to do. Everyone you know or love is going to wind up victims of that crazy cartel unless I take them down. Maybe that's what it's going to take to get your bosses on my side about the situation here."

"I had no idea you even cared what they thought. I'd worry a lot more about your problems if I hadn't just spoken with the cartel's negotiator." I tossed this into the conversation just to

"He probably threatened to kill you. I'll kill you myself if you give him the name of one person I have in town or tell him where D-Tech has their operation. I'm the only one who can pull you off the thin ice you have been skating on."

"You'll have to come out on that ice to stop me." I was beginning to wonder if my unconscious plan was to give the Deputy Director a massive heart attack. Kinkaid certainly looked like he was about to have one. He pulled himself erect and almost visibly swallowed the words that came to his mind in response to my scorn. The two men standing behind him opened the door to the dining room and formed the rear guard as Kinkaid began storming down the stairs.

Kinkaid paused halfway down the stairs. He turned around and jabbed a finger in my general direction. "I'll be here Monday and will expect to hear you say you're back on board."

"See you then, Sir." I remained standing at the head of the stairs until Kinkaid left the building. At least he gave me a more specific deadline to work with than El Carnicero did.

Tulip and Katie were standing beside the hostess stand at the foot of the stairs with Tony as Kinkaid stormed out of the bistro. They pretended to be deep in conversation with Joaquin, but their attention was entirely on Kinkaid and me as we came down the cypress staircase.

"What was that all about?" Tulip finally broke the silence after Kinkaid's party sucked nearly all the air in the building after them.

"Just the latest guy to threaten my life today."

"And what are you going to do when he comes back on Monday?"

"Hopefully one of us will be out of a job by then." I was smiling triumphantly, but my brain was busy processing what just transpired. Kinkaid wasted a lot of bluster while inadvertently letting a few things slip. His tirade left me troubled by his precise knowledge of my activities. Someone within the very small circle of people I knew was feeding him information I knew D-Tech did not have.

The possibility that Chief Avery or Captain Hammond chose to protect their jobs at my expense made too much sense. Bureaucrats make saving their jobs their primary task. I discounted this possibility because both of them were consciously distancing themselves from the dirty work they each asked me to do. I eliminated my sister and Tony out of hand. Tony was too loyal and Tulip believes I am far smarter than the people I choose to fight. Katie demanded full disclosure, but she was used to keeping secrets as a prosecutor. I kept the things I suspected she would report from her as best I could, but I did not believe she would betray me to the likes of Kinkaid

The Deputy Director's comments about El Carnicero threatening my life pointed to someone in the ranks of the criminal company I kept. Fernando knew the fate of those who turned against the cartel and The Butcher's arrival certainly reinforced that understanding. The Pistol Peetes were leaderless, but devoted to one another and my contact with them was minimal. The process of elimination left me with Willie Hawkins. His comments about knowing his nephew was safe while he was still looking for him gave me a clue. Ritchie was the perfect hostage to hold if Kinkaid wanted Willie's cooperation and Willie was privy to every tidbit Kinkaid just let slip. I wasn't going to discuss this with Katie, because I would have to admit it was how I would have handled Willie if I were in Kinkaid's shoes.

Chapter 50

Katie and I decided to take a break from the party to give Roux his evening walk. The French Quarter was packed and noisy. There were a number of celebrations going on, but mostly there was a collective inability to sleep and need for drunken comradeship as the clock ticked down towards the election and the Super Bowl. We sidestepped the crowds at Molly's and Coop's Place that spilled onto the sidewalk. Most of the drunken revelers already considered the Saints victorious just for being in the game. I wondered how many of these Saints fans would sleep through the polls opening the next morning. Their new politicians would be with them longer than any Super Bowl hangover.

"It looks like the entire city is out tonight," Katie laughed as we negotiated a path to avoid being splashed by anyone's drink.

Our path took us along Decatur Street to Jackson Square. Roux had a fan club among the tarot card readers and sketch artists making their living off Café du Monde's nighttime business. Roux also proved to be an icebreaker with the homeless population camped out in front of Saint Louis Cathedral every night. A couple of shaggy Vietnam veterans sleeping here were the ones to tip me off when Beignet and Top Gun began following me. I had not given a moment's thought to anyone following us on this evening's outing. I began to set aside enough of my distractions to pay more attention to the people and shadows around us. I had attracted enough enemies to worry about someone stepping out of a doorway and putting bullets in the back of both of our heads.

"I think we all need to take a vacation when this is over with," Katie suggested as we turned down Chartres Street and headed for home. "Your sister is a wreck, what with the FBI investigation and getting kidnapped today. She and Tony are still working through his story, and I am not fully comfortable with what I learned about you, either. I know what's going on has brought up some things you hoped were over and done with."

"A vacation sounds like a good idea. Any suggestions?" My neck began to swivel as I began to pay more attention to our course than to what Katie was saying.

"Maybe some place with a nice quiet civil war or a revolution." It took me longer than it should have to realize she was joking. "It would be nice to go someplace you felt more at home."

"Thank you for sticking by me," I sighed. I stopped and took her in my arms to kiss her. I wound up with one arm around her and having the other tugged by Roux. "I love you."

"I love you, too, but have to tell you it's harder to do than it was with Ray. He only imagined he's as tough as you, and you tend to forget that none of us are bulletproof."

"I don't go out of my way to get into these situations."

"Yes, you do." Katie slipped her arm in mine again and tugged me forward. I noticed she held my left arm, the same one that held Roux's leash. This placed her closer to the curb and away from the inset and darkened doorways we passed. She left my right hand free to reach the pistol tucked into my waistband. I wondered if Katie actually taught herself to do this, or if she were mimicking my mannerisms.

We walked past our normal turning point and now approached the bistro's parking garage. We would have walked another block and a half and turned on Esplanade if Roux had not sat down next to a black SUV illegally parked too close to the entrance to our garage. City code requires leaving twenty feet between a vehicle and a driveway. The front fender of the SUV passed that by several feet.

It was not the rude distance the driver left bothered me. Tony and I neither one planned to go anywhere the rest of the evening. The SUV would be gone by the time either of us ever ran an errand and needed to park again. What sent a shiver up my spine was that Roux sat down next to the rear tire and looked back at me. I gave a firm tug on his leash, but he refused to budge.

I patted Roux on his head and tugged his leash to have him

follow me around the vehicle. It was a black Humvee H-2 with tinted windows, identical to Richie's except for its color. The doors were locked, which I expected. It was also riding a little low on its rear shocks, as though there were a heavy load inside. I looked around to see if there were any occupied vehicles or people hanging about in the next block. It was hard to tell if anyone standing that far away was showing any interest in the H-2, but I did not see anyone sitting in a vehicle. I took it as a good sign that there was nobody waiting for me to approach the vehicle to detonate a car bomb, and a bad sign that my first thought when Roux sat down was that there was one. I pressed my left hand to the engine hood and felt its warmth. I looked through the tinted windows and did my best to see inside the cargo area. A cheap blue tarp covered whatever was there.

I took a quarter from my pants pocket and used the serrated edge to scratch at the paint on the cargo door. The paint peeled away with little effort. It exposed the factory paint job, in a glossy shade of white. I called the State Police headquarters in Metarie and asked a trooper to run the license plate. It came back as belonging on a Buick owned by a couple living in Terrytown. I tugged Roux to make him follow Katie and me away from the car. I led them on to the next corner while my finger hovered over the keys to my phone. I was trying to decide between playing it safe and calling NOPD's bomb squad, and being my usual self and trying to handle the situation without creating a different set of problems. Either decision meant raising questions I hated to answer. I could not involve NOPD in a situation lacking an easy or reasonable explanation. I sighed and decided to see if Tony minded brushing up on some old skills.

"Is there something wrong?" Katie asked as I walked her towards the restaurant at a considerably faster pace than we were previously walking.

"Nah. I just need to get that car towed."

"I thought Roux found a bomb or something." She sounded a little too serious. She definitely witnessed Roux's strange reaction to the SUV.

"Wouldn't that just make our day?" I forced a chuckle.

She and I re-entered the restaurant through the same side door we'd left. It was the delivery door to the kitchen and provided a path to the elevator without passing through the crowded dining room. I sent Katie to sit with Tulip and Tony while I took Roux upstairs and locked him in his kennel with double treats. Good dog. I then took the elevator downstairs and went to Tony's office. I pulled a battered red plastic toolbox from underneath Tony's desk and set it on his worktable before I rejoined my friends at our table.

The brick building that houses our restaurant and apartments stands three stories tall and vibrates when a transit bus passes by. The close confines of the corner where the driver left the suspected car bomb would amplify the force of an explosion. The concussion would be undeterred by the roll-down aluminum door on our garage. The blast would also probably detonate the fuel in the half dozen cars parked in the garage as well. The back wall of the garage was the opposite side of the back wall to our presently crowded restaurant. Even a moderate explosion would level every building in a fifty-yard radius and irrevocably damage any in the next fifty yards, as well, or more. Everyone in Strada Ammazarre was doomed. Suddenly calling our bistro "road kill" in Italian lost its irony.

"Can I see you for a moment?" I asked Tony in as casual of a voice as I could. Katie glanced at me before she turned her attention to Tulip.

"Sure."

Tony stood up and silently followed me to the kitchen. I hoped Katie believed I wanted to discuss something about the restaurant or that we were headed to my apartment to talk about something related to my case. I was steering the chef into the kitchen so we could slip out the delivery door.

"There's a car bomb parked outside our garage." I told Tony and picked up the plastic toolbox from the worktable.

"When was the last time either of us defused a car bomb?" Tony asked and grabbed my arm to stop me as I started walking towards the door.

"Ask me that tomorrow, if we're still alive, and you'll like the answer a whole lot more." I forced a grin and my partner followed me out the side door and into the darkness blanketing our corner of the world.

Chapter 51

The Hummer was parked exactly where it was when I pulled Roux and Katie away from the scene. They were no safer now as Tony and I appraised the situation. We both looked in each direction to see if anyone was sitting in a car waiting for a signal to detonate the bomb. There were people in cars, but everyone seemed intent on doing something other than blowing us to pieces. There were also no pedestrians hovering nearby, but nobody would place themselves within a mile or more of the SUV if they knew what was in it.

"I'm thinking in terms of a timer or a remote detonator. The men who parked this plan to blow up Strada, so they're probably only watching the front." It was a guess on my part, but one based on personal experience.

"Booby traps?"

"Maybe, but probably not. We wouldn't even know about this if I hadn't taken Roux for a walk and come back a different way than usual."

"I'm still worried about opening the door." I trusted his instincts.

We retreated to the same corner we came around to get to the H-2. We both crossed ourselves and said a quick prayer before I did what might have been the last stupid thing in my life. I leaned around the corner and fired two rounds through the passenger side window of the SUV's cargo area. The glass shattered, but the bomb did not detonate. That was the best result possible.

"How long before NOPD shows up?" Tony asked as we sprinted

towards the Hummer. We pulled the remaining broken safety glass from the rear window and dropped it on the sidewalk. I opened the passenger doors and used the remote hatch release to open the cargo door. This would nominally dissipate the blast if we did anything wrong.

"Tomorrow morning." I grinned despite the tension I felt. Gunshots are nothing new in the dead of night. Shooting one's pistol or shotgun was a traditional way for the city to express the joy in the air around us. I was much more concerned about a routine patrol happening upon us.

Tony grabbed the rear corners of the blue nylon tarp lying atop whatever was weighing down the rear of the vehicle and snapped it upwards before giving it a hard jerk to pull it out of the vehicle as though he were performing a magician's trick with a tablecloth. The bomb builder probably did not expect anyone to discover his handiwork so we worried less about booby-traps than we probably ought to have and began taking other chances we knew better than to risk. There was little comfort in knowing that neither we, nor several hundred of our guests, would know if we made a wrong decision trying to defuse the bomb.

It was a basic explosive device. That is not to say it was amateurish, just that anyone with internet access and the materials could build this device. We found pipe bombs duct-taped to a dozen propane tanks surrounded by five-gallon metal fuel cans. I gingerly opened each jerry can and verified they contained a mixture of diesel fuel and ammonium nitrate. A cell phone taped to the top of one can connected it to the detonator wires snaking from it like thin fingers of death. I shone my flashlight at the phone and breathed a sigh of relief that we were apparently confronting a remote detonator. This meant we had until the phone rang to defuse the bomb. A timer would have meant nobody could detonate the bomb while we were trying to defuse it, but also meant we would have only the time left on the timer to disarm it. There was no way to tell how long the bomb sat there before I spotted it. The warmth of the engine indicated someone parked it within minutes of Kinkaid's angry departure from the bistro. So much for his deadlines.

Tony and I took a few minutes to shine our lights over the entire surface and see if a second detonator was tucked anywhere. I gingerly reached into the cargo area and pulled the phone towards us. Tony took the phone and studied the wiring to isolate the detonator's link between the phone and the pipe bombs. It took him only a moment to use his wire cutters to break that connection and defuse the bomb.

"I've still got the touch." Tony said, mostly to himself. I took the phone from him while he studied the bomb's construction. The way he frowned at what he saw made me glad the phone in my hand never rang.

The phone was a flip phone that was probably five or six years old. The SIM card was unlikely to trace to any useful source and was archaic enough that random sources of electronic emissions, such as answering another phone, might cause enough interference to set the bomb off by accident. I assumed the bomb's construction resembled that of a specific bomb maker. The El Caminos use explosive devices to kill their enemies, or to make a point. Duplicating their handiwork was an obvious way to shift the blame.

I had a fleeting moment of concern that this actually was the handiwork of El Carnicero. I would not have been the first person he ever lied to before he killed them. I still wanted to believe he was going to murder me face-to-face. He also did not come to New Orleans to make things worse for his bosses. Whoever shouldered the blame for the bomb faced targeting by every law enforcement and intelligence agency from NOPD to the CIA. Nobody would question the conclusion by Deputy Director Kinkaid that the El Caminos detonated the bomb. Kinkaid's active oversight of any investigation into this bomb's damage meant Homeland Security would reach any conclusion he wanted.

"Now what?" Tony was looking at me.

We needed to do something with the bomb, or at least find a place to put the Hummer. It would have been smartest to call Parking Control and have it towed away. The odds were about even whether anyone in the tow lot would look inside and understand what it was they saw. The Hummer destroying the impound lot might complicate Kinkaid's attempt to implicate a Mexican drug cartel in the bombing.

"Let's put it in the garage and figure that out later. Right now we deserve a drink." I walked to the keypad on the brick wall beside the garage door and punched in the code to raise the metal door.

The keys were still in the ignition, but neither of us was prepared to test the limits to our luck twice in one night. I turned the key only far enough to loosen the steering wheel. I put the vehicle into neutral and Tony helped me push it into our garage before we lowered the overhead door and walked briskly back to the restaurant.

The Deputy Director's confidence that the cartel would kill everyone I loved suddenly boiled up out of my memory. Everyone in the restaurant would have died had Roger not trained Roux to sniff for explosives, or if I refused to adopt him, or Katie and I waited until later to walk the dog. None of us would have felt much of anything, but I was alive now and felt a level of rage I once hoped to never to feel again.

Tony and I returned to the restaurant the same way we left. Our dates expressed displeasure that we were gone so long, but neither of them asked us why. I saw no reason to tell Katie how close she'd come to dying twice in one day. I carried the flip phone in my jacket pocket and planned to examine it closer in the morning. Katrina noted our return and sent one of the servers to deliver a glass of red wine to Tony and a fresh Manhattan on the rocks, made with single-barrel bourbon, to me. She had a good bartender's exquisite instincts about her boss' moods.

I was finally able to relax a little and enjoy Lionel Batiste's party. His guest list included a couple of dozen important African-American businessmen, former City Council members he'd been counseled by as his campaign progressed, and dozens of city officials he would have to deal with during his first term on the Council. Chief Avery announced the incumbent mayor's arrival as he entered the party flanked by a pair of state legislators trailed by a municipal judge and all of their wives. Lionel Batiste's star was definitely on the rise if he won as everyone expected.

I nearly jumped to my feet when I felt the flip-phone begin to ring. Tony and I looked to one another in initial panic and then began to laugh a little uneasily. I reached into my pocket and took out the phone. I flipped it open and put it to my ear. There was no voice at the other end, but I could hear a boat's horn in the background.

"Boom," I whispered before disconnecting the call.

Katie and Tulip nonverbally questioned my one word response, but I was leaving my chair by the time either could ask what was going on. I made my way through the crowd to the front door and stepped outside in time to look in the distance and see an oil tanker making its way down the Mississippi River. A boat heading north, towards Baton Rouge, approached the Canal Street Ferry and sounded its horn. It sounded a lot like the one I heard over the phone.

I considered running back to the garage and setting an ambush. Someone would need to find out why the bomb failed to detonate and killed us all. It might have been fun to see the look on the scout's face when they found the Hummer was gone. Someone from D-Tech or Jack's operation would now be up all night listening to a police scanner for any report of a mysterious explosion involving a stolen car.

Chapter 52

It was nearly two o'clock in the morning by the time the gathering downstairs wound down and the guest of honor took a limousine home to the Lower Ninth Ward with his mother and aunt. There was probably a reception still waiting for his arrival there.

Katie asked me if I planned to leave when she noticed Roux was loose to wander about my apartment. I failed to realize I had developed this tell. I must have begun thinking of the pit-bull as a worthy substitute should anything happen to me.

"What's going on?" Katie prodded.

"What do you mean? We're going to bed." I was still undressing.

"I'm going to sleep, but you're going to go out and do something." She sat up and pulled her pillow behind her back. I sat down next to her on the bed.

"Not until you're asleep." I could tell from her expression that this was not an adequate response.

"Can it wait until tomorrow?"

"You heard the Deputy Director. I'm on a pretty short timetable to stop him." I sat up to look her in the eye.

"What can you do at three or four in the morning?"

"Things I can't do as easily at three or four in the afternoon. Do you really want to get into this?" I said this far more harshly than I ever meant to speak to Katie. "I need to do things you shouldn't know about. It's hard being your knight in shining armor and also do what needs to be done."

"Oh, I'm past thinking of you riding in on a white horse. I just don't want your sister to spend another month waiting for you to come out of a coma. I don't want to ever go through that, either." At least I finally understood what her main concern was when she saw me with a gun in my hand. My role in Operation Stoplight came to an abrupt end when Tony rushed me to a hospital with multiple gunshot wounds and skull fractures from the stock of an AK-47. Months of surgeries and painful physical rehabilitation rebuilt my physical appearance and agility, but now I live in a state of near-paranoia about ever losing another fight.

"I've got this. Tony's coming with me and we should only be gone an hour or so." Katie's face tightened at the mention of Tony.

"You doing anything with Tony at his hour is not going to help me rest any easier." Katie pulled me close and we kissed. She gently pushed me away and waved me off the bed. "Go, then. Go do whatever it is you think you have to do."

I opened my closet and dressed in jeans and a long-sleeved thermal pullover. I laced on running shoes instead of boots because I anticipated doing far more running than walking once things began. Katie watched me clip my Glock and spare ammo clips onto my belt before laying her head on her pillow in silence as I left the room.

I went to my office and loaded my Kriss bull-pup carbine into a canvas bag with multiple clips of .45 caliber ammunition. I added my Kevlar vest with its ceramic chest plate in place, a half dozen flash-bang grenades and a set of walkie-talkies. I paused for only a moment before I reached into the cabinet and added the Navy medic's kit. Roux watched me from the office doorway the entire time. I scratched the top of his head and he turned and headed into the bedroom. I thought I heard him climbing onto the bed.

Tony was waiting in the kitchen when I stepped off the elevator. He was also dressed in comfortable street clothes rather than like an Italian ninja. Joaquin and two porters were still tidying the dining room when we passed through. They looked up, saw the look of fierce determination on our faces and the heavy bags over our shoulders, and quietly went back to their cleaning duties.

I pressed in the code to activate the roll-up metal door on the garage while Tony scanned the neighborhood. It seemed reasonable to think someone lurked in the shadows to see if the missing SUV ever showed up. We hastily ducked under the rising door and lowered it before it reached waist height. It would have been awkward for an NOPD patrol to happen upon the two of us building a bomb in our garage.

"Tell me your plan again," Tony asked. All I'd told him when we left the party was that I knew how to get the dogs to fight one another as we'd discussed in my apartment earlier in the day.

"We'll torch D-Tech's Suburbans to pin down Jack's men and then use the bomb he gave us to blow the crap out of D-Tech. It should disrupt whatever it is that they have planned long enough for me to only have to focus on the El Caminos for a day or two." This was one of those plans whose best chance of success was when it was still nothing more than scribbles on a bar napkin. Its risks and consequences were almost entirely unknown because we lacked anything in the way of surveillance or practice.

Only a handful of especially skilled people searching our garage would give the range of things we keep in the cabinets very much thought, even though at close examination it would become apparent that most have little to no use in automobile maintenance. I softened blocks of paraffin from the cabinet in a metal canister I then filled with diesel fuel. I took four empty Heineken bottles from a cardboard carrier near the trash and filled them with gelatinous sludge from the metal can. Tony drilled holes in the top of four plastic champagne corks that were just large enough to accommodate fuses made from firework sparklers. I twisted the corks tightly into the top of the nearly full beer bottles and set the four newly made Molotov cocktails back into the cardboard holder. Tony set it on the passenger-side floorboards.

Police officers catching us with firebombs was the least of my worries. I was going to be the one driving a stolen vehicle while holding an automatic weapon and transporting a massive bomb. My main concern was that the Molotov bottles might tip over since that would be bad for my plan.

Tony removed the SIM card from the bomb's cellphone so nobody could call it. He programmed the phone's timer to serve as a detonator and located the wire necessary to re-arm the bomb. I taped the detonator to the center console. I needed to be able to reach it from the driver's seat as I left the vehicle. It was unlikely the bomb would trigger itself by accident. Then again, there were enough things to go wrong in my plan that I saw no reason to tempt fate.

"Why don't you follow me in the truck," I suggested as he

picked through the canvas bag for his share of the flash-bang grenades. Our Raptor pickup truck was a big target, but it moved very fast. My Cadillacs were too conspicuous.

"You're paying for any damage."

I sat down behind the wheel of the H-2. I put a clip into my carbine and racked a round into the chamber before placing the gun on the seat beside me. I then placed a pair of flash-bang grenades in the cup holders and waited for Tony to open the garage door.

I backed the Hummer from the garage and far enough up Chartres Street to allow Tony to back into the street as well. He hit the switch for the door and we waited until the garage was secure before Tony led the way out of the Quarter. I pulled around him once we reached Elysian Fields and turned towards the Holy Cross Neighborhood. I was worried that I might be counting too heavily on Jack not moving his men just because we tracked them back to Alex Boudreaux's rental houses.

I parked two blocks from the corner where we last spotted D-Tech's black Chevy Suburbans. Cones of dim light from the handful of working streetlights intermittently lit the neighborhood. We needed to retrace my steps from our last encounter, avoiding any dogs penned or chained outside. They formed an alarm system we couldn't defeat.

Tony parked and walked to my car door as he strapped on his own protective vest and checked the action on the Keltec KSG shotgun I handed him. He wore his own .45 pistol on his hip. Being able to share ammo was why I chose the carbine I carried. Running a night mission brought back memories neither of us particularly cherished. Our last such outing together ended poorly for both of us.

I picked up the Molotov cocktails and moved the pair of grenades from the cup holders to my belt. We were saving the four others for our next stop. I slid out of the Hummer and eased the door closed.

I used my burner cell phone to call 911 and report the fire we were about to set. Tony lit the magnesium sparklers on the bottles as we approached the first house and took off with two of the firebombs. Having our hands full put us in a bad position if anyone began shooting in our direction. The brilliant white light from the sparklers abruptly lit up the night. I tossed one against the nearest Suburban's rear window and was chagrined when the bottle broke without doing any damage. I never considered whether or not the vehicles were armored. The flammable mixture barely damaged the paint. Tony grinned at this first wrinkle in my plan.

Tony improvised and changed this part of the plan by throwing both of his Molotov cocktails through the tall window of the second house's front room. The window lacked any protective reinforcement and the burning mixture set the interior ablaze within seconds. I followed suit and set fire to the first house as Tony ran past me in full retreat. We made a hard turn between two houses and were out of sight when Jack's men poured out of the rental units with their guns in hand. We ran through dark back yards until we reached our vehicles. Our trucks sat illuminated in the firelight, but we had parked in line with those of the residents, and Jack's mercenaries failed to spot us getting into the vehicles. We waited until three fire trucks pulled up to block anyone trying to follow us before slipping back into the night, while Jack's gunmen dealt with the fire department.

We stopped on the shoulder of Paris Avenue and tried to plan our next move a little more thoroughly. The stakes were considerably higher now. The homeless security team would need a while to reorganize, and the success of our plan relied on denying them their mobility. I knew I damaged only one of the Suburbans. I hoped that the fire engines lining the street blocked any of their other vehicles.

"There will probably be forward observers at the intersection with Chef Menteur." I was reverse engineering the measures I would have taken after our first attack on D-Tech. "And there will be more guards at the lot."

"Do you want to come in from both ends at once?"

"No. I say we take out one observation post and then get the bomb in position while the main force is still setting up for an attack. They're going to expect us to come in shooting, not to blow them to hell with their own bomb. I'll park in front of the fence and put the Hummer between them and you. Then I'll jump in with you and we'll get out of there. We can double back after the bomb goes off and clean the place out."

"Brilliant. What can go wrong?" Tony looked nervous about the number of moving parts in the plan and the odds stacked against us.

"You're going to bring up that old line?" I tried to lighten the mood by chastising him for repeating the line he uttered at the briefing before that last mission in Iraq. I can now enumerate a great many things that can, and will, go wrong--even on a well-planned mission.

I lowered the window on the Hummer and checked the timer. I would have only twenty seconds to jump from one vehicle to the other, possibly under fire, and for Tony to get us as far away as possible before the bomb exploded. Setting the timer for any longer gave D-Tech's security team time to disarm or move the vehicle. The blast radius promised to be impressive because detonating the car bomb in the open meant nothing would slow or block the shock wave before it rolled through D-Tech's base. The broad, flat sides of the expensive recreational vehicles would act like sails on tall ships caught in a storm. I was prepared to accept that there were going to be casualties, but I did not think of D-Tech's personnel as being innocent civilians.

I spent some time visualizing the awkward shots I needed to take to neutralize the first line of defense. Tony drove past the first turn-off because we figured anyone waiting there would be at a higher state of alert than anyone guarding the back door. Instead, he pulled off Almonaster and began doing donuts in the parking lot of a closed McDonald's across the street from the security detail's unmarked sedan while I moved into position behind them.

Tony's antics distracted the guards just as I hoped. The sentries shifted in their seats to watch the pricey truck making senseless loops in the darkened building's lot. I had the lights off on the black SUV and was able to slam into the trunk of the Charger at nearly thirty miles an hour to send it careening forward. I figured I could crash at that speed without damaging the bomb. I only needed to drive another quarter mile and the Hummer could make that distance even if I flattened both tires. I immediately pulled forward and stopped next to the Charger. I leaned out of my window and tossed one of the flash bang grenades into the vehicle before I fired three rounds from my Glock into each man's protective vest. Murdering them was unnecessary; I only needed to protect the element of surprise. The slugs struck the plates in their vests with the impact of three football linemen jumping on a metal rod an inch in diameter. Ribs break under that kind of pressure and breathing becomes difficult, making it nearly impossible to speak into a radio to warn anyone.

I made a hasty assessment of the Hummer's condition and decided it was in better shape than the crumpled grille and engine seemed to indicate. My headlights were both smashed, but that was a good thing. Tony pulled behind me and we accelerated all the way to D-Tech's lot. It was barely a mile's distance and I watched our target the whole way. There were a pair of Suburbans positioned in front of the gate. My guess was that this placed at least four armed men in position to fend off any assault. Standard protocol called for at least that many to be hiding across the street as well.

I brought the Hummer to a screeching stop in the middle of the four-lane street slightly ahead of the gate. I positioned the vehicle ahead of the gate so I was not in the direct line of fire of the guards. Doing this put barely forty feet between the bomb and the Suburbans blocking the entrance to the lot, and left the farthest RV bus barely fifty yards from the detonation point. Detonating just the pipe bombs was more than enough to destroy the Suburbans. I had not done the math to estimate the precise blast radius the sixty gallons of home-made ANFO and any additional damage the propane added to the explosives, would create. I just knew it was deeply into the range of "serious overkill."

I triggered the timer and threw my door open just as Tony stopped with the passenger side of the Raptor slightly ahead of my position. There was no time to open the door to the vehicle. I hopped into the truck bed and aimed my rifle towards the armored Chevrolets as Tony raced into the open. The guards were still trying to decide what threat we posed when I began firing. They reflexively dropped low and hid behind the wheels of the heavy SUVs. I hoped they would stay there another fifteen seconds. I pivoted and fired in the direction of muzzle flashes coming from a parking lot across the street from the Suburbans.

The detail in the Charger we chose to bypass hastily abandoned their position to fall back in support of the men they heard were under attack. We passed the Charger barely two blocks from the lot. They braked hard to make a U-turn and give chase. I did not like our odds of outrunning the sedan's powerful Hemi engine.

I was taking aim at the Charger when the Hummer took care of that problem for me. Two-hundred pounds of explosives detonated less than a hundred feet from the Charger as it turned sideways in the road. I watched the vehicle lift towards us and begin tumbling like a child's toy. Bright light followed by a massive dust cloud obstructed my view of the two Suburbans and the parking lot they meant to protect. I had a brief instant to curse myself for not bringing ear protection before the blast wave smacked us from behind. Tony managed to drive nearly three hundred yards from the blast zone, but that barely cleared us of most of the explosion's largest pieces of debris. The immediate area went dark as the power lines snapped in two. Pieces of pavement and bits of other sharp things I found hard to identify in the dark pelted me. I felt relief that none of these involved either blood or actual flesh.

"Holy hell," I mumbled mostly to myself. Tony stopped and looked over his shoulder at the cloud of dust. We looked at one another and realized we were both imagining the effect this would have caused in the Quarter.

Tony turned around and drove as close to the blast zone as he dared. It would have been a very bad place to get a flat tire. I estimated our window of opportunity was less than five minutes before the first NOPD squad car arrived. We could not be reported anywhere near what we'd just done.

I placed a fresh clip into my carbine and then Tony and I sprinted into the carnage on foot. The Suburbans were burnt out hulks and identifiable only from memory. The fence was a tangled mess wrapped around the first of the buses, which was lying on its left side but surprisingly not aflame despite its ruptured fuel tank. We could hear pleading voices inside the bus. I felt little pity for those people but was glad they had enough strength to scream. The blast tipped the first bus into the second one, and the windows on both shattered and blew glass over the passengers. I spotted the movement of a flashlight beam in the third bus, but I saw no threat. The last two buses were severely damaged, but still upright. All of the glass was blown out of each of them and debris had penetrated their sides.

Tony set about lobbing the remaining flash-bang grenades into each vehicle for good measure.

I turned my attention to the damage the bomb caused to the cinder block office building. The front wall and most of the wall facing the line of buses collapsed in the blast. What was left of the roof remained in place from a mixture of surviving structure and dumb luck. Tony raised his shotgun and fired deer slugs into the chests of a pair of men carrying rifles when they staggered out of the building. Neither of us checked to see if they were wearing vests. It was sufficient to know that they posed no further problem to us.

"Help. Help me, dammit!" a male voice shouted from the rear

of the building. The voice sounded far too young to belong to any of the guards.

"Come on," I said, and motioned for Tony to follow me.

We climbed over a pile of shattered cinder block and followed the voice into the dark interior of the building. The cries became the sound of someone banging metal on metal and we followed the new sound with the hope that the voice and the noise were connected. Tony used the flashlight on his shotgun to spotlight a dusty hand pounding a metal plate on the side of a metal bedframe. Tony ran the light along the wall and gradually illuminated the shape of someone handcuffed to the metal bed. The young man wore an orange jumpsuit but no shoes. A leather hood covered the young man's dust covered head.

"Richie?" It was a guess, but one that suddenly made sense. I did not call out his full name initially because being that formal might scare him even further.

"Who are you?" We were nothing but new voices to the prisoner, and he may not have been sure if he was alive or dead after that explosion.

"Are you Richie Franklin?" I repeated my question because mine needed answered before I was going to worry about his.

"Yes."

I closed the distance between us and used my handgun to shoot through the chain holding the handcuff to the bedframe. I reached out and removed the leather hood. Richie raised no objection to walking through the rubble in his stocking feet if it meant he could leave. Tony took point and we hustled Richie Franklin out of the building and across the still deserted parking lot. The two men Tony shot were no longer lying sprawled in the dirt, but it was hard to tell if that meant they crawled to cover or other operatives moved them to safety. I covered our exit and kept one hand on the young man's shoulder while he clung to Tony.

Richie curled himself into the confines of the Raptor's passenger side floorboards, and I tossed everything but our pistols on the floorboards in front of me before Tony drove us away from the scene. We passed the first patrol cars responding to the commotion as he turned onto Chef Menteur Highway.

"Who are you guys?" Richie finally asked as Tony accelerated up an entrance ramp onto Interstate-10.

"We aren't even here," I said and pressed a finger to my grinning lips.

Chapter 53

Tony pulled into the garage and I hurried to close the door. I opened the trunk and retrieved our weapons while Tony helped Richie unwind from his cramped position. We have a small refrigerator filled with water and beer in the garage and I retrieved a bottled water for our guest and beers for Tony and me.

I was happy to have finally located the missing member of the Pistol Peetes, but the young man posed a unique problem. Jack's men or D-Tech would want to retrieve him as soon as possible, and we were high on their list of places to look. Sending Richie home, or to his uncle, only put others at unreasonable risk.

"Richie, my name is Cooter Holland. I'm a detective with the Louisiana State Police," I said to introduce myself. He did not seem inclined to believe me. "Your mother filed a missing person's report on you a few weeks ago and I've been looking for you ever since."

"She wouldn't file no report with the police." He took a long sip of his water and tried to decide if I was lying.

"She did after I asked her to." I needed to earn his trust to use him as I now intended. "You are a major piece in a very large puzzle."

"How so?"

"Do you have any idea why you were abducted?"

"They said I was collateral. They wanted to make my uncle spy for them." That confirmed my suspicion about Willie turning informant, and explained his comment about knowing his nephew was safe.

"Well, it worked." I took a drink from my beer and studied him. "The thing is, now they will see both of you as loose ends. The men holding you lost their leverage over your uncle when we took you. Now they have no reason not to kill you or Willie. You're going to have to be my own guest for a while."

"Why would I do that?"

"Here are a couple of reasons, not that I owe you any. First, we just saved your ass. The second reason is I am asking real nice, and the third one is that the only way to keep your uncle alive is for him to not know where you are. Bear with me and I promise to have you home in time to watch Zulu march." It was nearing dawn and I lacked enough patience to negotiate. "You need to decide where to hide."

"What's today?" Ritchie asked. I had not even considered how sensory-deprived the D-Tech team kept the boy.

"It's not Fat Tuesday." Tony was impatient as well. We were already deep into a mutual flashback of Iraq, where we were never this charitable towards our prisoners.

"What are my choices?"

"A private holding cell or your very own dog kennel." I pointed to the sizeable plastic and metal dog carrier Roux rode to his new home in from my mother's house. I still needed to hose the dog urine from inside the cage.

"I'll take the holding cell. Can I call my mom?"

"I need to talk to your uncle before you talk to anybody. Let's find you a new place to stay."

There were myriad problems with finding Ritchie a new hole. I would have trusted my own department to hold him, but the State Police have no jails of their own. Too many people knew Ritchie to place him in a parish jail. Neither of those scenarios would prevent Kinkaid from simply walking away with him.

Jack's men were going to be combing the city for him soon. Hiding Ritchie in my own apartment was too obvious, and using either Tulip or Katie's places to hold him meant finding someone to guard the place. I could not trust Ray not to turn him back over to D-Tech for a few pieces of silver. Getting Chief Avery or Captain Hammond involved endangered their careers. There was only one place I could hide Ritchie for a day or two that was not on a list of places anyone might think to look.

"It's four o'clock in the morning." Roger complained when he answered the phone in Audubon Place. I did not give Jack or his men credit for thinking to look here.

"I'm sorry, but I need a huge favor. Can I speak with my mother?"

Roger placed his hand over the phone and I heard only scratching and unhappy mumbling as he woke my mother and passed her the phone. My mother was going to be more upset that this call established she and Roger were sharing a bed than she would be about the purpose of my call.

"What is it, Cooter?" my mother finally came on the line to ask. She sounded remarkable wide-awake. "Is everything alright? Did something happen to your sister?"

"It's nothing like that, I promise. I need to borrow one of your guest rooms for a day or so."

"Whatever for?"

"I have a young man that needs a place to hide."

"Is he in any danger?" I was surprised that she did not automatically refuse to help.

"Considerable. Your place is the only one I believe won't be checked when some men come looking for him." My mother's comfort level with risk is a little higher than most because of her years living with a police detective.

"Who are these men you're talking about?" She was indeed wide-awake. I could not slide near as much past her as I might have if she were groggy. I had to assume she began to wonder about all of our safety when she moved into town.

"That won't matter if they never show up. Just loan me the room and you can hand him over if anyone does find him. I'm not asking you to put your lives at risk." Well, okay that was a lie.

"Yes, you are." She caught the lie just like that. "I'll help you, but I have to know what's going on, Cooter."

"He's the nephew of a gang member. He was kidnapped to pressure the uncle." This was all true, but only a fragment of the story. My mother knew this, as well, and made me wait for her next argument.

"Then give him back to the uncle."

"I can't. I need to use the kid for the exact same thing."

"Why *do* they let you keep your badge?" she asked with almost as much humor as genuine wonder.

"Because I'm the cop everyone needs to do things like this. Am I hearing a yes?" I was beyond feeling tired and Ritchie was getting antsy.

"Fine, bring him," she finally relented. She used this exact tone of voice when I asked her permission to first park Tony and then Roger Kline, and a murderous pit bull, in her boathouse. Apparently, that second time worked out much better than any of us expected, and it was perhaps the only reason she trusted my judgement a third time.

"I can't. Can Roger come get him?" I realized asking for this additional favor told her something else was amiss.

"Why can't you bring the young man?" Her willingness to get involved apparently stopped short of providing taxi services.

"Because that would leave a logbook record at the gate. The men that are looking for this kid might think to check that. It would be better if I was never there."

"True," she agreed a little more quickly than I imagined she would. I could hear her talking to Roger before she rolled over to go back to sleep.

"Where are you?" Roger asked.

"Meet us at Checkpoint Charlie's."

I hung up the phone and went to my Cadillac XLR. I keep a stockpile of things I might need, too much of it weaponry, in the trunk. Ritchie started to reach for one of the guns and I slapped his hand. He was only admiring it, but I did not want him to have a gun in his hand. Our level of trust was still low. We were nowhere near the same size but I found a clean shirt for him to wear over the jumpsuit. He wound up wearing a loose long-sleeved button-collar shirt and baggy orange pants with bare feet.

We remained in the garage until it was time to walk to Checkpoint Charlie's, which was Katie's hiding place the morning I rolled up Paul and his surveillance team. It is a 24-hour bar and grill, laundromat, lending library, and music hall all in one. Tourists have stepped inside for a beer and sent for their things because they had found a home.

I did not take Ritchie inside. There were video cameras recording the comings and goings of the patrons, as well as everything they did in between, and I could not afford any record of our ever having been together. I held him in a doorway down the street.

"Are we clear on what you have to do?" I considered it imperative that the young man follow my instructions without fail. "Make no phone calls, do not step outside, and definitely don't take off. I will not bother looking for you, but the men who find you will kill you and your uncle. Can you get that through your thick head?"

"I got it, man. Lay off," Ritchie complained. I repeated this warning to him every five minutes after I'd hung up the phone.

"And do not, I repeat do not, get my mother mad at you. Just stay in your room as much as you can until I come to get you." Ritchie was still trying to understand my instructions when Roger pulled up in front of the bar. I took hold of Ritchie's shoulder and hustled him to my mother's car. Roger was still dressed in his pajamas and a pair of slippers, neither of which he had ever owned or worn before moving in with my mother.

"Roger, this is Ritchie. Ritchie, this is Mister Kline." Roger and the young man shook hands a little stiffly. "Don't let him call anyone or let anyone see him until I come for him."

"Not a problem," Roger agreed while Ritchie adjusted to the fact that he was about to be chauffeured to safety in a top-end Mercedes sedan. Ritchie was in for a real surprise when he discovered where his new jail cell was located. Being my prisoner was the only way he was likely to get to spend a night on Audubon Place.

I walked a block up Esplanade and looked around. The mobile surveillance on me was absent. I could not believe D-Tech's surveillance on me was removed so easily. I assumed Jack and Jill chose to step up their timetable to wrap things up before I could find a way to interfere any further. I walked slowly around the block containing the parking garage and the bistro to see if anything indicated someone might have seen Ritchie with me. I paused for a moment by the garage to look at the ancient brick buildings and imagined, just for a second, what that bomb would have done. The shudder that hit me had nothing to do with the crisp morning air.

"I hope you're planning to sleep in," Katie grumbled when I found her reading in bed. She had obviously been awake since I left.

"That sounds like a great idea." I rolled her towards me and gave her a long kiss. She broke the kiss and gave me a very disapproving look.

"Go take a shower. You smell like gasoline."

I did not argue with her or explain the reason. The entire city would hear about it soon enough. She was asleep when I climbed back into bed.

Chapter 54

There was no way I could sleep in. I had far too much to do and not nearly enough time to do it. Stephan, El Carnicero, made it clear that I needed to deliver Jack to him before he sat down with Homeland Security's negotiator. I was embarrassingly slow to realize that Deputy Director Bradford Kinkaid must be the negotiator. He was holding me to a deadline of his own.

I felt confident that D-Tech was finished after the bomb blast. Their focus in the mission to push the El Camino cartel out of New Orleans ended when they provided Jack and his mercenaries the list of addresses for the cartel and the Pistol Peetes. They remained in town to do communications support for Jack and his henchmen. Jack's hand-selected contract operatives were definitely still in play and Tony and I had kicked a hornet's nest the night before. They would be looking for any chance to take their revenge, and Tony and I were always going to be seriously outnumbered. When it came to tough deadlines, I may as well add burning through my mother's patience asking her to hide Ritchie Franklin.

Willie Hawkins became disposable the minute Tony and I pulled his nephew out of the rubble. Kinkaid could not blackmail Willie if there was nothing with which to blackmail him. I now held that collateral, but now I needed to know Willie's expiration date. I had no idea if Kinkaid would chose to cut him loose or see him as a loose end needing eliminated. Ritchie was in my care, but there was very little that I needed to blackmail his uncle into giving me.

Tulip's legal troubles remained an Achilles heel for both of us. I would do almost anything to get her free from the serious legal jeopardy downloading that file placed her in, including coughing up Richie. Kinkaid was in a position to use the situation I believed he had a part in placing her into to punish me. I needed a way to extricate her from my problems, and to that problem go away permanently. I am obviously not the guy who handles anything involving legalities with a deft touch. I knew Katie and Tulip could explain her legal options to me. I dared not confer with them on what I was prepared to do illegally.

My brain began to hurt after thinking about all of this. It consumed the entirety of my circuit through the French Quarter as I took Roux on his first walk of the day. I actively looked for anyone who might be following me, and finally accepted that nobody was walking in my shadow. Roux sat beside me while I consumed a double order of beignets at Café du Monde, along with the first of a large number of cups of coffee. We jogged back to the restaurant to get some exercise, and because I was in a hurry to get to work.

Chapter 55

Willie Hawkins was wide awake when he answered my text two days later. Maybe what snapped him to attention was that I knew his personal cell phone number. I could have called him, but there was a slim chance his calls were still being monitored. I texted him a request to call me from a payphone because texts are harder to monitor, and because my typed words carried none of the clues spoken words can provide.

"How'd you get my number?" Hawkins demanded. That seemed to bother him far more than the fact a police detective used the information to text him.

"Let's get together and talk about that."

"I'll meet you at the lakefront in an hour." I assumed he meant the narrow stretch of open ground extending between Lake Ponchartrain and the levee. There was an amusement park there when I was a child.

"No, I'll pick you up in front of Home Depot in twenty minutes." I refused to meet him in the open, and I sure wasn't going to let him dictate the time or location. I hoped he knew which Home Depot I meant.

"I'll be there."

I was already parked in sight of the Home Depot on Read Boulevard when I texted him. He arrived five minutes early and positioned three cars to either block me in or follow us when we left the parking lot. It must not have occurred to any of his men to check the lot for existing threats. I waited until five minutes after I told him to expect me before I dialed his number. He answered on the second ring.

"Walk to the street," I instructed him and snapped him out of his smug confidence that he had any control over the situation. "I'll pick you up. Don't call or signal your men or I'm gone."

"Where are you?" He did not bother denying he was not alone.

"Start walking." There was no reason to answer his question. I watched him through my binoculars as he pocketed his phone and began to walk towards the frontage road.

I was parked in a used car lot next door and timed my exit to coincide with his arrival at the street. I was certain that his men were watching his every move and were probably confused by his taking a walk at such a time, but they saw him take my call and were at least bright enough to know something changed. I honked and pulled my Cadillac wagon to the curb. I threw the door open and motioned for him to get into the vehicle.

I moved my pistol from atop the center console to the storage pocket in my car door, and stomped on the gas pedal to bolt away from the Home Depot store before he was finished buckling his seatbelt. We seemed to vanish before his men's eyes.

"I have Ritchie," I told him as I slowed long enough to get through an intersection and onto the interstate. It was only a matter of time before his men split up and gave chase in both directions. They lacked the advantage I had of the blue lights flashing in the front window as I sped towards Slidell at a hundred miles an hour.

"What do you mean you have Ritchie?" He was not surprised, but my having him was an unexpected development.

"I mean I'm holding him, which means I can touch him and you can't."

"What's he done? You got no reason to arrest Richie!"

"I didn't say he was in jail. I just told you that I have him." I turned to the big man beside me and froze him in place with a look it has taken me years to perfect. The whole range of damaging things I could do to his relative flashed before his eyes.

"What do you want?" He was very quick to understand that his situation did not improve just because the police were involved.

"The same thing everyone wants. I need information."

"What do you want to know?"

"I want to know exactly when and where Bradford Kinkaid and El Carnicero are going to meet tomorrow."

"How would I know that?" The tone in his voice made his argument unconvincing, as did not denying the meeting.

"You can find out if you don't know already."

"You think I know a lot of things."

"You'll find the answer, and you know Ritchie and you are both safer with me hiding him."

"He's not going to be safe until he's with me," Hawkins argued.

We were crossing the new Twin Span Bridge to enter Slidell when I turned to look at him again. My expression was not nearly as combative as the first one I gave him, but it remained firm. He did not doubt a word I said.

"You are both dead men if I release him before something is done about Kinkaid. He will kill Ritchie if he can't use him against you, and he'll kill you the minute he thinks you don't believe he's got Ritchie. Kinkaid needs to believe he remains in control. Do you understand that?"

Hawkins nodded. He sat back in the seat and began to consider his options. Trusting me was going to be difficult. He betrayed me to the El Camino cartel without knowing whether it was a death sentence or not, and he knew that I was sure he did not care one way or the other what they did to me. That was not something he would have forgiven were the roles reversed. He also knew I was right about what the Deputy Director's response was going to be when he learned about Ritchie's escape. I was counting on his coming to the conclusion that his best interests involved trading this one piece of information for his own life and that of his nephew.

I dropped him off at a Cracker Barrel restaurant just off the interstate and headed back to New Orleans. He was already calling his men to pick him up by the time he closed the car door.

Chapter 56

Tulip and Katie were sitting in my office when I returned to the apartment. They had showered and dressed. They were looking at the notes and lines on the whiteboards while they drank cups of the chicory coffee one of them brewed in my kitchen. Chicory is not my own preference in coffee, but Katie loves the stuff.

"Giving my sister the grand tour?" I asked before I leaned over and kissed Katie lightly on the lips.

"Just looking at another one of the holes you've dug for yourself," Tulip said to emphasize her opinion of the latest investigation of mine she found herself pulled into.

"I'm working on filling all of them in. I need to know what I can do to get you out of trouble over that file." I sat between them and took my sister's hand in my own. "I know you were set up just to put pressure on me."

"At least we all agree on that," she said without a trace of sarcasm. "I think the only way out is to prove I was set up."

"She's right," Katie concurred. "The only way she can walk away from this is if the FBI believes someone set out to frame her for some reason. The reason isn't even all that important."

"I'll get right to work on that," I said and stood up. I was already doing so, but it was too early to tell either of them what I had in mind.

"I think I've seen enough of your work," Tulip said and stood up to block my exit. "I didn't read that report, but I'm clear enough on what's in it to know that you're one of the people I've spent a decade trying to bring to justice. I don't care that you only killed people while trying to protect soldiers' lives. What you did made the world a less safe place. Look what someone else using your nifty plan has done."

"I'm not going to apologize, and I'm not going to try to justify what I've done in the past. There is no way to explain things that will ever make you believe you're wrong about me, and what Tony and I did in Iraq. I am just going to point out that what I did there got me killed and I have tried to make amends for those sins with my second chance at life. I've just been trying to use my training and experience to bring a little justice to a city not noted for it."

"Your idea of justice, though, right?" Tulip continued to challenge. I wasn't going to argue that point because none of us believed the justice system worked in Orleans Parish, much less in the rest of the state.

"If Lionel Batiste taking Delia Adams' place on the city council or Roux not getting put down is my idea of justice then maybe that's not such a bad thing." Using two things that she truly agreed with as examples was unfair. She could have listed hundreds of others to prove her point.

"You two are just going to have to agree to disagree," Katie said, but remained seated rather than appear to take either of our sides. Neither of us were entirely correct about my actions in the past or present. I do what I do because it is the only way I know how to live. Chief Avery accepts that assigning me to a case means I will resolve the situation, and that my solutions may or may not involve putting anyone in jail. Tulip bases her view of how I should act in the world on a system of justice and a moral code that only applies in the world she and Katie lived in before I came back into their lives' it's one where the laws are far more black and white.

"No, I don't," Tulip snapped. "I guess what I have to learn to do is to live with my brother being a war criminal."

We watched her storm out of the room and heard my apartment door slam a moment later. Katie did not rush out of the room after her best friend, but she also made no effort to leap to her feet to console or encourage me. I sat on the bench, but left a few inches between us.

"It's really not you that she's mad at, you know," Katie strived to explain. "She can yell at you because you're her brother. She can't rip into Tony for doing the same things, and worse, because she still wants to love him."

My lips slipped into a crooked grin as I turned towards her. "Oh, that makes me feel so much better. How are the two of us, by the way?"

"You're my favorite vigilante, and I'm just glad you're on our side." She scooted next to me and laid her head against my left shoulder.

Chapter 57

K atie and I sat at the bar while she ate the Sunday breakfast Miss J set before her. We watched the election results on the TV behind the bar, and were glad to see Lionel won by a landslide. There was also a story that the "authorities" were still on the scene of Friday night's natural gas explosion at an unnamed business location on Almonaster Boulevard. It certainly involved exploding gas, but there was nothing natural about what happened. The reporter made no mention of any casualties. The damaged Suburbans were gone, and a temporary fence shielded D-Tech's lot from the street. The demolished office building was all that was visible in the frame. Anyone familiar with IEDs or car bomb explosions knew the hole shown on their TV screen did not come about from a leaking gas line. The news team made no mention of the house fires Tony and I set. They were mentioned inside the local news section of the morning paper. Nothing could bump the Super Bowl from being the top story of the day in New Orleans.

"Is that why you came home smelling like gas?" Katie asked between bites.

"I didn't smell like natural gas, did I?"

Katie gave me a hard blank stare. "We have a deal, mister."

"And you know better than to ask that sort of question," I reminded her. "I'll just say that the authorities reached the wrong conclusion."

"Just how bad are things going to get? You're mixed up with, what, three gangs and a band of mercenaries hired by Homeland

Security?"

"I have no idea, but I think it's all just about over. The Deputy Director from Homeland Security is meeting with the Mexicans and then with me sometime today or tomorrow. He will expect both of us to do what he says. If we do, then I'd guess everything will go back to normal."

"And if you don't?"

"It sounds like he'll make it go back to normal. He has created a very bad situation that he thinks only he can solve. He wants to be able to stand up and say he scared a ruthless bunch of Mexicans out of town and that this means the government really does care about New Orleans after all. There's a new President and everyone wants to put the last one behind them." I had divulged more of my conversation with the Deputy Director than I should have.

"So you think the new President ordered Kinkaid to put this together?"

"Hell, no. This started after 9/11. Kinkaid is trying to find a way to either cover his ass or feather his own nest."

Katie took another bite of her egg white and something green and leafy omelet. It did not look nearly as appetizing as my omelet and the tall stack of bacon I was picking at between sentences. Katie chewed slowly and focused her attention on the television rather than me. A thin smile started to form on her face.

"You really think Deputy Director Kinkaid framed Tulip?" I doubted that this thought just popped into her head.

"I would love to prove he did." I stuffed my mouth with bacon rather than pursue the matter.

"That certainly would be justice, huh?" Katie chuckled and filled her own mouth rather than say another word.

Justice began to prevail about the time Joaquin began seating the lunch crowd. Willie Hawkins entered the restaurant as our regular patrons began to arrive for their big meal of the day.

"Is Mister Cooter here?" Willie asked Jason as I approached him from behind. Jason pointed over his shoulder to me and the big man spun around in surprise.

"May I help you?" I was acting polite, but grabbed him by the arm and headed towards the door.

"The meeting's this afternoon at the Monteleone," he blurted out before we reached the sidewalk.

"Why not just call or text me that information?"

"Some things got to be said in person. There's more you need to know, too."

"And what would that be?" I let loose of him.

"That Mexican dude didn't come here to make any deal with that guy from Homeland Security. He's going to kill him to make it clear that the El Caminos don't fear nobody."

It took me a long moment to sort out the double negatives in what he said. I was very clear on the part about El Carnicero planning to kill Kinkaid. I was almost comfortable with his doing so, but saw the unforeseen consequences the Mexican either ignored or was not worried about. Killing politicians in Mexico is an effective means of instilling fear in the rest of the politicians and filling the leadership gap they created with people of their own choosing. Killing an American in Kinkaid's position would only create a demand that our government scorch the earth beneath the cartel. It was also going to give New Orleans yet another black eye. The irony was that Kinkaid's death would accomplish almost exactly what the Deputy Director sent Jack to town to accomplish. I didn't think Hawkins fully grasped the situation. He would not be the leader of the Baghdad Brotherhood if he worried about things like consequences.

Chapter 58

I was startled by the sound of my burner cell phone ringing about an hour later. It was a little disconcerting because only three people knew the number and the caller ID showed the incoming call was from a number not in the phone's recognized contacts.

"Hello?" I decided to take the call rather than smash the phone.

"I'm sending Jack to pick you up. He'll be there in ten minutes." I probably should have expected the call to be from Deputy Director Kinkaid as he had the wherewithal to learn the number to any private phone.

"Make it fifteen. I'm still in bed."

"Ten minutes," Kinkaid snarled and hung up.

Jack and three of his mercenaries walked up to the hostess stand exactly ten minutes later. I barely had time to change into slacks, a button-down shirt, and a sport coat with my State police badge hanging from the breast pocket. Being pressed for time did not mean I could not take the time to figure out a means of irritating the Deputy Director.

Deputy Director Kinkaid was ensconced in style. He was staying in the FJ Monteleone Suite of the Monteleone Hotel. My mood about his summoning me into the suite's opulent Napoleonic décor brightened with Kinkaid's inadvertent disclosure of both his own location and where he would meet Stephan El Carnicero. I was still deciding on the best way to use this information when Jack closed the door to the suite behind me.

I knew the layout of this suite better than the Deputy Director could have known. I used to bring the same paid escorts that accompanied Jack's men to the restaurant here, on my Uncle Felix's tab. I acted as if I were being nosy, but I knew the places to look that would make him nervous. There is a small office off the living room where I found an innocuous-looking piece of electronics I immediately recognized as a cell tower simulator, a device meant to intercept cellular phone calls. I began to wonder whose room this actually was when I found the doors to the spacious bedroom locked from the inside. I realized the tickling in my nose was from perfume and not the Deputy Director's after-shave. I knew only one woman who wore that particular perfume.

"I still need an answer from you." Kinkaid stated. My attention shifted to the dining table and its place settings for two. The empty plates held the last bites of someone's eggs Sardou and an assortment of croissants and fruits. The coffee smelled like a chicory blend so I poured myself a glass of the fresh squeezed orange juice. Kinkaid was not amused with my plundering his room service order.

"I thought you said I had until Monday to answer. I assumed you wanted to discuss D-Tech." Kinkaid was changing the timetable to remind me that he was the one in charge. The Deputy Director motioned me towards a chair in the sitting area.

"There really isn't anything to discuss, Detective." I took the seat, but did not appreciate the way he used my title. "You're either going to get out of their way or I'm going to crush you and everyone you love. D-Tech's doing important work for us here."

"And breaking about every law there is, which is why I'm not a part of this. Their operatives have torched houses and murdered at least two dozen men. They have also done at least one kidnapping and illegally wiretapped phones, including my own. Surely there are limits to what gets a pass as being part of national security." It wanted to remind him that what D-Tech did on his orders would not stand much scrutiny. I was still working on how to make him worry about anyone ever questioning what he did here.

"You'll have a hard time ever proving anything they may have done wasn't the result of a feud between the El Camino cartel and the Pistol Peetes. There won't be many of either gang left to round up or send to prison when D-Tech's mission is finished." Kinkaid seemed unusually confident that his plan was still on track to succeed.

"I have everything I need to convince a judge that this is just rehashing a questionable operation I ran in Iraq." Suggesting I had any pertinent knowledge was meant to get him to divulge even more details. "Maybe a Congressional hearing would work even better than a grand jury."

"Jack lost good men to your antics. A dozen of D-Tech's technicians are still in the hospital as well. Don't think for a second that they didn't know you were behind moving the bomb." Kinkaid was upset but seemed disinclined to discipline or prosecute me for anything I did. I found that curious.

"You're just admitted Jack planted that bomb in the Quarter. It sure didn't start out as my bomb."

"The bomb you're talking about was exactly the same as the sort that the El Camino cartel has used in Mexico." It was chilling how well the cover story he would have used to explain our murders served his purpose.

"Except the bomb was in Ritchie Franklin's Hummer."

"What difference does that make? The Mexicans were the ones who abducted Ritchie." Kinkaid was still working from his prepared script.

"Then why would the El Camino cartel stash Ritchie on Almonaster with the crew from D-Tech?" I took obvious relish at his lost composure. His reaction told me that I'd definitely underestimated the importance of Ritchie. I had undoubtedly seriously underestimated or misinterpreted other things about D-Tech operation. "No, better yet, tell me how in the hell things ever got this far. D-Tech is obviously running things because you definitely aren't in control of what they're up to. It just occurred to me that you want my answer now because nobody knows you're even in New Orleans, and you'll be missed if you're not at your desk tomorrow morning."

The Deputy Director moved to the table to refresh his cup of coffee. He did not give me the impression that he was preparing to answer my question. I think he was debating whether there was a way to make me disappear. I loosened my pistol in its holster while his back was turned. I might need the second or two this saved if he called Jack in to deal with me.

"That won't be necessary, Detective," Jill Bledsoe announced as she came through the bedroom door behind me in a haze of the perfume I smelled earlier. She was wearing a tailored suit, and a cast and sling on her left arm.

"Convince me," I suggested but left a hand in my lap as she poured herself a cup of coffee. I was not encouraged by her reluctance to sit down with us and kept a close eye on her. I'd already seen what a cup of hot coffee can do to a man.

"This began as a favor, nothing more." She was standing behind Kinkaid's left shoulder, perhaps because a right- handed shooter would hit the bureaucrat and not her. "The American government struck a deal with an insignificant band of smugglers from Mexico after 9/11. We would let their people go so long as they kept our intelligence services informed about what was happening on that side of the border. Bradford here inherited the situation when Congress created Homeland Security and made it their job to see terrorists everywhere. Unfortunately he forgot what happens to vermin when you take away the predators."

"So, they used this stupid agreement to go from being the weakest to being the strongest cartel." I paid attention in Biology 101. I held my tongue about the mess I thought this made of things.

"And now they've decided that since my territory has expanded they get to follow wherever I go," Kinkaid elaborated on his dilemma. "It was one thing to cover for them in a place like Arizona, where there's plenty of other cartel activity, but it's a lot harder in places where that isn't the case."

"So this is your own little mess. How did D-Tech get involved?" I relaxed a bit, but I knew she was not sharing this without planning to attach a massive catch.

"I was lobbying for contracts in D.C. and heard a rumor that the Deputy Director needed some help. This was a perfect opportunity for D-Tech to stay busy after you cost us our contracts in Iraq. We planned to demonstrate our potential value in domestic situations by helping Homeland Security send a message to the cartel." Jill was speaking to me as if she were making yet another sales pitch.

"That's not what you're doing, though. Is it?" I moved both hands to the tabletop, but my gun was still readily available. My eyes kept track of the doors to the hallway. I was still waiting for Jack's men to drag me off to some hole in the black-ops world with no name on it. Secret prisons are too valuable of an asset to shut down completely.

"The cartel has threatened to have their people testify in open court about the deal the Deputy Director made if any of them are ever put on trial." Jill finished her coffee and leaned around

Kinkaid to set the cup and saucer on the table. "So, they have taken the option of legal recourse off the table themselves."

"Now we are just trying to squeeze the toothpaste back into the tube and make them agree to stay in Arizona." Kinkaid still seemed to think I might rejoin his team if I believed in his mission. I am sure this all sounded logical, though annoyingly inconvenient, to him. I sensed his role in this mess was just to keep the operation under wraps until D-Tech forced the El Caminos to accept the original deal.

"How's that going for you?" I had to laugh.

"Well, they've sent someone to negotiate, right?" Jill demanded with just enough triumph and spite that I saw no reason to correct her misconceptions about what was really happening.

"And where is Ritchie now?" Kinkaid returned to our original conversation with forced casualness.

"Safe from you and your men. He's off the grid and his uncle knows you don't have him. That's going to cost you your inside man." Kinkaid gave me a look that would have intimidated anyone with more to lose.

"Here's the best deal you're going to get. You find something else to worry about until Jack wraps up his work, and never mention it to anyone in the future, and I'll make your sister's problems with the FBI disappear." The Deputy Director strained to strike a balance between sounding as gracious as he could while still doing his best to intimidate me. He was beginning to see I held more bargaining chips.

"That's a generous offer coming from the guy who probably framed her. I'm pretty sure I can't stand by while Jack and Jill burn my city down, but I'm positive that I don't trust you about anything having to do with my sister."

"Fine. How about if I put an agreement in writing?"

"You won't do that. Putting anything in writing means you wouldn't be able to deny any of this ever took place." I now leaned back in my seat, showing him that my pistol was now in my hand and not in its holster. "I'll give you a chance to show your good faith. Pick up that phone and call SAC Conroy at the FBI and order him to drop his investigation, or I'm going straight from this room to the Times-Picayune with everything I can prove, and a lot I can't, but will still make you deny on the record."

"You'll go to prison. You signed a confidentiality agreement."

"Prosecuting me for violating it only gives my accusations that the project exists merit."

I holstered my pistol and started to rise from my chair. The now frantic Deputy Director was quick to raise a hand and motion me to stay in place.

"Fine. I'll make the call." Kinkaid reached inside his jacket for his phone. I grabbed the phone after he dialed the number and set it on the coffee table before pressing the speaker button. The sound of the phone ringing filled the high-ceilinged suite.

"Good morning." I recognized the voice as being Special-Agent-in-Charge Conroy's weekend secretary. The man works seven days a week.

"This is Deputy Director Kinkaid. I need to speak with Michael."

"Right away, Sir." At least somebody was prepared to show him the respect he still felt he deserved.

"What can I do for you, Deputy Director?" SAC Conroy was also willing to show him more respect than I had yet to demonstrate that morning.

"There has been a change in the case involving Tulip Holland. You're to drop your investigation." I think Kinkaid believed that this was going to be enough to convince me that he was keeping his promise to me.

"It's a serious offense, sir. What's changed? Did she make a plea bargain? I'm sure we have a winnable case." The SAC's disappointment that he'd lost a means of causing me distress began to irritate me.

"The file has just been declassified. There's no longer a case, so drop it." I rather liked the wrathful tone Kinkaid used to get his point across.

"Done. Is there anything else I can do for you, Sir?" Conroy was not going to argue with a Deputy Director.

"No. Just let the poor girl know she's in the clear." Kinkaid looked to me to see if I was satisfied that Tulip was no longer his pawn in our chess match. I nodded, but only because I was now free to use her to make a move of my own.

"Thank you," I said with some genuine gratitude. "I'm still not very comfortable with what Jack is doing. What's going to happen when the Mexicans start fighting back for real? They've figured out it's not the Pistol Peetes or the Baghdad Brotherhood that's attacking them, and they believed me when I told them it isn't the State Police. They've brought in their best troops and are out there looking for someone to fight."

"And you know this how?" Kinkaid grasped that the illusion D-Tech worked so hard to create was collapsing. The bombing must have required an unexpected amount of effort to minimize in the press.

"For one thing, I told the Mexicans as much. You've also verified the story they've already told me about your deal. I can't let a gang war break out during Mardi Gras." The Deputy Director's expression when I told him this made me worry that he might have Jack's men shoot me after all.

"What do you propose?" Kinkaid began to pace about the suite, but never took his eyes off me. Half his thoughts seemed to be on what would neutralize me as a threat.

"You need to make whatever deal you can with the Mexicans and then both of you get out of town before anyone else figures out what's going on. Just give the state prosecutors their files back and NOPD will get credit for taking down the heroin ring on their own."

"And how do I know you'll keep what you learned here to yourself?" Trust did not come to him any easier than it did to me. Especially after I threatened to expose him.

"Everybody just wants their lives back. Your story is nothing more than one more tale of an ambitious bureaucrat. Nobody wants to hear that crap anymore."

Oddly enough, he seemed to believe that was a good answer. He knew he failed to destroy the El Caminos despite handing D-Tech millions of dollars in his futile effort to do so. I apparently convinced Kinkaid that the best he could do now was to maintain the increasingly untenable status quo. He and Jill would undoubtedly try something no less ambitious in Arizona, if they had not already done so. I needed to begin to nail the door closed behind him now that our conversation convinced him to leave.

"I could sit in on the meeting with the guy from the El Caminos if you want. I've at least spoken with him, which is more than you have."

"That won't be necessary," Kinkaid decided.

"I probably speak better Spanish than either of you do." I said this as a joke, but it was actually a feeler.

"We'll be fine. He'll be here this afternoon and his English is good enough for what we need to discuss." Jill exchanged a look with the Deputy Director that probably involved deciding whether to keep trusting me or not.

I choose not to give them a chance to reconsider letting me leave and headed for the door without another word. I'd managed to do more damage than I could have hoped, and I'd narrowed down the time frame for the meeting between the Deputy Director and The Butcher. I walked past Jack in the hallway without a word and checked behind me as I walked out of the hotel to be sure nobody followed me.

Chapter 59

My personal history with Michael Conroy, the Special Agent in Charge of the FBI's New Orleans office, makes it best that we avoid crossing paths. Our discord grew out of an investigation that uncovered the strong likelihood that a future FBI agent murdered my father after Hurricane Katrina and that Conroy was covering it up. The SAC remained certain that I played a central role in the car wreck that took that same agent's life days after that discovery. We were both absolutely, if never provably, correct in our assumptions about one another.

This means I need to be careful in the way I approach him. I knew that the easiest way to get him to do what I want is to help him convince himself it is in his own best interest.

"Do you have an appointment?" Conroy's weekend secretary demanded when I approached her desk. I had visited the SAC's office only twice before, but all of SAC Conroy's secretaries and agents know their boss most likely wants nothing to do with me.

"I have a time sensitive situation your boss needs to know about."

"And what could be time sensitive enough that you'd show up here in person on Super Bowl Sunday?" Conroy asked from his doorway. He must have spotted me through his office window and wanted to get rid of me on his own.

"A member of the El Camino cartel named Stephan, or El Carnicero, is in town."

Conroy acted nonchalant, but I could tell the name struck a

chord with him. He motioned me into his office and closed the door. He took a seat behind his desk and I politely declined the offer of one of the seats across from him.

"How do you know about the meeting?" Conroy asked with slightly less than even breath. It is not every day someone he despises shows up at his office with a tip that might catapult his career.

"I'm working on a narcotics case and his name came up. I only found out exactly how important he is late last night."

"How did his name come up?" Conroy was not interested in how I heard the name, only the credibility of my answer.

"I've been conducting an investigation into a heroin ring and have someone close to the El Camino cartel as an informant. He told me El Carnicero is in town to meet a mole in Homeland Security. Apparently this guy is covering for the cartel with the DEA and ATF." I paused until it was obvious Conroy was looking for a hole in my story. The FBI Agent could smell a trap as well as he could set one.

"Do you have the name of the mole?"

"I'd be talking to Homeland Security if I did. All I know is where the meeting is taking place and that it is today."

"Why aren't you taking this to NOPD or your own people? I'm pretty sure I'm not at the top of your list of people to bring this to." Conroy was beginning to let his ambition overtake his caution. The chance to be the agent who arrested a corrupt Federal agent and the cartel's henchman together was simply too tempting of an opportunity. He still needed one last push to his ego to take my bait.

"NOPD isn't equipped to handle a take-down like this and the State Police can't respond in time. Besides, they are both strapped for officers with Mardi Gras. You'd just swoop in and grab the guy from either of them anyway, so you may as well do all the work." I shrugged as if to say I accepted the unfortunate reality of the situation.

"And you know where and when this is supposed to happen?"

"I do, but there's a price for sharing it." I saw the smug look cross Conroy's face when I confirmed his suspicion that I had ulterior motives.

"Of course there is. What would that be?"

"I want you to drop the investigation into Tulip. She got pulled into something that has nothing to do with her." I saw no reason to let the SAC know I was aware that my sister was already safe from his threats.

"Fine. We'll drop it if your story pans out." He was not going to admit Tulip was no longer his own bargaining chip. "We can work out the details once the Mexican is in custody. Now tell me what you know."

"My source said there's a bad apple in Homeland Security who made a deal with the El Camino cartel after 9/11. The Mexican plans to meet the agent to in the Monteleone Suite at the Monteleone this afternoon to renew their deal. You just need to follow their room service order in to catch them both." I tried to sound as if I was sure of what my source told me about the place and approximate time.

Conroy was certain to contact the hotel and would learn what I already knew, that an offshore shell company rented the suite. Conroy would not have enough time to learn a company called D-Tech controlled the foreign-owned company, but using the shield would make the situation look shady enough to validate my accusations. Kinkaid did not have the budget for such accommodations and D-Tech would not put their name on anything that might connect them directly to an operation that blew up in their face once before. My story about a rogue agent in Homeland Security gave Conroy an excuse not to call the Deputy Director because Conroy would blow the meeting between Kinkaid and El Carnicero if the FBI tipped off the Deputy Director that they were going to raid the room. It was important to convince Conroy that he had only a few hours to deploy a tactical team to arrest the Mexican and expose the duplicitous agent. Conroy was not usually one to approach about making such a unilateral move, but I baited him with a chance to catch a high-level member of the cartel and embarrass his rivals at Homeland Security.

"Well thank you for bringing this to our attention." Conroy ushered me towards his office door. "We'll be sure to give you credit when we make the arrest."

"It might be better if you just call me an anonymous tip. I sure don't want the Mexicans coming after me." I could tell by the way Conroy smiled in reaction that there never was going to be any public credit for my role.

Chapter 60

I walked to the parking garage for my Cadillac XLR. I kept turning around and changing course as I walked what would have normally been a short distance from the CBD to the garage. I could not afford to be followed or abducted as I set the last pieces of the plan Tony and I came up with overnight into motion. I could feel the clock ticking down on El Carnicero's deadline to hand over Jack.

I asked Chief Avery to meet me at the Lakefront Airport with a half dozen of his best sniper-trained SWAT team members. I was sure that the best use for the Barrett rifle the cartel brought to town was to shoot down the Deputy Director's plane as he took off from the airport after his meeting with El Carnicero. The damage done to a jet engine by a fifty caliber round would be obvious to any FAA examiner after they pieced the wreckage back together. The Mexican might even act as though he had conceded to all of Kinkaid's demands because he would never have to do so.

"Why do you need so many snipers?" Avery asked as I approached the knot of uniformed officers standing in the city's helicopter hangar.

"I need them to find another sniper." It was indeed all that I needed them to do for me, but Avery gave a snort as though I was asking them to find a needle in a haystack. I was, but it was a big needle and only a small haystack.

"My snipers aren't good enough for you?" The men with Avery shared his amusement.

"The El Camino cartel brought a gunman and a fifty caliber

rifle to town this weekend. It's probably their intention to shoot down Homeland Security Deputy Director Bradford Kinkaid when his jet takes off from here in a couple of hours." Nobody was laughing now.

"Do you really think we're going to find this guy?" Avery blanched at the prospect of such a thing happening. "More notice would have been nice."

"I could have told you about this a year ago and it wouldn't change the timetable. The shooter will not be moving into position until an hour or so before Kinkaid takes off. You might have driven right past the spot he'll use if you'd started earlier." I did not want to argue or make excuses about the admittedly short notice. My real reason was I wanted to maintain operational secrecy by allowing only a small amount of time between the start of this search and the moment the Deputy Director was due to depart. "The best way to shoot down the jet with a fifty-caliber rifle is to take out either the pilot or an engine as it's taking off. It has a range of over a mile, but they'll probably be shooting from only a few hundred yards distance because of the jet's rate of climb."

"So we just draw a five-hundred-yard circle and start looking?" one of the SWAT team members asked. It was not a rude or dismissive question. He just wanted to confirm he understood what I was asking them to do.

"Not even a full circle. The shooter needs to be almost in direct line with the runway. I'd favor using a boat over shooting from somewhere on land. That thing is going to make a lot of noise when they fire it and they'll want to get away as fast as they can. You've all been trained to take a shot like this and the guy you're looking for isn't likely to be an amateur either." I had nothing else to offer them so they turned their attention to a map of the lakefront.

Avery and I walked away from the group to continue our own conference on the classified operation he felt I was drawing him into once again.

"How the hell did things ever get to this point, Cooter?"

"You told me you didn't want to know how I fixed the situation and I've kept you out of it." I knew that I sounded tired and frustrated. Avery was overwhelmed contemplating the consequences of failing in this one small part of my investigation.

We were out of the hangar before I noticed an executive jet designed to carry fifteen to twenty passengers nearby. A set of imposing Customs Service stickers marked it as having been impounded.

"What's the story on the jet?" I pointed to the maroon and tan jet.

"Customs impounded it last month after they found a load of exotic animals being smuggled out of Costa Rica by a fake tourist service. They'd fly tourists down for a week and then stash the birds and lizards with the tourists' luggage when they flew back."

"Who owns the plane?" I needed a means to convince both Jack and Fernando that their targets were able to leave town on short notice. Luring them to the airport was the easy part, but actually having a jet to use as a prop made my lie more credible.

"Right now it belongs to the United States Government." I could tell that Avery wanted to get back to his men and to take part in the search.

"I've tied you up. I'll tell you everything when it's all over and done with. Just let me know when you catch the sniper." I shook Avery's hand and barely waited for him to walk away before I approached the impounded aircraft and dialed the number on the Customs Service sticker.

Chapter 51

I was back in the Monteleone Hotel shortly after two o'clock. I took a seat at the Carousel Bar and ordered a Bloody Morgan, a Bloody Mary made with spiced rum instead of vodka, as a way to fill the time until all hell broke loose. I was not sure if I was early or late to the meeting between Kinkaid and El Carnicero, but there were men from each of their security details skulking about the entrance and lobby. I chose to watch them while acting like a daytime drunk at the revolving bar. The bodyguards were strutting about the lobby and making it look like a cage full of fighting cocks. The El Caminos looked uncomfortable in the new jackets and slacks they wore to try to blend in. The Brooks Brothers suits and buzz-cut haircuts on what I took to be Jack's men made them no less conspicuous. The dumbest part of their combined presence was that there is normally no reason for anybody to be in the hotel lobby at that hour of the day. It was past the point most people check out, too early to check-in, and anyone actually staying there had better places to be at that time of day.

I planned to lure Fernando and Jack to each join me at the bar. The last part of my plan involved both men, but the order in which I dealt with them was not important. The improbable setting of a fancy hotel bar designed to duplicate a carnival merry-go-round seemed somehow apt for the sideshow magician's act I needed to pull off. I also really needed a drink after the morning I had already endured.

There was a sudden flurry of activity at the door to the hotel, and I turned my attention from the conversation I was having with the bartender to see what was happening. El Carnicero entered the hotel surrounded by Fernando and a dozen heavyset bodyguards. I gave a small wave to Fernando as the tight phalanx passed the bar en route to the elevators. Fernando whispered something to Stephan and headed my way. I had not seen anyone who looked like an FBI agent in the lobby, but I counted the number of security cameras in use and hoped agents were monitoring the situation from the hotel's security center. I was counting on Conroy to play his part in my loosely scripted drama. Things would begin to unravel rapidly if the FBI failed to arrest El Carnicero before he left the hotel.

Fernando took the seat next to me. He made a point of letting me see the gold-plated .45 caliber automatic in his waistband.

"Is that your dress gun? Do you shine it up for special occasions?" Fernando did not laugh at my sarcasm and his face flinched when I insulted his gilded pistol.

"I believe you have something for me, or should I say someone?" He wasted no time getting to the point. "El Carnicero said I get to shoot you unless you give us the man that killed our men."

"Your boss said I had until tomorrow to deliver him. No matter, the guy you want is probably standing in the room with your boss right now. He's in charge of the Deputy Director's security detail." I said this and then casually took a sip of my cocktail. I enjoyed Fernando's momentary loss of composure. "But I'm sure he isn't going to kill your boss here."

Fernando started to leap out of his high-backed wooden bar stool, but I forcibly held him in place with a hand on his thigh. I leaned towards him as he snapped his head in my direction and reached for his golden pistol.

"You don't want to do this here. He is leaving town, along with his men who did the killing. They have a jet waiting at the airport at the lakefront. He tried to recruit me to work for him and said to meet him there at eight o'clock if I am interested. Look for a maroon and tan jet. He'll have a dozen with him." I was counting on Fernando preferring an ambush to staging a spectacular public bloodbath in an expensive hotel. I hoped telling him the men who killed his men would be at the airport was enough to tempt him.

"I can wait." I felt the tension leave Fernando's leg and let loose. He moved his hand from his pistol, while I clicked the safety off on my own.

"Good. Let me buy you a drink," I said with a sigh of genuine relief, and waved to the bartender for two shots of Patron anejo tequila. It was going to be best if there was liquor on Fernando's breath when the FBI locked handcuffs onto his boss. El Carnicero struck me as the sort of psychopath paranoid enough to believe Fernando betrayed him. It would be easier to sell that idea if he spotted his point man drinking with me in the hotel bar as he headed to jail.

Chapter 62

SAC Conroy's surveillance team planted a bug on the room service cart their agent rolled into the Deputy Director's suite with fresh coffee for his meeting. I would have truly enjoyed seeing the expression on Conroy's face when he realized he was listening to the Deputy Director of Homeland Security speaking so cordially with one of the FBI's most wanted international criminals. I am sure he taped more than enough of the conversation to satisfy anyone he might have to answer to later. The SAC is a real stickler for having plenty of evidence before making an arrest, and for people not betraying their country.

I have no idea what actually transpired, but standard procedure would have agents take the elevator to the suite's floor moments before heavily armed members of the local HRT squad barreled out of the stairwells and tossed flash bang grenades at the guards before bursting through the door to the suite. I hate to think what the FBI would have to pay to repair the room's heavy antique door and doorframe.

The version I heard of the arrests was that El Carnicero leapt behind the Deputy Director and put a gun to his head. He backed his way towards one of the towering windows, with its drapes still drawn against the mid-day sun and any prying eyes from across the street. He may have believed he could negotiate his way out of the room in exchange for the safety of such a high-ranking government official. Things might have gone differently had El Carnicero not taken the only other person in the room the FBI intended to arrest as his hostage. El Carnicero eventually accepted the reality of his situation and surrendered. He may have still harbored some notion of immunity and thought the worst that lay ahead was deportation to Mexico.

I can easily imagine him thinking about who betrayed him after Conroy placed him in handcuffs and hustled him towards the waiting elevator. Now came my opportunity to create the illusion of that very betrayal.

Fernando and I were still sitting at the bar, whose slow spin fortuitously placed us directly in front of the entrance for all to see when the FBI hauled El Carnicero and the Deputy Director to the van waiting at the curb. The cartel was not paying the man trusted with their local operation and El Carnicero's security to drink tequila shots with a State Police detective. Fernando and I both saw the expression on El Carnicero's face when he spotted us being chummy at the bar. My drinking companion knew he was never going to satisfactorily explain away how this appeared in the time he was given before being dumped into a wood-chipper or something worse.

"You set me up!" Fernando shouted and jumped off his seat with his gun in hand and pointed it straight at me.

"Put that away before somebody sees," I said and put my hands out ahead of myself to show I was not going to draw my own weapon. I could not clear my holster before he shot me anyway. The bartender froze in place. "I did set you up, but you can still be the hero here. I told you where to find the men who killed your men. Deliver them to your bosses in Mexico and they might believe you about being framed for ratting out The Butcher."

Fernando thankfully gave this a moment's consideration. The frown never left his face, but he did stuff the heavy pistol back under his belt. I sat back down but he chose not to join me this time.

"They will be there tonight? You are sure?" He knew delivering Jack and his men was his only way out of trouble. There were enough men and firepower at his disposal to overpower a dozen men in an ambush.

"Eight o'clock, at Lakefront Airport. Maroon and tan jet. You can't miss it." I kept my hands on the bar as he backed away and then shakily gulped the last two shots the bartender had poured before the commotion began.

"I don't think I could do your job, Detective," the bartender sighed as he grabbed the empty glasses. Then again, what he witnessed was probably one of the least interesting stories he could tell by the end of this last week of Mardi Gras.

Chapter 53

Conroy was still reeling when I approached him at FBI headquarters on Poydras. The full comprehension of what arresting a man far above him on his professional ladder could mean to his own career was beginning to settle in. The political bombshell on the audio cassette he sat holding in his hands nearly rendered him catatonic. I had to say his name three times to get his attention and make him look up from his desk. The agents who took part in the takedown were also unusually subdued.

"Well, this should make for one hell of a press conference," I opined and finally took the seat he offered just a few hours earlier.

"I've got calls in to the Director and to Kinkaid's boss at Homeland. I'm sunk if that meeting was authorized like he's saying it was." Conroy looked at me with a concerned face. Seeing me added a new level layer of rage to our relationship. "You set me up, didn't you?"

"Everyone's accusing me of that today. You've had bad sources before," I deflected the accusation. "Do you really think anyone above Kinkaid is going to verify he was sent here to negotiate a deal with the El Camino drug cartel now that this has gone public? People will be stumbling over themselves getting to the exits."

"You're right there," Conroy sighed in relief. Scandals happened often enough that he knew I was probably right. I do not think either of us really believed Kinkaid was an errand boy in this. He arrived over the weekend without his usual entourage in tow and I doubt anyone at DHS knew Kinkaid was in New Orleans until

Conroy made his calls.

"I'd say you're going to get to announce arresting El Carnicero and then have to put the Deputy Director on a plane to Washington to face the music there. Nobody is going to want a trial. That tape is your magic ticket out of here if you want." I did not think I was exaggerating his position. "I do have a favor to ask, though."

"I think we're even right now. I suppose Kinkaid had time to declassify that file she received like I asked." Conroy was a terrible liar and his face showed it. I knew he was lying about being the one to get the file declassified, which I doubted would ever happen. He was also still peddling the idea that he was the one who cut my sister loose. "You might earn another favor when people start answering my calls."

I saw no reason to confront him about lying to me. My sister was out of trouble and I still needed that favor.

"I just want to speak with one of the guys in Kinkaid's security detail."

"About?" Conroy still distrusted my motives in this. His own career was at risk until his phone rang.

"About other things. You won't want to record what we discuss."

"I think I have all the tape from you I want for one day, anyway," he said and tossed the toxic tape onto his desk.

Two of the agents brought Jack to one of the conference rooms still shackled at his wrists and ankles. I sat at the head of the wooden table and they placed Jack in a seat next to me before leaving the room and taking up positions outside the door. They left the blinds open and I could not close them on my own. Conroy wanted the agents present to be sure I was not beating a suspect in their care.

"Well played, Cooter. I think Director Kinkaid and I both seriously underestimated your ingenuity," Jack said and clapped his bound hands together. He accepted a glass of water from the pitcher in the center of the table. "What do we have to discuss now? Isn't your work here done?"

"Almost. I spoke with Fernando Rodriguez about you this morning. The cartel deserved to know what really happened to their men."

"They weren't buying that it was the punk kids in the Peetes, anyway." Jack didn't bat an eye at the mention of the cartel's lieutenant because he had to know who he was.

"You should have picked a much bigger donkey to pin that tail on," I said and cracked a grin. "I told Fernando I would trade you to him if the cartel agreed to leave town."

"Do you think the FBI is going to let you do that?" Jack did not sound all that worried about his safety.

"Who knows? You are part of a mess Homeland Security would like to have disappear. I know how it feels to be disavowed." I enjoyed my moment of gloating about the reversal in our roles before I leaned across the table and lowered my voice. "I hoped you wouldn't mind spending your time waiting for D-Tech to get you released talking with me about Iraq."

"What the hell. What do you want to know?" Jack took another sip of water and relaxed in his chair.

"You ratted out my team after the ambush, right?"

"That's a strong word to use. And, no, I did not tell the Iraqis about your entire team. I didn't mention D-Tech at all. They gave me the choice of providing the Iraqis with the names of Tony's men or taking personal responsibility for the problems you created not just for the Iraqis, but for D-Tech as well. You derailed the contracts D-Tech was about to sign with the new government," Jack explained. What he said about D-Tech changed my line of questioning.

"You told me we were working for the State Department." I knew this made me sound naïve but I didn't care.

"I may have extrapolated a bit. The information you gave me did wind up there, if that makes you feel better. The State Department used it to screen the Iraqis running for office. They wanted to be sure only candidates friendly towards the United States made it onto the ballots. They didn't have to influence the election itself after we chose all the candidates who were running."

"So, the mission wasn't about finding the people behind the attacks and stopping them. It was about keeping people who didn't like us being in their country from taking control." Knowing this made a great many things that bothered me about the focus he wanted on certain people I thought were only small players a lot clearer.

"Oh, we definitely needed you to stop the attacks. Doing that was how you had access to all those military assets," Jack seemed to be enjoying himself. He knew how much all of this hurt my pride and undermined the rationalizations I made to approve the mission's most ruthless actions.

"You knew the Iraqis would track my men down and kill them if the operation you sanctioned was ever discovered."

"I knew somebody was going to die if that happened, and I wasn't going to let it be Americans. I always had a way to get you out if it fell apart. Your pal Tony and his men were cannon fodder to D-Tech," Jack seemed unbothered by the consequences of this attitude in the aftermath of the ambush. "I specifically told you to have all of your suspects in custody by the time the new Iraqi government took over and you failed to do so. You didn't arrest the last one until after the Iraqis were back to ruling themselves."

Jack spoke to me as if I were a disobedient child and he wanted me to admit I was responsible for what happened.

"The bastard was no less guilty of paying people to kill our troops just because his relatives were running things."

"No, but he went from being a disgruntled former member of Saddam's regime to having a brother in the new government. Arresting him caused huge problems and I needed to fix them as quickly as I could." The way he said that struck a chord, and I realized something I never considered until that very moment.

"You paid somebody to ambush us."

"I've always wondered when you'd figure that out. I told them to grab your prisoner and leave. I will say, though, that nothing worked out like I planned. The last anyone saw of your prisoner was Tony shoving him into a car and one of his men driving away with him." Jack broke into a cruel grin and I had to grab the rounded edge of the heavy table to keep from hitting him. "What do you actually know about what happened after the ambush anyway?" Jack seemed intent on driving a wedge between Tony and myself.

"I missed some things, being in a coma and all. Tony told me he paid bribes to get us out, but we've intentionally avoided discussing everything that happened."

"All that American currency you found during your raids was looted from the pallets of cash our own Treasury Department sent to Iraq to help with the rebuilding. Tony found a list of offshore accounts where the guy you grabbed stashed millions of dollars his family stole under Hussein and from those pallets of cash. Tony emptied the accounts within hours of the ambush, but I made him transfer cash amounts equal to the part of those accounts the Iraqi treasury knew about so the two of you could leave the country. I let him to do that or you'd both have gone on trial in an Iraqi court for kidnapping." I could tell that Jack's role in those negotiations fueled a big part of his grudge against us. "I couldn't involve the State Department in what was basically a bad business deal for D-Tech, so I gave the names of your men to the head of their new secret police force after Tony skipped out with the rest of the money. It still seems like a fair trade to me."

Jack took another sip of water and then broke into a smug grin. "So, Tony never mentioned where he came up with the money to open your little restaurant?"

"He told me the State Department paid us a big bounty for bringing down the insurrectionist operations that targeted Coalition troops and diplomats."

Jack laughed aloud at the very idea. "Tony has thirty-five million dollars stashed somewhere. Not one dime of it came from the State Department, and you apparently don't know where it is either. The most State did was approve Tony's visa so he could move to New Orleans. They did that because I convinced them that it was going to be easier keeping tabs on the two of you together than to worry what you'd do separately."

"What makes you so sure Tony has the money?" I saw no reason to not go on believing the State Department story.

""Think how much money he paid for your medical bills, to open your restaurant, for those cars you drive. By the way, Tony is very good at hiding his accounts. D-Tech still has not found a trace of the money. Well, other than that damn restaurant you two own."

"You're telling me that D-Tech has been looking for the money all this time?" He could have admitted to being the one looking. I believed D-Tech should have lost interest at some point during the past five years.

"It's been an exercise for their research teams." Jack shrugged. "The most they have found is that Tony claims to do an extraordinary amount of outside catering. A restaurant must be a great way to launder cash."

"I suppose it could be." I never gave our business account any thought. Tony always handles anything involving the restaurant and its finances. I get a generous check once a month simply for having my name on the liquor license. "None of that really matters anymore."

"You sure had me fooled." Jack laughed.

"We both know they're going to cut you loose in another couple of hours, assuming you didn't try to shoot it out with the FBI." I raised an eyebrow in query and he shook his head to confirm his men had the sense to surrender without a fight. "They'll write you off as private security and tell you to get out of town while they figure out what to do with Kinkaid."

"Sounds about right," Jack said with undue smugness. He knew exactly how the FBI was going to process him. I think Jack was only concerned that I might tell Conroy everything I knew about his activities over the last few months.

"I am supposed to meet Fernando Rodriguez at eight o'clock tonight to tell him where to find you."

"Go on." Jack was interested in my story, but it was hard to tell how much of it he believed. We had reached the point that if either of us said the sun was overhead the other would immediately look skyward to verify it.

"Willie Hawkins says Fernando told him he is leaving town about eight o'clock. There's a jet already on the tarmac at the airport out on the lakefront. It's a big maroon thing with tan trim," I used his own informant's name to give him a reason to trust what I was telling him. "Maybe you should take one last crack at knocking them out of business."

"Why are you telling me this?"

"To be honest, I'm hoping they kill you. Failing that, you killing enough of them might make the cartel forget all about me," I suggested. He would believe self-preservation might be part of my motivation because it would have been part of his own. "If you do manage to kill their leadership and enough of their men, the cartel might decide New Orleans isn't a friendly place to do business and isn't that what D-Tech promised they'd do in the first place? The cartel will make the gangs they're in business with here start picking their stuff up in Houston and the DEA can pick them off on I-10.""

"Eight o'clock, huh?" Jack repeated. "You planning on being there to tell Rodriguez where to find me?"

"I was thinking we might carpool."

"Nah, I'll just meet you two out there," Jack laughed. I knew I was as much in his sights as was Rodriguez.

Chapter 54

Tony was in his kitchen office filling out Monday's produce order when I came through the doors from the dining room. Joaquin was sitting at the bar, working on the following week's server schedule. He was grumbling loudly about the certainty of no-shows among the staff during the last week of Mardi Gras. Our servers were not going to make near the money working for us that they could make working on Bourbon Street those few days.

"Got a minute to talk?" Tony looked up from what he was doing when he heard the tone in my voice.

"Here or upstairs?" He swiveled his chair to face me.

"Maybe upstairs would be better." Tony did not ask what I needed speak to him about. He just headed towards the elevator.

We rode in silence, but it was not an awkward or heavy one. We avoid talking on the elevator because we both know it is the last place before our apartments that somebody could plant a listening device. It is easier stay silent than to constantly sweep the elevator for hidden microphones.

Tony's apartment is a mirror image of mine in layout, but his sense of decorating leans much more towards Modern furnishings and more abstract art. It is hard to reconcile that our apartments started out as twins. I took a seat on the low red leather sofa and he sat on one of the wide armless chairs opposite me.

"I just met with Jack and he told me a few things I have believed were different all these years. He said you ran off with our prisoner, and he gave me a much different version of where our money came from. He says the State Department did not pay any bounty. His version is that you emptied some family's bank accounts."

"Do you believe him?"

"I don't know that it even matters. I am curious what became of our prisoner, but I'm more worried that D-Tech is still looking for the money from those accounts. I hope you can keep it hidden. Assuming his version is right, what did become of the guy we had?" I knew Jack was telling me the truth. Tony lacks the poker face it takes to be a convincing liar because he does not care what anyone thinks.

"I don't know what happened to him. I only know what I did with him." I hate arguing with Tulip or Katie because lawyers have an infuriating gift with the English language. I hate these conversations with Tony because he always tries to hide behind his supposed lack of vocabulary.

"And that was what?" I hoped we were not going to spend the entire day playing word games.

"I traded him to the Iranians so they would help get our friends out of the country. Jack turned everyone in, including you, after the ambush."

"I know what Jack did. So, how much money did you take?"

"I spent a lot of it. Money leaves faster than love, my friend. I gave a million dollars to each of our men that got out of Iraq alive. I paid all of your medical bills. We built this place and we have never made any money."

"Ballpark." I suggested. His brows furrowed at my choice of slang terms. "Roughly how much money is left?"

"A lot?" He held up a finger to tell me to be patient and then walked into his bedroom. I could hear him opening the safe under the head of his bed.

Tony returned a moment later and handed me a gold bar, with the troy weight stamped in English numerals. Gold is one of the few things you can place in anyone's hand and know they will never want to give it back.

"This is why they cannot find the money." Tony grinned and pointed to the glimmering troy-ounce bar. "I converted most of the cash to this before we left Italy. I keep it in the safes we have at the Security Center. I sell a few every year and tell our accountant it is money from big catering jobs. I take the cash back to pay bills we don't have."

"So how many do you have?" I now added tax audit to the list of things to fear in life. At least I never signed the bistro's tax returns.

"I don't know." Tony said this and immediately saw my frustration ramping up. "I paid twenty-six million dollars for the gold bars."

"That's all I need to know." I was relieved to have this clear between us and to know the truth behind our seemingly endless wealth. I was disappointed to hear that he was not running the restaurant as a means of making a living. Apparently, Strada Ammazarre was something between a laundromat and a hobby.

"That was twenty-six million dollars in gold five years ago." Tony was waiting for me to absorb the first number. "The price has doubled since then."

I looked at the bar with a new sense of wonder. It sat in a safe for five years as inert as a paperweight while the world changed around it. I looked up from my hand to smile back at my partner.

"Then why in the hell are either of us working this hard?" Tony and I both laughed heartily at the question.

"This is why I want to buy the pizza café the bank keeps offering to sell us. It could be very profitable as well," Tony said. I had almost forgotten about our banker making the offer on the building and the pizza business a block away.

"Christ, buy the whole damn block if you want to." He had to tug the gold bar from my hand and left me thinking of the nearly equal combination of possibilities and penalties our partnership held in store for the two of us.

Chapter 65

very called from the airport to say his team swept the area
three times and found no sign of a sniper. I thanked him for
spending the time the NOPD snipers undoubtedly thought
of as wasted. I wondered if the cartel recalled the sniper
because murdering a disgraced bureaucrat was not going to send
much of a message to anyone. Cancelling the hit on such short
notice would have meant the sniper and El Carnicero were in
nearly constant contact. I wondered what other operations the
Butcher was running while he was in town, and if his arrest
disrupted any of them. I saw no reason to believe that telling
Fernando where he could intercept Jack took killing me off the
cartel's list of things to do.

I risked exposing Ritchie's location by heading to Audubon
Place to check in on him. I had received no calls from my mother
about how things were going since I sent him to stay with her. My
mother is not one to hold any opinions to herself, so her silence
over the past day and a half was beginning to worry me. It turned
out I was worried about the wrong person.

I found Roger sitting in the library reading the latest edition of
New Orleans Magazine.

"Homework?" I jested. I liked Roger a lot, but his background
as a lowly dog-handler did not prepare him for life as a kept man
on Audubon Place.

"Not hardly. If you're looking for Ritchie, you should try the
conservatory. I think you'll find that situation pretty funny."

I could hear music as I approached the glass-enclosed room

overlooking the manicured garden and lap pool behind the mansion. The tall vine-covered masonry wall at the rear of the property keeps out the hoi polloi. I opened the door to the conservatory to confirm that what I was hearing was indeed music by a funk-inspired group from the Seventies named WAR. The song streaming from my mother's laptop was called The World is a Ghetto. I was left momentarily speechless by the incongruity of the music and my surroundings. The world would love to live in a ghetto as nice as this mansion.

Ritchie wore clothes my mother must have sent someone to Perlis to buy for her guest. This was possibly the first pair of pleated twill khaki pants he had ever worn. The button-down collar shirt bore Perlis' signature crawfish on the left breast. His shoes were leather lace-ups. If nothing else came from this experience, Ritchie now owned his very own Fresh Prince of Bel-Aire costume for next Halloween. I did my best to keep a straight face and he did an admirable job of acting comfortable in this new wardrobe.

"Well, look who's here," my mother said and crossed the room to give me a peck on the cheek. It also afforded her an opportunity to whisper in my ear. "Where did you find this poor child?"

"What do you mean by that?" That was just such a loaded statement coming from her.

"His clothes were a mess. He had not eaten properly in days. He was nearly feral." She has a capacity for sounding judgmental while appearing to be concerned for another's situation. A roomful of her peers is enough to make me head into their manicured gardens to scream.

"Well, mother, he was kidnapped." I thought for sure I told her this about Ritchie.

"Oh, I know all that. That was dreadful. And it's not much nicer that you won't let him call his mother or uncle." Ritchie was keeping his head buried in the laptop. He knew she had the best likelihood of making me change my mind about the safety protocols.

"That's part of why I dropped by. I think Ritchie can go home tomorrow morning. Things are falling in place better than I'd hoped." I was not about to explain what I meant by that. The less all of them knew of what my day entailed, the better off everyone would be. "I just came from the FBI and they've dropped their investigation into Tulip. I thought you should know as soon as possible."

My mother's face twitched as her emotions and muscles strove to coordinate an appropriate response. She settled on a relieved smile and slightly moistened eyes, but nothing that might smudge her mascara. She gave me a quick but sincere hug and then stepped back again.

"What are you doing out here?" I could not leave without knowing.

"I heard the horrid music Ritchie was listening to on the radio in his room and found out he has no idea how much good music came before it. I've been introducing him to some classics he should know about." I had utterly forgotten my mother was a music major before becoming an art major. She earned a degree in design when she graduated from Vassar without having found a suitable husband.

"Your mom's the bomb," Ritchie declared as she cued up the next song and Jimmy Cliff's voice filled the room.

"I think you've seen enough bombs." I tried to joke. He probably could not hear my response at the volume he was playing the music. I turned back to my mother, whose own hips were swaying in a way I was not entirely comfortable watching. "I had no idea you liked this music."

"Oh, Lord, I hate it. Your father used to take me to these concerts and I was always afraid we'd be stabbed. I just couldn't stand this young man thinking music for his people didn't start until he was born." I saw no point in addressing any of the manifest racism in that sentence with a nearly seventy-year old woman who could not hear herself speak.

"Well, keep up the good work. I'll take him home tomorrow."

"My psychic told me things would work out. He says you're one of those rare people who can dig themselves through a deep hole." I had long ago given up on ever being able to dissuade her from wasting her money on an internet swami. I was usually most dismayed that his disembodied advice so closely resembled my late father's way of thinking and speaking.

"Well this time that was a foxhole." I meant to joke. The humor was lost on her because she had never been in a foxhole. "I will plan on picking Ritchie up about eight o'clock tomorrow morning if that's alright."

"I cannot imagine why it wouldn't be." My mother looked at me as if I should explain what I had just said.

"I didn't know if you were planning to give Ritchie elocution lessons or planned something else I might interrupt when I take him back to his life as a gangbanger." It came out a bit more cruelly than I intended. I was just having a hard time seeing the young man she appeared to have cast in her own production of My Fair Lady as anything but the Pistol Peete I knew he still was.

I am sure Ritchie heard every word of our conversation. I owed him a small debt of gratitude for behaving himself while staying with two people with whom he had so little in common. He was certainly the first high school dropout from Central City to sleep in a guest bed over the history of the Deveraux family's century-long occupancy of the mansion. Perhaps my having found a way for people from both sides of the high wall around Audubon Place to come together was going to have a good effect. It was a far better thought than imagining Ritchie burglarizing the place after he went back to his more familiar ways. I didn't give a moment's thought to the possibility his time with my mother might inspire him to change his ways, because his ability to make a living and be accepted in his chosen community didn't allow for dreams about living a straight life.

Chapter 55

Captain Hammond obtained permission for me to use the Customs Service's impounded jet as part of my investigation. He had done so without once asking me what use I had for a jet that could not take off. The Customs Service also stipulated that one of their own pilots would taxi the plane to any location I requested. I did not want the State Police to have to pay for repairs to a fleet of civilian and commercial airplanes after the smoke finally cleared. I was holding onto a slim hope that the jet would not become a heap of smoldering scrap metal.

I asked Chief Avery to meet me at Strada Ammazarre after the last afternoon parade was over. His evening was going to be a busy one, with the Super Bowl and the hordes that would be up all night celebrating or grieving. Too much alcohol was going to be involved either way. He had a full evening, but I still needed to add to his worries.

"I heard the FBI caught the Deputy Director meeting with a honcho from the El Caminos at the Monteleone." Avery could tell I already knew about the arrests. The news must have travelled far and wide for Avery to know so many details about the arrest only a few hours after the FBI raided the hotel room. It was a sure sign that Homeland Security disavowed any knowledge of what its Deputy Director was up to when someone in D.C. finally returned SAC Conroy's calls. They may have asked Conroy to take him out and toss him under the nearest bus.

"Yeah, I'd say his career is over and done with. He's lucky

nobody will want a trial. Hopefully, there won't be any Congressional hearings, either."

"I take it that whole thing he cooked up here is over now as well?" Avery sounded optimistic about this possibility.

"Close. There are still some dangerous loose ends."

"Such as?" Avery's relieved and triumphant smile disappeared. He probably thought I invited him to the bistro to celebrate the Deputy Director's downfall. My situation report and facial expression popped that balloon.

"Well there are still armed men from both sides running loose and looking for a fight. The operators Kinkaid hired to do the dirty work that was supposed to look like a gang war haven't given up on wiping out the Mexicans and the cartel's reinforcements are now hunting for Kinkaid's operators." I waited for him to finish his first bottle of beer and take a firm hold of his second before continuing. "I've arranged for them to ambush one another at Lakefront Airport. I've tried to arrange things so nobody else is likely to be involved or get hurt."

"That's probably one of your very worst ideas yet."

"This is going to happen eventually. It's the safest place to let them have at it."

"Probably so. Will you need anything from me?" Avery hates any plan that incites violence. He offered no alternative plan because he did not see one any more than I did. He trusted that I based my decision to instigate a modern-day Gunfight at the OK Corral on what I knew of things he still insisted on not knowing. He also trusted me to find a way to keep our names out of the papers when the smoke cleared.

"I don't want NOPD officers to get caught in the middle. Can you find a way to have the District Commander out there ignore any 911 calls they'll likely get when the shooting starts?"

"I can have someone call him and say the Film Commission approved a movie shoot. It's the only plausible excuse I can come up with for what you're talking about." The city has been the backdrop for more than its share of motion picture gun battles. One more was not going seem at all suspicious.

"Tell him the film company is called D-Tech." Avery did not ask for an explanation as to why he should do so and I did not offer one. The idea of getting their name in the middle of the mess I was about to cause just made me feel good. Avery wrote the name down on a napkin. "I'll call you when it's over and you can send in whoever you want to clean things up. Maybe suggest that bounty hunters had it out with the Mexican cartel. Homeland Security will probably toss a heavy blanket over the scene so it won't much matter what story you use."

"Where are you going to be while this is happening?"

"Both sides are expecting me to be there. I'm sort of stuck."

"Even your worst plans aren't usually this stupid, Cooter." Avery sighed and took a long pull from his beer. "Do you want any backup?"

"I'm not going to drag anyone else into this that I don't have to," I tried to explain. I certainly did not want to endanger his life or Tony's. I needed Tony to survive in case I didn't, so he could settle my affairs instead of my sister or mother. They had already done so after I was reported dead in Iraq. Making them do so twice would have just been unnecessarily cruel.

"Okay," Avery shrugged. He was not about to volunteer. "So, the plan is that you'll call me when the coast is clear? What time is this happening?"

"Somewhere between seven and nine. I told everyone to be there at eight o'clock, but they'll both turn up early if they plan to ambush one another."

I had other reasons to use eight o'clock in the story I gave both parties than that it would be dark at that hour. The airport handles only a few flights once the sun goes down. I didn't want to make anyone curious by shutting down the airport entirely. I also wanted to give both sides ample time to plan and execute their ambushes. Mostly I wanted everyone living near the airport to have their attention focused on the Super Bowl rather than what was going on at this airport. If the Saints played well enough, people might mistake the shooting for normal celebratory gunfire.

"I'd usually lie and say it sounds like you know what you're doing, but this sounds suicidal. You need to stop trying to cheat death." I saw Avery was afraid that what he had just said would haunt him as being the last thing he ever said to me. He finished his beer in two gulps and gave me a long hug before walking out the door in silence.

Chapter 57

I loaded my ready bag into my Cadillac CTS-V wagon as soon as Chief Avery left the bar, while Katie and Tulip were still shopping at the French Market. The bag held my ballistic vest, with every ceramic plate I could fit in place, two of the pistols Tony and I lifted from D-Tech's surveillance team, and multiple clips of ammunition for the pistols. I also tossed my holstered pistol into the bag, but really did not want any of my own shell casings to wind up in an evidence bag. I changed clothes after speaking with Avery and left the restaurant in jeans, boots and a thick sweater. The sweater would provide some cushioning beneath the vest if someone did shoot me. The initial pain of a bullet's impact is not that much different whether you are wearing a ballistic vest or not. The vest just greatly improves the odds of surviving taking a bullet to the chest or back.

I asked Katie to record the Super Bowl so we could watch it together after a meeting I absolutely could not get out of attending. She forgave my absence only because she could tell I was no happier about missing a game I waited my entire life to see because of some adult responsibilities.

I met with the Customs Service pilot as he began to turn on the jet's interior lights and warm its engines. I fed him a scenario in which the plane was a prop in a sting operation I was fronting. We decided his best way out of the scene would be to tell the first person who approached the plane that he needed to go to Flight Operations in order to finalize his flight plan. I flashed my badge to convince the private security force responsible for patrolling the airport to make its final pass by the jet no later than six-forty-five and then stay away until I gave them the all clear. I did not want to see anyone without a stake in the outcome get hurt, or possibly be called as a witness about what happened.

I rode in the very comfortable jet while the pilot taxied to an open spot west of the main runway, placing the jet at the end of a concrete apron parallel to the runway and at the far edge of the fueling tarmac. I hoped that the distance and likely firing angles would minimize the chance of a stray shot hitting one of the huge tanks holding the airport's fuel supplies. The thick concrete floodwall behind the jet was going to take the brunt of at least half of any gunfire, and the wide-open space between the runways and the masonry terminal building could catch most of the rest. It was too much to hope for that the men who showed up would all be good shots and not miss their targets.

A black Chevy Suburban drove slowly past the jet just before seven o'clock. I could not see who was inside the vehicle, but counted four occupants including the driver. The SUV headed to the terminal and two men got out and entered the small light-toned brick Art Deco-era building. The Suburban then returned to the tarmac and parked about thirty feet away from the jet.

Jack discussed something with the passenger in the front seat before he stepped out of the back and began to walk in my direction. He carried no luggage and wore the same suit he had worn all day. As he came closer, I could tell there was a Kevlar vest under his dress shirt. There is just no way to wear one without it showing.

"Wouldn't you rather be watching the Super Bowl right now?" Jack asked and then laughed.

"Someone's taping it for me."

"You're quite the optimist," Jack snorted as he topped the jet's stairway. He located the jet's wet bar and poured a tumbler half-full of Johnny Walker Red. "You're not likely to live long enough to watch that tape."

"Why's that?"

"Because whichever side wins this is going to hold you accountable for their friends being dead." He had a point, but this wasn't the one he wanted me to see. "Now, me personally, I am going to shoot you just because you keep being a thorn on my side. I am going to shoot you and then ruin your pal Tony's world until he gives me all that money."

"You? Not the Iraqis it was taken from?" I caught his word play immediately.

"No. I have earned it. I've had people watching you two since you came to New Orleans, waiting for you to slip up."

"I guess it's true that you aren't paranoid if they really are out to get you," I tried to joke. All the same, I became deeply troubled by this disclosure. "I guess we didn't slip up."

"Not in any way I could make use of," Jack sighed and sat down in one of the high-backed seats. I sat down across from him, my hands closer to a pistol than I believed his were. He had the advantage of facing the jet's doorway. "So, I decided to just start messing with you until something came along to really get back at the two of you."

"Like this fiasco?"

"It didn't start out as one," Jack assured me. "And it didn't start the way you probably think it did. This did not begin with either Kinkaid or Jill. Your buddy Boudreaux is the one who set this in motion."

"No way," I argued. I could not see Alex Boudreaux being the inspiration for something of this sort. "Convince me. I am going to be dead soon anyway, right? Dead men tell no tales."

"You aren't a normal person Holland. You are a freaking cat and you have too many lives left." Jack seemed amused with his joke, but he kept talking now that the scotch was loosening his tongue. "Junior Hauser lost a bunch of money when you exposed his racket. He was set to blame that Boudreaux character for all of his problems, especially after the El Camino cartel came in and stole the deal Hauser wanted to make with the Black Knights. Boudreaux figured out the men I put in his houses were some sort of undercover cops, so he tried to make a deal with them. He swore he could help them get rid of the Mexicans if someone could help him with the charges he thought the Feds were about to drop in his lap."

"You're telling me Boudreaux is getting a get-out-of-jail-free card for tipping your guys off to the Mexican cartel being here? The DEA probably already had that figured out. I think you are just spinning tales, Jack. Maybe you are trying to keep me distracted. Maybe you're just seeing if you can make me mad." I stopped believing his story at the point he made Boudreaux into a criminal mastermind.

"He convinced me that there was a way to make some money out of the Mexican's muscling in here. I was still on good terms with people at D-Tech and drew up a plan to help the Fed's keep the cartel from getting a foothold here, only to find out Kinkaid was running interference for them. He had struck some sort of deal with them when he was still a DOJ prosecutor in Phoenix after 9/11. He was looking for some way to break the deal without doing so causing a big scandal. Jill and I approached him with my plan and he jumped at it. D-Tech hired me to arrange all of their local housing and I helped build that list of addresses Jill gave Ray. I needed him so I could find out what you were telling your prosecutor girlfriend. Things started getting out of hand after Boudreaux put D-Tech in bed with Hauser by having them use the Mob's incinerator in Biloxi. He used that to blackmail Kinkaid into getting the charges against him dropped. I'll bet why you got pulled into this has been bothering you more than anything else." Kinkaid felt we suckered him into a deal as bad as the ones he made with the Mexicans in the first place. He wanted you to figure out Boudreaux was involved and come up with some way of taking him down despite the deal we made." Jack's story took a much too credible turn with these disclosures. This made his threat on my life all the more serious as well. He was coming clean just to knock me off balance enough to distract me long enough to kill me.

"I'll check this out, tomorrow," I said as calmly as I could. I felt my hands growing uncharacteristically sweaty.

Fernando and his men arrived at seven forty-five in three panel vans. They parked along the floodwall, facing away from the jet. The van parked closest to us had a number of holes in it that led me to believe it was the second van in the ambushed caravan from the past weekend.

The pilot and I stepped out of the jet and stood at the top of the stairway until Fernando and I locked eyes. I told the pilot to start walking towards the terminal and not look back. He did not need told twice after stepping out of the jet and seeing the area teeming with armed men. He probably walked right through the terminal and out the other side.

"Where's he going?" Fernando demanded as he came to a stop at the foot of the fold-down metal stairs.

"He has to sign off on the flight plan." I shrugged.

Fernando lost interest in the pilot and turned his attention back to me. He spotted Jack staring at him from the interior of the sizeable aircraft.

"Is that the man you promised?"

"His name's Jack Rickman. He's all yours if you still want him," I said and stepped to one side in the narrow cabin doorway. Fernando was reluctant to climb the stairs and separate himself from his men.

"He came here without a fight?" He anticipated that I would set a trap, but he could not see it clearly just yet.

The tarmac was evenly lit by pole-mounted lights and floodlights mounted on the distant terminal, leaving damn few shadows around the jet and no obstacles anyone might use for cover. Fernando could have concluded that Jack's men were hiding below the level of the jet's windows as if they were concealed in a modern-day Trojan horse, and this might have worked, but all his men would have to do was shoot through the thin aluminum skin of the jet to kill them all. I really hoped he did not decide to do that without checking first because I was still responsible for the plane.

"I wouldn't say the fight is out of him." I motioned for Jack to come forward and present himself to his would-be captor. He was acting far too calm. It told me he had a plan up his sleeve for getting out of this situation.

"Jack, meet Fernando. Fernando, Jack. I think my work here is done so I'll leave the two of you to it."

"Stick around," Jack said and grabbed the back of my vest. He trapped me on the stairway. He used my shirt collar to move me like a shield to block anyone from taking a shot at him from below.

Fernando stood below us backed by nearly three dozen heavily armed gunmen. Each of his shooters carried at least two pistols apiece tucked into their pants, and they carried about an equal number of pump-action shotguns and AK-47s. Most of them also wore vests like mine.

Four black Chevrolet Suburbans screeched to a halt directly in front of the jet, blocking its forward progress. They meant to flank the vehicles along the floodwall, and to put Fernando's men in a kill box created by the sets of vehicles, the floodwall, and the jet. The airport's lights abruptly went out, probably thanks to Jack's men who entered the terminal earlier. D-Tech's mercenaries began pouring out of the armored SUVs. They all wore night vision goggles and made quick use of them to begin pouring gunfire into the gunmen still clustered around Fernando. The Mexicans were blind in the dark, but they instinctively returned fire towards any muzzle flashes they spotted. They were not nearly as skilled or disciplined in their tactics as the men they faced, but they were equally fearless.

The driver of the lead van sped forward before making a sharp U-turn and flipping his headlights to their brightest setting. This backlit the Mexicans and temporarily blinded Jack's men in their night-vision goggles. The Mexicans tried to exploit their brief advantage. Those who were still able to fight dispersed and attempted to outflank the Suburbans. Jack's trained operatives tossed smoke grenades in an effort to make themselves harder to see or hit. Fernando brought superior numbers and diverse firepower to the fight, but team discipline and years of experience on the part of Jack's former Special-Operations soldiers would win the fight.

The military-trained operators worked in groups of two and three to pick off their opponents, and seemed to disregard that they were easy targets as they fired in the open. The Mexicans returned fire either singly or in undisciplined clusters that were easy to pick off. Both sides had the sense to wear vests, but the Mexicans wasted the money on theirs. Jack's operators only aimed for the Mexican's heads.

Fernando leapt behind the stairwell when the shooting started and waited until the firing moved away from the plane before he dashed to the safety of the shot-up van. He opened the side door and then closed it behind it himself. I truly thought he had either gone into hiding or planned to drive away. I could not have been more wrong.

The Mexicans did not bring a sniper and a fifty-caliber rifle to town. Fernando flung the rear doors of the van open to expose a fifty-caliber machine gun bolted to the floor of the van. Short bursts of massive armor-piercing rounds made short work of the light protective plating in the Suburbans. I could see plumes of blood erupting behind the vehicles. The Mexicans fell to prone positions and tried to force Jack's men to fall back against their vehicles. Jack's men chose to run forward to close the distance to their adversaries and make the man firing the machine gun risk hitting his own men. Pistols and knives began to replace the rifles and shotguns.

Jack was still standing erect on the stairway, holding a Beretta in his hand. I felt exposed standing in the doorway, and hastily retreated to the interior of the borrowed jet. I pulled my MP-5 machine pistol from its hiding place and aimed at the open doorway. I was fully prepared to shoot anyone who stepped into the cabin. I had no friends here. Jack stood his ground and watched the bloody tableau unfold with the detachment of someone watching a war movie. He calmly set his cocktail at the top of the jet's stair ramp before circling behind the Suburbans to approach the van carrying the machine gun.

Jack chose his moment and then lobbed a flash-bang grenade inside. Noise and a brilliant, white light filled the van a second later and he calmly walked around to the open rear door to begin firing his pistol into the smoke emanating from the interior of the van. He pulled his phone from his pocket and spoke into it briefly. Moments later, the lights came back on across the airport grounds.

The Mexicans found themselves not just exposed but leaderless and clearly outnumbered, yet they continued to fight. Jack's remaining men divided into two teams and formed firing lines to attack the Mexicans with a wall of lead measured shoulder-to-shoulder. There was no longer any place for either set of shooters to fall back. The Mexicans found themselves with their back to the floodwall and D-Tech's gunmen fought backed against their own burning vehicles. The operators who manipulated the lights walked directly into the firefight from the terminal to outflank any fleeing Mexicans. They picked off the few shooters running in their direction from the fight. Fewer chose survival over a senseless death than I imagined would.

I looked at my watch when the noise stopped. It was fifteen minutes after nine. The firefight left the tarmac littered with smoldering and immobile vehicles and the bodies of at least three dozen gunshot victims. Jack walked back to me, executing any wounded Mexicans he passed along the way, while his own operators began patching up their badly wounded comrades. Jack's winning side suffered few losses, and surprisingly few injuries. Most of their losses came from the massive fifty-caliber rounds. The majority of them escaped injury altogether other than bruises and sore ribs under their vests. I thought I had seen two Mexicans climb over the floodwall. The lake was full of cold water and is over twenty miles wide, so it was a short escape.

"I guess that's that," Jack declared and holstered his pistol as I came down the steps from the jet and surveyed the scene. The jet had taken only a couple of rounds, which I was hoping missed anything vital. A little patching and painting would not be too much to ask Hammond to pay for, certainly not compared to buying the whole jet.

Jack and I returned to inspect the cartel's war wagon. We had both seen heavy machine guns mounted on vehicles as improbable as a Suzuki Samurai, but not once inside a panel van. You never mount a weapon so loud in such an enclosed space if you expect to hear again. The young Mexican firing the weapon wore earmuffs, which fell off as he tumbled backwards when Jack shot him at nearly point blank range. I could not tell where or how many bullets struck Fernando, but he lay covered in blood beneath the dead gunner. Jack and I turned to watch as men loaded corpses from both sides into the Mexicans' remaining vans. The vehicles were shot-up, but seemed to be drivable. Jack and I sat down in the van's open doorway.

"I guess you are who I need to worry about now," I said in a not particularly friendly voice. I certainly could not afford to take his earlier threat as some sort of bad joke.

"I always have been," he half-grinned. We both sat with pistols in our hands. I had only a slight advantage by being to his left. I could grab his gun hand with my own left hand when I twisted around to shoot him. I had reason to believe every gunman still alive had orders not to let me leave the airport. Killing Jack would be for my personal satisfaction, and the last good thing I did before I died.

"What a mess," I said as I looked at the carnage.

"It's just your tax dollars at work." Jack had managed to find a way to slip his favorite phrase into the conversation. I was about to respond when we heard a wet rustling sound behind us and turned to find Fernando was now sitting up and had his gilded .45 aimed at the two of us.

My trained instinct was to push Jack out of the line of fire. What I did instead was begin to raise my pistol as I fell out of the van and rolled three feet to my left to get out of the line of fire myself. Jack was on his own. He lost valuable time by looking at me as if to ask if I planned what was about to happen. Fernando fired three shots from his gilded pistol and struck Jack twice. The first round caught Jack as he began to turn around and struck his upper torso through a gap in his body armor. The bullet ripped through Jack's left bicep and entered his chest by way of his armpit. He would have survived that round as it missed his lung and the bullet came to rest against the inside of the body armor. The second round caught him in front of his left ear and dropped him where he sat. I was already in motion and fired three shots into Fernando's forehead before I gave a moment's thought about which of the two men I needed to shoot. I know to shoot the threat holding the warmest gun.

I used my sweater to wipe my prints from the pistol and tossed it into the van with Fernando and his companion. I stepped away from Jack's corpse as his men came running towards me with their guns leveled. Some of them witnessed the shooting and immediately absolved me of having taken out their leader. I am sure every one of them knew I would not be sharing any grief they might have felt over Jack's death. I could not read their reactions, but I cannot be the only person he ever crossed. I was not relieved to find Paul was the person who seemed to have taken charge of the remaining fire team.

"We have a problem?" I asked Paul. "Jack said I might not have a hall pass to leave here tonight."

"Go on. Get out of here," Paul said and waved his hand. "I think it's safe to say that we are both done with this."

A pair of semi-trailers arrived. They bore the logo for the same incinerator in Biloxi that disposed of the evidence of D-Tech's operatives' previous murders and arson. It was chilling to think D-Tech was in bed with Junior Hauser, if what Jack said was true.

"Sorry about Jack," I largely lied. "And I hope you can find a new job."

"Our oath about 'enemies foreign and domestic' covers a lot of things." Paul reminded me and grinned.

I might well have been among Paul's remaining nameless operatives, had I not been brought back to life twice on an operating table and found a different use for what I was trained to do. I felt much cleaner living by the rule of law instead of some military contractor's questionable rules of engagement.

I walked away and dialed Chief Avery's home number.

"For once it's good to hear your voice," he said with unrestrained relief. I envisioned him sitting with the phone in one hand and his rosary in the other.

"I'd say NOPD could respond to any noise complaints out here in another hour or so. The cleaning crew is hard at work as we speak."

"Everything work out as you hoped?"

"It all worked out as it had to. I would have hoped none of this ever happened at all," I assured him and began peeling back the

Velcro that held my vest in place. I found a number of perforations in the fabric and felt around for the slugs. The rounds must have been ricochets or I surely would have felt the impact despite the adrenaline I could still feel coursing through my veins.

Chapter 58

I checked myself for bullet holes or splatters of Jack's blood before I locked the vest and my weapons into the back of my Cadillac wagon and headed home. Avery was satisfied that I was safe and sound. He had a cover story he could use to dissipate any interest in the gunfight. I was not going to be nearly as fortunate dealing with the State Police. There were not going to be any reports to file, but Captain Hammond would not be happy that the bullet holes in the jet linked the two of us to whatever put them there.

I headed directly to my apartment. My original plan was to watch the Super Bowl without knowing the outcome of the game. Honking car horns and people running up and down their streets made it obvious who won the game. I was ecstatic that the Saints won, but now the only mystery left to me was how that happened.

I waded largely unnoticed through the euphoric crowd at the bar as I made my way to the elevator. I gave Katie a quick hug before hastily placing my heavy equipment bag in the office and closing the door.

"Seems like I missed a good game," I tried to make conversation while I opened a beer and moved to sit next to Katie on the sofa. I could tell by the accumulation of empty bottles and snack bowls that I also missed a good party.

"You did, but I think I missed the big action tonight. I've taped all of the post-game shows as well," she said and turned slightly towards me. She glanced up and down to assess the condition of my clothes and myself before she silently turned to face the television.

"What's that supposed to mean?" I asked, but I was not trying to start a fight. I survived one close-quarters battle that evening, but arguing with Katie was a fight I could win and lose at the same time.

"I was sure you'd gone off to get yourself killed again. I was already planning on taking Roux and sleeping at my place tonight if you weren't home by the time I finished taping everything." I wondered if this why she was still looking for things to tape when I came home.

"Why would you have done that?" I asked with considerable alarm, though I knew what she meant.

Katie hugged me tightly, but looked me square in the eye to tell me what she had apparently wanted to say for some time.

"Because, I didn't want to sleep in your bed if you were never going to be there again." There was no way to respond to that but to hold her.

I tried to kiss her as well, but wound up pressing my lips to her forehead before she stretched out on the sofa with her head in my lap. This was not the time or place for the discussion I could tell was coming, and she had already made her positon clear on making hollow promises about coming home.

She turned towards the entertainment center and cued the match-up I would have preferred watching that evening. It was a great game, and being in charge of my own replays actually made the experience that much better. Katie finally wrestled the remote from my hands to speed things along.

We had never argued, but the make-up sex was great.

Chapter 69

Ritchie Franklin was back to wearing jeans and a crisp white t-shirt when I picked him up from Audubon Place shortly before nine o'clock on Monday morning. Ritchie carried the clothes my mother bought for him in a plastic bag. I missed a Christmas card photo-op when the two of them hugged before she closed the door behind us. I noticed how she looked around before allowing this to happen. She did not want any rumors circulating about her snuggling up to what looked like the help.

I checked the morning paper and listened to the early news for anything about an incident at the airport. There was little in the local news about anything besides the Saints winning the Super Bowl. The absence of news is not always good news. I still felt safe about dropping Ritchie off at his mother's house.

"How much does a place like that cost?" Ritchie wondered as we pulled onto St. Charles Avenue.

"You could get a fixer-upper for about five million bucks. Are you in the market?" I saw no point in explaining the odds stacked against his getting past the homeowner's association.

"Maybe. A man's gotta have a dream, right?" Ritchie was not toying with me about the idea. In his largest Scarface dreams, he truly thought he was on a path to having the money it would take to live such a lifestyle. He had obviously spent too much time hanging out with the Mexican cartel.

"Well, I'll tell you what, Ritchie. If you ever want to be legitimate, I know a guy who can loan you the money to go straight." It would not be me, but Tony had plenty of money to invest.

"What do you mean by that?"

"I mean if any of the Pistol Peetes would rather open a corner store than keep selling death to your neighbors, then I know a guy who can front you the money to get started. It takes guts and some brains to do what you're doing now. Imagine if you applied those to something that wasn't going to get you killed or locked up." I was at a traffic light so I could turn and look him in the face to let him know this really was what I thought.

"You sound like your mother, man." Ritchie grumbled before he broke into a little smile.

"Don't you be talking about my mother," I laughed and cocked a finger to point it at him. He laughed at the gesture, yet I feared he felt his fate was set and nothing was going to change it.

Chapter 70

I called Tulip to invite her to lunch at the bistro after I dropped Ritchie off at his mother's house. Tulip accepted the invitation after an odd pause, as if she wanted to say something then decided it needed said in person. We talked about things besides my case and I was relieved to find that whatever Tony meant when he said that money and love are fleeting was not a sign that my sister lost any affection for him.

She arrived slightly before noon and we took a booth along the brick wall at the rear of the dining room. She was wearing a dark skirt and cashmere sweater and said she did not want to go back to work smelling of olive oil and garlic, as she always does if we eat in the kitchen. I am so used to those odors that I no longer notice them.

"How did you get the FBI to drop their investigation into that file?" She was being unusually brusque.

"That was entirely their decision." It was only a minor lie and the truth was just going to disrupt the world she likes to imagine herself living in even more. "What's crawled up your fanny today anyway? Why the third degree?"

"Well, for one thing, when that jackass at the FBI called to say they were dropping their investigation he said it was because the file had been declassified."

"That would be enough to make them drop it." I had to believe that this was Kinkaid's last official act.

"Mike Conroy personally delivered a copy to my office this morning and to say he was just doing his job. I've been reading it ever since."

I am sure I flinched, or at least blanched. She saw something in my reaction, but the waitress arrived with a bottle of wine and we both held off saying anything else until after she left with our food orders.

"I know you and Tony said you were involved in that operation, but your names only come up at the end when you ended the mission by arresting somebody you were told to leave alone. Most of the report is about your pal Jack and some company called D-Tech killing Iraqis suspected of attacking American troops. They just executed them, without a trial or anything. Hell, my tax dollars paid them to do it." I could tell by her tone that she found a new injustice upon which to focus her attention. I had Jack's taking credit for everything to thank for her not holding Tony or me accountable, although we had both unnecessarily confessed.

"I guess both history and after-action reports are written by the survivors." I chuckled, but I intended to never elaborate on the comment.

I almost laughed at the phenomenally bad timing Jill Bledsoe and Willie Hawkins had in walking through the front door of the bistro at that precise moment. Jill had a word with the daytime hostess and I watched as the young woman pointed in our direction. I stood to greet the pair as they approached the table.

"Detective Holland? I need to have a word with you," Jill said with her usual sense of self-importance.

"Miss Bledsoe, of course I'll make time for you. Hello Willie, I see you're still traveling in dubious company." I was not surprised that Willie failed to see humor in my joke. Jill simply ignored it. "This is my sister, Tulip. Miss Bledsoe here works for a company called D-Tech."

"Nice to meet you," Jill shook Tulip's hand and reached for a chair, but I placed a hand on the back of it to prevent her from sitting down. She nodded silently at the message this sent.

"What brings you by today?" I asked to hurry things along.

"I'm sure you're aware that Jack Rickman, our security director, left town rather abruptly." Jill's face was tight as she said this. I saw a slight moistening around her eyes.

"I saw Jack off at the airport." It was a needlessly cruel comment to make, but I did not like this woman and had few such opportunities to express it. Jill grimaced as though I had struck her, but only briefly.

"We still see opportunities here. I have a meeting with your mayor about future contracts and wanted to introduce you to the man filling the position that Jack's departure has created. A local connection always helps a sales pitch."

"Hopefully Willie here will give you that local face you need. He certainly needs to find some honest work for a change."

"You're the one that told me to get out of that other line of work. The Director of Homeland Security said he was still hopeful her current project could be completed." Willie was unusually quick to defend his decision to work for the company that kidnapped his nephew. I was sure he realized he was in way over his head with whatever was happening between Jill and me at that moment.

"I'm sure the Director is grateful for your role in arresting the cartel's favorite executioner," I said to Jill. He was probably a lot more grateful about the role D-Tech played in that than it did in creating a political scandal that might cost him his own job.

"Oh, we aren't taking any public credit for that. The Director is going to haul El Carnicero back to Arizona and let Deputy Director Kinkaid announce the arrest. The Feds in Arizona want to try El Carnicero on multiple charges and it was quite a coup to lure him across the border in the first place. I believe the arrangement is that the Deputy Director gets to take credit for the arrest right before he announces his retirement." Jill seemed rather eager to let me know the backroom maneuvering that took place with El Carnicero. Making the announcement in Arizona took the spotlight off his capture in New Orleans; Making Kinkaid into the public face of the arrest of the cartel's henchman would hopefully focus the cartel's need for revenge on Kinkaid personally. He not only broke their agreement, but his own agency put him forth as the agent who arrested their favorite enforcer.

"Well, if you're going to be in town for a while, maybe you could spare my sister here a few minutes of your time," I suggested to Jill.

"How so?" Jill was clearly uncomfortable with the proposition. She'd either come to my place of business to intimidate me with the suggestion that Homeland Security continued to support her apparently ongoing operation, or to see if I could be persuaded to keep what I'd learned about D-Tech's domestic activities to myself.

"Tulip's been reading about something called Operation Stoplight that the Deputy Director was kind enough to declassify."

Jill's neck snapped in Tulip's direction, letting me know she was familiar with the file, as well.

"That wasn't supposed to happen." Jill tried to swallow her words. I was surprised that Tulip did not seem to hear the comment.

"I think reading that file has convinced her to focus on the military-industrial complex Eisenhower warned our parents about. I thought you might have time to discuss any of D-Tech's other reconstruction contracts and exploits in the Middle East with her."

Tulip looked up at me as if she wanted to say something now that she knew whom Jill worked for, but knew to keep her mouth shut and listen. I decided against pressing Jill on the file, but I now had an entirely new theory about the file's release to Tulip in the first place. Nobody goes down alone.

"I'm sure I don't know anything about any of them." Jill frostily declared.

"Well I'm equally sure Tulip and her researchers will still be sure to ask you whatever's on their mind about D-Tech if they see you around town. I had to disappoint them by not being able to be of more help in explaining D-Tech's role in Iraq's reconstruction because of my own nondisclosure agreement. She's been fascinated with what she's read so far." Tulip spun in her seat to get a better look at Jill. Their eyes locked and I knew they had each found a worthy new adversary.

"I'm sorry, but I won't be staying in town much longer." Jill abruptly turned and walked away. She lacked a lot of the swagger with which she arrived and Willie Hawkins looked quite confused about what just happened.

"What was that all about?" Tulip asked as I took my seat.

"Honoring a vow I took a long time ago about fighting enemies foreign and domestic," I said and hid behind my menu until Tulip changed the subject.

Chapter 71

Strada Ammazarre was nearly empty when Roux I returned from his afternoon walk the next day. The kitchen was closed and Jason tried to find polite ways of encouraging the last of our regulars to take their drinks and head to the parade route. Tony had already headed there with Tulip and Katie. This particular parade was shorter than any Mardi Gras parade would be, but it was certain to have the largest crowd of locals. It was solely in honor of the Saints and their Super Bowl victory. The city was still in the grip of its Super Bowl euphoria. Even less enthusiastic fans were clinging to that glow for as long as they could, and the team and city were happy to oblige with this parade.

I barely took two steps out the front door of the bistro before I noticed Ritchie standing in a doorway across the street. I looked around for anyone else that looked either familiar or likely to be part of the Pistol Peetes. I felt safe from any near-term retribution by the Mexican cartel, but I hurt the Pistol Peetes and the Baghdad Brotherhood just as badly.

I crossed the street towards Ritchie, watching his hands for any movement. One was holding a beer and the other stood pressed against the doorjamb of the junk shop whose doorway he was blocking. I kept my own hands loose and free, in case someone else was going to be the shooter and he was only the decoy. I now spotted his uncle's conspicuous Chrysler parked in the next block with someone sitting in the driver's seat.

"What can I do for you, Ritchie?" I asked from a polite but safe distance. We were still not friends and I refused to shake his hand.

"You told me you'd loan me money to go straight."

"Something like that. I know a guy who would listen to any ideas you have that would get you out of your current line of work, but I'm not going into business with former gang members." I needed that clear between us. I had no problem using Tony as their banker, but I would not personally approach my partner with the idea.

"I'm not sure we can come up with something legitimate. Do you have any ideas?"

"Why give up the easy money?"

"It ain't all that easy, boss. The Mexicans are pulling back and that will make it harder for any of us to get product. Plus, we're losing their protection and you strike me as the sort of cop that's going to be after us until we're all dead or in prison." Ritchie was a smart young man.

"You're right about that," I assured him. "Do you like pizza?"

"Yeah, who doesn't?" he asked. I think he thought I might be offering to buy him lunch.

"Call Tony at the restaurant in a week or so. He's got an idea you two to can work on together."

"Okay," Ritchie said. He sounded a bit disappointed that I wasn't going to just write him a check.

"I'll tell you this. I'd rather see him pay you to get off the street than have to take you off the street as a cop."

Ritchie understood my point. I still refused to shake his hand, but I smiled and continued on my way without worrying about another ambush. I genuinely hoped he would call Tony. I was not going to give him long to do so before I went looking for him with handcuffs in my hand.

I could hear the crowd gathered on Canal Street even before I turned the corner onto Royal Street and saw the thick rows of spectators waiting for the parade's arrival. I made my way to where my companions had staked out a piece of turf and kissed Katie before I hugged my sister.

I had not seen Katie in a couple of days and it felt good to see that she seemed to have missed me nearly as much as I missed her. She moved home after the Super Bowl and told me her office was swamped because the District Attorney was going to resume pursuing the drug dealers in New Orleans East. I was without a case, but I welcomed a break.

The Deputy Director's announcement of El Carnicero's arrest

made national news. Homeland Security let the networks and newspapers believe the arrest took place in Arizona, but the cartel and I knew the truth.

I was desperately hoping they would decide against trying to rebuild their New Orleans operation without their blanket immunity deal. I had consciously not asked Katie to look into the status of the Federal investigation into Alex Boudreaux. I wanted him behind bars less than I hated the prospect of figuring out whom Junior Hauser sent to replace him. The city had quite enough problems without people bringing new ones to town.

The parade turned the corner at St. Charles, and Katie and Tulip pressed forward to position themselves to catch any throws the Saints players might be tossing. There had not been nearly enough time to make custom beads or doubloons. At best, there might be plastic cups from the team's own promotional materials.

Most of us were content to bask in the presence of our temporary demi-gods. This was a team that tested the city's loyalty to its football franchise for years and taught us all how to maintain an unreasonable faith in sheer possibility. A city with a more successful team might not have found the inner strength this city showed in rebounding from Hurricane Katrina's destruction and aftermath. Five years of hard work and relentless effort, and a crap load of money, set New Orleans on its way to being a better city than ever before and sent its team to the Super Bowl. The odds were they would not be world champions at the end of the next season, but we did not need them to be. We only needed to believe we could all be better, and different, people than we were before the storm.

Acknowledgments

Thanks of the highest order to my wife for her unflinching support of my dreams and ambitions.

Only in New Orleans would there be two investigative reporters with the same name. Special thanks go out to Jason Berry for his political coverage and Jason Brad Berry for his reporting on housing and political problems in the wake of Hurricane Katrina. I also need to give a nod to my friend George 'Loki' Williams and his Humid City blog for keeping me informed about the dilemmas short-term rental property have added to life in my beloved city.

OTHER BOOKS BY
H. MAX HILLER

Cadillac Holland Mysteries
Blowback
Blue Garou
Can't Stop the Funk

https://www.indiesunited.net/h-max-hiller

ABOUT THE AUTHOR

H. Max Hiller's first taste of New Orleans was as a cook on Bourbon Street at the age of seventeen. His resume now includes many of New Orleans' iconic dining and music destinations. These jobs have provided a lifetime of characters and anecdotes to add depth to the Detective Cooter 'Cadillac' Holland series. The author now divides his passions between writing at his home overlooking the Mississippi River and as a training chef aboard a boat traveling America's inland waterways, and is always living by the motto "be a New Orleanian wherever you are."